THE DIARIES OF EMILIO RENZI

FORMATIVE YEARS

"Splendidly crafted and interspliced with essays and stories, this beguiling work is to a diary as Piglia is to 'Emilio Renzi': a lifelong alter ego, a highly self-conscious shadow volume that brings to bear all of Piglia's prowess as it illuminates his process of critical reading and the inevitable tensions between art and life. . . . No previous familiarity with Piglia's work is needed to appreciate these bibliophilic diaries, adroitly repurposed through a dexterous game of representation and masks that speaks volumes of the role of the artist in society, the artist in his time, the artist in his tradition. . . . Piglia's 'delusion of living in the third person' to 'avoid the illusion of an interior life' transmogrifies us as well, into the character of the reader, and 'that feeling is priceless.'"

MARA FAYE LETHEM, *THE NEW YORK TIMES BOOK REVIEW*

"When young Ricardo Piglia wrote the first pages of his diaries, which he would work on until the last years of his life, did he have any inkling that they would become a lesson in literary genius and the culmination of one of the greatest works of Argentine literature?"

SAMANTA SCHWEBLIN, AUTHOR OF *FEVER DREAM*

"A valediction from the noted Argentine writer, known for bringing the conventions of hard-boiled U.S. crime drama into Latin American literature. *L'ennui, c'est moi.* First-tier Argentine novelist Piglia's (*Money to Burn*, 2003, etc.) literary alter ego, Emilio Renzi, was a world-weary detective when he stepped into the spotlight in the claustrophobic novel *Artificial Respiration*, published in Argentina in 1981 and in the U.S. in 1994, a searching look at Buenos Aires during the reign of the generals. Here, in notebooks begun decades earlier but only shaped into a novel toward the end of Piglia's life,

Renzi is struggling to forge a career as a writer. . . . The story takes a few detours into the meta—it's a nice turn that Renzi, himself a fictional writer, learns 'what I want to do from imaginary writers. Stephen Dedalus or Nick Adams, for example'—but is mostly straightforward, reading just like the diary it purports to be. Fans of Cortázar, Donoso, and Gabriel García Márquez will find these to be eminently worthy last words from Piglia, who died at the beginning of 2017."

KIRKUS REVIEWS, STARRED REVIEW

"In this fictionalized autobiography, Piglia's ability to succinctly criticize and contextualize major writers from Kafka to Flannery O'Connor is astounding, and the scattering of those insights throughout this diary are a joy to read. This book is essential reading for writers."

PUBLISHERS WEEKLY

"Where others see oppositions, great writers see the possibility of intertwining forking paths. Like kids in front of a stereogram, they are able to shift their gaze in ways that allow them to read the history of literature otherwise and, in doing so, write beyond the dead end of tradition. Ricardo Piglia, the monumental Argentine writer whose recent death coincided with increasing recognition of his work in the English-speaking world, was without a doubt one of these great visionaries. . . . It was said that there lay hidden something more impressive than his transgressive novels or his brilliant critical essays, a secret work of even more transcendence: his diaries. . . . In the tradition of Pavese, Kafka, and Gombrowicz, the diaries were the culmination of a life dedicated to thinking of literature as a way of life."

CARLOS FONSECA, *LITERARY HUB*

"It almost seems as though Piglia has perfected the form of the literary author's diary, leaving in enough mundane life details to give a feeling of the messy, day-to-day livedness of a diary, but also providing this miscellany with something of a shape, and with a true intellectual heft. In these pages we see the formation of a formidable literary intelligence—the brief reflections on genre, Kafka, Beckett, Dashiell Hammett, Arlt, and Continental philosophy alone are worth the price of admission—but we also see heartbreak, familial drama, reflections on life, small moments of great beauty, the hopes and anxieties of a searching young man, the endless monetary woes of one dedicated to the literary craft, and the drift of a nation whose flirtation with fascism takes it on a dangerous course."

SCOTT ESPOSITO, *BOMB MAGAZINE*

"As a fictionalized autobiography, it is, like the work of Karl Ove Knausgaard, of *My Struggle* fame, part confession and part performance. Renzi meets and corresponds with literary luminaries like Borges, Cortázar, and Márquez, and offers insightful readings of Dostoevsky, Kafka, Faulkner, and Joyce. . . . Fans of W. G. Sebald and Roberto Bolaño will find the first installment in Piglia's trilogy to be a fascinating portrait of a writer's life."

ALEXANDER MORAN, *BOOKLIST*

"In the long history of novelists and their doubles, doppelgängers, and alter egos, few have given more delighted attention to the problem of multiplicity than the Argentine novelist Ricardo Emilio Piglia Renzi. . . . Under the name of Ricardo Piglia he published a sequence of acrobatic, dazzling novels and stories that consistently featured a novelist called Emilio Renzi. . . . The larger story of *Formative Years* reads something like a *roman d'apprentissage*: the romance of a writer's vocation, in all its hubris and innocent corruption. . . . [T]he book's real subject is more delicate and more moving than the simple story of a literary vocation. It is the process of textualization, of the stuttering, hesitant way a writer tries to convert life into literature. In these diaries, Piglia is dramatizing not only the writer's split between a public and private self, but also the time-consuming, exhausting, delicious, compromised effort to construct that textual self: the self that exists only in words. . . . *Formative Years* is one of the great novels of youth: its boredom, powerlessness, desperation, strategizing, delusion . . . this journal impassively records not only a novelist's self-creation, but a society's unraveling."

ADAM THIRLWELL, *THE NEW YORK REVIEW OF BOOKS*

ALSO BY RICARDO PIGLIA

RICARDO PIGLIA

THE DIARIES OF EMILIO RENZI

The Happy Years

Translated by Robert Croll

RESTLESS BOOKS
BROOKLYN, NEW YORK

First Restless Books paperback edition November 2018

Paperback ISBN: 9781632061980
Library of Congress Control Number: 2018938474

Cover design by Daniel Benneworth-Gray
Set in Garibaldi by Tetragon, London

Printed in Canada

1 3 5 7 9 10 8 6 4 2

Restless Books, Inc.
232 3rd Street, Suite A111
Brooklyn, NY 11215

restlessbooks.org
publisher@restlessbooks.org

CONTENTS

THE DIARIES OF EMILIO RENZI

THE HAPPY YEARS

A life is not divided into chapters, Emilio Renzi said to the bartender of El Cervatillo that afternoon, leaning on the bar, standing before the mirror and the bottles of whiskey, vodka, and tequila lined up on the shelves. I've always been intrigued by the unreal yet mathematical way we organize the days, he said. Take the almanac, a senseless prison around experience that imposes a chronological order onto a period of time that flows without criteria. Calendars imprison the days, and this mania with classification has likely influenced human morals, Renzi told the bartender, smiling. I say so for my own part, he said, since I write a diary, and diaries obey only the progression of days, months, and years. Nothing else can define a diary—not its autobiographical material, not the private confessions, not even the record of a person's life. Simply, said Renzi, the definition is that what is written must be organized by the days of the week and the months of the year. That's all, he said, satisfied. You can write anything, a mathematical progression, for example, or a laundry list, or a meticulous account of a conversation in a bar with the Uruguayan man tending the bar, or, as in my case, an unexpected mixture of details, or meetings with friends, or the testimony of lived experiences; you can write down all of that, but it will be a diary if and only if you note the day, the month, the year—any of those three means of orienting yourself amid the violent currents of time. If I write, for example, *Wednesday, January 27, 2015* and then write down a dream or memory beneath this heading, or if I imagine something that hasn't actually happened but make a note before I start the entry that says *Wednesday 27*, for example, or, even shorter, just *Wednesday*, it has now become a diary and neither a novel nor an essay, although it can include novels and essays as long as you take the precaution of writing the date first, orienting yourself and creating a sense of serialism, but then, look out, he said—and he touched the index finger of his left hand to the lower eyelid of his right eye—if you publish these notes according to the calendar and with your own name, that is, if you assert that the subject who is speaking, the subject who is being spoken of, and the one who signs it are all the same person or, rather, share the same name, then it is a personal diary. Your own name ensures the continuity and ownership of what is written. Although, as we have known since Sigmund Freud published *The Interpretation of Dreams* at the end of the nineteenth century—a great autobiographical text, by the way—you are not yourself, never the same person and, since I no longer believe that a concentric unit called "the ego" exists, or that a subject's manifold ways of being can be synthesized into a pronominal figure called "I," I don't share the current superstition about the proliferation of personal writings. And so, it is naïve to talk about the writings of the self, because no self exists for whom that—or any other—writing can exist, he laughed. The "I" is a hollow figure, and you have to seek meaning elsewhere. For example, in a diary, meaning is derived from the act of organizing according to the days of the week and the calendar. Therefore, although I am going to maintain mathematical temporal order in my diary, it also troubles me, and I'm thinking about other types of chronology and other types of order and periodization, provided, of course, that the diary is published under its author's real name and that the person writing the diary entries is the same person who lives them and also has the same name, Renzi concluded. It amuses me to reread these notebooks, and my Mexican muse laughs uproariously, as she tells me, at the amusing adventures of an aspiring saint. All right, exactly, I say to her, a book of humor, yes of course, I always meant to write a comedy, and in the end, it was these years of my life that achieved the touch of humor I was looking for, Renzi said. Maybe I'll call them my happy years, then, because I was amused while reading and transcribing them to see just how ridiculous one can be. Without meaning to, I turned my experience into a satire of life—in general and in particular. Looking at yourself from a distance is enough to show you that irony and humor turn our stubbornness and departures into a joke. A life retold by the same person living it is already a joke, or rather, Renzi said to the bartender, a Mephistophelean prank.

Due to my de-formation as a historian, I have a special sensitivity toward dates and the ordered progression of time. The great mystery, the question that has followed me through these weeks spent transcribing my notebooks, dictating my diaries, and making, as they say, "clean copies," lay in seeing the points at which my personal life intersected with or was intercepted by politics. For example, in the seven years I'm dedicating myself to now, I am incessantly, exclusively interested in knowing how I lived between 1968 and 1975, my poor life as a young, aspiring writer or rather as someone aspiring to be a writer because I wasn't yet a writer in a full sense, though I had already published a book of stories, *The Invasion*, which was fairly decent, I can say now, especially compared to the story collections that were being published in those days; back then I was only young and aspiring to be writer, and now, in reading the diaries from those seven years, the question that has arisen, almost an obsession that won't let me think about anything else, is what part of any individual's life is personal, and what is historical, Renzi said that afternoon to the Uruguayan bartender of El Cervatillo, as he drank a glass of wine at the bar.

A key event was the army raid in late 1972, during which, in search of a young, unidentified couple, they leveled the apartment building on Calle Sarmiento where I lived with Julia, my girlfriend at the time. We were a young couple and so the army, or that patrol, which was "combing"—as they say—the area, was surely seeking to verify some fact, some piece of information obtained with the interrogation methods typical of the security forces, forces dedicated to intimidating and killing defenseless citizens. Who knows who that young couple was, what they did, what they were working toward; they were, surely, leftist students, middle-class kids, since they lived and were being searched for in a building on

Sarmiento and Montevideo, right in the center of the city. We weren't them, but we lived there.

I realized it because, when I entered the area, I saw army trucks parked outside and two soldiers leaving the building, and so I turned back and retraced my steps, as they say, and called Julia at the office of *Los Libros* magazine, where she worked in the afternoons, and I caught her in time, and we decided to stay in a hotel that night. The City Hotel. We'd had, Renzi told the bartender, some training on how to change our residence when the storm drew near; we knew that one tactic of the suppressive forces of the occupying army, as it would be called now, was to act quickly, by surprise, and then move away and surround another neighborhood. Though what happened back then can't be compared to the brutal, criminal, and diabolical methods that the Argentine army, or rather, the Armed Forces, used a few years later under the operational command of the Military Junta, as it was called after March, 1976. That time was much easier, but all the same, Julia and I erased ourselves, so to speak, for a couple of days. The army patrolled an area of the city rather randomly, or with fairly imprecise information; they would surround it and inspect house after house, seeing if they could catch some dangerous little fish. So we spent two days in that hotel near Plaza de Mayo, and then, when the storm seemed to have passed, we went back home. Renzi turned toward the entryway and, absorbed, commented with a tired voice, "this heat is going to kill us," and then, as though awakening, he resumed his conversation without changing position, that is, in profile to the bartender, looking out toward Calle Riobamba.

So, when I get back, the doorman tells me that they came through, people from the army, asking about the young couple who lived in the room on the sixth floor of the building, and, since we lived in that room, we gathered some things—my notebooks, my papers, the typewriter—and left, not meaning to return. I see an intersection, there, between history and personal life, because that retreat produced several effects in me, as critical as the move from Mar del Plata when my father was affected by politics and, unwillingly, we had to abandon Adrogué, the town where I was born.

The porters of the buildings in Buenos Aires were divided into two categories; 30 to 35 percent were retired policemen and another 30 to 35 percent were undercover activists for the Communist Party. The communists had undertaken a great project of planting old militants in buildings around the city as caretakers. The Argentine communists had used that technique in anticipation of an insurrection in Buenos Aires similar to the one that had brought the Bolsheviks into power; managing the buildings of the city was an excellent revolutionary tactic, but, since the communists had no intention of making a mess, the doormen had become informants for the party and were also used to protect sympathizers of the left who were being pursued by the police. And one of them was there for me, a kind man from Corrientes who warned me of what was happening when he saw me appear and helped me to flee.

I will never know if it was me the army was looking for, but I had to act accordingly, as though I, a pacifist and schizoid aspiring writer, were actually a dangerous revolutionary. That misunderstanding, that crossroads, changed my life, Renzi said that afternoon to the bartender of El Cervatillo. Everything changed, chaos came back into my life. And so, to impose some order onto the passions and impulses of existence and to turn the disorder into a clear line, I must periodize my life, and for that reason I find, in that young couple whom the army was trying to capture, in that serendipity, meaning.

Personal experience, as written in a diary, is sometimes intervened upon by history or politics or economics, that is, the private changes and is often controlled by external factors. In this way, it would be possible to organize a series based on the intersection of individual life and outside forces—or shall we say external forces—which tend to intervene periodically in the private lives of people in Argentina under political systems. A change of one official is all it takes, a drop in the price of soybeans, a false piece of information taken as fact by the State information or intelligence services, and hundreds and hundreds of pacifists and distracted individuals are forced to change their lives drastically and, for example, cease to be dignified electromechanical engineers after a factory is forced to close because the Minister of Economy made a decision one morning while in a bad mood, and they become bitter and resentful taxi drivers who only talk to their poor passengers about the macroeconomic events that changed their lives in a way we might associate with the heroes in Greek tragedies, controlled by fate. Another example could be me, Renzi said to the bartender of El Cervatillo, that is, a young writer who must leave his house and flee because of an incomprehensible decision by an army colonel who looks at a map of the city of Buenos Aires and, based on a vague piece of information from the army intelligence services, after a slight hesitation, uses a pointer to indicate a neighborhood, or rather a corner, in the city which must be searched to find the suspicious couple. An abstract, impersonal *factum* acts as the hand of fate and takes a young couple between its index finger and thumb, lifting them into the air and literally throwing them out into the street.

And so, in order to escape from the chronological trap of astronomical time and to remain inside my personal time, I analyze my diaries according to discontinuous series and, upon that basis, I organize, so to speak, the chapters of my life. One series, then, is that of the political events that act directly on the private sphere of my existence. We can call that series or chain or continuum of events Series A. On that afternoon when we left, covertly, trying not to be seen, like two thieves robbing their own house, loaded down with suitcases and bags and putting them in a taxi while a moving van driven by the doorman from Corrientes transported some furniture, many books, lamps, pictures, a refrigerator, a bed, and a leather chair to a warehouse on Calle Alsina, a new life began for me, very chaotic, with no fixed address, and very promiscuous, because the first effect of that intervention of political fate and the military search was my separation from Julia, a woman I had lived with, by that point, for five years. There, we have a new chronology, a temporal scansion, an incident

8

that changed my life; I separated from a woman not for emotional reasons but because of the catastrophic effects of the military's intervention in my little personal sphere. Figuratively speaking, an elephant's foot had crushed the flowers, the thoughts I had cultivated in my garden, Renzi said to the bartender.

He had often thought of his notebooks as an intricate web of little decisions that formed diverse sequences, thematic series that could be read as a map, going beyond the temporal, dated structure that at first glance ordered his life. Underneath lay a series of cyclical repetitions, equivalent events that could be followed and classified beyond the dense chronological progression of his diaries. For example, the series of friends, meetings with his friends in a bar, what they talked about, what they built their hopes on, how their topics and worries changed over the course of all those years. Let's call Series B a sequence that doesn't respond to chronological and linear causality. Or his relationships with women, would they belong to Series B, given that many of them had been his friends, a few of them, the most intimate, his best friends, or should that be an autonomous series, a Series C? Love, adventures, encounters with the women he has loved, would these be in Series B or Series C? However, it might be, that serial organization would define a personal temporality and would allow a scansion or a series of scansions and periodizations, far more intimate and true than the mere order of a calendar. After all, he didn't remember his life according to the scheme of days and months and years; he remembered blocks of memory, a landscape of plateaus and valleys that he mentally traversed each time he thought about the past.

He has spent several weeks working with his notebooks, never going out into the street, lost in the stream of written memories, with the intention of organizing the chapters of his life thematically—friends, loves, books, clandestine meetings, parties. He spent months copying and pasting fragments of his diary into different documents, obsessively going through each one and reconstructing, registering a single event, for example all of the family dinners over the years, following the ways that they repeated and changed without ever ceasing to be what they were, or it could be all of the meetings with a single person, how many times did David Viñas appear in his diary? What did they talk about, what was said, why did they fight? He said D. V., but he could just as well have said Gandini or Jacoby or Junior. What did I do with them, what had I written down after our meetings? I worked in that way for months, determined to publish my diaries by organizing them into thematic series, but—there's always a *but* in thinking—it would have lost the feeling of chaos and confusion that a diary records, as no other written medium does, because, in being organized according to chronology alone, by date, you can see that a life, any life, is a disordered sequence of little events that seem to be in focus while they are being lived, but then, when they are reread years later, they acquire their true dimension as minor, almost invisible actions, and their meanings depend precisely on the variety and disorder of experience. For that reason, I have now decided to publish my notebooks just as they are, making little narrative summaries here and there that function, if I don't deceive myself, as a framework around the manifold succession of the days of my life.

For me, of course, it was never about using the idiotic decimal sequence that is now in fashion everywhere in the world, in sensationalist yellow newspapers and in studies, theses, conferences, and panels of the academic world; now they've discovered that every decade means a fundamental change in the ways of things (in the first place), of people, of culture, of art, of politics, and of life in general. They speak of the decades of the sixties or the eighties as though they were separate worlds with hundreds of light-years between them. Since nothing really moves in the world and nothing really changes, the idiots invented the idea that people become other people every decade and the music they listen to changes, along with the clothing they wear, and sexuality, Peronism, education, etc. The culture of the eighties, the politics of the nineties, the stupidity of the seventies, and thus everything is ordered and periodized into these ridiculous timelines. They all believe that the expression is true, and they complain that they're from the eighties and are being viewed *now*, shall we say, for example, in the nineties, as romantic individuals and half-hippies, while the people in the nineties are cynical, conservative, and skeptical. Earlier, at least when I was young, time was periodized into centuries; the eighteenth was a century of light, the nineteenth was one of progress, positivity, the cult of the machine. Now, changes in civilization and in our collective spirit are given every ten years—they've given us a discount in the supermarket of history. I never saw anything more ridiculous; for example, a person is accused of being a product of the seventies, that is, of believing in socialism, in revolution. Some star reporters, who mark the lowest point of human intelligence and contemporary culture in their hopeless descent into decadence, have invented the terms "*ochentoso*" or, even worse and uglier, "*sesentoso,*" or even "*setentoso,*" as though the decades were categories in thought, the way you would say *the Italian Renaissance* or *Anglo-Saxon Protestantism*. The imbeciles reason by using categories, and in this way, they conceal their total lack of gray matter speaking as though they were intellectuals and thinkers.

It is foolish to believe that life is divided into chapters or decades or defined segments; everything is more chaotic, there are cuts, interruptions, passages, decisive events, which I would call *contretemps* because they bring about both forward and backward steps in personal temporality. And he stopped to drink from his glass of white wine. Contretemps, that's the word I would use to define the moments of fracture in my life, Renzi said to the bartender in a tone that was unfriendly yet polite and sincere. And he resumed, after a pause. When I was thrown into the street by the Argentine army, my life of course changed, but I didn't realize it, he added, now looking with suspicion at his own face reflected in the mirror that covered the wall of the bar, behind the bottles of whiskey, tequila, vodka, and Caña Legui that were lined up in front of him, half-empty or half-full. No, I didn't realize it, and it was only while writing down the events—and above all while reading the things I had written, years later—that I glimpsed the shape of my experience, because, whether we like it or not, we align what has happened into an ordered configuration through writing and reading, subjecting events to a grammatical structure, which, on its own, tends toward clarity and organization into syntactical blocks.

I realized, then, that something essential had been lost to me by my remaining, so to speak, naked in the city, carrying my papers, my notebooks, and my portable typewriter in its sky blue case from one place to another by taxi or subway. I have maintained the chronological order in the diaries that I'm going to publish, but I want to leave evidence of my conviction that because of that expulsion, or rather, because of that intrusion of political and military reality into my life, a change occurred, one that I can understand only now, in rereading my notebooks from those days, Renzi said to the bartender of El Cervatillo that afternoon. He also confessed to him about other matters, all of which had to do with thinking about what order, what form he should give his diary in publishing it, if he did decide to print it, if he overcame his qualms and the shame of exposing to strangers the intimate secrets of a happy, but also disgraceful, phase of his life, because, as he told the bartender, happiness can sometimes take on a criminal and despicable tone.

The thing that changed, after we were forced to abandon the house where we lived, was my emotional life; I entered a vortex with no center, promiscuous, an erotic cycle that had always been a means of flight or compensation for me in days or periods of drought when I was unable to write, and then beloved or unknown bodies would alleviate the void and give meaning to my life. Meaning or a state of being that didn't last, or barely lasted for a few hours, despite my searching for ways to make desire endure, with rituals and dangerous games that lasted until dawn, like ocean tides helping me to keep going onward.

When we abandon ourselves to the conviction of the body, we forget reality. In those days, leaving behind the certainties I'd lived with and venturing out into the elements, I lived in hotels or friends' houses with Julia, forced into a constant sociability, sharing places and conversations, because we were intruders or guests and so had to follow the rites of social convention, until one afternoon Julia suggested that we move into a vacant apartment that one of her friends from the College had offered her. It was a den in a stately building on Calle Uriburu, near Avenida Santa Fe, and during that move, as I've remembered now while rereading the notebooks I wrote in those days, like trade or barter, I began an intense clandestine relationship with Tristana, Julia's close friend, a beautiful and mysterious and slightly alcoholic woman, whom I had observed with interest from a distance because she had an unforgettable intensity. One afternoon, without thinking it through and almost without realizing it, we ended up in bed, Tristana and I, and we began a confusing series of clandestine rendezvous and conversations that reached a dimension I had never known until Julia discovered—by reading my diary, as will be seen—my version of the things I was living through.

There, in that series, in living, writing, and being read—when an event written in a personal notebook is later read, secretly, by one of the protagonists of the story—I discovered a morphology, the initial form, as I would like to call it, of my recorded life, day after day, in my personal diary. And so, having been discovered once, having been read treacherously more than once, I've decided to publish my diaries and exhibit my private life to the public, or rather, the written version of yours truly's days and works over the course of fifty years, Renzi said that day to the bartender of El Cervatillo. And, as he left the bar and went back out to the street after paying the bill, he added, as though talking to himself: those discoveries, those flights, those confusing moments have been turning points for me, and I've used them to construct the periodization of my life, the chapters or series into which I've divided my experiences, Renzi thought aloud as he walked upright, though limping slightly and leaning on a cane, toward his usual hiding place.

1

Diary 1968

January 31
I'm back. I tell stories from the trip to Julia and my friends.

The end of a month with some news. Jorge Álvarez asked me to manage a literary magazine (along the lines of *La Quinzaine*) for fifty thousand pesos a month. This proposal would have guaranteed my happiness three years ago, but now it leaves me (like everything these days, except Julia) cold, distant. Maybe it is necessary to work with others. Always working on art for others.

Series A. A meeting with Virgilio Piñera at Hotel Habana Libre, I bring him a letter from Pepe Bianco. "Let's go to the garden," he says. "There are microphones everywhere in here; they're listening to everything I say." He was a weak and fragile man. We were already unconsciously growing to like each other. He'd been friends with Gombrowicz and had helped him translate *Ferdydurke*, which was why we admired him, and Gombrowicz's touch can be felt in his striking stories. What danger or what wrong could that refined artist pose for the revolution.

February 3
She said: "But who can know how we've come undone, what things men have left after the first encounter."

Such astonishment, facing the void of this window that looks out at the street. I have everything to live for now, coming back, but always from the outside. These notes as well, their tone more than their style, I'll come back to them when it is too late, when it is the right time for decisions without motives. A ship's logbook.

Series E. In a notebook from '66, I find the record of a film by Michael Powell (*Peeping Tom*), with a psychopath who wants to grasp reality through the camera and ends up filming his own death. It seems very connected to *Blow-Up* by Antonioni. The concept of cinematographic technique as a magical eye used to capture personal reality, the same as the camera for still images. A diary too is a device for registering events, people, and gestures. *Live to see*, that could be the motto.

February 4
A harsh reaction after a family call; what had once been a peaceful, sheltered childhood, is now the experience of an invasion. I would rather not press this too far.

Wednesday, February 7
Coming and going, movements of solidarity. David Viñas and Germán García, letters to *Primera Plana*. I don't understand their responses. Then yesterday, a report on Channel 11 on TV: you can't even cross your legs, let alone talk about Vietnam. Then at home with David, another proposal: an article on American literature for the magazine David is trying to publish with the Centro Editor. The project is getting in the way of Jorge Álvarez's magazine.

Thursday 8
A series of meetings yesterday: José Sazbón, Ramón Plaza, Manuel Puig, Andrés Rivera, Jorge Álvarez, Pirí Lugones. Why do I make a note of this? Because I've changed my habits, and now I settle in at La Ópera bar and friends come to see me while I remain at the same table for three or four hours, or longer. A long talk with Puig, who gives me

Heartbreak Tango to read, a book that follows the path of his previous novel but deepens the poetics and seeks popular feeling and technical experimentation. I've always admired his ear for spoken language, his rare sensitivity for capturing each character's tone. The techniques in the novel are very original: using the melodramatic novel form involves thinking about the cutoff of each chapter like suspense in the classical novel. Once again, it is a novel in which the narrator is absent and can only be noticed in objective and clinical observations. Then dinner with El Quinteto de la Muerte. Pirí is quiet and capricious because of the presence of Andrés Rivera, who acts tender and charming around her, while Jorge Álvarez revealed to me both his intelligence (greater than I gave him credit for) and his turn toward Tercerista political positions, founded, as often happens, upon facts that prove the Machiavellianism and forcefulness of world powers (the USA and the USSR), as they play with the rest of the world. In that way, you end up as an absolute skeptic because anything you do is part of the superpowers' plans. Beside me, Julia was dazzling, her tan skin rising above a white *guayabera* dress that I brought her from Cuba, a braid over her shoulder, and all of the qualities of her alarming temptation toward *Doing Wrong* (capitalized and emphasized).

One day I'll have to take a look at my continuous, successive ability to keep up conversations that always seem the same to me, though I hold them with different people, all close to me, as though I were the only one who could unite them and make them coincide.

"The point is to permit the Germans not even a moment of self-deception and resignation. We must make the actual pressure more pressing by adding to it the consciousness of pressure and make the shame more shameful by publicizing it. Every sphere of German society must be shown as the *partie honteuse* of German society, and we have to make these petrified social relations dance by singing their own tune!" Karl Marx.

Friday, February 9

In literature, we know what we don't want to do, because what we do want to do isn't always accomplished in writing. On the other hand, this negativity allows us to write by casting aside everything that doesn't interest us. The pressure of fashion (Cortázar), which mires my contemporaries (Néstor Sánchez, the tone of the novel that Castillo is writing, Gudiño Kieffer, Aníbal Ford, etc.), will never draw me away from my projects. I know that it's something I never want to do, and thus a poetics is already defined. That doesn't mean adopting rigid guidelines as a defense (the way David Viñas does), leaving out all Argentine writers from all eras, but instead adopting a position that consists of thinking that there is no single way to create literature (and here it is Borges that one must break away from, along with his literary dogmas like "Chesterton is better than Marcel Proust," which become contagious and are repeated without analysis). Thus, writers who can discover the personal profiles of *their own worlds* (to reiterate the possessive) have at least secured a tone of their own, a music to the language that is imposed onto the era and not the other way around.

Some victories, certain circumstances in my life that would once have satisfied my dearest pretensions, are now commonplace, and their current relativity proves to me that my years of learning are now bearing some fruit. At the same time, my firmest certainties come from childhood. In those days, entirely separate from any knowledge that could correspond to my own future life, I adopted or created the convictions that now sustain me. It's as though my soul's defenses came before my soul itself, as though I were not allowed any knowledge of my life story until after the catastrophe. I had begun to live, not knowing anything about myself until the moment when I realized that all knowledge was useless when it came to doing what I wanted to do. That is why it's easy to remember the magic of decisions made in total certainty, with nothing to justify them, when everything came to me naturally. *That is why* there is no present time that can bring to life something that has survived for itself alone. Hence the perverse coherence that some of these notebooks acquire when they are revised, finding signs that lead to the central highway, unsuspected profiles of myself, which now form my way of being.

Saturday 10

Yesterday a visit from Germán García, an immediate verbal magic, taking off toward thoughts that floated in the air, Germán returning to his attacks against *Primera Plana*, since they praised him and then forgot about him.

Since we can only choose what is possible, the things that we choose—nothing can be rescued from the past now, not the paths or the meanings—are phantoms that guide us; strange portents arise behind uncertain intuitions, dark certainty, empty eyes, the blind gaze.

Sunday 11

A sudden, but not unexpected, appearance from Ismael Viñas, escaping from the emptiness of this rainy afternoon, and a long conversation about Argentine nationalism and the merits of epigrammatic and provocative style. We made a genealogy that began with El Padre Castañeda and went all the way to Aráoz Anzoátegui. From there, critiques of the left's journalistic style: they write poorly because they're always trying to be optimists. Only the negative shines in language.

Thursday 22

I'm in Mar del Plata, in the bedroom I've always had, with the window that opens to the tree that grows up from the sidewalk; I see old friends, and we reconstruct the years with Steve in Buenos Aires, his obsession with Malcolm Lowry, etc.

Friday

Yesterday a dangerous situation. Three boys in blue pullovers appeared in the hallway, followed by my brother; I thought they were his friends until I saw the guns. I was drinking maté with Julia in the kitchen. At first I was frightened, thinking they were police, and strangely I calmed down when I realized it was a robbery. They were looking for cash, but I of course didn't know where my father kept it hidden, and he wasn't home. The one who had the gun, a skinny guy with a cap and a face like a bird, was very nervous, more nervous than we were. I thought: "Something's going to happen if they don't find the cash," but we didn't have a single peso, no jewelry, nothing. The tension mounted until, suddenly, the one who had been standing guard brought in a round-faced man who had been looking for my father. They sat him down in one of the chairs and pointed the revolver at his temple. The man gave them all the cash he had, close to eighty thousand pesos. The one with the gun kissed him on the head and said: "You saved us, baldy." Suddenly they left, and we remained sitting at the table. The man they had robbed went out to the street and returned with the police. He thought that Julia, my brother, and I were part of the gang because we were so calm. We explained the situation to the policeman, and my brother took the opportunity to lodge a complaint because the thieves had stolen a tape player that he really liked. My father came back that night, but he didn't place any importance on the matter.

Monday 26
Novel. A moment of tension and expectation. Caught in a trap, as the police sirens cross the city, they are all silent. Malito: Speak, say something. Costa: What? Malito: Something, anything. Costa: When I was a boy, I saw my uncle coming in through the country on horseback . . .

I realized yesterday, during the robbery, that, in the middle of a tense, violent situation with an armed, nervous man looking for money, any dialogue can work well because no one refers explicitly to the situation they are experiencing. That's how to make a narrative scene work: If the situation is strong, the dialogue acts as a soundtrack.

Recorded scene in the novel. Four or five people are talking about the Englishman. They let slip hints, pieces of information about him and his history, though they're talking about other things at the same time.

X Series. "They lived in conditions where the unusual may be dangerous," Joseph Conrad. (That seems to capture Lucas's situation, the clandestine man must live a "normal" life and avoid what seems out of the ordinary to him.)

March 2
A novel. Imprisonment, outside of time, floating action, several unidentified narrators.

Realism. Balzac was not a realist in spite of his theocratism but rather precisely because of it. That was the condition of his critical view of bourgeois society. One's way of seeing social issues is defined by one's status and one's way of life.

Sunday 3
There's an obvious preconception that leads "university thinkers" to dispel oppositions and disagreements in favor of always thinking about halfway solutions. It is the neither-nor that Barthes spoke of. Balanced thinking that opposes all positioned, "biased," localized thought: they seek the truth in high places, in the middle ground. They imagine that not taking a position in a conflict is the same thing as being objective, while they actually hold the position of one who disengages and thinks outside of social matters (as though that were possible).

You have to look behind the criticism of *Hopscotch* for what has been offended, which is first of all the idea of what a novel should be, as though that were already determined; the critics don't perceive the fluid nature of novelistic form. Other critics reject the novelty of the technique and argue that it has already been done before, etc. Of course, the model of the encyclopedic novel can be traced to Flaubert's *Bouvard et Pécuchet* (going no further), and of course also in Borges's structures ("Tlön," for example) or in Macedonio Fernández's novel that is always about to begin. But to find precursors is not to say anything about a book's value.

Little contact, even with unreality (these days).

Series A. We have moved very carefully, as though conserving energy, because we have no cash, and, it goes without saying, money guarantees many movements and changes. We have five hundred pesos, and that must be the measure of the distance we can traverse. Or, in any event, the material choices we can face. I am discovering, then, a secret relationship between *economy and space*, or rather, between the velocity and amplitude of subjects' movements according to their wealth, etc.

Tuesday 5
I'm in La Modelo, always in this bar, which I will try to describe in a story someday. The lattices darkening the air, the blades of the ceiling fan turning slowly. The light of the afternoon, muted, filtering in through the picture windows onto the wood-paneled walls. I used to meet José Sazbón here now and then to read the chapter on fetishism in Marx's *Das Kapital*.

I believe that everything I describe is autobiographical, only I don't narrate the events directly.

"All Gods dead, all wars fought, all faiths in man shaken," F. S. Fitzgerald.

"That those who can, do, those who cannot and suffer enough because they can't, write about it," W. Faulkner.

Friday
Someone reads your absence on the palm of my [left] hand. A daydream that no one must discover [but for me alone].

Reading early Hemingway is crucial, definitive; he refuses to accept "depth" and narrates the surface of events. The fragility, the brevity, and the transience of action in some of his stories put the integrity of reality in danger. He acts toward reality as though he were blind. He takes the linearity of the story to the point of exasperation, and does not write what lies before or what comes after the events. He seeks the pure present, narrating the invisible effect of the action.

Suicide. His father had attempted suicide two days before. He learned about it that night, when someone called him several times on the phone and finally managed to reach him. "I'm a friend of your father's," she said, and there was a silence. The father attempts suicide. They save him. He stops talking. He saw his father sitting in a living room armchair, covered with a blanket of uncertain color, and he seemed . . . not bothered, more distracted. They looked at each other without speaking. (A man's "reasons" for killing himself are never known.) During the journey by bus, he tried not to think. It was raining. At one of the stops, in a desolate area, at the entrance to a town, by the side of the road, it seemed to him that the men and women traveling with him knew each other and were talking too much. He went back and sat in the empty minibus, drowsy. Dawn came. He sat down in a bar to wait for the sunrise to end. In the taxi he could see the sea. He stays with his father that night. Grows bored. Goes back, leaving him alone.

Sunday 10
Suddenly, a couple days ago, like a gust of wind, I envisioned the story of the father's suicide, entire, complete. Basically, I'm thinking about narrating that nocturnal journey home.

Novel. Work with footnotes that interrupt the narrator. Confirming or denying the events. Adding information. Micro-stories at the foot of the page.

In Beckett, always the attempt to write. A post-Joyce literature, that is, a story that moves between the ruins and the void. "It seemed to me that all language was an excess of language," Molloy.

I've always thought with a delay; the experiences were there, but when I wanted to *say them* it was always too late, they were out of place.

Monday
X Series. Lucas appeared. He always seems the same, but between one visit and the next what takes place is brutal (a bank robbery, the kidnapping of a businesswoman), but he never describes any of that, I find traces of it in newspapers, in notices, and in police reports.

Monday 18
Last night, I unexpectedly ran into a friend, Mejía, in Pasaje de La Piedad. He lives there, a fantastic place. I haven't seen him since childhood, in Bolívar. That alleyway is another world; it is circular, with large houses and trees, at the end are a church and a sign: *Exit for coaches*. Mejía played the bandoneon and my grandfather would always ask him for "Desde el alma," and he would play the waltz with great feeling, sitting on a bench, a cloak of black cloth wrapped around his thighs, where he rested the bandoneon. His father and mother were communists, and they read Russian magazines and scathingly criticized Peronism.

Thursday 21
Series A. Bogged down and penniless. I'm working on the story "Mousy Benítez." It will never be known for sure . . . That's how it should start. Miguel Briante offers me two editorials in *Confirmado* for twenty thousand pesos, I tell him no. An uncertain future, but not so different from that of former years. A personal economy always in crisis.

Today on TV: Hitchcock. Cinema on the small screen, as they say, becomes something else when interspersed with advertisements from reel to reel. It seemed as though there were two interwoven narratives, a collage between a painstakingly made story with fully-conceived and almost perfect images and, in parallel, happy people with tyrannical images attempting to sell a number of objects in brief microscopic stories. This double game causes a detachment, dissolving the illusion that cinema creates in a theater. On the other hand, television is watched with the lights on, and people can talk and move around. Something has changed in the reception of images.

Monday 25
I was born on November 24, 1941, and I've looked in the papers for news from that date. I looked in the National Library for everything I could find. The war took up all the informational space. It was six in the morning, and, according to my father, it was raining.

Novel. With the three gunmen already inside the apartment, the informant managed to leave the place for a few minutes under the pretense of buying provisions and took the opportunity to notify the police that everything had gone according to plan, and he then returned quickly to the place with his orders, coming back out after a few minutes for reasons he did not reveal. (*From the newspapers.*)

Saturday, March 30
Novel. Investigation using a tape recorder. The storyline appears from the beginning (they have been surrounded and cannot leave the apartment). It is about narrating the pauses, three recorded monologues, oral syntax.

Sunday 31
In a decisive hour of the early morning (around four), I try to reverse my life and start working at night. I isolate myself even further. I go out into the city with a different spirit than at other times, more attentive to myself than to reality. Ready to return home and work through the night, without interruptions. The discipline of work is a way to organize passions like any other.

I wake up at two in the afternoon, shower, shave, and have breakfast. I go to the Biblioteca Lincoln and work there for a while in the afternoon.

"No one can describe a man's life but the man himself. His inward being, his real life, is known to him alone; but when writing of it, he disguises it . . . he exhibits himself as he wishes himself to be seen, but not at all as he is," J.-J. Rousseau.

Tuesday, April 23

Nonfiction. Up all night reading *Treblinka*, a testament of the descent into hell. The first thing that makes an impression in this investigation into the workings of a death camp is the use of technique, a recognition of a change in the use of mechanisms of destruction. A certain historicity of the horror and forms of slavery appears. Formally, it is along the lines of Oscar Lewis and Walsh: it is a "novel" like *The Children of Sanchez* and a narrative judgment in the style of *Operation Massacre*. Today, anyone who wants to respect critical realism has to employ the tape recorder, reportage, and nonfiction. This new way has as much documentary importance as cinema. It constructs a reality through the use of new methods and language. Narrative experience with forms of investigation, using the techniques of true (or testimonial) stories.

"Only make the reader's general vision of evil intense enough, I said to myself—and that already is a charming job—and his own experience, his own imagination, his own sympathy (with the children) and horror (of their false friends) will supply him quite sufficiently with all the particulars. Make him think the evil, make him think it for himself, and you are released from weak specifications," Henry James.

Julia awoke from her sleep at noon and started to drift around the house, half-covered in my pajama top, her magnificent legs exposed, which was enough to rouse me, so I got up to have some tea with her. Then I took a cold shower, and even though my body remained dead and elsewhere, I couldn't escape the beginning of the day.

"Destiny is character," Heraclitus. "Character is destiny," Novalis. The modern concept of experience is contained between these two definitions, and emphasis on one or the other defines a vision of the world. The quote from Novalis (closer to psychoanalysis) escapes Heraclitus's magical, ritual, tragic meaning, which sees a design in character, a proof of the existence of fate. In Novalis, by contrast, there is no distance: a man "freely" chooses according to his character, that is, his impulses, his repetitions, in other words, his destiny.

A Christian conception: consciousness of original sin, initial guilt and the fall into mundanity (and into contingency), nostalgia for the paradise lost, prior to the division of the sexes, a sense of the supernatural. Transcendence.

A tragic approach: personal guilt does not exist, but judgment and fate do. Each person's destiny is written and dictated by the gods, but, by reading it in the many signs (oracles) and being mistaken, the tragic subject is condemned (in pure immanence).

Octavio Paz is mistaken in *Alternating Current*; it is not our art that is "underdeveloped" but our way of understanding art, that is, our colonial way of seeing, blinded by certain models. In Argentine literature, this moment covers history until Borges: since the beginning, our literature felt itself lacking compared to European literatures. Sarmiento says it precisely, and Roberto Arlt says it ironically: "What was my work, did it exist or was it ever more than one of those products that they accept around here for lack of something better?" Recently, after Macedonio and Borges, our literature—in our generation—exists in the same plane as foreign literatures. We are now in the present of art, whereas, during the nineteenth century and until quite a way into the twentieth century, our question was: "How can we be in the present? How can we become contemporary to our contemporaries?" We have resolved this dilemma: Saer or Puig, and even I, are in direct dialogue with contemporary literature and are, to put it metaphorically, at its level.

Wednesday, April 24
Series B. Sometimes I feel that I am "letting go" of certain friendships (my relationships with José Sazbón or León Rozitchner, for example), distance from the world and other people, and an apathy that always postpones actions.

Sometimes I worry because I've gone several months without writing, marked by vertigo and social circulation. Meetings, parties, entertainment. I'm determined to have done with this farce and finally sit down to write, come what may.

Novel. Maybe the whole account of the events could be structured as an interrogation or a conversation with Malito, the chief, alternating with third-person narration, not in chronological order.

"What?"
"Because talking with that thing on bothers me."
"The tape recorder bothers you?"
"I get all shy, it's like that thing makes me shy."

Series E. Neither the historical essay nor literature, strictly speaking, has succeeded in registering the microscopic changes of private experience. A narrator talks about himself in the first person, as though referring to someone else, because he habitually reconstructs his life from the end of the series that he is narrating, that is, from the present time of the writing. The best parts of the genre are the drafts or remnants or plans for a future autobiography that is never written. Life is momentum toward what does not yet exist, and, therefore, to pause in order to write it is to cut off the flow and leave behind the reality of experience. For its part, literature is a way of living, an action like sleeping, like swimming. Does this idea take away the sense of deliberate construction that literature possesses? I don't think so; the mistake is to seek the ashes of experience within the book when you should instead seek them in pauses, in fragments, in short forms.

Thursday 25
A hectic afternoon; I went to the Biblioteca Lincoln to look for Melville's complete novellas in a single volume, and then I got Raymond Queneau's article on *Bouvard et Pécuchet* from Galatea to use as a preface for the translation of the book. Then I went to Tiempo Contemporáneo to collect

ten thousand pesos so that I can go on spending, and finally I ended up at Jorge Álvarez; not much new except for Y. Mishima's book *Confessions of a Mask.*

Friday 26
"Because I'm creating an imaginary—it's always imaginary—world in which I would like to live," William Burroughs.

I'm at La Paz, a bar with modest delusions, annoyed because I'm over-dressed and overheated and also because Jorge Álvarez didn't come to our meeting, so I don't have enough cash to make it to the end of the month. I interrupted my note because B. appeared, wanting to write a script with me based on my novel in progress about the struggle in the hideout in Montevideo. I don't have much interest in using the subject for another parallel story, but Carlos is insistent and offers me so much money for the script that, in the end, I write the first scene, very much in the tone of my short stories.

Saturday 27
Surprised and uncomfortable after news of the publication of *Gazapo*, a novel by Gustavo Sainz, which, according to Monegal, was written using a tape recorder. The same as my story "Mata-Hari 55" and the novel I'm writing. I hope I don't have to deal with an unintentional precursor.

Series C. A woman appeared in the brief moments of early dawn as though pulled along by the wind or the morning, dressed in a strange leather jacket, a dark mantle to command the night.

Novel. Among the theories to explain the betrayal, a possibility emerges that the Englishman chose the apartment knowing that the police would come.

Toward an aesthetics of the typewriter. To write with a typewriter means to introduce the fixed reading into the moment of writing, since the act of tapping out words is distinguished by the possibility of reading what is being written simultaneously, though in another register and in another position of the body, without having to withdraw from the paper or stop writing (as happens when writing by hand). At the same time, the sound of the keys creates a rhythm, directed at both the ear and the eye, which can be sustained or altered. The keys with their printed letters create a musical score of language, a key that one must know how to perform in order for the music of language to be heard (but I, of course, write by hand in a notebook with a black ink pen).

Wednesday, May 1
Series B. Last night a multitudinous gathering to celebrate Pirí Lugones's birthday. At some point someone—I don't know if it was a man or a woman—gave her a dare, and a moment later Pirí was kissing Laura Y. in the middle of the living room, and it was like a flash of lost desires and secret fantasies. We stayed all night, attending to the little neurotic nuclei of the party, and came back home at eight in the morning.

Thursday, May 2
I entertain myself in every way possible, he said, and always with people whom I observe with a stranger's gaze; every once in a while, I head out into the streets in search of an adventure.

I'm not so sure, but the risks are minor in any case. The risks are always minor. I think: "There are too many people in my way." I think about Zelda, who died the same way as any of her husband's characters; she refused to leave the hospital, as if she had been waiting for the fire.

A story. One early morning at the Atenas club in La Plata, the body of Mousy Benítez lay strewn across the floor, face up as though floating in the flickering light of dawn. // In a cracked and yellowed clipping from *El Gráfico*, covered in rags, The Viking's fine, illuminated face looking at the camera head-on, his eyes opened wide, next to Archie Moore, who was laughing with his serious eyes.

Monday 6
Series A. A period similar to the last days of 1964; he talks about himself as though he were a historian reconstructing some long-lost past.

Today I didn't do any writing on "Mousy Benítez" (it is ready now) because I couldn't see it. The (verbal) image is everything in a short story: the gym at the Atenas club, a boxer feinting in front of a full-body mirror.

A desire to escape from here and to go out alone, with no baggage, to rent a room at a hotel downtown, to compose the inner logic of my life.

Series E. Diary: collage, montage, short forms, tension. "Killing oneself seems easy."

Smoking marijuana calms him. Rather, it relaxes him. He was always very tense and alert. Through the window the city full of lights, and below, far below, the dark street.

The father's suicide. The telephone tore him away from sleep, he sat up in bed, and he struggled so much getting dressed that he thought he was dreaming. Then he went to the hospital: it was there that he realized what he already knew. (Maybe it's better to begin when the nun comes in.) A dry tone, terse, *without* metaphor.

Karl Marx. Historical creation of the categories of understanding. Philosophy takes up the rationality of the means of production at a linguistic level. The historical process is not thought of as content but rather is based on the categories produced by the process itself. Example: Nation. Example: Social class. Is literature also a concept produced by historical experience? In any case, we don't call the same texts literature in different periods.

An economy. "The money which I got in exchange for sex was a token indication of one-way desire that I was wanted enough to be paid for, on my own terms," John Rechy, *City of Night*.

Saturday

Series E. Drastically changing lives, another name the same as other passions, seeking peace, leaving this empty chaos.

In Cuba, during a long and talkative walk with León Rozitchner along the Havana pier, León pauses and asks me: "But would you live here?" His philosophy is founded on the claim of an accord between modes of thought and ways of life. He calls this throwing yourself in. I recalled the habitual challenges in gaucho poetry—what I say with my lips I defend with my neck.

Novel 1. For me it was like returning to the town, pretending those hooks in my wrists did not exist, while the faces of the passengers in the train car watched me fleetingly, a woman across from me in a polka-dot dress did not know where to rest her blue eyes. I was returning to the town, as always, bound, with a policeman attached to me.

Novel 2. Costa comes to me and says: The Englishman told me you're staying here, but I just saw him leaving Acapulco, going to Suipacha. We've been sleeping on the La Plata-Buenos Aires train for three days, back and forth, back and forth. I tell him: some day we'll end up in the railway sheds, a day and a night, Costa says to me, sleeping. We were hitchhiking to anywhere we could go, we would cross the tracks and already be traveling backward, to the south.

Saturday

Series A. In El Foro. I write in bars, spend my hours here. Once more the vertigo, turning in wider and wider circles around a center that changes with the clock. Yesterday with the newspaper classifieds, I go back and forth (as they say), from one end of the city to the other, and finally find an apartment on Pasaje del Carmen. I look for a guarantor, that is, a guarantee. I pay for three months as a deposit. Last night, turmoil with Pirí because of my leaving. The coming weeks seem difficult. If I manage to land this place (or another), I'll try, after ten years of hotels and single rooms, to begin to live in a stable environment. Otherwise, my economic problems will start up once again. I prefer them to the others . . .

Series A bis. Another bar, now on Carlos Pellegrini, cold air filters in through the cracks of the poorly-closed window, to my left a woman speaks quietly in French with a man who seems to be her father, she laughs at him and he tells her a dubious story about an Algerian making the crossing to Gibraltar. The older man, who perhaps is not her father but rather her lover, who perhaps supports the woman or is supported by her, repeats "Gibraltar, Gibraltar" several times like a litany.

Sunday, June 2
Settled into this bright apartment, in an alleyway that comes from the past, the rear-guard, last bastion, last defense. An end to the journey. How many places in recent years? Some economic security to let us survive for a season. I was lucky. Out on the sidewalk there was a fair, lots of noise starting at four or five in the morning, but to my good fortune they changed places and moved away from here . . . as of yesterday. All is calm now, waiting.

The structure of Puig's novel is Faulknerian, choral narration based on narrators who at once participate in and witness the events. It is the reader who must reconstruct and synthesize a hodgepodge of faltering sentences, fragments of conversations, letters, and diaries, finally building a story that is not located anywhere, that has not been told but rather alluded to. A coming-of-age novel, great skill in the use of orality.

"A woman once left me stunned at the concept of 'corny' when she wrote to me in tears. These laments and protests of mine will seem corny to you. Corny is all sentiment that is not shared," Ramón Gómez de la Serna.

Tuesday, June 4
Series E. As always, my tendency to blame my lack of solitude on "presences," my difficulties with entering the game, are in reality an excuse. I

think about empty spaces as places where I can cease to be myself, like someone in the corner of a station waiting room who changes his glasses, uses fake documents, and transforms himself.

Just now a walk down Santa Fe to the Supervielle bank to cash the check and stop by the bookshop to find *Cabot Wright Begins* by James Purdy.

Thursday 6

Series B. Yesterday I ran into León Rozitchner, who offered me a bookcase to organize my books, and I walked with him down Florida, with everyone frightened after the assassination of Bobby Kennedy. Finally at Jorge Álvarez I ran into David Viñas, who has a striking ability to change the subject and draw me into the world of his concerns. In this case, our friendship is founded on what could be called a shared velocity for thinking about several things at the same time, avoiding obstacles. Impossible to have a conversation if it doesn't come out of a dense series of implicit understandings and common ground.

In Puig's *Betrayed* . . . a phenomenon of stylization occurs, a sort of visible distortion that can be viewed as a "defect" of the composition (in the manner of Onetti's clashing and stylistic affectation). Yet this is its greatest merit; the novel reveals the extreme nature of a world that moves around within a common language based on forms of expression derived from Hollywood cinema—photo-novels and sentimental letters—which mold lived experience (and exist outside all literary formulation or high culture). What is striking is that he controls this form of verbal realism with such skill that he transforms language into the lived expression of life. That language is now a form of life. The novel, then, works with reality that has already been told (by the mass media).

Series A. I cross Viamonte to buy croissants, walking quickly to beat the cold, with the wind and sun in my face. The alleyway opens onto Calle Córdoba to the left and onto Viamonte to the right, and it runs parallel to Rodríguez Peña. Long ago, these shortcuts were passages for cars or the tram. The street is silent, and I feel well here.

Friday 7

Yesterday I worked out the matter of the newspaper pieces with old Luna. I arrange ninety dollars per month (a stipend). My dream of living off three dollars per day . . . I have to be in the editorial office for three hours every day, which I don't like.

X Series. Later, Lucas comes to my place dressed like a banker; he always follows the walk signs when he crosses the street, but he goes around armed and carrying fake papers. He came with beautiful Celina, and I imagine (love notwithstanding) that she also serves as an alibi for him, or creates the natural image of a married man strolling along with his wife. Everything is fake, except for the danger. He sits down, and we talk calmly. Celina was my student at La Plata and is much more intelligent and sensitive than he is, but perhaps isn't as brave. (I ask myself: does she know? Or, at any rate, how much does she know about Lucas's clandestine life?)

Hamlet = Stephen Dedalus = Quentin Compson = Nick Adams = Jorge Malabia. The young romantic, the aspiring artist, who faces the world as it is and can't bear it. The story told is how each one reacts to the weight of an unbearable (and adult or adulterous) reality. Creating, then, a story of the *imaginary writers*.

Saturday 8

Series B. Just now a visit from José Sazbón, he's my oldest friend from my new life (which began in A.D. 1960). I don't know anyone more intelligent or more cultured (from the culture that interests me), no one shier or friendlier. Veiled conflicts about five thousand pesos, etc.

"It is not that one expresses anything when writing. One constructs another reality, the word," Cesare Pavese.

"Literature is not a mirror that reflects reality but is something added to the world," Jorge Luis Borges.

"Economy and interest are at the base of behaviors, beliefs, systems of neurosis," Roland Barthes.

Dostoevsky. In his novels, the action moves forward for reasons that are hidden to the reader, and it is only when catastrophe approaches that the hidden cause is made clear by means of an extensive confession. Underneath, there is always an inability to remember or name "The Crime" (which is different for everyone and is secret). This outmoded exposition is the theory of the crime and the superior man, which Raskolnikov communicates only after the murder. It is the Legend of the Grand Inquisitor that functions as Ivan Karamazov's novel. Stravrogin's confession in *Demons* belongs to the same method.

Sunday 9
I saw Godard's *The Carabineers*, a fable about war, a silent film, an air of Beckett and Borges creating a story full of surprises, vertigo, earth, magic, etc., with photographs of everything in the world (style of *Bouvard et Pécuchet*) wrapped up in the violence of war.

Tuesday 11
Puig's poetics. "Without a model I can't draw," says Toto. Then there's the magnificent chapter with the school composition describing the experience of seeing the film *The Great Waltz* and retelling it. The letter that ends the novel is the same one that Berto tears up in the first chapter.

It is striking to observe the treatment of seduction in Stendhal and Laurence Sterne (*A Sentimental Journey Through France and Italy*). The same situation in both: Julien Sorel and Sterne's autobiographical narrator hesitate to take the hands of the women they love for the first time. Nothing more. A touch, the gesture of moving toward . . .

"It is time the reader should know it, for in the order of things in which it happened, it was omitted: not that it was out of my head; but that had I told it then it might have been forgotten now;—and now is the time I want it," L. Sterne (seems like Macedonio Fernández).

Wednesday
Series A. A visit from my father, always cheerful and distrustful, with an air of helplessness but strong convictions. Disheartened because I'm not interested in politics (that is, in Peronism) like he is; we have dinner together, and he makes me recall moments of my life that I had forgotten. (My attempt to put a bomb in the UCR headquarters in 1956, in what had been Carlos Pellegrini's old house in Adrogué, when I was fifteen and did everything in secret, or so I believed, though I see now that my father knew the score. I planned it with my cousin Cuqui, and it seemed natural to us to do something like that in response to the catastrophe caused by the Revolución Libertadora.) My father amuses himself by telling that story and, in the same way, silences the story of his own "exploits," which put him in prison.

I read *Absalom, Absalom!* for the second time with astonishment and admiration. From a used bookshop I get the Mexican series *Los narradores ante el público*, autobiographies of writers from my own generation who describe ways and routines from their lives that are very similar to my own or those of Saer or Miguel Briante. A generation is a scattered, non-chronological series of shared readings and rituals, which will age along with us.

Thursday 13
Celina L. comes to see me with a proposal for a lecture in La Plata. She is sick but perseveres despite her bleak outlook and goes onward, intelligent and firm. I left and went down Corrientes in the light rain. In Jorge Álvarez everything is going along well, he brings me Rojo's book on Che. Many anecdotes with no great importance, critique of Guevara's foco guerrilla theory.

I am working on possible topics for my lecture at La Plata, maybe I'll talk about Puig and Cabrera Infante: spoken language and choral narration of an ever-elusive story. An alternative is to give a talk on Puig, Saer, and Walsh: Walsh's nonfiction and his pieces in the CGT newspaper at one extreme, and Saer with his writing that tends toward lyricism on the other. Puig in the middle. All three reproduce the experience of Peronism in their own ways. Walsh in *Operation Massacre*, Puig with the diary of the girl talking about Eva Perón, and Saer in *Responso*, a novel in which Peronism is the context behind the protagonist's "player" lifestyle. These are the three who can be read in Buenos Aires today (see Walsh's short stories).

Friday 14

Series E. It is five in the morning, another hollow night, going from bar to bar. I always have the same conversations even though the friends sitting at the table are different. I go out and drink whiskey until dawn in order to erase some fixed ideas that have always pursued me, ones that I prefer not to name. A very cold night; I walked alone until I made it back to this corner by the window, through which the dawn air filters in.

Saturday 15

Series Z. I want to record what is happening to me. Slight hallucinations that trouble me. First, I have a feeling of fullness, a ferocious happiness, and then suddenly a veil is unwrapped and pulled away, and I see reality as it is. I don't know what is happening to me, and all I want is to name these visions. If I can. I don't know if language suffices to describe these vistas.

For many weeks I've been coming to the library every afternoon and working on Tolstoy, and now I'll say why I do it. My eyes are exhausted; according to the doctors, I don't blink at the normal rate and my eyes are dry, like a well without water one of the specialists told me, and he gave me a prescription for tears. Not to help me cry (something that is hard for me), but to use as eye drops. We'll see.

Sunday
Series Z. That dryness may be the cause of my disrupted vision. In the extreme aridity of the desert, mirages appear.

Notes on Tolstoy (1). In the company of his younger daughter, Alexandra (who will die in the sixties in the United States), and his personal doctor, an ancient Tolstoy sets off—like a King Lear fleeing with Cordelia—on an erratic pilgrimage with an unknown destination. He is looking for Father Albert, he says, a *starets*, a holy man (the model for his short story "Father Sergius" and for Father Zosima from Dostoevsky's *Karamazov*), who has been a sort of Mephistopheles for Good to him and is the one who converted him to Christianity, in a past encounter.

I must continue onward, recording what happens to me and never ceasing to register my life day after day.

Tuesday 18
Series B. Yesterday a long stroll around the city with David Viñas, circular and amusing conversations, maneuvers, estimations, the early stages of a friendship. I don't let on to him about what's happening to me, though I take his arm when we cross the street so that I don't take a plunge. He doesn't notice anything and goes on talking.

Wednesday 19
Yesterday a frustrating meeting for the magazine, Andrés Rivera's confessions, sadness in the Royal Garden. I see Andrés's face like a distorted mirror and comment on the Japanese park. I tell him: it was night and the faces distorted, he was surprised.

Two hours later the crisis has already passed. The memory is funny. Andrés's face was like elastic, inflating and deflating. Now I'm working on Hemingway for the book *Balance de E. H.*

Hemingway saw the same things I'm seeing, and they gave him electro-shock treatment at the Mayo Clinic, but he tried to throw himself out of the car when they took him back home. Funny and unbearable.

I am well and at peace; it is ten at night.

The mass media and journalists have found their hero in Hemingway. An image of the writer who doesn't write and spends his life off hunting in Africa or fishing for sharks. It has to do with a cult of personality, putting literary figures in the place of movie stars, so that what is valued is the picturesque aspect of their biographies. Underneath lies the superstition that life legitimizes literature and replaces it. Soon there will be no need to write; it will be enough to lead a turbulent life and say you are a writer. His early books are, of course, examples of a very intentional writer, close to his experiences on the front lines, who created an extraordinary prose based on brevity and the cult of the unsaid.

Series A. When Henry Ford built the V8 engine, powerful enough to outstrip police cars, gangs began to develop. The automobile became a weapon of war. Gunslingers practically lived in their cars. In those years, the car replaced the horse as the symbol of the outlaw and, in a sense, Westerns evolved into gangster films. (From a description of the genre by the film director Arthur Penn.)

A laborious night, as usual these days, fighting against my own visions. It is written in the body, that is, in the posture; exhaustion can be recognized in multiple areas, in the stiffness of the fingers: a pianist with gloves, a hunter with dark glasses. Something about that. What is extreme lucidity worth if your body feels like it belongs to someone else?

Sunday
We're going to set ourselves in motion, and, even though I'm cramped, I won't think of leaving the table, by the typewriter, sitting in this wooden chair, with its high back. (You also write with your ass.)

A story. A heavyweight boxer, elegant, charming, who moves with a lightweight's speed.

Novel. A tape recorder is hidden in the apartment; the police know the layout. They changed their hideout. In any case, the narrator reports: this is a tape submitted by the police (a fragment of a telephone call can be heard).

In Pavese there is an opposition between "the business of the classics" and "the dialectical tumult of our time." There is no language common to everyone now, but was there once? The language of the classics is in reality the literary language that functions as a social model (for us, Borges's style, copied in the weekly magazines).

Monday 24
Series B. An unexpected visit from Andrés R. during an amorous moment. A theory about interruption must be made: who or what interrupts, and which is the situation that is "curbed" and must change direction. For the better, Andrés comes with his emotional misfortunes, so Pavesian (his woman left with his best friend, a poet, for a change).

For me, the interferences are the vistas (I don't mean to speak of visions) that lie in wait for me. They are off to the side; I see them in the corner of my eye. Situated on the northeast edge of the room. They murmur like the whine of a taut wire in the night wind. I cover my ears with my hands or sometimes put on music to drown them out.

"Literature sustains me." I like Onetti's early prose, less baroque. I'm reading *No Man's Land*, a nervous style, sensitive, tense, which incorporates echoes of Faulkner but above all a certain air of the "hard-boiled" novelists: Hammett and Cain. You can also see the connection to Roberto Arlt there; the Argentine era of Onetti is a bridge, crossing the void of the forties after Arlt. Borges is there like a light dazzling everyone, and Onetti takes many of his stylistic turns from him. Going against the short form of Borges and Rulfo, Onetti seeks to establish a story of longer duration, which doesn't turn out well for him until *A Brief Life*, although what he writes in those first novels is very good.

I'm going along well, and only the altered, arrhythmic beating of my heart keeps me alert while I write so as not to think, seeing nothing more than my hand gliding through the pages of the notebook.

It is possible to detect the way certain invisible writers embody the tone of an era, later crystallized into what we call "a great writer" or "a great book." This can be seen with José Bianco, Daniel Devoto, and Antonio Di Benedetto himself, and also with Silvina Ocampo and María Luisa Bombal or Felisberto Hernández, finally concluding with or flowing into Onetti. Of course, it isn't about someone "consciously" reclaiming a tradition, but rather a sort of contemporary tone or horizon in which several writers, though unconnected, seek "the way." (The one among us, who is it or who are they?)

Series E. As can be seen, this notebook tends to mark my intellectual biography above all, as though my life were being sketched with no other motion than that of literature. And why not? You always have to choose work over life or, rather, the work creates your way of living. For me, the lonely assailant now no longer demands "your money or your life," but rather, more light-heartedly: "your work or your money." Otherwise, in the other register, there are contingent events, which I give some meaning to by writing them down, although there's a risk of introspection, the nonsense of "interior life" (what could be exterior?), for example, talking about today's stroll with Julia, tangled up in a rhetorical and circular argument, trying to find a way to get along together. Impossible.

Series E bis. But, at the same time, there is a simple moral; the point is not to turn literature into a superior world, not to take part in the game where it is considered a sacred territory that only the enlightened or holy can enter. If, on the other hand, life is subordinated to literature, the risk is such that it doesn't occur to anyone to "become an artist," there is too much at stake, or too much has been set aside not to take on projects that have classical criteria, coming from Aristotle: the artist is like a carpenter who knows intuitively how to work with the wood and therefore chooses that profession and tries to learn how to make a table. That is all.

Novel. When I say spoken language, the use of oral syntax in narrative, I refer to the origins of modern Argentine literature, that is, to *Martín Fierro*, a story that is sung, from its vocabulary to its tone. This was the discovery that Borges made. Conversely, Arlt's is a purely written language, a language fascinated by literature, translating Russian novels into cultured language. At times it is more "literary" than Borges. You have to wait until Manuel Puig to find their intersection, with his wonderfully fine ear for oral language and his experimental choice to write using techniques and forms that often come from elsewhere and not from the literary tradition in the strictest sense (and in that sense Puig is very Joycean).

Betrayed by R. H. and *Mad Toy* are coming-of-age novels. Arlt defines his poetics in the first sentence of that book ("I was initiated into the thrilling literature of outlaws and bandits"). That sentence constitutes all of the books that follow that first novel. In Puig's case, the constitutive moment is the grade school composition that Toto writes about the movie *The Great Waltz*, retelling it. Bovarism, which consists simply of preferring fiction to reality, is present in both. That is what unites them and defines their education.

I spend the night awake, eavesdropping on the noises that come from the apartment next door. Once again come the murmurs that I alone can hear, a woman (a voice like a woman's, a pretend voice) says something about an uncle who has bought a house in the country. That single mention troubles me. The womanly voice (that is the way I define it, as though it were a moo) keeps repeating the same thing but sometimes laughs with a little worn-out song, am I hearing voices? I have to do something, I don't want to wake Julia up or tell her what has been happening to me for the last fourteen days. I furtively escape and take a little excursion down Corrientes to the bookshop. I discover the Spanish edition of Gombrowicz's *La seducción*, which I had already read in Italian as *Pornografia*, lent to me by Dipi Di Paola. A little bird hanging from a wire, a sparrow?

Notes on Tolstoy (2). A shared dream between Anna Karenina and Vronsky in the novel: an old man with a bag says incomprehensible words in French, which—as Nabokov has already pointed out—is tied to a personal memory of Tolstoy's. An ancient blind man, who had worked on the estate as a storyteller for many years, would come into his grandmother's room at night, while she was lying in bed, the candle already snuffed out. He would sit on the inside sill of a deep window, eating some of the food left from dinner out of a bowl, and then, in the wavering glow of the nightlights that burned before the icons, he would begin a tale. Long-haired, with a large beard, he resembled other mujiks and wore a black wool tunic, both inside the house and outdoors, following the customs of peasants. He has Homer's eyes, but how different he is from the ancient bard and his sublime songs, bathed in the blue of the sea! The old man mixes together stories that have not come to him through books (he is illiterate) but rather through orality, dating back along the Volga, coming from the far end of Turkestan, farther even, from Persia. One night, Lyovochka—the Russian diminutive that they called Tolstoy in his childhood—snuck into his grandmother's room and listened. The mystery of the scene left an impression on him because of the storyteller's unseeing eyes. He always says that it was one of his first memories.

Tuesday
I think about Martín Mejía, who would play the bandoneon for my grandmother Rosa on the dirt patio, behind the country house in Bolívar.

I can see myself at age eight or nine, watching Martín's serious face as he played with his eyes closed.

Wednesday
Series B. I woke up at three in the afternoon when David came knocking, as though I needed help from some danger he could perceive in me, though he doesn't know what it is either. Half-asleep, I received him but, as usual with him, he gave me the sense that he was already talking to himself in the elevator and then continued his private-political-literary monologue without realizing that I was still asleep. He came to help me, but I scared him off despite his visible attempts to stay and chat with me all afternoon. I have to be alone in order to think.

There came a night when they locked me out of that house, lost in the country, and I jumped over the mud wall thinking the key might be the problem, since I always had trouble getting out: but on the other side of the door I found the padlock, and it was like a robbery in reverse. Above all because my books, my clothing, and especially the original versions of my short stories were on the other side of that padlock. And then I had to jump back over. Filled with anxiety, having nothing more than the front door, no place to sleep, Julia and I went to stay at a horrid hotel near the station, in a tiny little room.

The initiation. Without trying to prove anything, I found myself making love to a woman for the first time. I was fourteen, and she was a neighbor, the same age as my mother, and was one of her friends. To confirm all of my half-mystical theories, she, Ada, had red hair. I've always loved redheads.

Series E. Another landscape outside: balconies with bars, dark houses, always a different image in the window beside where I sit, writing. Every now and then, I raise my eyes and look off to the left, and I remain still like that while the words come and go until suddenly I start to write them down once again. That tiny room, painted white, on Riobamba, on the second floor; the high-ceilinged bedroom with a picture window that went all the way down to the floor, on Montes de Oca; the room shaped like a cross on Avenida Rivadavia; the wall painted by a Fine Arts student in the boarding house on the diagonal street in La Plata, where I would listen for the paperboy coming from the end of the street at dawn and get dressed to catch the newspaper from the balcony—they have remained fixed in my memory, places that come from a motionless time.

I do not exist in any place, and fortunately I do not belong to my generation or any classification of current writers. I am saying this because today (Wednesday, July 3, 1968), my absence from the overview of new Argentine narrative presented in *Primera Plana* is outrageous, and once more I feel the same anger that sustains my writing, the same sensation that I'm writing against the current. There are signs that reach me, even though they are very faint, and I alone can see them, ready to maintain a silence that has already lasted five months.

Monday
Of course, I'm trapped in the whirlwind caused by my move out of Pirí Lugones's house, with her organized system of constant meetings and parties. In the vacuum of publicity, there is always a tendency to set aside more time for promoting a book than for writing it and, as an obligatory reference and measure of value, to put the same people in charge of managing that publicity.

Friday
I saw the beggar, her face bent to her breast, talking to herself, stubbornly walk past and turn onto Calle Viamonte as though she were escaping. She sleeps in a doorway and I observe her behavior, waiting for the right moment to approach and talk to her.

The narrative experience of boxing. Verbal description that moves among three planes: a rapid account of what is taking place, a lucid analysis of the technique and strategy of the fight, and, finally, the cries that filter in from the audience around the ring. I could write a novel by using those first two levels: narration and analysis in a single story. This all came to me because I heard the story of the fight between Bonavena and Folley, with ironic and picaresque moments: "Bonavena looked out at the stands, and his rival was furious."

The workings of the narration. All of the characters appear as narrators, putting the story, so to speak, on the table. The role of the narrator, that is, a person describing something, must circulate among all of the characters, including the one writing the story. The point is to value the act of telling (conversing) over the simple act of writing.

All explicit reference made in literature itself to the void, to the absence or end of literature, invades the territory of ethics and is idiotic.

"The English . . . kill themselves without one being able to imagine any reason that would cause them to do so, that they kill themselves when in the bosom of happiness," Montesquieu.

On Puig. In his work, there is no ironic distance between the writer and the speech of the characters (as there is indeed in Bioy Casares or Cortázar, who clown around, spurning the use of the subordinate classes' language). There is a sentimental relationship between language and character. They tell themselves stories without discerning any meaning. Puig immediately understands the need to write without parody. Instead of ironically observing from the outside, the narrator moves among the characters like one of them. Puig avoids aristocratic satire, the kind of speech that creates a facile complicity with the reader; instead, Puig establishes a complicity with his characters.

Series E. Ultimately, like it or not, these notebooks will be an archive or register of my sentimental education, and so they will basically be composed of reflections on my feelings, barely intersected by actions or events or words about myself. At the same time, these notebooks form a narrative with little significance on the level of plot, but they have a tension that only arises from the reading yet to come: as in any novel, what takes place in the moment, brought on by chance and contingency, will be viewed as immutable once it has come to pass. I tend now to intersplice the narrative with analysis of the actions and with pure description of the events.

Saturday 13
Solidarity with Viñas and his reserved and violent speech, rejecting what he calls "the seduction of the media" (which seduces him too much, I say). He's right, he has captured the change in the intellectual climate. Literary validation no longer passes through the traditional systems (*Sur* for example), but instead through the mass media; journalists are the new intellectuals or, at any rate, they're the ones who fulfill the function of intellectuals.

In the year before I published my first book, beginning a new story was an exhausting effort; my nerves were frayed, and I would catch perilous glimpses of the right names and spend a whole morning calling everyone, men and women, "Ramón." One afternoon, which I experienced as though it were a sunrise, I watched the sunset through the window three hours after I'd gotten out of bed. I was hungry and listening to a strange radio story about a desert region in the north of the country. At the time I was living in a room in a large boarding house near Parque Lezama, on the corner of Martín García and Montes de Oca. I was calm, waiting to see nightfall before going to buy ham, cheese, and sardines at the market to eat with fresh bread and wine, letting the night pass without surprises. Now, by contrast, a year later, I live besieged by momentary visions or—as I call them—vistas. It's as though I had a private TV channel activated inside my head, making me see a sequence of blurry, real images on the edge of my mind. At this stage, closing my eyes does nothing for me. Are they mental images or forgotten memories?

Monday 15
Light rain. I'm getting started. Fiction for B. now, then a meeting for the magazine with David Viñas, pushing forward well, on my side, but the rest is ambiguous, unclear. We'll see what happens.

Novel. Tone before storyline, inner voices before plot.

"The author? For me, the author is the one who puts on the title," Juan Carlos Onetti.

Thursday 18
Series B. Yesterday a walk with David through Boca, the little houses that I almost never saw while I lived there. A world mixed with tango and anarchist tradition. A brotherly meeting with him, his way of understanding reality is very akin to my own (more so than anyone else's). Then, in the end, we have ravioli with wine in a tavern looking out at the boats, between the clamor and the painted walls.

Sunday
Series B bis. More visits from David, his attempts to attack Borges that I blocked elegantly but unsuccessfully, dinners in Bajo, meetings for the magazine, and meanwhile I'm working on Puig, many ideas.

Monday 22
Bursts of insomnia, rare for me, and no great results, a conflicted month. Today I saw Boorman's *Point Blank*, with Lee Marvin, the loneliness of gangsters.

Series A. What enchants me about the indifferent figure is the decision to drive oneself to live without others. Living in a closed circle.

A complicated day, but so are all days, unless I decide to live on an island.

Sunday 28
Adventures with David, who lambasts Borges again and again. We went to a lecture by Sabato last Thursday to stir up some trouble. Apprehension, but I am happier, riding out this period of my life without drama, with little clarity and much exhaustion, with nothing lying ahead but my own confusion, empty certainties, repeated mistakes. Disorganized reading. Fleeting elation.

Thursday, August 1
The month ends with no great internal cataclysms, with Pirí, with Julia, with reality.

Friday 2
I don't tell anyone what I see. Even here, I take care in writing about my "vistas" so as not to give them validation. What is happening? Hallucinations, visions. It is not a secret, they are not secrets or anything like that, but they're so vivid that I can't describe them (still).

Notes on Tolstoy (3). "Poet, Calvinist, fanatic and aristocrat," Turgenev defined him with these four words. In the end, the categories of "Calvinist and fanatic" canceled out those of "poet and aristocrat." After his crisis and conversion, he progressively distances himself from literature, learning how to make shoes with the cobbler in the town. "A good pair of boots is worth more than *War and Peace*." As has become clear, in another context, the opposition of literature vs. boots had a tradition in the political and social debates in Russia. "Pisarev . . . following Bazarov, had resoundingly declared a shoemaker to be more useful than Pushkin." The Peronist slogan of *shoes yes, books no* seems to be a creole version of the same tradition (extreme populism).

August 8
Disoriented, I realize that it's been more than a week since I've paused to write about what is happening, the nights that stretch on past noon, altered sleeping patterns, working on the essay about Puig that interrupted

a letter to Cabrera Infante. Meetings for the magazine, a certain sadness that came and took me two days ago. The worries continue, yesterday it pained me to cross the entryway with the woman sitting there, so I turned back and waited until I couldn't see her. She wears a navy-blue cloak, and she even knows my name. She is fat; I have seen her in dreams, and she reappears to me now.

Friday 9

Yesterday David came over, assuring me that he felt "very good, better than ever." Beba Eguía was already on the way to Europe, neither Julia nor I knew what to do for him, in my case due to my excessive shyness, in hers out of respect for my excessive shyness, until he finally left, as though it pained him, and agreed to call me on the phone. The light is low; my eyes are tired, and now I'm reading Gombrowicz's *Diary*.

Tuesday 13

Series E. I get up early in spite of the cold and open the window, and on the other side of the street, against the wall, two old men are warming themselves beside an improvised campfire in an oil can which has already turned red from the heat. The flames rise and envelop the precarious container, and they shift around it and laugh, tapping their feet on the ground. The day is at once gray and clear.

Tuesday 20

Hard work to get five thousand pesos in advance of the fifty thousand for the book of three *nouvelles* by Melville, with a preface by Carl Olson! Earlier, a doctor gave me a prescription for eyeglasses. We'll see if, by seeing more clearly, I can see more clearly. It would be amusing to prove that a pair of glasses modifies reality. According to the ophthalmologist, peripheral visions of figures or objects is a result of excessive reading. He treated me like an idiot: what do you see here? he asked me, and he lit up the wall with a little flashlight, pointing to different sized letters on the eye chart poster. Nothing, I told him, I mean, basically nothing, I can see the light from your flashlight. We went on like that for a while because he wanted to verify whether I was seeing those figures, but I only see them when I'm alone. This specialist is very expensive. Junior recommended him to me.

Series E. Someday, I will have to motivate myself to *revise* all of the notebooks I've written, selecting from within them and making clean copies. I am afraid, among other things, of misrepresenting the past, of deliberately forgetting, of choosing poorly, leaving out things that—in ten years, let's say—may seem fundamental to me. I come and go with the style; sometimes everything is very fluid and other times I fall into private shudderings. The fundamental thing is the fatigue in my left hand, the stress from writing, and that's why, I think, I see too much.

Thursday 22
The effects of reviews are always insubstantial; it seems as though they are talking about something else and that is in fact the case, but what can you really expect? Something that can never come, and so you have to keep writing. There is no way to gain certainty in what you are doing, unless you come back from death. All this hot air because the Centro Editor's chapter on this generation was published yesterday (which generation is mine?). Exclusions, little hostilities, etc. To overcome my abstract anger, I have to sit down and write, projecting myself toward a future that seems uncertain (but isn't that the essential quality of the future?), because I've been in this dry spell for two years so far, writing to forget.

Series A. A splendid lesson, in any case; I'm here but would prefer not to be, which confirms some half-glimpsed truths. If I had the courage (I could barely make myself write down the above, I should never talk about myself or my relationship with the critics), I would keep coming back to this period but would write everything in third person: everything since I arrived in the city in 1965, my trip to Cuba, my stay in Piri's house, my work with Álvarez, my book release, my economic problems and solutions. This whole process is a sort of novel of education, and I still haven't written about it because I find it hard to step back, despite mentioning this distant attitude as my most legitimate pretension. Maybe the fundamental work lies in finding the tone to narrate my passions with distance. Knowing how to let the incidents come. All the same, it is evident that I've spent my life asking for more time, looking for ways to postpone the moment of informed decisions.

One unexpected afternoon, his wife—the woman he considered to be his wife in his imagination—spontaneously appeared at his room in a boarding house in La Plata, along with the father (his father). He was in bed with Constanza; they weren't doing anything special, they'd only gotten into bed because it was very cold. Inés came up the staircase first, and when she opened the door she stood there motionless, not entering, and only told him that she'd come with the father (his father). Confusion; Constanza took a moment to get dressed and put on her shoes and then went down the stairs, calmly (trying to seem calm). He remembers nothing of that day. Inés told him that his father had turned up, looking for her, and the situation was so confusing that she'd decided to come to La Plata with him, without warning. He imagined his father trying to seduce Inés, he'd already tried it with Helena, and he felt so wounded that he decided right there to leave everything behind and go to live in Buenos Aires with Inés. He remembers the journey on the bus, he and Inés were speaking in low voices, maybe he was making promises, and his father traveled in the seat behind the two of them.

Sometimes, the reality of an action is manifested to us in its consequences (I should say: it is always manifested in this way). On certain occasions, great crimes have been committed easily, as if in a dream. Then came the desire to wake up, but it was too late. I would not like to say that this has been the story of my life.

"I am not an entertainer . . . I'm concerned with the precise manipulation of word and image . . . to create an alteration in the reader's consciousness . . . to make people aware of the true criminality of our times," William Burroughs.

Trouble concentrating and reading, a certain undefined restlessness; my *sidelong glances*, as I call them, persist. Now I'm reading André Gide's diary, which I remain outside of, as if he were accountable for raising a fence to isolate his life, or rather, the everyday story of his life, presenting it as the experience of a man too aware of his privileges and virtues (and also his beautiful imperfections).

Friday, August 23
Alone, with Julia, at an event for Felipe Vallese in Avellaneda, caught up in excitement and anger.

I finish a draft of my essay on Puig, read Gide's diary, and agree to write some articles for Luna under the pseudonym of Trekiakov, caught up in the narrative aspects of journalism; I finish two pieces, one on social delinquency and another on the military. In this voluntary work, I foresee a more and more efficient and impersonal mechanization.

Good times, at any rate, despite some indeterminate sources of restlessness that I put aside until suddenly, as I turn my head, I am surprised, seeing them in front of me as though catching myself, spontaneously, in a mirror. In such cases, of course, experience does nothing. If I could get them to leave me alone, I would not spend so much time gazing into this unexpected mirror.

Series B. David arrived last night.

Series A. Nervous about my visit to Jorge Álvarez in a little while. Why so many problems? I can't bear economic favors, both because of my delirious relationship with money and my resistance to "entering" reality (and the two movements are just one). I would like to receive enough money—out of thin air, as they say—to work for a whole year in peace without seeing anyone.

I resist describing last night's dinner and my meeting with David, a certain shared nostalgia for past times.

Sunday
Today I spent the day alone without any surprises. Decent work yesterday, although the piece about Puig is still twenty centimeters short of the final. Correcting a piece of writing seems like one of Zeno's paradoxes. Further still: to correct a text—with each modification—is to open a new path, finding another passage that moves the entire structure and opens a new balance and a new imbalance, which, in being modified, will open a new balance, etc. At any rate, if there's time, I hope to correct the beginning and end before I type it all up definitively.

Monday
A good meeting for the magazine at David's house. Discussion of some weak materials (by Ismael on intellectuals), prior tensions that David experienced after his conversation with me the other night (which I didn't want to relate). Raúl Sciarretta has good critical sense, though he's excessive sometimes: his joining, with David and Walsh, along with my momentum (how long will it last?) may work out.

Series E. Clearly, I struggle to write down here what I'm living through in the present; the experience takes on all of its newfound weight in memory. Anyway, I must demand greater continuity and less direct style from myself in these notebooks. But how can I write about crossing Carlos Pellegrini yesterday afternoon after taking LSD, with my super-heightened senses and a kind of velocity that went beyond the events themselves? Or Friday afternoon in Plaza Lavalle, reading an article on Gustavo Sainz in *Mundo Nuevo* and thinking about how I was the same age as him but still hadn't published a novel? I think about how old writers are, what they did when they were twenty-six years old, my age. Better still, I thought about this while sitting between an old asthmatic man and a lady opening her lunch bag.

According to Julia, I talk in my sleep; last night, for example, I said: "But, old man, you know this issue is a spiritualization." Before that, on Friday, according to her (if I must believe her), I said in my sleep: "For me, Erdosain is the literary unconscious, so to speak."

Tuesday 27
Series B. In a bar filled with light on the corner of Lavalle and Rodríguez Peña. A convoluted morning that began badly, an argument with Julia that grew worse to the point that I left home and came here to calm down. The people in this place come and go, leaning over me to talk on the public phone on the wall at my back. When I saw a beautiful free table by the window, I didn't consider the risk of the telephone located behind it. After a while I started to entertain myself with their conversations: a blue-eyed girl was announcing her father's death to a friend, who asked her to repeat the news twice. Invasions of trusting ladies who covered my table with purses and objects, while they complained about the time and the state of the country.

Saturday
Noon. A meeting for the magazine yesterday. A good editorial written by David and decent reception of my article, although David took the opportunity to criticize Puig and insinuate that he didn't deserve an essay like mine. For his part, Ismael said that while my article was very good, I didn't ever say whether the book was good or not. Then David, with a mischievous air, said to him: "Ismael, that isn't done anymore." For his part, Sciarretta critiques my article for lacking a critical element and literary theory. What is literary theory to him? I don't know how to put it. Croce, maybe, or Della Volpe. Is literary criticism knowledge that is lacking from a book or knowledge that is already there? Sciarretta believes it's what is lacking, which the critic must include in order to "complete" the meaning. Finally we find a middle ground; we will introduce my essay on Puig as part of a book, and in this way they can calm down because what is lacking can come later. All of them praise the prose and the level, but we're in different worlds.

The difficulty comes not from what the words say, but from what is said between them. This means that the syntax matters more than the lexicon.

Suddenly, in the middle of my work preparing for the course on Arlt and Borges, an attack of terror comes upon me: fear of being unable to write any longer, of failing, etc. I am rational with literature and irrational in my relationship with literature.

Monday, September 2
Series B (or C?). I'm at La Modelo in La Plata, at a table by the window, in the sun, on the left side. Outside, you can see the trees, the wide streets; my past lies in this bar. The succession of afternoons when I was the only regular customer. Today I ordered sausages with fries and a bottle of white wine, just as I used to. And suddenly Lucía Reynal walked past, beautiful as always, on the other side of the glass, smiling and greeting me with an affectionate wave. Then she came into the bar and sat down with me and we were quiet. We had a history six years ago, which I imagine neither of us will forget. She wrote down her phone number for me on a scrap of paper and told me to call her when I came back here. But I won't do it, I prefer the memory.

Tuesday, September 3
I looked at my face in the mirror and it was 5:30. I looked at myself again, and two hours had passed. Now I'm drinking maté to combat my hunger. And it is 8:30.

Wednesday, September 4
Now I'm watching the street through my "round pair of glasses" (heavy, with black frames), unsure whether they help to clarify things for me or erase them completely. The things I'm trying to forget can be seen more precisely. The images are clear and yet oblique, appearing as though blurred. The family dog, which had become rabid, had a black coat and was named Duke. They locked him up in a room, and we watched him

through the skylight. He jumped around and growled furiously, and a fat policeman climbed up onto a table and killed him with a bullet.

Notes on Tolstoy (3 bis). *Ostranenie* [defamiliarization] as the difference between showing (making seen) and telling. In this way, Tolstoy broke away from the allegorical way of interpreting the Old Testament and the Gospels and imposed his detached ("Rational") reading. Everything is built around the question "What must be done?" And, laterally, "Who am I?" Compromise as a theory about use, about the relations between art and life, about the rejection of artistic autonomy as false religion and false art. Against the kitsch that is possible in profane illumination, *ostranenie*, and epiphany.

Series E. When I manage to assemble my notebooks from the last eight years, I will type them up. I always run the risk of trusting more in my past than in my future. Anyway, it would be interesting to publish all of my diaries from 1958 to 1968.

Thursday 5
I wake up at five thirty, get out of bed. Now it is six, and the clear light of the sun enters through the window. Uncertain about my perception, I wonder about my eyes, certain that my glasses are overly focused; my sight has started to grow cloudy, and now I struggle against a pained vision, *sensing* my own eyes as though they were made of glass. It is interesting to observe my way of seeing, understanding the contingency of the world; a pair of glasses can change the visible texture of reality. Of course, I can also go to the ophthalmologist to confirm or deny the excessive focus. But just what is *focus*?

Seeing one thing at a time.

Description of a mental state. My head paralyzed, a pain in my eyes, an emptiness, as though floating in the air, a weight that pulls my head to one side; I've always distrusted my body, which I cannot entirely control; that is where my rage at illnesses comes from. I undergo these states like rebellions, metaphysical experiences through which I confirm the existence of my body.

If I let myself be carried away by mysteries, so easy, so attractive, I would find a magical relationship in my encounters with certain books: *Mad Toy*, Hemingway's short stories, Pavese's diary, which I've never been able to "let go of," which I've come to rediscover again and again, finding some quality that I hadn't noticed but made me love them in the past. It is clear that these were the encounters that made me into who I am, and so I see them as encounters and not as origins. And that works for any magical idea about destiny; we always think we're seeing events and things for the first time while, unknowingly, we've been learning to discover them.

Friday 6
I continue my confused testing, trying to ascertain what is happening with my glasses. For example, I look at my face in the mirror without them on, and I recognize myself, but with the contribution of the prescription lenses my face changes, changing from one moment to the next, maybe because of the motions I make when I see myself in glasses.

Saturday, September 7
Series B. Yesterday confessions and misfortunes from Luna; I see in him that ferocious duplicity of all humbled. At night, David comes over and we walk down Corrientes in the insane atmosphere of the city on Friday nights and finally see *Accident* by Losey, with a script by Pinter, with all the snobs in Buenos Aires enraptured in the entrance hall, gaping at each other.

Series E. I would like to fill these notebooks more quickly, to systematize the information, to write about the everyday and analyze it, but—and I've already said this many times before—how can I write my conversation with Luna yesterday without making "literature" in the worst sense? The difficulty of writing openly in these notebooks arises from their lack of deliberate construction, which is both the virtue and the meaning of a diary. But, since I don't believe in spontaneity or sincerity, it is clear that this diary will be no more than sketches, notes, a way of looking down at myself, leaving behind details with which to later reconstruct certain periods, certain states. Therefore, what they need is not "more literature" but more swiftness, more of a *snapshot*. What is important is to search for these tones, to practice them, to write "with the flow of the pen."

A surprise last night on finding the drunk and half-crazed ex-boxer, who greets me every time I go down to the street, sleeping in the entryway to the building. I tried to step over him without waking him, but he spoke to me as soon as I opened the door. A frightened conversation with him ensued, throughout which I was trying to calm myself down more than calm him down.

I recall my experience yesterday in the carpenter's shop. As I enter, I witness an argument between a blue-eyed workman and a laborer with a bored expression who was holding up a decree that banned long hair on men and miniskirts on women. "It's a good thing," he said, "that they passed this." The other was looking at me, surprised and amused. "But you're an enemy of mankind," he said to him. "You should be sent off with the prisoners." Finally, when the one with blue eyes crossed the street to check my opinion, the other watched me without stopping work. "Now. That guy doesn't want to talk to me. Just got out of jail. He was a prisoner for five years . . . " It was a clash between the free man's defense of military repression and the ex-prisoner's defense of liberty. For me, scenes like this are the ones that condense experience, because they're left open and you can construct the complete story (which you don't know but can imagine).

Just now a boy's voice through the window: "I'm in such a hurry, I don't know where to go."

Sunday 8
Series A. A cloudy noon with a pale sun in the sky. Today is my father's birthday, and I feel the same indifference as ever toward this man who was beaten "by history," as he himself would say. He felt political anger and hatred as personal matters; that's what Peronism was to him, a private matter, as though he was trying to be faithful to a friend (Peronism turned politics into an emotional matter, that's why it has persisted). I called him on the phone; he always tries to seem euphoric and busy with projects. *When will we see each other?* is our leitmotif.

Yesterday, by contrast, was a splendid day with a clear sun, a walk down Calle Córdoba in the late afternoon, the warm air; the jacaranda trees had bloomed and my senses were heightened, maybe because of the conversation with Dad, who insisted yet again on my coming to live in Adrogué now that the house is empty. Worried about Nono's archives, could I take over? "Maybe," I said to him, "I should file and publish the old man's secrets and the dead men's letters." The men in the family pass on these mournful remains from one to the next. And so I walked through the restless city, amid the warm air and the voices of the people.

"All science would be superfluous if the outward appearance and the essence of things directly coincided," K. Marx. There's an element of Platonism in this sentence that opens the way toward an analysis of fetishism, that is, of the reality that is illusorily revealed in capitalism. And there is also a poetics of detective narrative; the philosopher is a detective investigating confusing traces in order to decipher the occult world. Only one who has a naïve and optimistic (or conservative) viewpoint can think that things are as they are.

A group of boys is playing with a ball in the ravine: one kicks it aiming for the goal that they've set up precariously. The ball goes off course and breaks a window. "I passed it sideways," one says, "and it bounced off you." "Yeah, well the redhead didn't stop it." They accuse each other, looking for the guilty one, and they all individualize, thus "separating" themselves from the group and also differentiating themselves from each of the members in particular. It is the inner mechanism of social matters, children learn it quickly. The guilty parties are individuals, collective responsibility is dissolved, and no one thinks about how they set themselves up to play on a narrow field with many windows for the ball to hit. A splintered way of seeing the world, and one that is learned in childhood.

Inevitably, literature works based on a situation (a non-verbal context) of reading: the interpretive delirium is measured in accordance with readers' greater or lesser ability to understand the things that will limit their reading.

Monday 9

A peaceful day, brutally cut short by the arrival of Luna with a stupid, shifty excuse (work problems that could be solved another time, a project of a new publishing house that is an underhanded jab at my working relationship with Álvarez). He sets in with an idiotic stubbornness, invading the space, occupying it completely, talking to himself, always telling the same stories in the same way, with the same professorial, schematic tone. I feel bursts of rage, and I'm on the point of cursing at him, laughing, escaping. He goes on like that, waving his arms, slow, satisfied with himself and his own anger and resentment.

Two hours later, still irritated, I made some maté and drank it slowly with the imbalanced feeling that the act of drinking maté alone can cause, as though missing someone who could sustain the cyclical rhythm of the ancient ceremony of getting together to drink "*unos amargos*," something bitter. As always, it is the little things that worry me, trivial matters, phone calls, ill-timed visits, avoided responsibilities, making me uncomfortable. It is very simple; for me, the only way out is absolute isolation, living outside of everything in a locked-off space, without a future. The only path left is to shut myself away, seeking refuge in an area of my own, high and walled, and working as though the world did not exist.

All that matters is knowing the limits of the outer wall, but this learning takes a lifetime. Now the cool air is coming in through the open window with the dry noise of crates, below, and the wheels of a car on the mismatched cobblestones.

Yesterday, an epiphany: In the empty street, Martínez (the crazy, drunken ex-boxer) with an air of "seriousness," his expression docile, "well-behaved," was standing next to a watchman, smoking fearfully, holding a package wrapped in white paper in one hand, his shirt open—and leaning in a doorway behind him, another vagrant, quite old yet with a fierce gleam still in his eyes and a scar on his face that gave away his real age—walking with a sluggishness I've never seen in anyone, immobile, moving imperceptibly, going slowly with the rhythm of a man who's lost his way in the darkness, moving away, led down by another policeman, who paused every two steps and waited, bored, to let him catch up.

"I am Ricky Martínez, boxer, I have a beautiful young wife," he applauded himself, looked for any wine left in the empty bottles, went on shouting insults: "Policeman, knob, snitch, animal." The row of boys provides him a chorus: "Martínez is the greatest boxer in the nation. Martínez *corazón*." He raised his arms with his fists closed, lowered his head, and danced around, on guard.

Tuesday 10
Seven in the evening on the almost empty bus, about to leave for La Plata. Where does this restlessness come from? As we know, I've always seen things "from above"; it bothers me to think about a group of idiots, condescending to the "lecturer." Maybe I can't stand to live in this time, knowing that no one knows anything about me. I can't stand the middle ground. We shall see.

Wednesday 11
Series B. In La Modelo, empty, with the clear sun on the other side of the window. I ordered, as I always have for many years, sausages with

63

potatoes and a glass of white wine. A certain stillness and peace. Then I give my first lecture. Everything goes well, some hesitation as I start, but then comes the feeling of controlling the subject, apart from some empty stares among the women in the audience. This first experience proves that my best tone comes from improvisation, almost without any notes; I go with the ideas and fall into the void, and after a while I feel the people coming along with me. The best part was my unexpected theory on translation (conceived of as social practice), which determines the literary style of an era more than any person can. For that reason, books must be retranslated every so often because, without realizing it, translators repeat the models of what can be said "literarily" at a given moment. They are working with the foreign language but also with the present state of the translation's target language. For them, this state marks possible turns of style, permitting them to say certain things in a way that is acceptable for the era. Thus can be seen, implicitly, the traces of social and literary style. Books are translated into an already-formed language, with its rhetoric and "aesthetic" grammar.

Beforehand, a professor, a poet and journalist from the SADE, gave me an Arltian introduction, speaking about global knowledge and my fame "beyond the frontier"; I looked down at the floor and now and then glanced at him, trying to raise me up onto some kind of pedestal, at a vast table, far away from everything.

Ezra Pound says: Flaubert is Joyce's immediate precursor. Joyce learned the encyclopedic form that structures his *Ulysses* from *Bouvard et Pécuchet*.

Tension between baroque style and classical style, defined by T. Wolfe in a letter to Scott Fitzgerald. I am a "putter-inner" and you are a "leaver-outer."

Thursday 12
The difficulty in the morning is not to think about what lies outside, almost as though I were piling up all of the senses, the events, into what begins after two in the afternoon, when I finish working. Today, for

example, stopping by J. Álvarez, paying Pirí back what I owe her, dealing with everything for Gide's diary, and also the many likely meetings with friends, acquaintances, etc. Then going to Luna's place, enduring his gossip, his complaints.

Today I'm working on the script for B. In two hours, I unenthusiastically lay out three scenes—still very schematic—for the outline of the story about the criminals who escape to Montevideo. Then I take notes on Gide's diary and Kafka's diary, and I'm also reading Musil's diary. What do they have in common, and what do I have in common with them?

In the short stories from my book, I have discovered, without knowing it, the difference between dramatization and story-telling. On one side are the "objective" stories, which tend to be narrated in the present tense, while the events and dialogues are taking place ("Tarde de amor," "La invasión"), and on the other side are the monologues, which are defined more by tone than plot ("Tierna es la noche," "Una luz que se iba"). So, when Héctor Alterio read "Mi amigo" aloud, it easily turned into a theater monologue. "Mata-Hari 55" is a reduced novel: recording, documentary, juxtaposition of voices (a model or plan for the novel about the criminals who escape to Montevideo). Present tense. Spoken prose, the act of storytelling, the form of the (false) nonfiction novel based on real events.

Friday
Series A. Last night with my brother Marcos, a stranger whom I struggle to recognize. "Grown up," more legitimate than I have ever been, determined to leave this country behind and take his family and my mother to live in Canada. Conflicted about my father's (his father's) weaknesses, a fragile tone that my brother can no longer endure. They drove from Mar del Plata together, with Dad confessing his crises, seeing no way out; politics is a crime, he says, and he lays his misery on Marcos, as he used to do to me in Mar del Plata, making me be his confessor at age eighteen. I learned from him that you must never let yourself be blackmailed by people who put history on their side and justify all of their own weakness or failures

with "historical" reasons. My father experienced the misfortunes of banned Peronism as though they were directed at him personally. At the same time, I recognize my own conflicts in him: being trapped by future events, refusing to accept reality. And so how can I, his mirror, blame him?

I'm reading Scott Fitzgerald's letters: "Don't worry about popular opinion. Don't worry about dolls. Don't worry about the past. Don't worry about the future. Don't worry about growing up. Don't worry about anybody getting ahead of you. Don't worry about triumph. Don't worry about failure unless it comes through your own fault. Don't worry about mosquitoes. Don't worry about flies. Don't worry about insects in general. Don't worry about parents. Don't worry about boys. Don't worry about disappointments. Don't worry about pleasures. Don't worry about satisfactions." Only concern yourself with doing things well, and seek compensation in the work itself (not even in its result). You'd have to be a saint to follow those rules, she said.

Saturday
At noon I ran into David with Edgardo F., and we went to eat at the restaurant on Montevideo and Sarmiento, talking about Eva Perón, the working girl who held a unique position. Condemned by the middle and upper classes, her rage and resentment transformed into an extraordinary political rhetoric, never before known in this country. Later with Luna, who takes note of the writing he finds in bathrooms and calls the phone numbers written there, and last with B., good ideas for continuing with the script.

Series E. Danger: replacing memory with these notebooks. Only living the experiences through writing.

When I'm working, I can't read. Either nothing catches my interest, or everything seems connected to what I'm writing. The books are trapped by the passion of the novel and transformed into superfluous objects or contagious objects. They are either worthless or they say what I haven't finished writing better than I can. A strange situation, the writer as the enemy of the reader. You become so sensitized by language that everything that is written seems either personal or personally addressed. A superstitious thought of the artist who feels as if the whole world—not just the books—is speaking to him privately, in service to the subject into which he is pouring the hours, the days, the years.

My other way of reading consists of having five or six books at hand and burying myself in them, a way to not think and not remember that I owe a debt to what I've left unwritten.

Pavese had decided to commit suicide; he was in the Hotel Roma but paused to write a few letters and entered the dead time of language, leaving his suicide in suspense. "The gods arranged all this, and sent them their misfortunes in order that future generations might have something to sing about," Homer. Pavese's suspended time before he killed himself has a likeness to "The Secret Miracle," the Borges story in which a man asks God for the time to complete his work before he is executed. To finish writing before entering death.

Popular storytelling, the serial novel. They possess, in particular, a precise functional power and invariably match with their meaning, which is, first of all, the desire to be read. But the point of these novels is not to be read at the level of their style and the typical dimension of language; they want to be read for what they narrate, for the emotion or fear or pity that their words are obligated to transmit, which they must communicate with pure and simple transparency. The prose has to have the absolute seriousness of the narrative, it must be no more than the neutral element of the pathetic. That is, they offer nothing in themselves. There is a fever of expression, an informative language. This gives rise to their complementary opposite, which we would call parody, an artificial expression that employs this language of excessive passions for comical effect. But this effect doesn't lie in the language but rather in the way it is read. Inversion of the reading, not of the meaning of the text.

Sunday

The best part of yesterday was my discovery of Doris Lessing, a lateral writer, the same as us. She was born in South Africa, was in the Communist Party, and had a daughter, whom she took with her to London after she divorced. She looks at English culture obliquely and thus writes what we might call a poetics of the left. First rate: great use of autobiographical material, looking at herself as a dynamo that receives many rays. The protagonist of her stories is always an aspiring writer. Thus, there is always a tension between life and writing. I read her work for hours, as happens every time I discover a writer. I'm going to read all of her books. But now I am turning, as happens with these "excitements" that won't leave me in peace (but what peace?), and moving away from the true path, as the mystics say. It is dark outside, gray. Ahead lies the end of the afternoon, *public relations avec* Mr. R.: we're going to watch Czech films. "La" Lessing distinguishes herself from Andrés R. and all of the ex-communists because she doesn't place blame on anyone, just observes their reactions ironically.

Monday

Series A. My ignorance of the past is clear, my complete forgetting of my childhood days. Because I'm here, I cannot remember them. Yesterday, a flash of the times I would go out with Grandfather Emilio, and his death, so close that it doesn't seem like it happened. Almost nothing beyond that, fleeting remnants; it's almost as though Nono conceals everything else, until he alone remains in my past.

These days I'm rereading all of Chandler, and I very much enjoy the combination of adventure and irony, a sedate epic. Marlowe is always looking for lost objects, facing many obstacles. He experiences this tiresome work (that of a private detective) like one of Kafka's heroes, with humor, seeing death up close and viewing money as a key that gives meaning to the game. He pretends to accept these rules as a way to conceal his attraction to the constant movement. There is formidable narrative technique, intended to incessantly bifurcate the paths; the action always moves two steps ahead of the hero, who always comes across the consequences of events but never the events themselves. Many times, I've felt tempted to write the *Don Quixote* of police novels. A single protagonist who would have to be Don Quixote and Sancho at the same time, a slightly insane ex-commissioner accompanied by inner voices that talk only to him (or that only he hears) with Sancho Panza's common wisdom, sayings, refrains, unexpected solutions to the mysteries. He solves them "on hunches." To have a hunch is to guess at the future, imagining how things will progress. And that is what this investigator's method should be, out on the edge of the genre.

I'm interested in the way that Chandler operates with a single hero-narrator in his novels, in such a way that the books can be read as a single, vast novel. I like this technique.

Tuesday
Series B. Yesterday conspiracy, commiseration, an affectionate and secret huddle with León R. and David V. They've adopted me as the heir to their way of thinking. Why? Maybe because of the editorial I wrote in the first issue of my magazine *Literatura y Sociedad.*

First phone call with León, aggressive and hurt because of what happened to him that one Saturday in the German pub before he went to the airport, when everyone (and David most of all) was criticizing the way he lives—too comfortable, he's a homeowner now and we don't like that—but also the way he thinks about Marxism, too personal. Several weeks of silence since that day. Yesterday my affection for him returned along with the memory of that month traveling around Europe with León, our long conversations in Havana.

There was a meeting for the magazine, a number of arguments, full of tension (David and Ismael against León), which I observed with the clarity that comes from understanding three or four levels of a situation. The editorial will focus on the ways that the dominant classes think about and define themselves. What Brecht called "the idealist customs" of the bourgeoisie. Capitalism with delusions; what they're doing never coincides with what they think about what they're doing.

Intense work. I write copy for three book covers (Mailer, Vargas Llosa, and French writers of today) and several biographical notes (Robbe-Grillet, Claude Simon, Le Clézio), and now, tired, I look forward to a long trek: go to the bank, collect a check, pay the rent (very late, with a warning notice attached), see Jorge Álvarez, stop by *El Mundo* to see the photos, chat with Luna about future articles, and finally come back home.

Obviously a confusing panorama, what will we do? Overwhelmed, I think about suicide as a way out for me. The scars on my right wrist that I used as a mark of my past life (I got them as a boy by punching through a glass door, but I have always used them for seduction, showing that trace as proof of my decision to have done with everything). The insane order of my life is going to break apart . . . like the glass of the door.

Wednesday 18
I'm rewriting "Mousy Benítez," it works well because the story is an implicit investigation, and the mystery is not deciphered (who or what killed Benítez?). The love among men in a hypermasculine world: boxing.

I went to bed with Julia at noon and stayed there all afternoon, until now.

A note I made on the white inside of the cover of a book by Pavese. I find an annotation dated August 15, 1966: *I've always wanted to find a style that defines my way of living. Language depends on the way one lives one's life.* That note is there, hanging in a vacuum, so I went to my notebook from that year and found a note from the day before. *I am with Julia at El Jockey, I decide to go back to La Plata with her and spend a while there, hidden, writing.* Then, on August 16, I wrote that I had already found a room: *a house with a patio and rooms that open onto the garden, and on the front side balconies over Diagonal 80. I settle in here with no one knowing where I am.* A strange game of mirrors.

If I decided to admit that my life, shall we say, also changes and "evolves," I could remember my profound stupidity in the beginning (1957), before I came to the end of that period of learning, ten years later, one year ago that is, when I published my first book. Those ten years could be the living material for my autobiography—if I were to write it.

A short story, beginning like this: "Later, my father killed himself."

Thursday
Series C. Women viewed as apparitions at distinct points in my life, sharp turns, until I reached that fleeting vision—a woman in a white raincoat— as though watching the form of my own life passing by.

Luna's perverse conversation yesterday, a wicked passion for misfortune (both personal and external) that he disguises as generosity, as good intentions. I reject his piety because of the element of spectacle, of bad faith, that finds all of its reasoning in this vicious puppet, with his air of a helpless hippopotamus, jumping up to spy through the window and collecting the juicy news, reading pornographic books, betraying, all with the greatest "good will" and love for his fellow man.

Just now to David V.'s house and back. Preoccupied with the prospect of work, he critiques the literal line of *Primera Plana*, the ease of presenting autobiographical writing as an example of experimentation.

Series E. Rereading Pavese's diary, I rediscover my old obsession with his self-construction of life (as a work of art), his businesses (of living, of writing, of thinking), his techniques, and his rules.

Fast bursts of images from the books I've lost in the times I've moved, in my "separations," the same books I need to have today, on this table, which are—let's say—on Jorge Álvarez's desk or at León's house or in some bookshop I don't know. There will always be new (and old) books to read, but there will always be a book I'm looking for and can't find. My hope is to have all of the books at hand so that I can use them when a practical need demands it, so that I can choose one when it's the right time for me to read it and I'm ready for that book and no other. Therefore, my library and the books I buy are not meant to be read now, but rather are meant for a future reading, one I imagine will find its place in a volume I've bought years before. This idea is sustained by my tendency to see traces of the future in the present (and to be prepared). The library persists as a place I return to: the same books, the same ideas that have been repeated for years and will be repeated in the future as well.

I think the best things I've written in these notebooks have been the result of spontaneity and improvisation (in a musical sense); I never know what I'm going to write about, and sometimes that uncertainty is transformed into style. I defend the perplexed author trying to understand a hostile world. Letting myself be guided by an intuition, a hunch, a *pálpito* (a beautiful word that refers to palpitation and also to the imagination of what is to come).

Everything I've thought or tried to think comes from ignorance or from the attempt to write in its place. For example, when I reread Faulkner and wrote a profile of his life, I discovered the novel as investigation. I was only able to think of that because I was led to that insight while preoccupied with working on other matters.

Series A. I've always been afraid of thinking all the way to the end, worried about the effects that this thinking might have on my body. To escape the pain, I avoid thinking about myself entirely. To put it better, I think from myself but not about myself. And in that lies the revelation that it is always someone else—not me—who is writing.

Viewed from another angle, there is my choice to postpone, to pass on what is troubling me now to another day: to create a pause, a waiting. That's why the collapse is so unexpected, because it breaks into the cease-fire when no one expects it (the surprise is the catastrophe).

I began to earn my living at age twenty-two. What did I do before? Nono's patronage. And before that?

A discontinuous temporality—never linear, in which there is no pro-gress—can be seen in what I write (and in the way I write): There are raptures, happy moments, inspirations, and I'm always writing in spurts, in streaks, struggling to establish a stable working rhythm, a discipline. It is an incessant search for the perfect moment. I have too much confidence in the future, and that is what defines my life, the way I think and write (and love). What is to come, that imminence, allows me to go onward.

I've started rereading Conrad under the pretense of putting together a selection of his stories for my classics collection. I quite like the way he places the narrator, who is recounting the story, in the center of the scene. He always defines the situation that makes the story possible. For exam-ple, the ebb of the river, the calm girl who halts the journey and brings together the idle sailors and the narrator (who is or was one of them).

"Marlow (at least I think that is how he spelt his name)." This is the distance between the writer and the narrator, but also the relationship between the writer and the narrator, who already knows the story and is telling it in his own way, in conversation, to a group. What fails is his confidence in the spoken tone of the story. What he needs to tell the story is less calm, more narrative confusion, fewer direct dialogues. And that is what Faulkner does, coming directly from Conrad but creating a narrator astonished at the story he is trying to tell.

Every morning, before starting work, I open the window slightly to let the light of day come in, without waking Julia, and then I clean the table, making an empty space for the typewriter, and begin, without rereading what I have written.

X Series. A. P., whom I've known for years, appears in an article about the arrest of a group of guerrillas in Tucumán, and therefore Lucas T. M. as well. I discuss this with David V., needing to support them "morally" despite the fact that politically we disagree with their methods, etc.

Monday 23
Walking around the city with David V., we made it as far as La Noria bridge and went in circles around the slums that surround it, the dumps, Boedo to the south, ending up on Corrientes and then in the Alvear theater to watch *Bajo la garra*.

A note about my nonfiction novel. As I have said, I became aware of this story through the newspapers, I thought there were unclear points and decided to investigate, etc.

Series E. I'm reading Gide's diary, and I don't like the self-satisfaction, the way he lives in the spotlight. For me, only diaries written in opposition to oneself are valuable (Pavese, Kafka). In my case, what I most often find are moments that—in reading them today—I would have wanted to live another way. It pains me to reread them because I discover what was undesirable in myself. Not because I may have said so—or understood it—explicitly, but rather because of what can be seen from the present. A gesture would have been enough to make everything different, but in that moment I was blind: we never see what we meant to do until ten years (at least) have passed, and so we live blinded by the events, never finding the way out that we seek, even though it is right in front of our faces; it is not a problem of physical distance, but of temporal perspective. When I reread these notebooks, I can clearly see the moral quality of the man I was.

Commerce is the motor of the peripeteias in Conrad's novels; the interchange between distant regions acts, in his stories, like fate in a tragedy.

X Series. Taco Ralo guerrilla warfare. In the foco theory, the margin of error melts away and is minimal; only total efficacy would allow possible action to develop in the future. And so they fall too early, due to minuscule errors. In this case, what is new is the Peronist character of the politics (but not its methods).

Tuesday
Series B. Last night with David. I went to see him about a meeting with León. He greets me with an enigmatic smile. "You like Borges, no?" I keep on walking toward the middle of the apartment and see a book on the desk. "What trap are you setting for me?" I ask him. David throws himself backward, grabbing the book and hitting me on the arm, offended. "No, old man," he says. Then a great confusion on my part as I try to exaggerate my thanks and dispel the misunderstanding. He has given me a first edition of *The Language of the Argentines* as a gift, with an inscription from Borges, to which he adds another, written in large strokes. I realize that he stole the book from José Bianco because I know the way Pepe binds his books, but I don't say anything. So the situation is multiplied. David steals a book and then gives it to me, and as he establishes a *mise-en-scène* without telling me anything, I act defensively because I know his tricks. León is late (in the end, he doesn't come), and David once again shows me his friendship by recalling our trip around the city the previous Sunday. I go back, walking slowly down Viamonte, and León is waiting for me at home, a surprise, a reprise of the previous scene: León offers to give me a bookcase (because I have my books piled up on the floor), and then I try to be impartial.

Relationships with writers from other generations are always complicated because each one speaks a different language, and so we end up understanding one another through an invented jargon with fragments of each person's private language, and all we accomplish is incomprehension and unease.

My distrust of overly effusive and obvious outward performances of affection is the first thing that separates me from my Sartrean friends, León, David, Ismael, even Massotta. They act out their childhood readings, seeking "authenticity," turning sincerity and explicit words into proof of a conscience open to the world. For my part, I have had other readings; the true emotions are the ones that don't show themselves, and passion is too strong to be exhibited as though it were an object in a toy store window.

Even better, I find this quote from Borges in the book that David gave me: "The subject is almost grammatical, which I announce as a warning to those readers who have condemned (in the name of friendship) my grammarianisms and requested a human work. I could answer that there is nothing more human (that is, less mineral, vegetal, animal, and even angelical) than grammar."

Another from Borges: "Someone who does not work to earn his living finds himself a bit outside of reality."

Thursday
The bookcase León gave me arrived, I set it against the wall, and now the books are there in rows, too many to see in a single glance, too few for my fantasy (to read everything).

Sunday, September 29
I get the volume of Pavese's letters, so expensive (nine thousand pesos), the chance nature of what he writes, I can fill in the voids between one letter and another using his diary and his stories. What am I looking for? Always the same thing, to know why he writes, who or what it was that led him to write—just as it did me. The result: when I'm interested in a writer I read everything. There are not many who have this good fortune. And Pavese was one of the first.

An impression from that reading helps me understand that we are in a situation of breaking free from the exterior nature that has defined us from the beginning. Now we no longer look at other literatures or foreign writers as though they had more opportunities than us. We read as among peers, that's what has changed.

Series E. I imagine myself based on three or four clear, not-so-distant memories, as though my life began not long ago and before that—the rest—was the lost paradise of my over-prolonged childhood. The decision was made impulsively, and my closest friends (Diana, Elena, or Raúl's sister) insisted that I couldn't dedicate my life to literature, far too risky a gamble. For a few years, my father and his cronies began a campaign to convince me that I needed to make sensible decisions, and that was what ultimately had me cornered in a suicidal defense of a future about which I had very confused ideas. I recall and look at those scenes as a way to understand my subsequent vengeance (literature as revenge), and above all as a way to understand why I write this diary. For years, it was—and still is—the only place where I could support myself in maintaining this delusional decision. *All or Nothing* would have to be the title of these notebooks if I ever published them.

This all comes because of my shock in confirming in Pavese what I haven't realized about myself, shall we say, "consciously," something I only understood long after I decided, once again, "to be a writer" before I had ever written anything to justify that delusion. The advice I wouldn't listen to was trying to convince me to admit that literature must be a "secondary occupation" for me. I saw all of that—almost psychotically, I saw my whole life already lived—in one instant that afternoon, as I sat on the tiled floor of the hallway, my back leaning against the wall, writing furious words in a notebook. I must have thought: "If I write the things I want to experience here—and not, stupidly, only the things that I do experience—then I'll be able to experience them like prophecies come true." Just like that, I bound writing and life together forever. I was never worried by the idea that literature can distance you from experience, because things were the opposite for me: literature created experience.

Protect yourself well from making art a secondary occupation, because the gods who watch over general mediocrity will punish you, I thought without realizing it. I saw it at age seventeen, when I had done nothing so far to justify that belief. That was why I was intrigued by the lives "of writers," I was seeking their moment—or moments—of decision. I remember reading Proust's *Recherche* one summer and seeing the epiphany of that discovery in the Guermantes's library, when at the end of his life Marcel understands that he has lived through everything so as to be able to write the novel you are reading. In my case, the matter was reversed; I made the decision before I had lived, sitting on the floor in a hallway of our dismantled home.

I set aside all excuses (studying law, looking for stable work, making, as they say, a family, etc.) before anything else, in the same way that Marcel understands that his fascination with social life, parties, and the aristocratic world was nothing compared to his will—put better, his desire—to be a writer.

There is something strange in that decision to choose the imaginary as a reason for life itself. A flaw, a fracture that no one has seen, the consequences of which can be felt in the language, in a murky and troubling ability with words: None of that justifies anything, and you can have that certainty and never get as far as writing a single page. And so, without realizing it, I have also started to continue the creation of imaginary writers in fictional texts. What kind of writers do writers invent in their novels? What do they do? What is their work? The first in that lineage for me was Nick Adams, the young aspiring writer in Hemingway's stories, and then came the great Stephen Dedalus, the young aesthete who looks at the world—at his family, at his homeland, at his religion—with contempt because he has chosen to be an artist, and we never know whether he succeeds because, at the end of *Ulysses*, Joyce leaves him walking half-drunk through the Dublin night, with Leopold Bloom, who brings him home with the secret intention of adopting him as a son (and also, perversely, as his splendid wife Molly's lover). I read this succession fervently, as though it were my own life: Quentin Compson, Faulkner's suicidal character, who kills himself before he has done what he imagined he wanted to do (to be a writer). The list goes on, and I'm on the way to attempting a gallery or an encyclopedia of the lives of imaginary writers: They all seem to have a certain immaturity in common—they never manage to become adults (because they don't want to). Here, I could use Gombrowicz's novels, where the artist resists maturity. That is the limit, since maturity is the transformation of the artist into an assimilated man. That is what happens at the end of *Don Quixote*, once Alonso Quijano has forgotten all his delusions and resigned himself to a trivial life. That is why the lives of artists in novels end quickly and, in general, they all die or commit suicide so as not to resign themselves and admit the weight of reality.

I respond to an almost surreal scene: A woman asks me to lend her a novel and asks if I've read it, and a few weeks later I'm writing these notebooks. That would become clear if I thought about the situation in which—"without realizing it"—I gave Vicky my diary instead of my class notes. And she was clearly the second love of my life (for that reason).

Everything would be in place if I dared to live as though I were about to turn (not twenty-eight, as is the case, but rather) eighteen years old. Then I would indeed be able to wait, to be calm, to let myself go, ready for my formative years. But, of course, the temporality worked backward in my case.

Monday, September 30
While reading Pavese's letters, I once again felt the desire to compose a story that takes place in Turin, an invisible collage made from fragments of his diary and my own. Narrating Pavese's life (or one day, or the end) and at the same time a few days—or a few hours—in the life of the protagonist, who is an imaginary writer (and that's why he has gone there to see images of Pavese up close). One possible beginning (if I write the story in first person): "I do not understand why I am here, how I have come to be in Turin, with nothing to justify this journey to a city that

I do not know, one that I only feel close to because my father and my father's father were born here. I came on a fellowship to study Pavese, or rather, I came here to write something about Pavese's diary, but that is a pretense. As always, the reasons and the causes are something darker. Sometimes, some afternoons, when I am more disoriented than usual, I find a place in this room at the Hotel Roma, open my suitcase, and reread the notebooks in which I write, here and there, about what I am doing or thinking. I am alone in Turin, I scarcely know three or four people, the waiter who serves me in the restaurant, the girl who comes to clean the room, a circumstantial friend I met in the café where I go for breakfast every morning. My Italian is slow and hesitant and my acquaintances think I'm a bit slow in the head, not really a foreigner, more a stranger, an outsider . . . "

French and English Books
Art-Science-Medicine-Literature, etc.
Extremely low prices
. . . .
Don Bosco 3834 (Rivadavia and Medrano)
Tel. 89-6098 / 6099
Monday to Friday from 2 to 5 p.m.

October 1
Now the sun, which is always reflected in the window at the same hour and gets in my eyes: a white brilliance, moving away and blinding me; then everything is silhouetted clearly with a gleam that gives the city the guise of a photograph.

Pavese also deals with the key to all of us (or put better, some of us, or better still, only me); literature is contrary to life, and that is its virtue. For example: what it is that he does in that city he doesn't know, studying an author who spoke a language that was his father's and his grandfather's but not his own. Maybe it would be better, instead of getting lost in duplicating forms, to simply devote himself to translating some of Pavese's stories that he likes ("Wedding Trip," "The Leather Jacket," for example). In that way, his residency in Turin would be productive, and he could present a report at the end, justifying the money from the fellowship that had allowed him to travel. For example, to say: Pavese was an unbelievable man, which is not to say that he was a valuable man.

Yesterday a long meeting for the magazine with David, Ismael, Rodolfo, and Andrés; we finished at two in the morning in Munich, near the port. Argument about the publishing house, the issue is how we'll fit in what I call the foreign series. I'm trying to capture the multiple meanings of a lateral position with a single term. A nation on the margins of the central currents. Sarmiento already saw it, but we now think that such a position does not prevent us from establishing direct contact with the current state of culture. We are synchronized with contemporary culture for the first time.

Andrés gives himself a clear conscience there. He looks to others for the source of any ambiguous action that implicates or complicates him. A slightly out-of-focus image of any one of us, resentful; he seeks security, revolutionary verbalism, and imagines that experiencing everything in a complicated way is a demonstration of sincerity. A beautiful soul that conceals what we might call, in his words, dark temptations.

Very excited about the project of writing a story about Pavese, I rediscover old notes that have been inside me since '64. Suddenly, a phenomenal lucidity allows me to see the whole story and its title in a single image: a fish in a block of ice.

A fish. I came to Turin with the snows of January and saw the glimmers of the pale sun on the waters of the Po. To get to know a writer, you have to turn him into a part of your life. That is why I am here. (Use my own name to signal a fictitious narrator, inverting the mechanism of the pseudonym.)

Destiny. The texture of unconsciously chosen events. A path only seen in its entirety at the end, when it is already too late.

Wednesday, October 2
Unwanted entanglements yesterday. It's Luna every time. Now he's spinning an ambiguous web around some women and—especially—several men he wants to take his revenge on. Intent, ritual desire, repeating his own misery, able to be (after so many times that he's played that role) a "prestigious" bastard, deceiving, usurping a friend's wife, abandoning the "honest" but miserable side of the wronged, faithful husband deceived by his comrades.

Sartre's face, framed, half-bearded, his eyes watching the corners of the room; imagine the moment when he looked at the camera and felt the tension preceding this fleeting immortality, and what came immediately after that pause, which I have hung on my wall, the photographer and Sartre in conversation, saying goodbye, while I was somewhere else in the world, not knowing the photograph was destined for me.

Now I'll drink the tea that I let cool while the crisp morning air brushes by my face and a woman sweeps the sidewalk below, a familiar sound that carries me off to childhood. I am in bed, I must be six or seven years old, gliding the tips of my fingers along the wooden railing that crosses the wall at face level. It is seven thirty in the morning, and, as though wanting to make this moment eternal, I struggle to begin this pause in which everything is yet to happen and I am alone, free, in the middle of the city.

Why didn't my failure with "Los días futuros" in 1965 change anything in me? Everything stayed as it was, the same certainty, the same emphasis despite the amount of time it took me to write any stories that still last for me. What place, what blindness did I extract my confidence from in those days? Then the failure, partial, momentary, coming back to me with the certainty that it is only fools who triumph and come out ahead. (You need 40 percent mediocrity to be able to succeed in art. A decrease in those stupidity quotas condemns you directly to failure.) This theory is the direct realization of the way I think about reality.

Series E1. What is in play is the opposition between form and sincerity. An old polemic that has taken many names over the course of the years and has resurfaced in this present time, when people sing the praise of ignorance and celebrate the spontaneity of the noble savage. Meanwhile, I am alone, rowing against the tide and trying to create my literature by inserting that tension—life versus literature—into the themes of my stories (and also into these diaries). Creation in art and creation in life. Giving form to experience.

Series E2. Certain periods of my life that I've experienced with angst reclaim their true reality when I "go back to read them" (not the same as going back to experience them): some good insights, certain happy quotes that betray a healthy "movement of the soul," despite the suicidal tedium with which I sustained them, as though I were looking at a painful wound without seeing the beautiful texture of the flesh that is visible thanks to the division of the skin. The passage from wound to scar. And so, today, tense and with a strange lucidity, I see no reason to allay the burden that holds me away from (my own) mandate to write, every morning, my novel in progress.

Series E3. And what if the best thing I have ever written, the best thing I will ever write in my life were these notes, these fragments, in which I record that I never manage to write the way I would like to? An admirable paradox: infuriated because he is unable to write what he wants, a man dedicates himself to recording the story of his life in a notebook, always going against himself, and sustains himself on his notebooks, observing himself, continuing to fail, never knowing that he is writing the greatest literature of his time in those notebooks. He dies, unknown, anonymous, with no one interested or able (even despite knowing their value) to publish them. Notebooks in which an unknown man talks about his life, recounting his frustrations day after day, writing the deepest testimony of his era, about the fate of failure. It would be Kafka's life in reverse, the secret of a quality that is completely ignored, a great literature ignored, or rather, unknown even to its own author.

Thursday 3
It is raining, seven in the morning, the damp air comes in through the open window, and I'm troubled because I can't read now, waiting to go out to the street in the afternoon after writing all morning, going to see friends, have drinks, and seek adventures in the city until late at night.

Notes on Tolstoy (4). In his later years, Tolstoy struggled intensely to free himself from the bonds of his social life and from conformity, and therefore he fascinated a great number of men and women around the world who—like Gandhi—wanted in all sincerity to "return" to a simple and pure life and practiced nonviolence. Tolstoy himself was tragically unable to bring about this return, and his final attempt was, in its own way, a suicide.

Don Quixote. "All in the style of those his books had taught him, imitating their language as well as he could." In Cervantes's novel, there is always an aspiration to move on from life to literature, to the future novel: "When the veracious history of my famous deeds is made known, the sage who writes it, when he has to set forth my first sally in the early morning, will do it after this fashion: 'Scarce had the rubicund Apollo spread . . .'" and he goes on, showing how his story will be told. That is, he indicates the true meaning behind his actions: they are meant to be read. What he does by living is to indicate the rhythm of the wise writer who will write his life. In short, he speaks and acts in accordance with the novels he has read (which is what defines his madness), and, at the same time, he aspires to become a writer who would write things in the future according to how he has experienced them (which will define his sanity). And his peace, when he dies, sane, as Alonso Quijano once again, will lie in the hope that he has left his (written) mark, while the author speaks through the pen with which he is writing.

Friday 4

Yesterday, a brief exchange with David around four in the afternoon, very emotional, with unusual antipathy and helplessness that he tries to conceal behind his emphatic gestures, his rhetoric, and his intelligence.

Working since seven in the morning, always in intermittent stretches, with the temptation that everything I write must be "consumed" in a day. For me, concentration is synonymous with swiftness. I must cultivate the virtue of continuity.

Just now, my face pressed against the foggy windows, I watched the water falling against milk bottles piled up in wirework boxes on the sidewalk next to "Provisión San Miguel." The whole street was dark under the rain, and I once more felt the calm of certain mornings when anything is possible because the dawn, the rain, blanket me and hide me from the future.

Sometimes I have doubts, unsure whether this unscrupulousness—writing for an hour, completing one scenario, pausing—is the maturity I've hoped for, or laziness. Before, writing used to be a passion, something that carried me, that required certain rituals, certain exact times. Now I've found a discipline for my work, the first hours of the morning like a blessing, leaving a page half-finished and resuming it the following day and moving on ahead. I don't think I've lost the enthusiasm, because I like nothing more than to be sitting and writing, but I think I would like to turn it into a practice or habit that is picked up and set down, as in the days when I used to swim in the pool at Club Temperley and would break records, or improve my time, every day, not waiting for ideal moments.

Writing is like swimming. The stories have the speed of a front crawl stroke, a hundred meters at top speed, but for a while I've wanted to write as though swimming at sea, with no limit but my own exhaustion urging me to return to shore. A while ago, I wrote a story called "The Swimmer," relating the experience of a man I met on the beach who swam out three kilometers to a sunken ship and delved into the interior of the submerged boat, hoping to find treasure. For me, that could be a metaphor for the novel.

In any case, I think I could always go back to my old "pure moments of creation" and write stories, but I want to acquire a swimming rhythm that would allow me a longer term, "extended" concentration. On one side is the experience of "Tierna es la noche," written in six hours; on the other is the work that goes in circles around itself, my "Italian" *nouvelle* with Pavese at the center of the plot.

Saturday 5
Learning about Pavese in 1935, in total confinement and with three years of exile ahead of him, with no news of the woman he loved, alone, under the elements, he writes in his diary about his poetry, about the way he works, and never lets himself be won over by the "tragedies of the soul." I mention this because yesterday I worked all morning, until I was lost, "addled" by exhaustion, a ring of iron around my head. After that, nothing until evening except for my "mundane routine," which was barely a pass through the editorial office yesterday because Luna wasn't there, and then I went down to the city for a walk around Plaza San Martín. As I was getting off the bus to go to Air France, there was an explosion in the Círculo de la Armada; fear, everyone running for the park, even though it had only been an innocent short circuit that filled the sidewalk with smoke "like a bomb."

"In writing, the difficulty is not in what to say, but in what not to say," Kipling.

Sunday, October 6
Series C. We might say that the books I write are the price I have to pay for distant mistakes, sorrows that no one could have allayed, slow hours erased by a woman with a red skirt, black stockings, and a sweet smile. What is the point in distrusting and lamenting a history of which not even ashes now remain, from which only some lost books survive, a

library that was divided as though the books were precious objects that warranted a dispute, when really they were only symbols of the love that was left behind, imperishable moments, monuments to past joy. For I have never escaped from the books, and so these books are all that I can lose and lament and ponder. For example, one day I would like to write a story about two lovers' separation using only the titles of the books they fight over.

Since a precise moment (1957), everything has come to me easily, as though the forces had been accumulating since that time and everything had come all at once: the redheaded woman (Vicky was the third in that streak), the decision to live alone, the money I needed (thanks to the work that Grandfather Emilio invented for me), and no effort, finally reaching this place where I live, in a corner of the city. That explains my conviction, the certainty that, of course, I've never doubted, going past the "failures." An absence of the meaning, confused and always postponed, that I find in reality, in my love for the profession—and not in its results—which has allowed me to live for all these years.

So now what? A life always discovered afterward, the decisions, the changes, the subtle choices that have led me to this need to organize everything around literature. Never thinking about other possible paths.

I'm reading *Marks of Identity* by Juan Goytisolo. Of the writers of his generation (Viñas, Fuentes), he is the one who seems to have recovered best from the crisis that brought about "commitment" and the social novel. Here, he progresses in a new direction, political in the best sense of the word.

Wednesday, October 9
Yesterday I rediscovered a core part of my education, the English, French, and Italian literary magazines through which, in the Library of the Universidad de La Plata, I discovered contemporary literature and its debates and "learned" to become what I am. There was also my experience

in the Historical Archives of Buenos Aires Province, in the basement of the Galería Rocha, where Barba was my Virgil. One learns quickly, with the instantaneous velocity of a bird of prey, and a few seconds are enough to clearly perceive a path in the woods of culture.

Once again Andrés R.'s confessions, he's obsessed with the Viñas brothers, with their girlfriends, with their stories, which he tells me as though they were his own. Ismael, hiding his father's death from his brother David for two years, to prevent him from suffering. The descendants. Ismael, according to Andrés, asks David: What is it we have that makes our children turn out this way? A complaint, a lament.

I spend two hours listening to music on Radio Municipal. I have at last perceived the dual logic of live concerts: the spectators applaud and scream for ten minutes as though that noise were the music. I think: "That is the concert." Now it is time for the intermission, that is to say, the music. Now Schubert.

Not much work today. I am waiting for Julia now, so we can go out to eat. A strange thing. I just started reading intensely, two hours ago, and now the letters dance before me, I can't see.

Earlier, a lovely walk at noon after a talk with Álvarez and a haircut. Stops at all of the bookshops in Buenos Aires (Dinesen, Akutagawa, Les Temps Modernes), and then I sat down outside a bar on Avenida de Mayo. Later, in the plaza, a woman was chasing pigeons and I, alone on a bench, was trying to decide whether I really would like to be a father. I decided that the decision I made ten years ago was best, no family. Last, I met Korenblit about the lecture on Arlt and Borges that I'm giving at the Hebraica on Friday for five thousand pesos, which I look forward to with little enthusiasm. Álvarez offered to have me compile an omnibus, that is, an anthology of David's work. Will it mark the end of our friendship? I mean, could it become his will (his testament)? We shall see.

Saturday 12

Last night everything went well, the room was full and I "watched myself" walk out toward the people, remembering my body, and theirs sitting there, stirred by my youth and my brilliant speed. Afterward with Julia at Arturito, celebrating the five thousand pesos for my first paid lecture.

A very good era, I'd have to look hard to come up with another period this clear and smooth and "creative."

"My passion began the day that my soul fell into this miserable body, which I finish consuming by writing this," Michelet.

Series E. I walked in the sun through Buenos Aires, deserted because of Día de la Raza (as it is called here), trying to find the desire to write the article on translation that I have to turn in on the 21st. An urge to pass through Mar del Plata, despite all of the family ceremonies, to look for the notebooks that I keep there and start transcribing my diaries from '58 to '62. See what can be salvaged from those times. And what will that rewriting be? A written reading of writings lived?

Sunday 13

Nothing worse than mornings, nothing worse than Sunday mornings. I listen to Mozart, watch fragments of sunlight through the slits of the window, the swishing of a broom below, gradually leaving the oppressive opacity of the morning, rediscovering certainty, convictions to hold on to and pull my head out of the water to breathe. After a while, everything is set into motion, the work that begins at dawn, the books to be read. Ahead lies the end of night, the day to come . . . I always regain my drive.

"An autobiographical poem . . . portrays an idealized image of the poet, not what has occurred but what should have occurred," Tomashevsky.

Series C. Battles, ups and downs, there are times when this woman crosses from the other side, taking refuge in a strange ceremony that turns me into a strange guest. The two of us sitting, kneeling, lying in the bed, crying. Pausing to find new paths toward destruction. Strangers striking out at each other, their only motive not to know each other.

Monday 14
I suppose what bothers me in André Gide's *Journals* is a certain fascinated contemplation of nature. His sanctimonious optimism irritates me: birds that eat from his hand, mountains that let themselves be scaled, fish that develop their lives before him, etc.

Were my surprising tears at reading Pavese's terrible final letters a way of "posing?" Above all, who knows why? Something that a relative wrote to him, naïvely congratulating him for his "great prize" (that year's Strega), as though I had seen in that the clash of his own reality against abhorrent sentiments. A way to appear sensitive, worthy, crying for Pavese as though for myself. An aristocratic way to make myself be seen in that pain by the chosen, those whom the world crushes.

"If the science of literature wants to become a science, it must recognize the 'device' as its only 'hero,'" R. Jakobson.

Every day, at ten thirty in the morning, the sun destroys my things, my books, my desk.

"It is difficult to describe a character who has nothing to do in the story," L. Tolstoy.

"An artist's fate, in its ultimate analysis, lies in his technique," Heimito von Doderer.

Wednesday, October 16
Today the whole city in chorus: students from La Plata are intercontinental soccer champions. Car horns, confetti, noise, and chanting. Earlier with León R., his ideas about Freud are good since they confirm

my intuitions; along with that are the trials, his skirmishes with David, which catch me off guard.

At times I catch myself trapped in a blind vertigo, in the trivial chaos of the everyday, which I can't control, which crushes me: calls, visits, interviews that use themselves up and invade me, paralyzing me. Once I react it is too late, gone are the times when I imagined a space of my own, as though my days became that confusion, my work a continuous postponement.

Thursday, October 17
A bomb in the Biblioteca Lincoln. I thought: "I hope they didn't lose any books of literature."

A crisp morning, certain rituals interfere with the joy of launching myself into the Jakobson book, as I am learning to relate to my own body. Certain games that I play with reality have become a kind of rhetoric, and at the same time there is something fragile, theatrical about them. An effort of willpower, of intelligence, always leads me to be a rather cynical witness of the events that involve me (or someone close to me). I'll never entirely know whether this pretext of ironic objectivity is anything more than an implicit production of bad faith. A bit like Andrés, who always gives away what he's really thinking, denying any meaning behind what he says, though his words allude to it directly. It's as though the most resilient ghosts were the opposite of the motions we make to exorcise them. I mean my inability to control myself has turned me into a sort of schizophrenic, leaping from extreme self-control and irony to confession. Anyway, I could write a series of performances: my grandfather's death, accident in the army, attack in Mar del Plata. Incidents in which I have rehearsed a performance of myself. The old story about the sad songbirds.

Friday, October 18
My usual places: just now someone's voice reading science fiction stories at Pirí's house with a distant, passive affectation, the empty afternoons

at those school desks that open up, a house full of invisible spiderwebs, unexpected visits, painful objects. From there come the searches, the meetings, that broken music (an oboe?), Cortina on Radio Municipal, which I listened to in La Plata, and in Medrano that woman's voice reading a science fiction story, and before that the corner in Mar del Plata, a strange ritual with another woman when the only thing we had in common was the Montecarlo show, and before that the programs I used to escape from my adolescence—modern jazz, with Basualdo—which I've rediscovered in the afternoons now, here.

I prefer to know about myself through others, through the reflection of a gesture, from a phrase on the face of someone close to me. Knowing about myself through the mirror that startles me suddenly as I enter a room, showing me a threatening stranger who watches me watching him, astonished.

Yesterday afternoon, the way I dealt with all (or almost all) of my ideas about a possible history of translation and was unable to resist the temptation to seem more lucid than I am in front of Roberto C., is proof of my several lives: one of them is the way I let myself go in order to be sincere. The lives I speak of are ways of being, and they always remind me of a quote from the Austrian philosopher: "The world of the happy man is a different one from that of the unhappy man." Changes in outlook and perception of reality, then, are complicated by a certain point of view (like Henry James). And so, yesterday, I mentioned all of my theories that might seem brilliant, although the instant that I exhibit them could hold a high price: there is no need to speak about what is being written, and the luster is no a guarantee of quality. In this way, I have introduced a harmful rhythm into the tempo of my own maturation, as long as I need others in order to think.

X Series. Yesterday a fleeting exchange with Lucas, always elusive and evasive, more "secure" than at other times, his face marked by his newly shaven beard, some certainty that sustains his life. "And what if they catch you?" He smiles: "They won't catch me." But if they do catch you, what can we do. They won't catch me. Conviction is everything; nothing can be done without that. He also made some analysis and recalled his history. He was in the Taco Ralo guerrillas, after the EGP, these are previous experiences that began in 1961. At the same time, I perceive in him a demeanor of spying, of boredom, of falsehood. The man of action.

Series A. On Tuesday I waited, anxious, for the shopkeeper across the street to open for business. That waiting unsettled me, isn't it strange? It seems that every change in my plans or in my will, however small, microscopic, produces a greater effect in me. Finally, after two or three false starts, I went downstairs and saw him opening the metal shutter with both hands, his back to the street, and then I crossed and bought a bottle of milk. I paid with fifty pesos, there was no change. I accepted this, quickly, to avoid causing an uncomfortable situation, emphasizing my indifference about the fact that the shopkeeper still owed me eighteen pesos. This morning, I was the one who had no change. I put together thirty pesos in coins, but I was missing two pesos. Several times, as I slid the coins around, I came close to reminding him about the debt. Finally I held out the thirty pesos to him confusedly, asking him to trust me for two pesos. Without listening to his response—amiable—I went back as though escaping. For me, economy is a kind of secret passion, and I can never act with money "in the light of day"; in any situation, it feels like I'm handling counterfeit money and making unfair trades. A man without a personal economy. Or, better still, a man who has a personal economy, private, that is, who can't share with anyone, in the sense that he has no people to talk to or figures to "do business" with.

The violent reactions (see Sabato's letter in the magazine *Análisis*) in response to any theory about the marginal character of Argentine literature provoke an outcry that proves the truth of my arguments. Clearly, it doesn't have to do with talking about an "inferior" literature, but rather thinking about the temporality of culture in a territorially defined field. My argument was to say that, since the origins of the Literary Salon in

1837, Argentina thought about itself as a culture out of sync with the present, arriving late to the contemporary situation. What causes the outcry is my opinion about us, the writers who have begun to publish in recent years; we have broken from that imbalance and are now in the same literary temporality as European or American writers. The outcry comes from the fact that culture has been the space in which our relationship with the central countries has been most deliberately concealed and diverted. We have seen that things changed after Borges and Cortázar. Today, any one of us, Puig, for example, can exhibit the full contemporaneity of his writing and now has no need to go on about our "delayed" situation. It is about not accepting that mystification and using all contemporary literature, without any sort of "difference" or inferiority.

A tortuous walk under the merciless light that filters in among the clouds and shines on the cement like a knife of sun, avoiding meetings with other writers (for example, waving to Rozenmacher from far away and going on at a distance), until I dock at a bench in Plaza San Martín, under another sun, now clear and softer.

Saturday
If I were dragged out of paradise by age, when everything is worn away, and I realized it, how could I look outside of my experience for the certainties of that incomparable time? Our capacity for happiness depends on some balance between what our childhood has denied us and what it has granted us. Completely fulfilled or completely deprived, we will be lost. Maybe I am suffering the consequences of a too-happy childhood (too happy?).

People who still explain the crisis of the tango as a result of the embellishment of themes fall into a realist mystification. They don't see the tango as a genre that had a clear origin (1913, "Mi noche triste," recorded by Gardel) and has had a glorious end ("La última curda," 1953, sung by Goyeneche). Something shared by all the great genres (tragedy, for example): they are connected to certain conditions that make them possible, and, when those conditions change, the genre doesn't adapt and comes to a splendid close. The lyrics that sustain the story had a short duration that, nevertheless, made it possible to tell a story in three minutes, but that duration was intimately tied to the dance. Tangos were danced to, and when the singers intoned the lyrics, the audience would sometimes stop dancing and move in closer to listen to them. Troilo, for example, sometimes shortened the song to a minute and then the music would fill the space. It is rock that has put an end to that logic; that is where young people find what they need to dance, and tango has become a music to be listened to and not to be danced to. Piazzolla is to tango what Charlie Parker was to jazz. Faced with the presence of rock, jazz also stopped being a popular, danceable music and took refuge in clubs or in bars where people go to listen, as in a concert, to the development of a sophisticated music, popular in its history but rarified in its new situation. The same thing happened with tango; the typical orchestra disappeared, and these days you go to Caño 14 or Jamaica to listen to duets like Troilo-Grela or Salgán-De Lío or to Piazzolla or Rovira's Quintets. But now there are no lyrics, and people don't dance to them the way they did in the great dances of the forties, which had allowed them to support a complex—and expensive—orchestral ensemble.

Sunday, October 20
My verbal anticipations of my own reality continue, my readings of the future; the project of writing about Pavese, in Turin, is a way for me to prepare for my journey to Italy, which today resurfaced as an imminent possibility. An escape.

X Series. On Friday Lucas T. was here, brief and mistrustful as always, rigidly clinging to a stubborn rationality, which reminded me of some pianists I've known who always seem to be practicing the next piece. Lucas is always in action, never relaxes, comes to see me as a way to rest, to change conversation, lays down his weapons on the table and converses with me. "A man who's worn out politically doesn't talk," he says. And the torture? "He doesn't talk." And what certainty can there be? "Ideological certainty, ideological work. I know what I'm telling you. I was a prisoner, as you know." I grew furious, that's metaphysical, I told him, pain is a leap into the void, like death. "I have absolute faith in myself and my companions. You know who they are, they'll never betray me." But absolute trust is the reason for failure. It is the opposite of voluntarism, reality doesn't exist, you triumph or fail through errors, never through political matters. Lucas smiles. "If I thought the way you do I'd be working as a lawyer, I'd be living in Paris, spending my family's fortune, if I wanted to." A guy who acts tough and clings to the feeling of power that ideas give him. In his case the reasons make me ashamed: he has been betrayed, chased, his name put in the papers, accused of murder, all of the gates are closed, his only escape is by going forward. I love him like a brother, but he seems further and further away from me, even though I believe I'm the only friend he has left from his former life. We stay together until morning, shooting the breeze. If I read that line somewhere, I would say: "But why the breeze? Why shooting it?" Lucas would start a poem that way if he were living in France, free and away from danger.

The city was empty today, as though he were imagining it, a clear sun predicting the arrival of summer. A stranger watching himself walk along the streets that lead to the river. "A city of no one," he thinks.

Roman Jakobson has taken on the task of demonstrating the relationships between the translator, the cryptographer, and the detective, insofar as all three decipher messages in another language, in another code, or in an implicit language that the murderer has erased in order to leave no tracks that could let his presence be read in the "scene of the crime."

Series A. In relation to Perón's attempt, Onganía's dictatorship is in crisis not due to political reasons but rather because of a lack of politics. It is a demonstration of what Gramsci said: "the dominant class" has lost consensus and is no longer the "leader" but just "dominant," only boasting coercive force.

A strange day, wandering, at intervals, around this empty apartment; Julia is in La Plata facing her mother and her daughter, and I am distant and neutral, in this place, as disconnected as everyone, listening to music on Radio Municipal, working at intervals on the essay, which seems to be on the right track and puts me at ease, thinking that tomorrow I'll begin to give shape to these insights, which I leave hanging for now. Empty, exhausted, with no desire to read or to make the slightest motion, what am I going to do with the time left before she comes back?

Tuesday 22
Series B. The friendships that interfere with my reality are like a bridge that connects me to things, to the actions I must undertake in the near future, which invade and cancel out any present goal (the imagined actions, not my friends).

X Series. The covert man, who immerses himself in armed conflict and becomes invisible; his life is duplicated, he lives in the light of day as any one of us, but at night he lives in the inevitable revolution, behaves deliriously or—to keep up the consonance—bravely. In the early years of this notebook the subject under study was Steve, the secret American writer who seemed to live in two worlds. Then the years passed, and the hero was Cacho Carpatos, the man outside the law who broke into the houses of the powerful and was surrounded by the necessary figures of his own life (Bimba, the call girl, "the fence" who moved the stolen objects). Now, for a while, the figure under my gaze has been the man of action, the clandestine revolutionary who works in the shadows to bring about changes in the course of history. The one who observes this varied species of men, his friends and the people he admires, he is the indifferent, tranquil man (this one would be me, in a sense). These are the characters in my life, my friends. The other series is that of the women I've loved: the redhead, the married girl, the tempestuous woman, the young girl of the night (the girl with the Vespa).

Wednesday, October 23

A murder in the neighborhood and a gaunt, slight man with many verbal tics is raving: "She was fifteen, but he bled her dry. He bled her dry, all bled out. I was in front, there, and I heard something I thought was fireworks. Didn't even realize it or see the people crowded around because I thought it was fireworks. Now, a boy told me he saw them turn the corner, arguing, from what I saw they were stopped there, in the doorway." A couple, nearby: "They're going to close down the hotel," she said. "No, why are they going to close down the hotel?" And her: "Don't you think that's too much?" she said. "What I saw was, it happened on the sidewalk. What does the hotel have to do with it?" Later, in the store: "What can you tell me about the crime? Now, she was kind of a bimbo. Every time she came I realized she was kind of a bimbo. But it takes all kinds . . . " And as I was leaving several people crowded around a woman holding up the *Crónica* newspaper, which showed photos. "She looks about the same," she said with a mix of stupefaction and secret envy, as though the news belonged to her. And a man to one side said: "He gave her a kiss and she went like this," with a gesture of wiping his hand over his mouth, "like she was cleaning herself off . . . If a woman did that to me I'd . . . " And the others looked on with a mix of compassion and irony. Meanwhile, on the corner, two kids were carrying some machines (photocopiers?). The one who was further away said, skeptically: "Nothing. See? They already cleared it away. What do you want to see?"

The storm comes, breaking the bright afternoons that made way for the summer. It is noon, and in the street the darkness flattens the fronts of houses as the rain begins to fall violently, a classic scene, already seen many times in the repertoire of images of nature in the city. Now the rain has come down relentlessly (has the rain come down relentlessly?) and the fresh air carries the heavy smell of wet earth. The lamp traces a white circle on the table and warms my left arm while everything is dark in the world. A strange feeling of dispossession forces me to close the window to prevent the rain from dampening the notebook that I'm writing in, isolating me still further from reality. I am empty and alone, going in circles on a Ferris wheel, doing nothing but looking at the axis, immobile.

Thursday 24
Yesterday as I was getting off the subway there was a throng of people looking on with a strange mixture of satisfaction and shame. An acrid smell of burnt rubber, employees running from one end of the platform to the other, the train conductor, pale, pausing every time someone looks at him or suggests a question. He is a bald man, wearing glasses, with a pockmarked face and a strange object in his hand, some kind of handle. He pauses suddenly, as though having found what he was looking for, and explains that he couldn't brake. "I couldn't brake," he says. Then he takes off running again. And then he pauses once more. I too peer around the edge of the platform and look through the gap left between the coaches, toward the dark opening of the rails. I try to imagine the woman below, silent and alive. She couldn't have killed herself. The scene is extended. There's a sort of continuous motion inside a static scene, some people moving and running around, the rest peering around the edge of the platform (like me), still others surrounding a man with an honest face, fat and dark, with gaps in his teeth, who has climbed up the stairs, onto a podium, and speaks slowly, seeming surprised, stunned. "I cried out," he says, "if I'd seen that she wanted to throw herself off, I would've grabbed her, but I cried out because she went too close to the rails, she had a checkered purse and skirt, she was in line on the platform with the purse in her hand, standing there, next to me, and you could see the light of the oncoming train and after it hit the brakes she was nowhere to be seen." The firemen came a half hour later. She was alive. "Destroyed," said the policeman, who seemed inflated and spoke in a slow, almost childish voice that grew hoarse when he wanted to be authoritative and made the curious people circle around. I let myself be carried toward the surface by the escalator. I'd left home after the storm thinking specifically about "suicides," but I was thinking about the metaphysics of that decision and not about the dark track where a body throbbed below, strewn across the tracks, where everyone was anxiously

looking for her. The body of a woman who had clung to the edge of the precipice, thinking about what, about who . . . and had jumped into the void, breaking one storyline and opening another, more terrible, but distinct.

Notes on a suicide. Everything takes place as though the horrific image could naturally give rise to a concept. There is a mysterious relationship between terror and thought. What lives becomes nature. Dying in the subway (*sic*), in the bowels of the city, run down by a silent vehicle that lights up the sorrow.

We lived on a stage, facing the furtive but attentive eyes of our neighbors, residents who spied on our everyday routines: they peeked through the windows, pulled back the lace curtains, the latticework, the netting, the blinds, *voyeurs* spying in through the cracks. To kiss, we had to hide behind the doors or—almost always—in the bathroom, an enclosure where we finally settled in for good. (*A story.*)

Sitting in an airplane seat, taxiing along the damp runway, and flying over the rainy city toward the sun.

We could say that what scandalized the critics on the right or on the conservative left in *Hopscotch* is its explicit, visible poetics, the fact of its deliberately being a work in progress. Cortázar has tried to cross the narrow bridge that unites short form with vast novelistic structures without hiding the inner workings. Cortázar's novel narrates certain renowned processes of cultural consumption. In a sense, he establishes a moral hierarchy in the interior of artistic products, and those critics felt provoked, seeing themselves tied to the "female reader" (the unfortunate name that Cortázar gave to conservative consumption).

What if I were the subject of my collection of essays on literature? Criticism as autobiography.

You're Lonely When You're Dead by J. H. Chase is a great crime novel because it is very aware of the techniques and traditions of the genre. It is a cynical novel that uses them coldly and, in that sense, is the opposite of Chandler's *The Long Goodbye*, where the awareness of the history of the genre is romantic and nostalgic. The scene with the girl contorting, half-naked, her stockings with long runs in them, in front of the agent who writes on the typewriter, not looking at her, and she can't insult him for fear of losing her chance to get a job, it's sensational. On the other hand, the scene of brutal physical violence to elicit a confession stands out because Chase narrates it in the present tense, making it elapse over the same length of time that the reading lasts. We might say that the failed genre elements are the excessive expressivity and the use of coincidences to solve the investigation. Also the too-visible awareness of the rules of the crime novel. "'This scene has gone a little sour,' I said, for something to say. 'The detective always gets his girl. If you shoot me the story will have an immoral ending,'" J. H. Chase.

Series E. A good day of work, agile, full of ideas. Advantage: these notebooks are born "so that nothing can escape," but they immediately show our "inner poverty," while there's nothing that can escape, and so I must attempt to think in order to "have" something that will not escape. A poetics of thought.

Friday, October 25
Series E bis. There is also subservience to the space in these notebooks: often, everything improves when there is a blank page and grows worse when I'm trying to fill the end of a page. Spatial arrangement is also a mode of thought. In literature, I think, the means are ends.

In Andrés Rivera, I confirm his intuition for writing, which functions well, a less stylized but more dangerous poetics, and in rereading all his stories I discover his use of ambiguity, of midtones, few examples of which can be found among us (perhaps Conti's "Every Summer," Walsh's "That Woman"). The key is not to close off the meaning when concluding the story. Of course, these virtues have their flaws and their limitations, and the material always seems on the point of losing its way. These writers (Wernicke, Rivera, Conti) hit their mark in one out of every five attempts, but they struggle to go beyond the limits they impose upon themselves. They are deliberately naïve, the opposite of Hemingway or Borges, because greater awareness comes with greater risk but also greater achievements. Rereading a few pages from these notebooks is enough to make me think about "spontaneity." A need, then—or rather a desire—for an alert consciousness in the narrative, particularly when the technique consists of stating everything that happens, as I do here, as much as possible, while it is taking place.

Saturday 26

We went in circles around the room at two in the morning, thinking it was eight, and then I fell asleep holding Julia, and we awoke unexpectedly at ten after six, confused as we saw the hands of the clock but read ten to twelve on the upside-down alarm clock. Confusion in the springtime night, an effect of the passion that keeps us from sleep. We finally went out into the street and walked around in the icy drizzle. We found an English version of Dostoevsky (*Notes from Underground*) and ended up at La Fragata, on Corrientes and San Martín, having café con leche and croissants.

I would like to recapture my wanderings with David Viñas around this same apartment; we talked as we moved around the room and then continued at his place, and later we had lunch together and ended up walking down Corrientes.

Sunday 27

Series E. This notebook also suffers from the effects of yet another static time, in which all I can do is look for a way out, as though I were swimming underwater in the hold of a sunken ship.

Monday 28

I watch the days passing, one after another, unable to do anything that would lend them meaning. Julia said: "In ten days, you'll still think you're burned out. You'll look for more excuses so you can say: 'I'm ready, I am at the bottom of the sea.'" All of that, said sweetly.

Twenty-five years had passed; some women who had been very beautiful when they were young now exhibit the traces of time on their proud faces, and they hang Jeanne Moreau's photograph on the walls of their hearts. But this is only the wall across from the glass table where I sat in one of its high-backed chairs, not taking off my jacket, looking at a woman with blue painted eyelids as she told stories with metaphors that included me in them and talked pejoratively about herself. Finally I left, made it to the ground floor without an umbrella, went back up, walked into the empty place until she appeared with my umbrella, wearing a terrible smile, a smile that awoke an endless sadness within me, the light rain still wetting the streets.

Series A. In this notebook, I leave a record of the sixteen hundred seventy-two (1,672) copies of my book purchased by presumed readers. Mathematical exactitude that was converted into sixty thousand fifty pesos (60,050), with which I settled my account for books at my publisher's bookshop, books that had allowed me to survive by reading for the last two years. And so, to celebrate, I bought no. 11 of *Communication* magazine and Libertella's novel.

Thursday, October 31

I saw David going past in a taxi, upset, aggressive, wearing those glasses that look like a mask, suffering from dizziness and headaches, with his touching attempt to "objectify" and distance himself, as though his fear of old age had turned him into someone else. A speculative interpretation, because David looks too much like me.

Monday, November 3, 1968
I managed to wake up at five thirty in the morning, and now I sense the engine of the garbage truck below, on Carmen, mingling with the noise of bins hitting the sidewalk and the voices of workers yelling to one another.

Too much alcohol last night for me not to feel this oppression in my head, slowly clearing away in the crisp morning air.

Tuesday, November 4
Confirmation that I've been constructing my life against my better judgment. From the time of the photo that shows me smiling timidly at age six (dressed in overalls, short pants, and a shirt behind which you can glimpse my—heartwarming—fleece shirt with buttons, standing to the left of the blooming jasmine, in the open entrance to the hall where you can see the hard chairs of pale wood) all the way to this warm November night: narratively, it would be delightful to seek the paths, the detours, the good decisions, the accidents that lead from one image to another.

What seems undeniable is my learning of humility—that is, control over my emotional nature in order to face the extreme expressivity of family life. That may be where my interest in skeptics comes from, those elusive figures who conceal sentiments under irony. A learning that may end up in desolation, silence, if I'm unable to retrace my steps and rescue my emotions.

Wednesday 5
Series E. In reading my diaries from 1957, some constants appear: an evolving relationship with Elena, getting myself caught in everyday ceremonies (I went to play chess every day. Discovery of voracious reading, three books in one week). Narrative experience, double consciousness, and a schism between who I was in 1957 and who I am now in 1968 as I reread these events. Retrieving the events because of the value they may come to have in the future, an unforeseeable time for one who is

living it. I let myself be dragged along by the rare excitement of reading my own life.

Julia walks and moves around, taking off beautiful dresses, trying on an orange-colored one, holding it against her body and looking at her bare feet.

My excessive expressiveness in my early notebooks, in my letters to Elena, proves the spontaneous motion of an introspective nature, created in the expressionist atmosphere of my family.

Friday 6
Suddenly, like a wind in the night, whispers of my adolescence return: furies, fears, and tears that represent a search for that time when I owned the world in my ambition and imagined how I would conquer the city with my books.

José Agustín's *The Grave* interests me because of his frantic handling of a rough language that captures the vertigo and inescapable world of adolescence. I'm not interested in his use of very dated language, an argot that is too lexical, words that grow old overnight. The best part is how he uses Anthony Burgess's strategy, inventing a language of undefined territory, without a set timeframe.

In the detective genre, certain scenes are repeated. For example, the bad women; Marlowe comes across the daughter of a millionaire who sucks on her finger and stares at him, beguiling. In Chase, the detective seduces the invalid daughter of another millionaire, and she tries to make him come in through the service door. In that sense, it's possible to uncover a certain rhetoric. Millionaires in predicaments, generally married to actresses or ex-ballerinas who abandon them or die and leave them alone with their daughters, crippled, rather dumb, or nymphomaniac. Cynical butlers, very wise, great for creating atmospheres and delivering ingenious retorts. A multitude of secondary characters, all characterized by some singularity. The "other" fundamental element is the often-repeated moral code of the detective. As Molley says in a novel by Chase: "I enjoy my work. Maybe it isn't very productive, but it's original enough to inspire me."

Thursday 7

I recall Valéry's theory: the story must be told from an idea and not from a passion, and I think that, if *Discourse on the Method* is the first modern novel, then Marx's chapter on fetishism of commodities in *Das Kapital* is the *Ulysses* of our time.

Friday

Yesterday I saw Miguel B., the "delights" of the atmosphere, unnamed things that betray our differences, gossip. Miguel, meanwhile, is lost in the brutal world of journalism, or rather, literary journalism, a nest of resentful people, omnipotent mediocrities devoted to proving themselves through injury. I wanted to cover my back by making my code of ethics clear. All the same, he carries his resentment, his youth, his awful, insane father, his brilliant entrance into literature, like a bulletproof camera. Difficulty conversing with me since I come from the other side and find his literature to be one of salvation, of escape from this sinister realm.

All of this metaphysics in the editorial office of *Confirmado* with the bold young people (Mario E., Horacio V., Andrés A.) who practice "preemptive journalism." Amid the tumult, I saw a copy of *62: A Model Kit* on a table, Cortázar's latest novel, a sort of guide that draws its aesthetics from *Hopscotch*; from what they tell me, it has already sold twenty-five thousand copies.

Dream. I call Montevideo and travel to the south, where I'm supposed to work as a mathematician for fifty thousand pesos per month. Mountains covered with snow, abysses into which I could be silently lost, drawing the buzzards to destroy my body with their talons and then clean their beaks on my beard.

A certain relationship with women, certain ceremonies, parties in dim light that repeat over the course of time; they are the cipher of my life.

Saturday
Last night I went walking near the river, drinking wine and eating grilled steak in the open air. Before that to La Plata and back, collecting an unexpected four thousand pesos.

Series E. I'm making a place of my own for the first time, somewhere I can put my body and know where the friendly parts will be, a celebration that I discover in the mornings when I get up during the sunrise and write or read at this desk by the window. On the table are Cortázar, Paco U's *Adolecer*, Pavese, and Onetti's short novels.

In some places I am slightly sickened by the elegant and contorted prose of Cortázar's latest book, *62*. At first glance, we might say, all of the characters are the same or, at any rate, they correspond to the same "figure," as Cortázar calls it, a ubiquitous space (city, area) that is all of the characters and none. A novel that should be read in the same corner as *Hopscotch* along with other passages and stories ("A Yellow Flower," "The Other Heaven," "All Fires the Fire") and Persio's entrances in *Los Premios*, because of their kinship, their thematic similarities: a secret theory about narrative causality and motivation that, in this case, tends to be aleatory and spatial. An autobiography (in chorus), sixty-two voices through which each of the many narrators sketches the silhouette of an elusive figure.

Pavese, a story. I had chosen to go to Italy because that was what I was most familiar with; I was obsessed with Pavese, but it might have been anyone else, Osamu Dazai, let's say, as long as it was someone half-defeated, an ally who could help me to take action. But I chose *This Business of Living* and applied for a fellowship at Dante Alighieri and installed myself in Turin.

Tuesday 12
The use of pseudonyms is very common in popular literature. In this respect, the detective genre is the highest-quality narrative that I've read. I assembled lists and lists of titles for my project of making a collection of American crime novels. The production is vast, so I'll have to read twenty books for every three that I select. I'm going to start with an anthology, and then I'll publish Chandler's short stories.

Friday 15
Yesterday I saw Marcela Milano, whom I mentioned the other day. A judge requisitioned *Nanina*, accusing it of being a pornographic novel, and I spent the afternoon helping Germán make sense of the difficult ordeal. Finally a meeting for the magazine (Ismael, Andrés, Rodolfo W.), with many ideas circulating about the political situation.

Series C. "You used to deny your body, now you deny your feelings," Celina said to me. A woman's great ability to capture and expose masculine affectations. In slang they'd say *she nailed me*, the way someone would check a fruit to see if it's ripe.

Tuesday 19
Some tones, the melodies of certain prose (Chandler, Céline), mark the cadence and the rhythm of the story. You have to break yourself free from those tones, the way jazz musicians improvise on the piano over standards, trying to forget them.

Wednesday 20
"The Relatives of E. R." came out, an essay by Beatriz Guido about the writers who published their first books with Jorge Álvarez. We'll see what happens in the next ten days, remembering that my maturity is slow to come.

Saturday

A striking rediscovery of Dostoevsky's best while I'm revising the edition of *Notes from Underground*, the first book in my classics collection for Jorge Álvarez. This *nouvelle* will be a revelation; it has never been published as an individual book in Spanish. Floreal Mazía's translation does a good job of capturing the irascible tones of the prose; it is based on the English version by Constance Garnett, which I read many years ago in Mar del Plata at Steve's recommendation.

If, as G. Lukács notes in the preface to this edition, "Raskolnikov is the Rastignac of the second half of the nineteenth century," then the man who wrote these memoirs is the antecedent of the great first-person prose of this century. Beckett in first place, but also Sartre's Roquentin, Camus's *The Fall*, and of course there is the atmosphere and acuity of Kafka's monologues: "Josephine the Singer," "Investigations of a Dog," "A Report to an Academy," etc.

Series B. Sadness as I say goodbye to David, who is traveling to Cuba and Italy, sympathy with his cutting of ties; he sold his library, emptied his apartment. A feeling that I'm losing the only person I can talk to freely.

In Puig: the omniscient reader. (The absent narrator.)

Monday 25

Saturday was a complex day. A visit from David. My friendship with him is growing, facing the deadline of his flight. His demolished apartment, the sisal twine for bundling books, the helplessness of goodbyes. In the afternoon I have a meeting for the magazine, struggling to complete the third issue, which seems to be almost ready now. An unexpected invasion by Paco U. and Pepe A. at three in the morning like a police raid; they yell up at the window of my apartment from the street, asking for the Bola de Nieve record that I left at Pirí's house more than a year ago. Hostility that I have no response for, since I'm not going to get into that locker room game, and I have enough education and experience to tell when the "boys" are drunk. One more lesson learned and they're gone . . . I have to trust my intuition and mistrust insecure, anti-intellectual, populist associates. U. traveled to Cuba with me last year and we had several conflicts on the trip; for me, the first impression is always the one that matters.

Wednesday 27
Last night at the Teatro Apolo on Calle Corrientes. A Beat concert, Almendra, Manal, Javier Martínez. It's the music of the future, and I listen to it with the distance that comes with my age, so to speak. I went with Jorge Álvarez, and this seems to resolve the intersections we see in the bookstore, Pappo, Pajarito Zaguri, Miguel Abuelo, long-haired kids who smoke hash along with Jauretche, Pajarito García Lupo, and other birds.

Thursday 28
Yesterday, a journey through the city to pick up the 158,000 pesos for Andrés and our secret, or almost secret, publications, on which I collaborate sporadically and anonymously. I finally found several volumes of detective novels that they brought for me at the Costa agency in Belgrano. I'm making progress on the anthology, which will become the first volume of the Serie Negra, beginning this year, onto which I am placing all my literary and economic hopes. I ended up at the publishing office, dying of heat, looking through several boxes of crime books. The production of novels amazes me; authors like Ed McBain, Richard Prater, Chase, etc. write two or three novels per year for a fixed audience that buys for the genre and not the writers as such.

Thursday, December 2
Yesterday, with the ephemeral quality of cinema, I was disappointed rewatching The Man with the Golden Arm, which used to be legendary to me but has not stood the test of time. The best part is Eleanor Parker, the hysterical woman who pretends to be paralyzed in order to tie Sinatra down, the striking narrative value of the whistle she uses to call when she is alone. I remember the first time I saw it in Adrogué after reading

the novel by Nelson Algren, which I'd liked despite its naturalistic tone. Cinema ages more quickly, but literature is more easily forgotten.

Tuesday 3
Manuel Puig came to visit me, describing the passionless brothels for men in Tangier and Roberto Il Diavolo, whom he recalled with fascination on the Paseo de Julio, an unforgettable man, Manuel said; he managed to meet him before his death. Yesterday a conversation with Conti about his first novel, his current projects. I am reading badly, wanting to get the two anthologies over with and have the summer free.

Wednesday 11
X Series. David comes to say goodbye to me because he's leaving; as always with him, it's hard to write about the reasons for this flight. Later with Lucas T. M. at a bar in the Mercado del Plata, drinking beer from Denmark to give meaning to the meeting. He's in hiding, and his returns to the surface are always connected to me, visiting me as a way to rest. Despite the heat, he wears a jacket and tie, intending to look like an office clerk, but he is armed. He tells me about a bank robbery to confiscate funds; the cashier doesn't believe him when he points a Beretta at him, "Get out of here, don't kid around," he says. Lucas threatens him, saying "I'm going to kill you" as he backs away and leaves the bank, empty handed.

A check today from Jorge Álvarez (fifty thousand pesos) for the English chronicles. And twenty-five thousand from Tiempo Contemporáneo for December and the promise of another twenty-five thousand in January. I hope to live comfortably for the whole summer with this money.

Thursday 12
A meeting for the magazine and an argument with Andrés and Ismael about the implications of David's trip. A.'s hatred toward D. is very clear in this. He took charge of passing this judgment, inciting Ismael to betray him.

Carlos B. tells me a couple of stories. His father, buying newspapers from the revolution in '55 to "read when he retires." His mother, institutionalized and weeping. The father steps out into the hallway with Carlos. "I haven't shot myself because I don't have a revolver." Another story, an Argentine man and a Swedish woman look at each other, and he, unable to communicate with her, takes her to his apartment and there, not saying a word, she undresses. The next day, he thanks her and says goodbye.

Friday
X Series. Last night with Lucas, transformations—physical as well—of a person who has kept himself in shape for ten years despite successive transitions (rural guerrilla in Taco Ralo, a metal worker, then an ally of Casco, a Trotskyist leader). The only one in my generation who (despite his title as an attorney) hasn't returned to the fold. At the same time, he has a way of burning bridges, getting caught up in the inevitable whirlwind of unchecked violence around his life. He is learning to have courage, to not run away despite the bullets, to feign the "astonishing calmness" that the newspapers describe. It's also certain that I'll have to write about him again, here.

In Gide's diary (which I always come back to reluctantly), he has a good insight in comparing the museum to the library. He points out what is perishable in literature, the changes in time that become changes in space. The museum, a pure space, confirms the juxtaposition between the way some forgotten painters are reborn and certain fashionable ones come to inevitable ends. Confirmation or superimposition of what seems new and what has been forgotten, which are synthesized in a single space: the museum.

In Pavese's admirable "Primo amore," reticence becomes a tone, a level of awareness, but not, as in Hemingway, a void or a silence; what is unsaid in Pavese turns into something halfway spoken, into a restraint that defines the character.

I am going to make a note here of all my movements today. I got up at six, wrote until ten. From eleven to one, I read all of Pavese's *August Holiday*. Then Néstor García Canclini came with a letter from Cortázar and other nonsense. Next I went to Andrés's house and finished a piece about the CGTA for *No Transar*, signed as Sergio Tretiakov. Now I'm reading a book by Pierre Macherey, and in a while I'll go to bed.

Saturday 14

It has been raining since last night. I find a striking handling of the abstract second person in James Cain's *Double Indemnity*, the reference to an invisible interlocutor allows him to strengthen the narration and structure it.

"The author does not make the materials with which he works," Macherey. In that sense, he or she is not a "creator" who extracts something from nothing. A history of the motives, themes, techniques, and forms should be made, and a work should be inscribed in the space of that history in order to be understood.

Monday 16

Strikingly, some European writers (Gide, Sartre, Pavese) dismiss Faulkner; they see a great writer appearing and don't want to believe it. They look for ways to discredit him, to "diminish him." Today, the tendency is to use his techniques but talk about something else, the *nouveau roman*, for example. It's impossible to understand a writer like Claude Simon without Faulkner's prose, but they prefer to say that his poetics only results from a rejection of the traditional narrative of the nineteenth century. The same thing happens with present-tense narration and the rupture of narrative continuity which, of course, were present in Faulkner.

As for Chandler, his greatest merit is the way he handles romantic irony, set against a cynical and cruel world. The naïveties of his novels are typical of the crime genre; for example, there must always be a character who has looked through a window and witnessed scenes that the detective—who is also the narrator—could not see.

Just now, a walk down Corrientes to the offices where two books by Chandler were waiting for me as well as another two by David Goodis and a novel by Ross Macdonald, free of copyright, in Spanish, which we're going to make an offer for.

Tuesday 17
I should reflect on the use of parentheses in a narration (they are a pause, or they are an interruption that must be pointed out).

Ever since I went to see José Bianco, a few weeks ago, to give him the book that Virgilio Piñera sent him from Havana, dedicated to him (and with a photo), we have begun a telephone friendship; we talk early in the morning or in the evening, a way for me to start or end the day by talking to someone with whom I have an understanding, almost without having to explain anything, even though he comes from another generation.

I looked at my face in the mirror and decided that I shouldn't have a beard. Immediately some issues came up, and now I'm sure I'll keep my face the way it is.

Thursday 19
In the morning I stopped by Jorge Álvarez's place to drop off a list of books and had a very good talk with him, as is usual these days; he always has many projects and unexpected ideas. We go forward with the plan for a crime collection, in which we'll publish American novels distinguished from the model of the English mystery novel. In the bookshop I ran into Walsh, who invited me to see *The Hour of the Furnaces* on Friday next week. Then I got lunch with Schmucler and we organized some things for next year. He brought me a very favorable review, published in *La Nación*, of my anthology of autobiographical texts. From there I went to the magazine meeting without much energy, trying to put together

the program for a meeting among intellectuals of the left at the end of the month. Finally back at home with Daniel and B. having a very good discussion about the script, with compromises and agreements that allowed it to progress quickly.

Friday 20
At night I see Manuel Puig again, always infallible in his selections, he sees "the Argentine" in Isabel Sarli and Armando Bo's films. There, he finds what he was looking for: passion and social politics, everything taken to an extreme and beyond. He also sees "the national" appear in Silvina Bullrich and in radio dramas, more clearly than it appears in writers from the left, who deliberately try to reflect reality.

Today I reread Chandler's *The Long Goodbye* in almost one sitting, it has all of the mystery, the mythical atmosphere, and the tone of a great novel like *Gatsby* or *Fiesta* or *The Glass Key* by Hammett. In a sense, all of his novels form one saga structured around the adventures leading up to the meeting with Marlowe; a character's past becomes a novel you have read before. This heightens the sense of reality in the everyday life of the protagonist, whom you already know. Soon after the beginning of *The Little Sister*, after his meeting with Maioranos on the last page of the previous novel, he would have taken a shower and gone to his office to wait for a phone call. Rather, the structure of the novels allows them to be linked as a succession of Marlowe's adventures as he grows old, not learning from experience.

Saturday
Last night a thwarted attempt to see *The Hour of the Furnaces* covertly. It was raining and we all crowded into El Foro. I'm writing the cover copy for Mailer's *Complete Stories*.

Sunday 22
Amazed at the Americans' arrival on the moon, which I watched on television yesterday at Daniel's house.

Before I go to Mar del Plata:
M. Milano.
Miguel Briante.
Tiempo Contemporáneo publishing.
Chandler.
Magazine.
Boccardo (meeting Thursday).

Buy:
Agenda.
Notebook.
Shoes.

Tuesday 24
A year ends, its merits reduced to money. I earned one hundred thousand pesos per month instead of the thirty thousand I earned last year. Autonomy, free time.

A meeting for the magazine (which is coming out on Thursday), then at the publishing house, nothing else.

Wednesday 25
I spent Christmas Eve alone.

The end of the year, empty days, not reading or writing, waiting for something to change, not quite knowing why.

Thursday
An interview with Borges on Monday; my idea is to have him select a set of short stories by Conrad and write a preface for the classics collection.

Tuesday
Yesterday a visit with Borges (brief, hindered by María Esther Vázquez), which will be repeated next Monday.

Monday

At ten thirty I meet Borges. I arrive and the maid opens the door and lets me in. Borges is having breakfast, the tablecloth is an English flag, he seems to be eating ham. He gropes around in the air and bends forward in greeting, and the bones of his face are visible under his transparent skin. While responding to the imperative questions of a young man, trying to "make him talk" about Perón and about Russian communism, Borges confirms what the other man says but then starts talking about Stevenson. Finally, as he is leaving, Borges tells him not to put in anything about politics except for one line that amuses him: "What we need in this country is a good-natured Swiss dictator." Finally he comes toward where I wait for him in an upholstered armchair by the window, carrying a piece of furniture in front of him, and he says: "It's very dark. Is it still raining?" We begin to choose the stories by Conrad. "The Duel" is the first, and then I was able to see the mechanism of Borgesian fiction almost laid bare. First, he talked to me about Conrad's story; his reading emphasized the symmetry between the duelists' private war and the Napoleonic wars that went along with them. At the same time, he insisted on the difference between the duelists, they're different, not similar, he said. One of them doesn't want to fight and the other forces him to. Immediately, the theme of "duels" starts to be organized as an uninterrupted succession or an endless chain. He describes them as though they were his own and constructs a series linked by thematic unity.

1) Sainte-Beuve condemned duels. He was fat, very tall, and bald, and he snuck around with Victor Hugo's wife, disguising himself as a woman to enter his lover's house. Someone challenged him to a duel one day, but he couldn't accept since his convictions forbid dueling, but at the same time, he had to accept so that people wouldn't think his stance came from a fear of combat. He accepts, and on the field of honor, Borges tells me, he grips the pistol in his right hand and a yellow-painted umbrella in his left hand as a way to mock the whole procedure.

117

2) In the middle of the war, Julius Caesar was challenged to a duel by a general from the enemy army. Julius Caesar would not accept and told him he would send a gladiator if he wanted to die. Napoleon did the same thing, saying he was very busy and offered to send a fencing master.

3) Dr. Johnson, in a tavern in London, had a coarse argument about theology and his opponent, enraged, threw a glass of wine at his face, Dr. Johnson looked at him, "That is a digression," he said, "I await your arguments."

4) Conrad was about to fight B. Shaw, who had said that he didn't like his novels and couldn't remember the reason why. H. G. Wells intervened, convincing Conrad that he only wanted to fight because he didn't understand the rules of English humor.

5) An employee at the National Library told the story of a gardener, Narciso, who had fought with a man and killed him. They went out into the street to fight so that they wouldn't make a mess of the house (the unexpected gentlemen did this even though they were in a brothel). They fought for half an hour, and Narciso received serious wounds on his left arm but killed his rival. The whole town attended the duel, even the watchman. They fought near the drug store, Borges clarified, so that they could be treated.

6) A lion tamer named Soto comes to San Antonio de Areco with a circus. Everyone in town is amazed at his courage: the man puts his head between the lion's jaws. A tough guy named Soto, whom they call "Toro negro," challenged the tamer every time he came near the small village and went into a bar to have a gin. "There's only room for one Soto," he said, and in the end he killed him in a pasture, even though the other refused to fight.

2

Diary 1969

January
Looking at the relationship between writing and stigma, the scar in the form of the sword, my Uncle Sergio's face covered with a cloth. He imagined that he had a skin deformity and didn't want anyone to see his face for two years. One day he decided he'd been cured and returned to his usual routines.

Thursday 2
Notes on Tolstoy (5). The logic of Tolstoy's morality must have led him to complete inaction, to a refusal to confront any concrete problem, to the *epoché* and *apatheia* of the stoics or to a passive contemplation of the mystery of being, typical of the Buddhist monk. All evil, he sometimes says in his *Diaries*, comes from doing. Thus, Tolstoyan morality is a negative morality because it is based on negation and the renunciation of all values recognized and exalted by society. Logically, the critique of society is not accompanied by any concrete alternative for a fairer society. His fundamental ideas about common ownership of the land, the exigency of manual labor, the abolition of any form of violence and any State control over the citizen, vegetarianism, disavowal of alcohol and tobacco, nonviolence, and the vote for the poor actually seem to be forms of religious life without transcendence or faith.

Friday 3
Yesterday a covert, discrete walk on San Telmo with Dalmiro Sáenz, Ricardo Carpani, Lorenzo Amengual, etc., until we entered an apartment and all crowded in to watch *The Hour of the Furnaces*, a very good film by Solanas, a documentary in the same vein as the *agitprop* of the Russian avant-garde.

Sunday 5
Yesterday an unnecessary trap: Daniel invites me to have dinner and look at a series of slides from China, but after a while Roberto C., the boss, unexpectedly appears with a heavy pedagogical lesson about the "Great Proletarian Cultural Revolution." In the middle of his dissertation—according to Julia—I jump up, fall asleep, and go out to the balcony, annoying everyone by leaving when I shouldn't have. A repeated lesson: I don't like the language of the politicians on the left, although I try not to dismiss their positions. I must defend my solitude and isolate myself (not only from politics, though politics is too present these days).

I don't like the affected styles that circulate in my generation's narrative either: everyone writes in someone else's voice (especially in those of Borges, Onetti, and Cortázar); for my part, in spite of everything, I use a personal voice that may not necessarily be my own, that is, the one I speak with in my life. I write with the sincerity of a subject I don't know, who only appears—or shows his face—when I write. Call him "H," as people now habitually say in Buenos Aires when they can't talk accurately about a topic.

I'm interested in the way Scott Fitzgerald writes about cinema and the experience of a screenwriter in the studios. He uses a key, for example, in the story "Pat Hobby and Orson Welles," mythologizing Welles in the title, not only through the formal similarities between *Citizen Kane* and *The Great Gatsby* (via Conrad), but rather because both are metaphors for the failure of the artist in the United States, something both writers have described over and over again: geniuses, famous before age thirty, broken, forgotten after forty. "There are no second acts in American lives," F. S. Fitzgerald.

Half a day spent organizing the classics collection for Jorge Álvarez. *Notes from Underground* with a prologue by George Steiner, *Robinson Crusoe* with a prologue by Joyce, *Bouvard et Pécuchet* with a prologue by R. Queneau. Also *Les Liaisons dangereuses* with a prologue by M. Butor. I prepared a draft of the general introduction for the series and decided on material for the covers.

Then to the movies. *The Charge of the Light Brigade* by Tony Richardson. De-dramatization, Brechtian handling of crowd scenes; romantic heroes, rather naïve and poignant, destroyed by the absurdity of their own heroism.

Monday 6
I rose early, took a walk to clear my head through the empty plaza, its unforgettable shades of green from the trees. I also quite like the art deco streetlights in Plaza Rodríguez Peña.

Series E. "I understand," I said, but she knew how to shop. "So," she said, "deep down, understanding is the same thing as buying." I understand that everything must be linked to my personal history, and I buy the idea of my own life (but what property could that mean?). We could use my early morning walk as a metaphor: a writer traverses his territories, which may be an infinite plain, or the sea (as in Melville), or a circular walled cave (as in Kafka), or a plaza in the city. What is important is to have one's own ground and to delve in there.

The need to be on top of language is the same as swimming, moving forward over the sea (the depths hold a temptation that must be watched). A superficial prose, a short-distance swimmer; in all my life, I've never written stories longer than fifty thousand words. The impression that I'd get lost if I strayed too far from the shore. I remember the feeling of swimming in the sea at night, the terror that I could be lost from view and go farther out even while thinking I was going back.

I have a place that I can only lose if I let myself get excited by the kind of poetics I deplore (automatic writing, spontaneous prose), which is in fashion this season (the effect of Cortázar's writing and gravity toward the Beat Generation).

It is clear that, in order to survive the Boom, one has to remain apart. Keeping still, writing stories that go against the grain of the growth that is leading Latin American literature today. Writing without being interested in circulation (with luck, I'll never exceed three thousand copies). Less is more. Waiting. One who can stay calm amid the avalanche will go further, not burning up along the way. We shall see.

Tuesday 7
I awoke in terror, seeing strange creatures running along the wall, an effect of the heat, or who knows, a dream in which all of my fears organized themselves (I was crossing a weak and narrow bridge in a storm that pulled at me, moving one foot and then the other on the moving surface suspended in the air). Once I got up, I tried to get away while I recalled the details of the nightmare, sitting facing the window, drinking maté, and feeling that it was absurd to attempt anything in such heat; the whole city is an oven after six in the morning.

In the late afternoon I found my intuitions confirmed in a mysterious meeting with Walsh to see the first and second parts of *The Hour of the Furnaces*, which interested me less than the previous time. In the second part, the ideological arbitrariness becomes an aesthetic error. Solanas has invented the Peronism of the left.

Wednesday 8
The cultural industry's renewed, multitudinous criticism (Briante, De Brasi, Espartaco, González Trejo, Sebreli) forgets that art can't be thought

about in terms of the circulation of works or its effects on the media and that it is crucial to think about it in the moment of creation.

Friday 10

Back then—I will one day say—I discovered that it was a beautiful thing to go out early into the streets and walk through the empty city in the crisp air of dawn.

Write about tragedy cynically, write the love story in an anti-sentimental way. Irony, detail, and distance to conceal vulnerability. A schizoid style to write about passions. Style isn't made from *"belles lettres,"* but rather from changes in direction over the course of the sentence. A form that is an attack on "natural" feelings. A language that only *shows* the—disguised—intensity of the emotion.

Saturday

Bouvard et Pécuchet II. An unfinished novel that narrates the attempt to write the world. In that sense, this singular volume is tied to some of the most exemplary modern works (Kafka's *Diaries*, Musil's *The Man Without Qualities*). A current of reading runs underneath: Flaubert read five hundred volumes of different wisdom and specific techniques of useless erudition in order to write a book about a firm with two "copy-clerks" classifying their readings.

Monday 13

Last night with Lucas and Celina: the past. Luis Alonso, Junior, Casco: lost in trying to establish a coherence that could rescue them from the disorder of the world. The years in La Plata were critical for me. Using summary judgments to counteract any nostalgia.

Earlier, in the theater, *The Detective* by G. Douglas, a very good film, with Sinatra in the role of an "Officer" Marlowe who comes up against corruption. Once again a pure hero, brusque and efficient, lost in a world of traitors. Like all detectives in the genre, he is misogynistic, violent,

123

solitary. In contrast to *The Boston Strangler*, which I saw on Friday, all of the fetishes here (psychoanalysis, telepathy, schizophrenia) are employed in order to strengthen the American world in which social murderers are mental patients against whom the pure (and religious) nature of liberal values is raised.

Tuesday, January 14
I went down through the city toward the river and sat down on a bench in the sun, in La Costanera, in the middle of an entertaining *cour des miracles* that is always fresh and surprising with its characters: the fisherman who spends hours watching the river, the woman talking to herself, the young exhibitionist who changes his mesh leggings several times so as to be seen naked from time to time. The river is the final frontier where outcasts and suicidal people come to port.

Wednesday, January 15
Yesterday I ran into G. L. in the Álvarez bookshop. I'd gone there to finish up the classics collection and so be able to spend the rest of the week in peace, without *public relations*. But Jorge wasn't there and I found myself with G. L., who nearly drove me to hell all afternoon. We had a coffee and, when I wanted to escape, he came with me all the way to Córdoba and I had to sit down in another bar. Courtesy is a form of masochism. I stopped in the bar so that he wouldn't plant himself in my house for the whole afternoon. He seems like a lost man who will cling onto any acquaintance he sees in his vicinity and start going on about his readings and projects. As always, his compensatory ideologies, his obsession with himself, quoting from memory, textually, the reviews of his novel. Behind that mesh of wire glimmers a very alert intelligence, which works well in some areas and scrambles in others. Extreme narcissism is visible as the armor over very sensitive hearts. He talks about himself because there's no one there, to put it one way there isn't a "himself," there isn't an "inside himself," and everything is flat. A broken surface, everything is lost between fashionable reading and persistent delusions. When I managed to get myself free it was two in the afternoon, poor me, there's

a charitable soul inside me whose quality lies in enduring the monologues of friends who are slightly delusional. In that way, I defend myself from my own madness; for my part, I'm always looking for a place where I can be alone but never find it, and so I wandered around the bars for close to six hours with G.

In a biography of Tolstoy, I find the story I've always wanted to write. A couple—he writes a diary and gives it to her to read (a variant could be that she reads it in secret): "Tolstoy gave his wife the tormented and explicit diary of a bachelor to read." Tolstoy writes: "The thought that she is always there to read over my shoulder restrains me and prevents me from being honest." She, Sophia, a middle-class girl who aspires to become someone in the world of aristocrats, gets married at a very young age to this attractive, fascinating, and above all dangerous and manipulative Count. When she reads Tolstoy's diary, she is horrified and never recovers from the "truth" that she reads there: there are clear allusions to Tolstoy's homosexual experiences and also explicit narrations of how Tolstoy entraps young women of rural origins, his servants or his working staff, overpowering and conquering them like a sexual predator. Sophia is forever marked by these acts and throughout her life she views Tolstoy sometimes as a homosexual, seduced by the men who surround him, and sometimes as a despotic landowner who abuses the young women in his service.

Series E. I think that was what fascinated me about the possibility of writing a diary. Sketching down my life in a notebook for a woman to read. Thus, my first love story left a mark on my entire life. I can say that I wrote this diary for Elena, although she never found out. She asked me for a book I had read, and I immediately thought of becoming a writer for her. What is written for her, he said, are not the works that I've published, but rather these notebooks that no one has read except for some girlfriends, who secretly read them to see what I'd been up to.

Some information would be needed (my own experience wouldn't be enough) to prove the relationship between reading and life; it would be enough to think about Kafka's diary. It's one thing to live and another thing to secretly read the private notebooks of one's own life. In Tolstoy's case, *Anna Karenina* began with the enlightenment caused by reading Pushkin's narration of a party. That chance reading one night, unexpectedly, immediately led him to sit down to write a novel about a woman who follows her desire and abandons her husband and children for a cynical seducer, very similar to the person Tolstoy imagined himself to be.

We could say, following Lévi-Strauss, that society outside of the established circuits can be seen as a "primitive" society and that, as such, it is observed from the outside. This "outside" is what Borges theorizes in "The Argentine Writer and Tradition." It is situated at the margin of the central currents, in a no-man's-land that can only be defined from the outside (by those who are inside it). A quandary of frames, the outlines and subjects are both inside and outside of their country of birth.

The external view. Lévi-Strauss says: "In observing it from outside, we can estimate according to some number of indices and thus determine the degree of its technical development, the volume of its material production, the number of its inhabitants and so, successively, very coldly give it a grade and compare among themselves the grades we have given to different societies." On one hand, it has to do with the extra-local condition of that culture, which is always compared to another, and also with its asynchrony with the present. A culture that is far from its contemporaries (they say that it's "behind"), out of sync, in another place. That's what historians call an "underdeveloped" or "dependent" or "semi-colonial" society. It is defined in relation to another society that appears to be more developed or modern. From this I've discovered the importance of distance, always being outside of the context, halfway between the colony and the metropolis: the key is the empty space that separates them. That is where Borges situates his form of reading: reading obliquely, observing two realities at the same time; it is the cross-eyed view ("keep one eye on Europe and one eye on the interior of the country," as Echeverría wrote). It is seeing double, a metaphorical viewpoint that always compares one present reality to another superior and external one. It is a version of Gödel's theorem: no closed system can guarantee the certainty of a truth, but must be verified in another system, external and at a distance, and that series is interminable. Reality is verified outside of the system of internal proofs, outside of itself.

Thursday 16
Manuel Puig came over yesterday afternoon, tense, confused, wanting "to please," to be liked, submitting his books to the impossible test of validation. There will always be someone who doesn't like what he writes, and that obsesses him and persists more than any recognition or success. He remembers the bad reviews, the gestures of disdain toward his work. In the midst of these complaints, he brightens up when he relates his experiences and his steps upward as though he were an eager, emotional girl. He tells me about Jorge Álvarez's plan to release *Heartbreak Tango* as a serial novel and his goal to write a detective novel about the world of art and cultural critics, whom he views as assassins murdering the sensitive, countercultural artist. He has decided to take refuge in Italy, to move away from ungrateful Argentina forever.

Later I find myself with Héctor Schmucler, newly returned from France and desiring to start a magazine (model: *La Quinzaine*); he's dazzled by Cortázar, whom he frequently saw in Paris, and is fascinated by the "novelties" that are circulating, basically the tide of structuralism (following the wave of Barthes + *Tel Quel* magazine).

At night *The Dirty Dozen*, an excellent film by Robert Aldrich, very good control of irony and above all violence, with almost fascist and "adolescent" touches. Twelve men selected among those condemned to death in an American prison undertake a suicide mission: they're all psychotic and have a strong bond.

"One can only lose what one never had," Borges. I will use this quotation as an epigraph for my next book.

Artificial Respiration. My experience, today, in the bar: everyone was talking to me as though I were stupid, in a sickly-sweet and faltering tone. I don't like argots, established and closed-off languages; I speak another tongue. Remember Saussure: "A man who speaks another language can be easily considered incapable of speech." That can also happen within the same language. The Greek-derived word *barbarian* seems to have meant "stutterer" and is related to the Latin *balbus*, and in Russian they call the Germans *nemtsy*, mutes.

Words suffer a torsion when they say the same thing in different languages: "No inherent relationship binds the sequences of sounds in sister or sœur or hermana to the concept 'sister,'" says Saussure. In the translation of a novel by Chandler someone replaces the diminutive Little Sister, or *hermanita*, with *Una mosca muerta*, meaning two-faced (which synthesizes the image of the protagonist: a simple and yet dangerous girl). This torsion mechanism is what defines Arlt's language. He writes ugly horse as "equino fulero," where *horse* is made Spanish and *ugly* is Lunfardo.

Friday
I'm excited about the epic that can be written based on real events in the script for *Encerrona*. Tough and direct men, placed into an extreme situation, are turned into tragic heroes, but I'm working listlessly, not in sync with Daniel (who gets distracted to the point of the Argentine stereotype ridiculously easily) and B. (who has a dramatic but very aestheticized sensibility). You have to tell a story without falling into aestheticism or vulgar demagoguery—which are the two principal threads of Argentine culture.

In this age I have money raining down on me without having to work. Yesterday, Jorge Á. and I agreed on fifty thousand pesos per month and twenty thousand worth of books (that I can take from the bookshop) for my work on the classics series. With Tiempo Contemporáneo publishing I closed on fifty thousand for the Serie Negra, and then there are the thirty thousand from my collaborations in the newspaper (via Andrés and

Junior). At the same time, I'm working on the possibility of a magazine with Schmucler, intended to confront the culture imposed by the mass media. Meanwhile, I'm contemplating a great project for a novel based on real events, falsely using the techniques of nonfiction (the tape recorder).

I'm working on the story about the suicide of the father (of a father).

Schmucler comes to see me and we move ahead on the project of the new magazine. Possible team: Del Barco, Aricó, Germán García, José Sazbón, Aníbal Ford, Jorge Rivera . . .

Saturday
Yesterday *The Graduate* by M. Nichols, a character out of Salinger, an outcast in a family of millionaires, devoured by the matriarchy and the society of comfort. The myth of the pure adolescent crushed by the social structure, defined by blind rebelliousness (Teddy Boys, Beat Generation, rebels without a cause), habitually flees toward nature (Nick Adams in Hemingway) or commits suicide (Quentin Compson in Faulkner).

Sunday
An unexpected appearance of a highly favorable review of *La invasión* in *La Prensa* newspaper. Who knows the reasons why it was published a year after the book was released. As always, it makes me uncomfortable to see articles or read essays that take my writing as their subject; it's the same feeling as reading a letter that isn't intended for me and finding dark revelations about myself.

Monday 20
I only work well when I have the whole day free and can concentrate on a single objective. Now I'm toasting two slices of bread to eat with Gruyère cheese and a glass of cold milk.

Tuesday 21
It is strange, but what really constitutes a working atmosphere for me isn't the tone of the prose that I'm looking for but rather something previous, some events in the lives of writers I admire (Hemingway, Beckett). The confirmation that they too have had doubts and have been on the point of failure, etc. Identifying not with a style, but with an attitude. "Being a writer" precedes the act of writing. For me, those ways of being are more important than the narrative techniques or methods of those authors. In that way, I can "justify" my depersonalization while I write (that is the condition of prose for me, being someone else when I write, or rather, being someone else in order to write). I justify my (slight) schizophrenia in that way; I come apart, but that is the most difficult part, and thus the work is justified (not for its content or for its result). Literature is a directed dream. For me, its condition is leaving the being that I'm imagined to be. The same as in a dream.

Wednesday 22
"There is no trap so deadly as the trap you set for yourself," R. Chandler.

Thursday 23
Yesterday, while I was recovering from the enthusiasm of the night before, with J. D., old memories from '60 and '61; in those days everyone already saw him as the successful and recognized writer, while I was still trying to learn to suppress description in narrative prose. Now he's broken, so I keep giving him an advantage, like everyone I knew in my distant youth. A kind of blood pact among brothers; a non-aggression pact.

An exasperation can be found in Chandler, showing the narrator that he exists as an autonomous character (through rather affected touches of the prose), while at the same time he's there to tell a story that isn't his own.

A meeting with a weak and mustached puppet who bore down on me when I was trying to cross the street without greeting him. Gestures of surprise and recognition, and he hurries to tell me that he's bought a "club" in Palermo and says: "I already know things are going well for you." Meetings that are connected to my notebooks from 1959. It was Jorge S., always with his conceited distance, back in the years at the Mar del Plata high school. Like a flash, that first afternoon in the courtyard of the National school came back to me, with him talking about anti-discipline, and now I see him returning like a ghost.

Friday 24

I've started taking amphetamines again, seeking chemical euphoria and a brilliant lucidity that lasts as long as a match flame (during which one can, nevertheless, burn out one's mind). A risk that I take, certain that I'll be able to find this artificial blankness whenever I want.

Sunday 26

Yesterday and today with Roberto Jacoby, who proposes a pamphlet dedicated to certain misunderstood symbols: crime, soccer, Peronism, etc. A sort of mimeographed *agitprop* publication using Roland Barthes's categories (*Mythologies*). It could be given out to passers-by on street corners in the city, or "*panfleteadas*" could be organized after movies ended or after a boxing match in Luna Park.

Monday 27

Series E. I am thinking about the pseudonym and the double as non-corporal forms of suicide. Losing oneself in another identity, splitting in two, letting someone else do (one's) dirty work. Both adhere to the enigma. In a sense, the evil double manages to become one, and wickedness or shame can be narrated as something personal. Grammatical solution for suicide. (Come back to that.) The issue of the verbal double (the false name), two names, two utterances.

In relation to the problem of colonialism, remember Lévi-Strauss's analysis of primitive societies. Various series of access to the model of civilization. In every society, that model corresponds to an idea accepted at a certain time. In the majority of human societies, the proposed category (the Western world, developed, modern, etc.) lacks sense and is devoid of meaning. The key is that this category (Western civilization, that is, capitalism) is not proposed, but rather imposed (through force).

Tuesday 28
I slept for less than six hours and awoke dead tired, and I've been turning over for two hours, unable to wake myself up. I read the newspaper sitting in Plaza Rodríguez Peña and then went to have a café con leche at a bar on Charcas and read a—stupid—article by Mario Benedetti on Cuba, and just now a story by Chandler ("Nevada Gas"), but I'm still sleepy, hopeless. Then I worked on the detective series and got the rights to *The Thin Man* by Hammett, a turn toward an ironic detective story.

Wednesday 29
3:00 p.m. For the first time in more than two years (I wrote "Mata-Hari 55" in October of '66) I've written a good short story; the story about Pavese captures my relationship with Inés. I still have to adjust the dialogue, but it's there. As always, I have too many "other problems" to find the time to be happy.

Thursday 30
I returned home and finished the Hammett novel. *The Thin Man* is one of his books that I like the most: a comedy concealed in genre. The girl is a striking character: ironic, intelligent, autonomous, a dangerous companion, and attractive to the hero, who gives up being a solitary man. The detective in love thus becomes a parody of the genre. Then I started another splendid thriller by Raymond Marshall (under the pseudonym of Chase).

Friday, January 31
Yesterday I got confirmation from Capelutto, Álvarez's accountant, of the arrangement for the classics collection: a salary of fifty thousand pesos per month. If I work things out with Tiempo Contemporáneo publishing, I'll have another fifty thousand for the detective series; I'd like to be able

to free myself from Luna and combat his bureaucratic adherence to the calendar. Switching to a maximum of thirty pieces per month, that is, one per day. Four pieces that I write on Tuesday (which I bring to the paper on Wednesday) and two more on Friday (which I bring to the editorial office on Saturday). Then he'll cover the remaining four (he is slower) to complete the selection. Yesterday, my credit for twenty thousand pesos worth of books started working as well: I bought Pavese's *Racconti* (his complete stories published by Einaudi).

A great variety of readings: Foucault's *The Order of Things* (the demon of analogy). Steiner on *Tolstoy or Dostoevsky* (I like the system of condensing the state of a literature by using two opposing poetics: Hemingway and Faulkner, Arlt and Borges). Attentive reading of Freud's *The Psychopathology of Everyday Life*: an extraordinary new form of autobiography in the personal analysis of Signorelli's case. The subject of the autobiography splits in two and sees himself captured by invisible waves, as though he were someone else. The temporal distance between the present of the writing and the past of the subject is the basic theme of the genre. Another example is *The Words* by Sartre.

I write the outline for "The Glass Box." I find Genz's diary by chance and now read it while I'm alone. It is strange that he writes one, I never would have expected it. I've found several notes about myself. He carries the notebook with him. The story would start more or less like that and at the end there would be the story of the accident in the tower that I've wanted to write for years. I have to build up a relationship between the two.

I worked on the script for B., moving ahead by myself with the section in the paper (I wrote twenty pieces, the majority unsigned or under a pseudonym). Luna insists on transferring me to the crime news section or "local gossip." I put together an excellent introduction for the classics series. The first book is *Notes from Underground* by D., which has never been available in Spanish as an individual book before. I went to the theater a lot and didn't let any movie that came through here get past me. A very good critical reception of my anthology of Argentine autobiographies, and finally a proposal from Schmucler that I make a new magazine with him that will go out in the kiosks, confronting the cultural sections of the newspapers and magazines. Why do I make these mournful summaries? Who is it that I want to tell to pay close attention to everything I'm working on? I make lists of the things I've done as though I wanted to settle some debt, but with whom? Questions in the dusk of a summer day in 1969.

Monday

After a slight hesitation I take advantage of the rain to shut myself in and take drugs. I want to write a story about the shades that I see. A vague and sorrowful impression. A lucid and horrible old man. The boy he lets fall. Will I write anything more than that fall? I don't have the story yet, and I'll see what tone I end up using. Nothing in two hours. Instead a desire to work on the story about the man reading a diary in secret. Maybe I can connect the two stories?

Tuesday

The city changes color as low clouds block out the light. I wrote one page of the story. I still don't know its "objective." I'll see how I can bring the accident into it. Possibilities: it happens to the narrator, he steals the notebook or Reinaldi writes it in the diary.

It is six in the afternoon, and we could say that I've set up the story. They live together. Reinaldi writes a diary, Genz wants to go to the plaza. He lets the boy fall. Reinaldi appears. He has it in his hands, writing versions of the accident in the diary, forcing him to pay. The tone is still missing, I think. I have to find a more realistic connection for Reinaldi's appearance. Maybe it can be solved in this way: Reinaldi doesn't show up until much later, but nevertheless he describes real events in the diary. I've finished a very schematic draft, developing the internal threads.

Sunday, February 2
As always, eagerness, restlessness, fear that I won't repeat the miracle of yesterday. My romantic passion for literature is clear, two or three days like yesterday would put everything into place.

Tuesday 4
A walk with Julia through Retiro, the descent toward the river, the market in Bajo, the rather shady area filled with both bookshops and bars where the city's distinct Bohemian tribes meet. Moderno, Florida bar, the Di Tella, and Galería del Este. Before that, the world of the French collective (formal, hypocritical, affected) in the Biblioteca de la Alianza Francesa, reading Foucault (the simulacrum). On the way out, I ran into Conrado C. and felt, as with S. and I. before him, the ambiguity of old acquaintances who show me their horror roll (no longer an honor roll): "I'm translating Barthes," he tells me. "I bought myself an apartment in Palermo," his façade. "I'm funded by the College," they tell me respectively. They're looking for security, they settle themselves in and stare at me, uncomfortable because of "my activity." I could have been like them if I'd been distracted for an instant and hadn't been able to set everything aside and pursue a clear, impossible goal. Another thing: it seems difficult to have friends from my own generation.

Wednesday 5
For me, to write means "to be financed."

A visit from Roberto Jacoby, sickened by populism. Always very wise, intelligent and creative.

Conversation with Julio:
  "You know what finished off my old man."
  "No."
  "He wanted to commit suicide, and it didn't turn out well for him."

Tuesday
On *"sincerity" in literature*. "In language, one who speaks is never confused by his words," C. Lévi-Strauss.

Back and forth, to and from Tiempo Contemporáneo and Álvarez: I return with ninety-two thousand pesos, magical, as always. I see Jorge Á.'s change in direction, seduced by the rock kids and the underworld of Buenos Aires. Squandering the money from Scott Fitzgerald and also throwing everything he's got so far out of the window. He goes to Mar del Plata in a taxi with the guys from Mandioca.

Thursday 13
"In some sense the mark of the true writer is the impossibility of writing," Michel de M'Uzan in his article on Freud and artistic creation, *Tel Quel* No. 19.

Deleuze: For Proust, to write is to "read the inner book of these unknown signs . . . There is no logos, there are only hieroglyphs. To think is therefore to interpret, is therefore to translate."

Writing. Válery's condemnation of the novel is a rejection of the vertigo of possible narratives that open before each situation and before each sentence. It is impossible, he says, or rather, it is pointless, to write the sentence "the marquise went out at five" (to begin a novel), an unjustified decision. The marquise (or any other subject, for example, the dog) went out (or any other verb, for example, came in) at five (or any other time, or any other entrance of time into the fiction). The dog came in at three in the afternoon. That sentence has the same value as the other. The novelist must choose one way or another. It is a contingent grouping of replaceable components. The narrator can't cast aside the vertigo of possibilities because it's an arbitrary decision, that is, because of a convention that doesn't belong to the order of fiction. The possible narratives lie at the center of the poetics of the novel. Georges Perec's potential literature, or the intrigue of the novel in "An Examination of the Work of H. Quain," which branches apart and doesn't set any option aside, or the endless successive novel from Borges's "The Garden of Forking Paths," or Macedonio Fernández's novel that is always about to begin, they all deal with this issue. The novel is a combinatorial art form. To write is to make decisions.

One of the paths toward the renovation of the novel lies in making it visible and saying that it is a novel, a convention that gives itself away. Günter Grass: "Let's say that it was five in the afternoon." Or Néstor Sánchez: "On this afternoon in this novel it was raining." I don't like this way of making the connection between the words visible as though this were the only possible world. One must never forget that mimesis is what defines fiction. Something of reality always enters a story in such a way that belief will act to resolve the arbitrariness of the choices. We have to believe that one thing happens instead of another for reasons that the narration doesn't tell but rather shows, that is, makes visible.

One example of the awareness of conventions is *Tristram Shandy* by L. Sterne: the form and techniques make themselves visible by way of the violation of norms, and that becomes the content of the book. He plays with novelistic arbitrariness, just like Macedonio Fernández.

Literature and politics. Culture is seated in repression, but literature is a constant struggle against limitations and against taboo. The novel is situated on the psychological frontier of society, in which the individual is transformed into someone else who isn't allowed. The term for this activity on the border of censorship is: acquiring a language. It has to do with confronting reality, understood as writing and not as spectacle.

I go to the theater to see *Tony Rome* by G. Douglas, with Frank Sinatra. Yet again a solitary and skeptical hero who deciphers all the mysteries in exchange for payment in dollars.

Friday 14

Series E. I'm attempting three different registers in these notebooks. Ironic, with the events narrated directly, without elaboration. Introspective, that is, looking at myself as though I were someone else being observed in the past. Conceptual, for some still-unthought thoughts. I don't write these with the same spirit that I use in the prose I'm going to publish. I have a vague hope that one day I'll take the time to transcribe these notebooks—the image that arises is that of a person who in the moment of death, as they say, sees the main events of his existence like a movie—but here the point is not to see but rather to read.

Yesterday Edgardo F. suddenly appeared, a short conversation and light sarcasm to erase his deterioration. Brilliant ex-young people who crowd in a pack to hold out, never apologizing for having chosen (unconsciously, but until the end) a secure life, unconnected to hopes and dreams. For example, I say to him:

"Maybe I'll buy myself something."

"You want to make sure of your old age."

"I'm following your example."

Series A. If I analyze yesterday and the dialogue I've just transcribed, I will understand certain levels or layers of what I imagine that I am (for others). When E. arrives, I lower my guard, "excited," thinking that since he has come, I must be generous. In turn, he feels uncomfortable for having taken the first step and attacks me. I, who am not prepared, am left with no response and spend part of the afternoon meditating on a revenge that I'm only able to work out now, when he is no longer here, and then only in my imagination, or rather, in what I write. A clear metaphor for my relationship with the unforeseen, which, nevertheless, is always the same as what I already know.

I'm not interested in the detective genre; I'm interested in writing stories in the form of an investigation. Likewise, I see the detective as a modern

Ulysses lost in a labyrinth (facts, clues, crimes) trying to decipher something through inquiry.

It is clear that what interests me most in Chandler (or in Ross Macdonald) is the construction of a series of novels in a saga that always has the same character as its protagonist (Philip Marlowe) telling the story. The last in the series, *Playback*, begins with Marlowe's marriage (he is now no longer worried by the threat of losing his license). A marriage that can only be understood if one has read *The Long Goodbye*. At one point, *Playback* forms part of that novel and allows all of Chandler's books to be linked together as a long series of investigation that culminates in Marlowe's retirement. That's what I would like to do myself: to write a series of books that have "X" as their protagonist or narrator, a saga of diverse themes that always alludes to the life of a single character.

The story I want to tell. The life of a man in different situations over the course of fifty or sixty years. A series of stories or novels with the same secret protagonist.

Pavese. I'm not going to complete a conversation in the airport and several allusions in the narration (a woman who is taking photographs; sex in a hotel), and now I can think a bit better about the Italian situation. "Objective facts": Inés leaves in a taxi (let's get married, he says to her). Pavese. Conversation. An airport. A journey. A note in Turin. An article (someone who knew Pavese or was with him a few days before his suicide).

Saturday
Kafka's most definitive and Kafkaesque act is his attempt to erase his work: a decision that, for having existed, would have to be felt in what has survived. Proving this hypothesis automatically turns into a Kafkaesque fiction (without an end).

Sunday, February 16
Yesterday, another encounter with the admirable film *Le Deuxième Souffle* by Jean-Pierre Melville: an elegy to honor, the epic of our time. The only "possible" heroes are those who refuse the system (guerrillas or criminals); on the other side are the losers.

Analyzing the social situation of reading: the conditions of possible meaning are a material space that ultimately decides the significance of the text. That situation is not only social, but also historical. It makes some books legible and others invisible. A key procedure in the relationship between works and their conditions is, for us, translation. That is, access to the foreign series. It would be possible to recreate that space in three key books, *Betrayed by Rita Hayworth*, *Fictions*, and *Hopscotch*, which, in an elliptical way, tell their own relationships to contemporary culture.

Monday 17
All art constructs its technique and form through the wisdom of time and takes its methods from knowledge outside of its sphere (for example, Joyce with psychoanalysis; Borges with mathematics).

Tuesday 18
Series E. The protagonist writes in his diary what he is unable to think, what he cannot drive himself to say or to confront; those notes are the opposite of his will. Always out of context, his notes register what he believes he is living through and what he believes he remembers from his childhood. The imaginary scene in which the hero is always present. The diary is like a dream; everything that happens is true, but it happens in such a condensed record, so charged with subtexts, that only the person writing it can understand it. Literature tends toward that direction: its sphere is private writing, which deludes itself with the idea of being written for no one to read. For that reason, Pavese's suicide is also a theory of or a solution to what he has written in his personal notebooks. Kafka said: only one who writes a diary can understand the diaries that others write. Whereas Pavese says: only one who plays with the idea of suicide

can write a convincing diary. The conviction given by the certainty of killing oneself.

6:00 p.m. I make progress on a possible structure for the story with the diary. I find that I can resolve the connection between novel and essay. That's what I am looking for. Thinking about the interior of the narration.

The imaginary guarantees of literature. Society's question is always: what do you need in order to be able to write? A variety of answers can be read in works, referring directly to the place of writing in society. The basis that guarantees the form in each case is: 1. Erudition 2. Lived experience. 3. Inner demons. 4. Mimesis of reality: "This is how it happened," the writer says, I recount what was (as if that were possible). He says: "People talk like this," and then he explains his use of language. It's like what they say in bullfighting about the courage of the bullfighters. ("It's taken for granted," and then all that is discussed is the art employed in the performance), it's idiotic to show off one's talent—and even genius—because that is taken for granted, and something that is implied should not be spoken. Only what is shown is analyzed (from the basis that guarantees the form). Inspiration is a name for writers' ability to forget themselves and pass over to the other side (of language) while writing (the difference between writing and editing). Work on the notion of "support" and value in the economy of literature.

It's striking to see how two writers, who refer in their work to the sacred (that is, unverifiable) quality of those guarantees (Sabato, etc.), also establish that exceptional quality (or a subject who defines himself as exceptional) in the time that it takes to write those "masterpieces." The others, Borges in first place, visibly prove that support (quotations, cultural inheritance received from dead parents). In one case or the other, it is always about negotiating with the specters.

The body speaks the language of action: a narrative key to literature that interests me. It's enough to look at the role of the mime in significant moments in dialogue (for example in the detective novel); gestures and mannerisms allow the unstated—non-verbalized—thoughts of the other to be seen. To put it another way, the record of physical behavior is the hallmark of Hemingway and the substitute for the other's thoughts. Showing but not telling (what is thought). Forms of an underground language directed toward reading thought (which always remains unarticulated, that is, bound up, confused with the action itself). Never saying anything about oneself, as though the hero were under surveillance. This language—the syntax of which is enacted—is deciphered and reconstructed through investigation. In popular literature (and in dreams), these gestures are categorized: turning pale and blushing are direct ways of showing what is thought or felt (fear, shame) but not explicitly said. There, the function of description in a story is gambled. That is how V. Woolf's line can be understood: "God—or the devil—is in the details." What has no function is what functions as a revelation. For example, while talking without really saying anything, a character looks at himself—too much—in the mirror at the back of the room. Those quick glances that tend to go unnoticed are the evidence that he is talking about himself and that he is "nervous" (the description must show that he can't stop making that gesture, pointless, repetitive, for no reason). For example, a pregnant woman's "cravings." My father had to get up at dawn and go out like a madman looking for strawberry ice cream for my mother, who wanted "that," and he had to get it so that the person who was about to be born—me, that is—wouldn't have to endure a strawberry-colored mark on his face. He doesn't state it but acts it out. In the best writing, for example in Kafka or Tolstoy, that gesture is seen but we don't know what series it belongs to or what it means. It is there to open a question and give the story a non-verbal density. The investigation is the way in which those minor actions, almost invisible, form a significance that is only discovered at the end of the story. Then there is a double moment: blind, "unbound" actions that, once articulated—a syntax links them together—give rise to an investigation that reconstructs and supports what those invisible gestures say (if taken in isolation).

In the great first-person stories (for example, *The Stranger* by Camus or *The Sun Also Rises* by Hemingway), the awareness is always at the same immediate level as the action. Narrators never recount what they already know. Therefore, we could say that they don't narrate, to the extent that they don't establish causal connections, always tending to narrate in the present.

In reality, literature shows the opacity of the world. One never knows anything about people, even about those to whom we are close and those we love, and we only know what they tell us but never what they think because they can always lie to us; in that sense, we read novels because they're the only way to see another person from within. I know Anna Karenina better than the woman I've lived with for many years.

The great writings of Beckett or Tolstoy or Kafka, then, form a continuous and unconnected succession of small incidents. Action plus action plus action, disjointed, without causal connections. The nexus is made visible because the syntax or grammar establishes relationships that are not cause and effect. They display and offer up for judgment but do not explain, only place in relation. Why, after all, does Mr. Samsa awake one morning transformed into a horrible vermin? Kafka never says why but shows it. So, who institutes that syntax? Treating the story as investigation is one way. It begins in reverse: a family friend arrives at the house and is faced with a very confusing situation; something has happened to Gregor Samsa, but no one says what is happening, and something has happened in the other room as well, where Samsa is apparently resting. The friend spends the day in the house, collecting information, little clues, indirect accounts, and with that uncertain web of facts he constructs a hypothesis and says, without opening the door to the room: "I think Gregor awoke transformed into a vermin." This reality is inferred, and it is told in reverse. The truth is approached in an uncertain manner, feeling around in the dark, and not everything is known. But what kind of animal has he metamorphosed into? The story can go on.

All novels constructed in this way are a single thought, hidden and denied and lost and disguised in the action. In the case of the crime genre, the detective only attempts to read the murderer's thoughts. Because that form of action—that of the murderer—is erased and the proof is altered, mixed up in the opacity of reality, and the investigator must invent an order, going from the effect to its possible causes. The genre is always about investigating a violent act, and that is its only identifying feature.

Wednesday
Series E. Just now I repeated a motion, and that is the only valid explanation of this diary: a ceremony that is repeated. I went out to the street to buy the black notebook with a rubber cover in which I am now writing. For years, everywhere I've lived, I've gone out to the street one day to search the neighborhood for a place where I can find this specific type of artifact (a Congreso brand notebook with one hundred pages). The bookshop on Calle 1, near the university dining hall in La Plata; the bookshop in Boca, with old books from Losada publishing and a little old man who kept a box in the basement with a hundred notebooks like this one (Casa Liscio. Olavarría 624. Tel. 21-4461); the other bookshop opposite the boarding house where I lived, crossing Calle Montes de Oca, and now, this morning, in the office supply store (connected to the courts and lawyers) on Viamonte and Talcahuano. Every time I come back home with a new notebook, I'm certain of the "great changes" that will have come in my life when I start to write the future on the blank lined pages of this magical object in which everything is possible, before I start to write in my nervous hand the incidents of my life that, in order to justify the notebook, I must write down.

Yesterday I saw *Bullitt* with Steve McQueen: a cop's everyday life, the density, the fatigue. Going through trunks full of clothing, spying in a hospital, running and running after a guy in an airport and, in the midst of all that, there's a barely suggested relationship with a woman, which is constantly being interrupted (phone calls while they are making love); it gives the tone of a broken life, overtaken by violence. Reality "blocks" and covers that aperture toward excitement. Lots of dramatization, a heavy atmosphere, dead time, and a formidable car chase along the streets of San Francisco in the middle.

Now with Julia, who lost her contact lenses. Desolation, superstitious fear; any loss of an object is experienced as a sign or a warning. And so she too moves slowly, as if lost.

Yesterday I saw Edgardo in Tribunales, a fleeting wave, and as always I felt tense in the face of the unforeseen. Later, at home, he—without knowing it—reframed the situation for me.

"What happened today when we ran into each other? It seemed like you were afraid of jeopardizing yourself."

"Actually it was the opposite," I told him. "I didn't want to jeopardize your image as a lawyer by letting people see you with me."

The joke brings the matter to an end, but it leaves one fact standing: there is an ambiguity in incidents when one is not alone. A need to quickly impose an interpretation on actions, a reading (always opaque) for others, without any precise significance. Aggression is a way to elicit the hidden significance and discover the meanings that the other keeps hidden.

Cacho's phone number: 72-5237.

Thursday
Notes on Tolstoy (6). Self-examination, in the sense of protection of the self, as mutilation. The subject against the world and the subject outside of the world overlap. In his *Diaries* (which then become the "Work" that replaces his work), particularly during his last ten years, you can see his struggle against all feeling of self-affirmation and even of joy, so much so that he is ashamed for having felt happy to see his granddaughter Tanechka or for having been moved while listening to good music or even for having felt more distraught at the death of his daughter than at the death of any peasant. The only joy he allows himself is caused by criticism and insults and his feeling of disgust and

guilt toward himself. Happiness sprang forth from pure negativity as an expression of being an agent of God's will. And so the last note in his diary, from November 3, 1910, four days before his death, reiterates the position. It defines the idea of absolute solitude that Gorky perceived when he went to see him: nihilism, indifference toward other men, incurable desperation, and a solitude that no one had ever experienced so lucidly. "Real love is only that directed at a non-attractive object" (see entry from 10/8/1910). Alexandra Tolstaya made a note of this quote from her father (10/10/1910): "Exceptional love for children is a sin. If they bury my Masci, I suffer, and if they bury another girl it does not matter to me."

Friday, February 21
Just now through the window I saw a tow truck pulling a car: I'm amused by the owner's astonishment, his feeling that his property has been questioned. He can't bear to watch the agents taking the car from its space as though it belonged to them. A procedure in which having a "mislaid" property makes a person see that the whole country is the great possession of someone else that no one knows, whom the police work for.

Being on the favorite side has its advantages, at least in this indifferent time when our military has laid down a shameful quilt that covers the whole country with the same torpor. A boy who lives in hotels around this block deflates the wheels of all the cars parked in the alley. His little rebellion amuses me. For me, then, reality consists of the news in the papers (today in Uruguay the Tupamaros carried out a spectacular robbery and left a note with their regards), and the things I see through the window of the apartment if I raise my head to look out into the street. So I could imagine a narrator who only sees what is right in front of him or things that he reads in fragments: the rest, he imagines.

After an afternoon spent reading, taking notes, and searching for a common thread in my ideas about Borges, I ended the day eating in the restaurant on the corner with Julia, sensing the sumptuous presence of a couple behind us who were exhibiting themselves along-side a bottle of champagne set to chill in a bucket of ice. Despite the theatricality of the scene, the woman complained about the cost of the bill in the end.

Saturday 22
Julia and I walked down Corrientes, which was half empty at the end of summer, all the way to the sidewalks of Cerrito, trying to guess the story that came to us in fragments and bursts as though the whole city were a fabric of little histories. An old man was interrogating a hard-faced woman and asking her, rhetorically, for explanations; he went back and forth about some shared past, but she kept her lips sealed.

I saw the poet Alberto Szpunberg; upset, with nothing to say to one another, we shook hands ceremoniously, promising phone calls soon.

Monday 24
An easy debut of the work with Luna, who was waiting for me to read a story of his in which he repeats his rhetoric of false modesty in a nonsensical "literary" history. He left at once, as could be expected, and within the hour I finished the work, two pieces about education.

Now I'm reading, inattentive, mired in this humid heat that the light from the lamp adds to, creating a heavy atmosphere.

Tuesday 25
A strange day, everything twisted and halfway done, back and forth to the publishing house without finding Jorge, and then I go to the paper and work with Luna.

Later a visit from Germán García with a magazine project (yet another) to critique *Primera Plana*. It isn't bad, a way of participating in the debate about the media, which decides the march of culture today.

Thursday 27
A decision to run the necessary risks. I have to talk to Luna about restructuring the work, getting out of the bureaucratic formality of three hours a day. If he can't do it, I'll throw away the salary of thirty thousand pesos even if I have to go back to the era of undignified hardship. The risk is living only on the salary from Álvarez, who's always on the brink of bankruptcy, but I prefer uncertainty to that closed-off working time.

Friday 28
A little while ago I had a silent run-in with Helena, with a swift little wave on my part to avoid another meeting; a woman I wrote about in the old notebooks from '59, who now seems to be a stuffy housewife.

Saturday, March 1
Since eleven I've been unable to pull myself out of the cynical prose and oppressive atmosphere of Nabokov's *Lolita*.

Last night at B.'s house, the woman was describing the illnesses of her soul, the story of her grandfather, handsome and drunk, who fell into a tar pit and came out black, covered in the guilt of having lost his grace. Then, as always, I felt an irresistible boredom from being in the middle of a group.

Series A. A meeting with Borda: Minister of the Interior, with the director of *Semanal* magazine, asking for censorship of the reflections of the "alarming evolution of traditions." The military government wants to change not only cultural customs, but also any mention of a reality that it doesn't view as Western and Christian.

The bars along the coast, under the trees, with music, the disc jockey announces that Pascualito Pérez is there, "let's hear some applause for him," Julia and I face the river, eating barbecue with iced wine, while the wind makes the paper tablecloths fly up to show the glossy surface [*illegible*] carved by the knives in our hands.

Tuesday 4
X Series. Sunday night seeing Lucas, always furtive and cautious, drawn by events that he can't talk about and that isolate him. A marginalized man, he reminds me of Manuel; both of them bury their real worlds, which they must protect. In his case, armed action; in Puig's case, furtively picking up men around construction sites, the same mistrust. I also have to hide my reasons for adhering to secret agreements. Never asking.

Earlier I saw Néstor, wavering between everyday mediocrity (College, etc.) and the snobbish fascination of the cultural consumer (Grotowski, Cortázar, the people he's seen in Paris). At its root, this synthesis defines the archetype of the Argentine intellectual, attentive to the official cultural hierarchy, dazzled by the avant-garde (the future academy), consumers with no imagination.

Earlier León Rozitchner, who had been in Israel, confirms David's return. Rather intrusive, self-pitying because he hit his head, repeating the motions of guys from his generation, wavering between lucidity (abstract) and a temptation to show his control over things (real).

I was with Luna, I wrote two pieces and went to an old film studio on Calle Riobamba (where I had seen *The Lady with the Dog* in 1963). Torre Nilsson made everything revolve around him, silences, glances. Earlier, Beatriz Guido tells me that "Actas del juicio" was selected among the ten best Argentine short stories.

Wednesday 5
Enjoying the cool air, the lovely time, without the eagerness of summer, without the nightmare of a day that ended at two in the afternoon because I had to go to the newspaper office. I'm enjoying *Lolita*, which has an excellent tone.

It's interesting to see the distinct behaviors of individuals when isolated and when included in the family drama. They seem like different people;

on one hand there's a kind of social automatism, stereotypical behavior, and on the other hand a decision, often not thought-out, not to show how norms are followed but rather how they can be changed. I say this because people in my family change whether they are in groups or alone, my cousin Z. for example, who is effusive and cordial when he's by himself and reserved and timid when he's with the family.

Daniel came to see me, and I felt uncomfortable having to tell him that Álvarez rejected his book of stories. Then we saw a great film by Melville with Julia: *Le Samouraï*, with Alain Delon.

"I seem to speak (it is not I) about me (it is not me)," Beckett.

Thursday
The culture of neoliberalism is spreading more and more, organized as a means of "worshiping" everyday modern life. The world is a spectacle, a never-ending party.

Tuesday
A letter to Jorge Álvarez from David in Italy, he's planning a magazine in Rome. "In fourteen months, E. R. will come here, he's the only one who can direct it after I leave."

Wednesday
Last night a visit from Héctor G. He recalls the splendor of May in Paris, the discovery, the happiness; now that he's back here the opacity crushes him and buries him as it does all of us. There is no place for beautiful generalizations, everything is politics here, literature is as remote as the past itself. Between earning our livings and ignoring reality, our youth leaves us.

Wednesday 26
A letter from David repeating his offer for me to go to Italy to coordinate the magazine about Latin America that he's putting together.

Social variations. First with León. R., chatting about David's project, and then Elías and Roberto C. came over with two guys from the College of Philosophy to propose a course at the College in May. Last, Héctor Schmucler is back from Paris; very generous, he proposes that I start a magazine in Buenos Aires with him in the style of *Quinzaine*. That is, a monthly magazine that would be tasked with reviewing all of the books that are published in Argentina, and also, as I propose to him, staying abreast of the debates about literature and opposing journalistic criticism and the cultural supplements.

A joke that's going around these days: "What are you doing?" Learning Chinese. Why? "I'm a pessimist."

Friday
I write a cautious letter to David anticipating his current state of optimistic euphoria. I ask him what he means by starting a magazine in Italy and having me direct it.

Then a meeting with Walsh, Cossa, Rivera, etc., discussing a variety of matters and projects.

The best part is my conversation with Walsh about Borges and my subsequent, unexpected encounter with Borges himself while I'm getting off the bus near Retiro. I see him passing and call out his name, and he pauses a moment and smiles toward me.

April 1
My literature begins with a performance of writing a novel (copied from Verne), in which I recounted a voyage to the moon. A fuzzy memory of a class in school, I was telling someone an adventure about having a treehouse where I would take refuge to write. Two events before that, a reading competition in third grade against McDonald (who beat me), trying to seduce the teacher, whom I was in love with, and later my defeat by Castelli in a "composition" tournament, and the charitable praise to make up for it.

In the afternoon with Luna and at night a poor profile that I'll have to correct: I made professions of literary faith for the dumb boy and pretty girl who interviewed me, and my veiled and chivalrous competitiveness (with Walsh and Puig) led me to be attentive and impartial.

Wednesday 2
Passionately bound up in Marthe Robert's biography of Freud, a novel and, at the same time, the vertigo of a man thinking against the very limits of reason. A history of a "madness" that consists in discovering a secret logic that reverses the history of philosophy. Interesting to analyze the role of money in his discoveries. Economy turned his life into destiny and gave retrospective meaning to all of his discoveries. He seems, at times, to have forgotten the trajectory of his knowledge, but he largely obeyed the path indicated by his needs. A grant for six hundred francs, a journey to Paris, Charcot, hysteria. Another circuit, the economic status of his patients, especially the women (and their husbands).

In dreams we see ourselves as though we were characters. We attend to the adventures and misadventures of a hero whom we see traversing magical forests. Borges reconstructed this space and distance, but at the same time his work is a careful elision of sexuality and the body. Something we might term, using an oxymoron, the chaste dream.

As always, my response to any contact with reality (always slight) is euphoria and the rhetoric of desire. A quick back and forth to the bookshop. I meet Jorge Álvarez and Vicente Battista. Another letter from David in Italy, still going on about his project of a magazine based in Rome. Uncertain information that seems to lie at the root of my discomfort with the present, as though something was about to happen. I have to come back to this feeling of immanence and think about it with more order, that is, narratively.

In a way, my ideal has always been *Robinson Crusoe*, the isolation, the boundaries of an interior space that cannot be bridged (least of all by me). I remember the effect of projection that reading the novel produced in my father when we were still living on Calle Bynon (would it be in the year '54?), his fantasies of happiness on a desert island.

Series E. In my notebooks (1958–1968), the years pass by, the dates take place, but the temporality is motionless, static time. Rereading my conclusions from May of 1960, it is possible to understand the accidents I made in 1965. In a grammatical sense, what I call "temporality" is a sort of transference, semantic substitutions for lived experience.

Thursday 3
An uncomfortable day from the morning onward, interruptions, cutoffs. I've always thought that interruption defines experience for me, breaking the continuity of language (when I stop writing or stop reading) or at least that of written language, which seems to be the only one that matters to me, although conversations occupy a very important place in my life; but they belong to the order of reality, while the other language (solipsistic and intense) belongs to the order of literature.

My schism, narratively speaking, is an attempt to reconstruct my childhood home, a space without history where I knew "consideration" (with all of the meanings we can give to that word). I, the considerate person, that is, someone who thinks too much about others, but also someone who is thought about, considered (though he isn't doing anything).

Sunday 6
Why do I have this difficulty in "leaving" one subject and moving on to another, as though my interest were fixed with such intensity on an object that it then seems impossible to move on to somewhere else? Leaving my essay on Borges (I still have to make a final copy) and starting on another subject (resuming chapter three of the novel). In this transition, there are always mediations or bridges or focal points (Conti, detective stories, the courses).

In summary, I hope to make progress on the novel, correct the essay on Borges, prepare for the course, write notes for the publishing house and the prologue for the Serie Negra anthology, write the article on Conti, and think about the first issue of *Situación*, the magazine that Lucas managed to get me to agree to direct last night.

Series E. Night, self-destructive crisis, compassion. My conflicts with reality, my phobias, the seclusion that isolates me and prevents me from acting with fluency. I should be able to reconstruct that plotline in the narrative continuity of these notebooks.

Monday 7
A quick visit from León R.; I feel troubled without knowing why. I'm more aware of my words than his, while León, as always, settles into a space without distance, very near, something he can't think without, as though he needs confidants more than people to talk to. Things are going well for him all the same, bearing in mind the usual difficulties, the same as the start of my friendship with David. Some mistrust and some distance on my part when faced with the barrier between generations; in fact, it is a problem of convictions more than a problem of ages. They've read Sartre and believe in authenticity and sincerity; they are suspicious of bad faith and performances of a social character. For my part, I'm "an American," that is, I have a certain set of readings and an anti-sentimental, distanced, "objective" poetics, and I'm suspicious of interior life and sincere "confessions." I have read Brecht and Hemingway, but above all I escape from the melodramatic excesses of my family, where everything is sentimental, emotional, and tragic.

To write reviews of foreign books is to critique the version, the translation, as though it were the original. Even when one reads authors in their own languages, one never understands the same thing that someone for whom that language is a mother tongue understands. I read Faulkner in English but understand something other than what an author of my age born in the southern United States understands.

Tuesday 8
Another case. I run into G., walking down the same sidewalk as me opposite Tribunales, which causes me to turn toward Plaza Lavalle. I sit down on a bench, go back to the Álvarez bookshop, and on the way out I run into him again at the door. He hesitates, greets me with great affection and the necessary dose of smiles that is the style in such matters. I run off quickly so that I don't have to greet him, but when I return I run into him once again, as though it were a dream.

If I thought about the real-life dream of my encounter with G., I could begin to interrogate the events using an oneiric logic. It was reactive behavior, and thus an attempt to resolve a conflict that was not specific to him; the same thing would have happened with any acquaintance crossing paths with me. A sort of surrogate connection, experiencing what I don't know as though it were external to me. On the other hand, that enigma is not present either, but rather has some meaning that I don't know and causes a reaction. As Freud says, quoted by León: "Delirium is an attempt at the restitution of reality."

Wednesday 9
I need to train myself for the complex time that is drawing near, so that I can handle four or five issues at once without losing my calm. For the first issue of the magazine that Schmucler is planning, I'll write a review of *Catch-22*, the novel by Heller.

A long walk, first with Jorge Álvarez, setting the stage for tomorrow, putting strong pressure on Omar for the fifty thousand pesos I expect to get paid. Then with Mario Szichman in La Paz, talking about his novel based on Walsh, and last with Schmucler and Willie Schavelzon discussing the magazine, which is coming along very well. The same, at first glance, as my relationship with Willie, for whom I'll put together a book about Malcolm Lowry.

Sunday

On Friday night a long talk with Manuel Puig. On one hand there is his varied and rather surreal work experience (dishwasher, receptionist in New York, hitchhiker), all intersected by his sexual hunt. On the other hand, there is the quality of his literature, very original, infrequent, extraordinary. In the middle there is a fragile, insecure, rather theatrical figure. The thinning hair that worries him, the weak smile, the jokes that help him keep a hold on reality and practice his seduction. Deep down, he confirms my old certainty that it is experience, real behavior, the novel in Puig's case, that defines a person; the rest is empty gestures, brilliant masks to wear on a shallow stage.

Monday

A long phone conversation with José Sazbón, and I rediscovered his usual intelligence and humor. A secret mutual understanding unites us, abstruse for others but clear to us. As if we formed a sect with only two members. Sometimes I think José is the most intelligent person I know.

Tuesday, April 15

As always, random reading allows me to seek out the most enigmatic and revealing news without any preparation. Today, in the obituaries of *La Nación*, I find out about the death of Manolo Vázquez, who was crucial for me and my destiny, so to speak. Professor of Literature and History at the Adrogué National High School in 1956 and 1957, he had a pronounced influence on my choices, and so we might say that it was because of him, in a metaphorical and more or less incidental sense, that I dedicated myself to literature and history. In the way that important things happen, I didn't realize it; who knows in what obscure place I identified with him. I still remember a poem he once recited, which was his own, dedicated to his dead father: "Alone, no light, no shadow, no heart's beating." That's how it began, and I don't think it was very good, but I still remember it all the same. He was forty-five, and I always thought that once I became known I should go visit him and thank him. I remember that first afternoon when he read the poem as though it were someone else's and then, with a smile, admitted that it was his own. Neither he nor I knew where we would end up in twelve years.

I spent the morning going over notes from the sixties and rereading my diaries; including this one, there are 37 notebooks.

Saturday 19

My relationship with Schmucler keeps adapting because of the magazine. I didn't agree to co-direct it with him, but I did commit to handling a critical section in which I'll review all of the books published in a month in a sort of micro-criticism. The shared work improves my relationship with him, and he seems ever more intelligent to me.

Friday, April 25

Several successive meetings to devise the magazine, which I think will work out well if we manage to counteract a certain tendency toward absolute immediacy, which turns "the news" into the axis of the magazine; it's essential that we find a tempo that isn't the same as that of the weekly papers or *Sur* magazine.

A visit from Manuel Puig, who brings a beautiful copy of the French version of *Betrayed*. He's a professional novelist, the first one I've known, and he's determined to make a living from his literature. No one I can remember among us has had that goal since the days of Manuel Gálvez. Manuel clearly knows that he needs to expand the circle of his readers, to reach Latin America and Spain and to be especially attentive to the circulation of his books in translation. He uses the morning to catch up on his immense correspondence, keeping up contact with publishers, translators, and critics. Then he takes a nap, which he calls a *siestita*, and then writes from two to six in the afternoon every day. Then he spends a couple of hours watching movies with his mother and, after eating dinner, goes out, as he says, "to take a spin," that is, to pick someone up, going around the city on risky, adventurous walks. Then you see him and he doesn't look like a writer, and that's what distinguishes him, because he's more of a writer than any of the frauds who play that role; and then, as fragile and timid as he is, he walks into the Buenos Aires night to pick up men in the street with a courage that I admire, which never ceases to astonish me, a person who tenaciously pursues his two central desires (which in reality are one and the same).

In detective novels there is a condition of reading that defines the genre itself: the readers know or imagine what awaits them when they read the book, and they know it before beginning. That knowledge, that previous understanding, functions as a protocol or a way of reading that defines the genre itself. This understanding of the books that exists *before* is strengthened by mass-consumption reviews, which try to define this situation with such intensity that the reading ends up becoming unnecessary. In a way, the field of opposition to this mechanism seeks to reverse or refute that previous knowledge and thus produces effects of parody or innovation. This literary transformation consists in going beyond the condition and expectation of the text; for example, the mystery detective novel is crystallized in such a way that we already know the suspect isn't the murderer before we've read it, so that the hardboiled American detective novel doesn't concern itself with the enigma but begins directly with the preparations for the crime.

Monday
X Series. The fetish of the written word, there is news in the papers that I'm almost certain is false, but it makes me uneasy all the same. Although maybe it isn't false and has real consequences, even for me. Not to write about the visit I received on Saturday night would be to suppose that the police will be able to read this notebook, but, then, what sense is there in caution? Better to capture literarily the atmosphere of this morning after Lucas's visit, which raised my spirits. We had whiskey to celebrate his freedom, laughing at the newspapers that assumed he was arrested, but then, after a terrible afternoon, reading *La Razón* and *Crónica* last night, I used logic to shake off the fear that was confirmed this morning in *Prensa* and *Nación*. All that remains is to hope, trying to know who among my friends really is in prison. I make a fire in the bathtub and burn some

papers, compromising documents, as they say. Now my eyes are stinging from the smoke and the acrid smell of burnt xeroxes.

Series B. I'm in Castelar, the old café on Córdoba and Esmeralda, back after many years, resting from an afternoon spent walking circles around the whole city, weighed down by this prolonged summer, doing nothing but letting myself be carried away, captured by thoughts about Lucas, who may be in prison once again. I'm waiting for the afternoon papers, as though that were any way to stay informed.

Tuesday
X Series. Lucas's arrest was confirmed; the police were waiting for him when he returned home. They called him by name while he was waiting for the elevator, but he kept going on as though it weren't him. He went up to the twelfth floor with them, trying not to be recognized and to sneak away. When the porter recognized him, they took him away. "Tough luck," they told him.

Wednesday, April 30
I spent the afternoon in Galerna working on the magazine and trying to get *Los Libros* started; I discuss everything with Toto, who lets himself be led by opportunism and tries to keep the magazine "in the loop," as he says.

We wait for news about Lucas.

Thursday, May 1
Last night with Carlos B., the script taking shape. Carlos has a deliberate way of being a cynic, propping himself up on what he can so that he doesn't collapse, but behind that lies a kind of melancholic sadness (suicidal).

Friday, May 2
La Negra Eguía (who came back from Cuba before David) confirms some suspicions: giving no handicap to the "leftist" Argentine liberals, they ease their conscience.

May 4
At noon Carlos B. came over; our mutual understanding is growing, basically because of his determination—like all of my friends—to insist or call in order to see me and break through my desire for isolation.

"Literature . . . is not at the service of revolution, but it is the revolution at the level of words," Edoardo Sanguineti.

Monday 5
A strange dream today (dreamt between seven, when the alarm went off, and eight thirty, when I finally woke up: almost a daydream): I was writing an article about Fitzgerald and suddenly came up with a sentence: "If Faulkner's myth is born from the novels he wrote in four weeks, between midnight and dawn, taking advantage of pauses in coal shoveling, if the key to Faulkner is failure, in Chandler it is the fate of a writer of great talent, consumed by the detective novel and by Hollywood, whom we have to uncover." I can't remember now how the passage concluded, but I know I saw it structured together with Lowry, forming part of the theory. A dream of literature while not writing.

Tuesday 6
Yesterday I wasted the afternoon in Galerna with Toto Schmucler, who wants to make me share leadership of the magazine; I have to find an argument that will let me bow out gracefully. The magazine seems interesting to me in general, since it wouldn't use certain people who are too closely tied to cultural journalism and I could also take it in another direction (more tied to a critique of criticism in the media).

Pavese. "He had made a mistake I would not have expected of my literature professor: confusing biography with criticism and applauding some texts for documentary reasons. By contrast my idea of literature is this: to represent a world in which the author enters as a simple character and with the self-important security of a lyric sung to oneself." *Letters*, 1932.

Wednesday

Notes on Tolstoy (7). The idea that religion lies in feelings and practices and not in beliefs is a recurrent theme in Wittgenstein. [Primitive] Christianity is the only certain path to happiness, not because it would promise life after death, but rather because it provided an example in the words and the figure of Christ, a behavior to follow, which made suffering endurable. Religion as practice. (To become Christ.) In Tolstoy, the ethical takes precedence over the personal and the aesthetic, leading him to sacrifice his wife's happiness, his comfortable family life, and his elevated literary position in exchange for what he considered to be a moral imperative: to live according to the principles of rational Christian morality, to live the simple and austere life of humanity in general instead of the enticing adventure of individual art. And when he realized, in 1910, that as long as he went on living on his estate, at the heart of his tempestuous family, he would continue to betray his ideal of simple and pious existence, Tolstoy, an octogenarian, abandoned his home and set himself on the road toward a monastery, but he would never arrive, and he died in the waiting room of a little train station.

Thursday

Both arrive at the same time: a letter from David (coming up with projects based on his stay in Europe) and David himself, ringing the bell with the mischievous expression of a guilty man. Clear metaphysics, if such a thing exists.

Sunday

A long walk around the city with David, ending at a movie theater on Calle Corrientes where we watched a watered-down Soviet documentary about fascism.

I spent the morning throwing out unusable little papers, old loves.

Tuesday

Last night, all of the bad faith from being with David as he idealizes his attraction toward Europe, which awakens the rage of Julia and Beba, and I listen, impassive, without making too much bad blood for myself.

Wednesday 14

Last night I dealt a low blow to myself: I weigh 72 kilos (above my average of 65). A feeling of being controlled by my body, which takes on weight of its own accord.

Series C. As I left the publishing office I ran into Inés, absurd, a kind of ridiculous stranger, and I said goodbye to her as soon as we reached the sidewalk, brushing her off so that I wouldn't have to accept the stupidity of having spent three years of my life with her.

Style, for me, consists of seeing the events I am living through now with the view through which I will see them five years from now. Clearly, that is cynicism: critical control of what I have in my hands. In literature (at least), it is infallible. I also exaggerate that view with women. A kind of definition, carefully examined: add five years to the present to calm down the commotion. Just as effective as my theory that flaws (when made worse) are transformed into virtues. God knows.

Saturday

David returns after two or three days of "absence" because of the argument with Julia and Beba about his trip to Europe. (He enthusiastically suggested that we all go live in Europe.) He is depressed and, as always, defines reality according to his own condition; he either has faith in literature or rejects it according to his state of mind. In any case, he lives out his situation tragically and is too intelligent not to turn his compensatory ideologies into brilliant dissertations, in which what matters least is the subject. He sold his novel *Cosas concretas* to Tiempo Contemporáneo for twelve hundred dollars (five hundred thousand pesos), but he has no desire to publish it and even less to rewrite it, and so he quarrels with himself without making any decisions and talks about the abundance of books that are inundating the country and its surroundings.

Sunday
Friday with Nicolás Rosa and Schmucler at the magazine, trying to differentiate the few from the rest.

I come up with a regimen to lose weight; even if it refers to the regimens of the armed forces, there's no doubt that it's a ridiculous and rather useless activity (not to mention the hunger).

Yesterday a letter from Mom, who reproaches me for having forgotten her birthday and on top of that tells me that Dad had a relapse of his ulcer and will need an operation. What bothers me is the situation that I'll have to endure: a visit to the hospital, solemnity, comforting; I would like to be able to isolate myself without it being seen as something it is not, a lack of love.

Monday
At the magazine I ran into David. I walked back down Corrientes with him, after getting a coffee at Paulista, while the neighborhood filled with people in the darkness and drizzle. David is doing badly, with no desire to work on the novel, worried because of the collapse of the publishing houses that everyone predicts (the breakup of Schapiro and the Centro Editor, the retirement of J. Álvarez), obsessed with his fears: he imagines seeing his books on the bargain table, becoming an old writer who everyone knows but no one reads, lost and forgotten amid juvenile successes (Gálvez, Verbitsky, Castelnuovo). If it doesn't happen, suicide always remains, because David's true fear is suicide. Rather, he fears the events that could make suicide imperative. That explains his ideal to go to Europe as a "rebirth," starting there anew, forgetting, and leaving this reality behind. His eyes were shining as he told me about the shops in Rome where he would go alone for lunch, like someone who has left his parents' house and is learning how to live.

Wednesday
At the publishing house, news that Álvarez "kicked Pirí out" in order to save himself from the collapse, a way, I guess, to find a scapegoat or give up a hostage and so outlive his Beat Generation kids and survive economic hardship.

Thursday 22
The conflicts between students and the police go on, with three dead so far this month. Yesterday in Rosario the students took control of the city center. I have a strange feeling when I think about how I'm looking at them from the outside because they're twenty years old. My age back in 1960.

Correcting *Cosas concretas* with David. It's incredible, instead of cutting down he adds more text, he doesn't have the slightest idea of what structure is.

Friday, May 23
In Rosario the students force the police to retreat, one more killed, the fourth, several casualties, the army intervenes.

I put up little signs on the door that say I'm not home, trying to prevent "visits."

Saturday 24
"There is only one thing a writer can write about: *what is in front of his senses at the moment of writing* . . . I am a recording instrument . . . I do not presume to impose 'story' 'plot' 'continuity,'" W. Burroughs, *Naked Lunch*.

Sunday 25
I worked all day, happy but with few results: a review of Pynchon, the back-cover copy for the Bruce Friedman novel, and a piece for the magazine about the latest university conflicts. Later I ended the night at David's house while he worked ferociously on *Cosas concretas*; he wants to replicate the tone from a year ago, but he has lost it and so is ruining the novel.

Friday 30
Yesterday in Córdoba the workers and students took control of the city from 11 in the morning onward, forcing the army to intervene. The struggle continued until midnight. Undoubtedly the activist groups moved through the city like fish in water, with help from everyone.

Saturday 31
"The writer needs a capacity for critical reflection, familiarity with speculative texts and thought that the writer of yesteryear could dismiss. The work of Joyce or Beckett cannot be conceived without Freudian theory and the reading of philosophy," E. Sanguineti.

I have a cold; my stomach hurts. I ended the night by watching *The Human Condition* with David. We left halfway through because David was shifting around too much in his seat. He doesn't like American cinema but doesn't like the rest either . . . In the bar, David was very fired up about the events in Córdoba, needing to frame that struggle as a qualitative leap and a validation.

David has an interesting project to write a novel whose subject—and title—would be editing: *La redacción*. The text of a political manifesto devised collectively with a group of Latin Americans; working with language as political material, a novel that is ultimately nothing more than a text.

Wednesday 4
It is very clear: when I have a lot to do, I let myself go. I sit there with my head in my hands (metaphorically). I don't do anything. I let things pile up. Now I'm writing a piece on *Catch-22* (for Monday), preparing a lecture on Arlt for Friday at the Teatro Sha (Hebraica), finishing the section with information about all of the books published this month for the magazine (comments on every book), writing a manifesto about the events in Córdoba for the intellectuals to sign at the meeting of *Los Libros*, writing a piece for Luna by Thursday, visiting Lucas T. (in jail) at San Martín. Preparing for tonight's recorded roundtable with Onetti, Sarduy, and

María Rosa Oliver, and meetings with Schmucler, Jorge Álvarez, and the guys from Tiempo Contemporáneo publishing. Besides that, dealing with the surprise appearances of visitors who've been coming to interrupt my peace for the last week, an average of two people per day. Overextended, I get up late (today at eight thirty), work badly on the novel, a mess, but it's no use complaining. Imagine if Robinson Crusoe were visited by a cruise ship full of tourists every afternoon . . .

As soon as I come round and have some distance, I start to feel better and get excited about my work. I'm reading Walter Benjamin's extraordinary essay, "The Work of Art in the Age of Mechanical Reproduction," and some of my intuitions about the current state of literature are confirmed. The key, more than the market (which doesn't exist in Argentina), is the mass media. Sabato and Cortázar expand their audiences thanks to *Primera Plana* and *Siete Días*. I could write something about that this afternoon for the magazine if I can set the morning aside for the novel.

Thursday
What I said before about cultural journalism once again reinforces my idea that *Los Libros* magazine should be dedicated to critiquing the review pages in the newspapers and magazines, analyzing their cultural sections, etc. We live in the age of critiquing critical critique.

In Malcolm Lowry, the theme is *written* fate: not the man who is writing but rather the man who is written by another novelist, whose life is a text. In this sense, Lowry changes the tradition of novels that relate the life of an artist (as in Joyce with Stephen Dedalus or Faulkner with Quentin Compson): S. Wilderness, the protagonist in his final novels, senses that he is living the life written by Lowry in *Under the Volcano*. Isn't the same thing happening to me?

Friday, June 6
Meeting Onetti. Much taller than I'd thought, very well dressed in a dark flannel suit that accentuated his long hands, white and fragile.

A face like rubber, a certain difficulty breathing that cuts his words short, a furtive air, never looking straight ahead. I had imagined him fat and much shorter, disheveled and with an air like Dylan Thomas has in the photographs from when he came to New York to die. His wife imposed with a mixture of fear and strength, almost forcing me to stay for lunch because he felt bad being among old people (M. R. Oliver, José Bianco, Sara de Jorge) and wanted a young man sitting at the table: he looked at me without saying anything, and I felt more uncomfortable and timid than I ever had before. We looked at each other across the counter, and I tried to defend him against that strange imposture. I thought about him while he talked, but it was only at the end, when we started to talk about American literature, that I could really respond to him as needed. Then we turned toward the detective novel. He's an obsessive reader of the genre; we both consider David Goodis to be the best of all. Let's not tell anyone, he said, with a complicit look in his dark eyes.

To understand the situation, maybe I should recall that when I arrived at María Rosa's house and entered the living room, I approached Onetti, who was sitting in an armchair, and told him how much I admired his story "The Stolen Bride" and started to recite it from memory because I knew the beginning by heart. I asked him about publishing it in the collection of nouvelles that I'm doing for Siglo XXI, and he agreed that I could send him some questions and include his responses in the book.

Wednesday
A little crisis when they told me I had to talk to Jorge Álvarez, since he had paid me four hundred thousand pesos so far, and they might cut off my supplies. Today, all the same, Jorge, charming and intelligent, took my side, talking about "slight difficulties," payment installments, etc. He is very enthusiastic about the Serie Negra.

A time of chaos and fury.

Saturday
Whenever I happen to get paid (and wherever: yesterday at the Hebraica),
I feel that in that precise moment when I collect it, I really am "earning"
it, as though everything depended on the impression that I can give to
whoever is about to pay me. A metaphor for my general relationship with
money: it is always given in the present, and so I try to convince people
of my merits in that pure present, as though I had no depth or past and
they were paying me for my performances in the moment when I receive
the money (and not for the work that I did).

Yesterday everything went well in my lecture, with many people in the
room, I spoke well and without pausing, without reading, and almost
without looking at my notes. Afterward, to celebrate, I went to eat alone
at Arturito, on Corrientes near 9 de Julio.

Monday 16
I spent the weekend inventing epigraphs to describe every book that
has come out in the city this month. Interesting work for the future; a
reader leaves behind a record of the impression caused on him by all of
the books that come out in his time.

Tuesday 17
I've never been able to control reality, and what I call my schizophrenia is
nothing more than my inability to choose with clarity, out of the tangle
of events, only those that correspond to my central project. I've always
put literature first, and that is why I now have the feeling that I'm being
carried by Toto, who "forces me" (?) to publish a magazine with him that
I don't believe in. That feeling of being forced has always followed me. It
is connected to my lack of any anchor to reality. Since I don't have needs
(I never have), I foster my desires to the point of turning them into my
only way of living (in short, into a simulacrum of real need). I live as
though it were always Sunday, and I had enough money to satisfy any
possible need: the step after that is having no time to live, since "everything" seems to take place in a single holiday. I turn from side to side

and announce fundamental changes that I'll make tomorrow (how long have I been doing this?).

Wednesday 18
Today I bought an agenda, a space to organize the chaos.

A hellish journey: at eleven with Toto in Galerna trying to finish up Issue 1 of the magazine. While there I run into Alberto Lagunas, a short story writer from Zárate, who is moved by the "strength" of my work and says some nonsense in the tone of the "illuminated creator," typical of *El Escarabajo de Oro*. From there I went to the Álvarez bookshop: four hours waiting for a delivery boy to bring a check so that I could pay my rent (crossed and unsigned).

In the middle of that I meet Víctor Grippo, intoxicated, pursued by the CIA, obsessed with money. Then Germán García comes, undergoing a serious crisis with his second novel; alone and against the world, he appeals to me to decide (after reading it) if it makes sense to publish it or not (it seems to me that he puts on that whole circus just so I'll read his book). To complete the day David comes over, after dinner, looking for me at home "because La Negra is really messed up," he lies to cover up his own depression, his need to be with people makes him talk to me in a fraternal tone, objectifying his own dependence on others when things are going badly.

Further confirmation that either I'll have done with people or vice versa.

Friday, June 20
I know clearly, with perfect certainty, what I'm looking for, an aggressive and self-deprecating tone, making an analysis of my life as though it belonged to someone else, "drawing conclusions," citing some events and experiences as examples.

Taking a real biography and writing it as though it were my own. Introducing my personal tone and my own consciousness through that jumble of strange information would be a way to escape from myself and be left with style alone.

Friday 27

I go to the CGT action in Plaza Once. A turn to the left from Peronism, according to the CP. Combative speeches, rioting, police oppression. I have to run; I turn down Yatay and I'm alone.

Saturday 18

X Series. It is raining, and the storm erases a late summer that bothered us all week. In *La Nación*, I find out about the death of Emilio Jáuregui, born in the same year as me, in 1941. Some differences: an excellent political cadre, great military training. He was assassinated by the police, soon after the event. I think about Lucas in prison. Three years from Onganía's coup: that night listening to the radio, and then later in La Plata, Julia on the stairway of the University. Oh, the past.

Sunday 29

Last night a meeting for the magazine (Schmucler, Sazbón, Ford, Lafforgue, Romano, N. Rosa, J. Rivera). We discuss the upcoming issues, and I insist on the need to place the critique of the cultural vision of the media at the center. Some of them, Romano, Ford, Rivera, want to study the media in the past but not deal with discussing it in the present.

July

Yesterday news that unsettles the country, it grows harder to live here with every passing month. Five men cut down Vandor's guard at the Steelworkers' headquarters, they enter the office and kill him with three shots, blow up the building, and leave. They seem to have been the same ones who blew up three Minimax supermarkets at the same time. A while later I see David (who seems to be going around looking for Coordinación Federal). And then lunch with the guys from Tiempo Contemporáneo publishing to discuss how the book sales are going.

Wednesday 2
Yesterday, after lunch with TC, a long walk with David through the empty city to the publishing office of Álvarez, who was in his office, alone, writing letters and listening to a portable radio with a broken case.

Andrés and Susana are terrified by the oppression, more than five hundred arrested. They lock their doors, look at each other intensely every time they go out into the street, and obsessively come back to the subject of safety mechanisms.

Thursday 3
Julia and Susana, acting very bravely, entered Emilio Jáuregui's house as family friends and came out carrying grenades and automatic weapons in their handbags. Meanwhile, the men waited for them in a bar under the pretense that the girls would pass unobserved by the police more easily. Julia was enthralled by the danger and wanted to go back in to get a Russian machine gun that she'd seen in the bathroom.

Friday
Last night with Juan M., a tender adolescent with a mixture of genius and melancholy, a sort of consul like Lowry, almost asthmatic, just as impotent and drunk, who writes beautiful verses about love and lives amid the chaos like a stubborn old man or someone who invents strange omens by reading tarot cards. Jealous, cultured young people crowd around him (as happens in such cases), trying in vain to guide him, but he insists on drinking one whiskey after another and writing sad profiles meant for the hands of nighttime performers. Then he played several tangos by Cobián on the piano, based on the arrangements that he plays in the Sexteto Mayor.

Sunday 6
A walk with David through downtown, the frozen air from the south blowing against our bodies. Bent over himself, dreaming that he is still in Europe, afraid of old age and of repeating himself as a writer, he talked,

unable to come up with the "adventures" that could excite him. Won't this be my fate in twelve years?

Wednesday 9
Last night David, Andrés, Boccardo, and company in the restaurant on the corner until three in the morning. Raving conversations in unison under the lights of the city.

This weekend we will write the introduction for *Los Libros* magazine.

Wednesday 16
Last night in Edelweiss, clusters of golden and frivolous young people; Julia and I had run into Miguel and Nélida and also Pirí with her ex-husband Pérez, the fashion photographer, who was trying to seduce Miguel's girlfriend and insisted that we go to his house so that he could show us some things; once there, he kept on courting Nélida, saying that his girlfriend was in Punta del Este and fascinating her by showing off modern and luxurious dresses; the funniest part was when she said that the clothes didn't go well with the shoes and Pérez told her: "Don't worry, *Nena*, you can go barefoot"; she was immediately head over heels. Then we ended up at Edelweiss, and at some point the barefoot contessa got up to buy cigarettes and the photographer followed her. They didn't come back. Miguel, drunk by that point, was very crestfallen, but then Enrique Pichon-Rivière, the psychoanalyst, greeted Pirí from a table nearby and sat down with us. He had grasped the situation on the fly and started talking softly and consoling Miguel and, in the end, when he left, he gave him the pipe he was smoking as a gift. "There you have it, a great performance," laughed Pirí, and she asked Miguel to lend her the pipe and started smoking it, never once mentioning that she too had been abandoned.

Friday
I want to write a story in the style of a tango: a man lets himself die because his woman left with his best friend.

My father was waiting for me that morning at the grill on Viamonte and Montevideo, frightened by his loneliness and the buzzing of the city. He'd been calling me all morning, but I wanted to go on sleeping or making love (I don't remember now) and finally he said he wanted to drop off my scarf as an excuse to come visit me again, to be with me, to kill time until his train departed.

Thursday

As always happens in times when I'm working well, I move away from these notebooks, my "interior life" dissipates. This afternoon David came in, content because he sorted out the movie adaptation of *Amalia* with Ayala for one million pesos and a script about Varela, the officer, for five hundred thousand. Roberto C. was also there, going on about the latest political changes, the importance of the freedom struggles, for which Mao is the Marx of the Third World. Then, at the magazine, I see Toto and Roa Bastos, who is working ferociously on his novel *I, the Supreme*.

Sunday 27

I'm reading *The Man Without Qualities* by Musil, the presence of a controlled, intelligent humor, setting up a puzzle that recognizes the irony of technocratic myths, the "delights" of everyday life, the splendor of science: a fervent rationality, I would say, impassioned.

Series B. Yesterday I spent the morning in La Paz reading at a table by the window, alone in the empty bar. David stopped by at noon looking for me to get lunch, euphoric and at the same time depressed about his work on Varela with Ayala (he's getting paid fifty thousand per week).

An unsettling observation by Scott Fitzgerald, who lay on his left side every night—as he said—in order to more quickly wear out his heart.

Thursday, July 31

I can live on a hundred thousand pesos per month without much effort. If I manage to use the afternoons happily and efficiently to earn my living, everything will take on the rhythm that I, "mentally," have asked of reality. Also, I'm using my intelligence to fight against the stupid aggressive ideas that are nothing more than a depraved reaction: suddenly I see enemies coming from every direction.

Anxiety is the key to my peaceful madness: I can't deal with the future, going to the barbershop, seeing Jorge or Toto, writing the introduction for the magazine, anything.

Series E. Every time I come close to finishing one of these notebooks, as I have now, I grow philosophical about my life. These endings, dear God, my hands stained with ink, my fingers wasted away with yellow nicotine stains, my head heavy after lunch at the restaurant on Calle Sarmiento with dirty glass doors through which the noonday sun filters in and further slows my movements already affected by the wine.

"It is certain that I don't know how to write, but I'm writing about myself," Juan C. Onetti.

By rereading my old notebooks, I find confirmation yet again that one only writes about what is taking place in the moment of writing, as though one were a device registering the world in the present and, at the same time, I find that a vast collage has been constructed, from which I alone am absent; I disappear among words that form a path, the meaning of which can only be understood much later.

Series C. I have to go out to the street, stand in front of a kiosk, say hello to the woman there and buy condoms because Julia has stopped taking the pill this month. This worries me strangely, as though I lacked the strength needed to go out to the street, or as though I feared that, after buying what I am going to buy, I would lose myself in the city and never return.

I have reached the end of this page, as one must.

August

I walk through the empty city at eight in the morning, envisioning this moment: sitting at a table by the window in an empty La Paz, writing notes and trying to capture what is taking place.

Series E. I seek a writing that erases itself as it goes along, light and quick and so fleeting. But if I'm unable to achieve that here, where could I? I recall that I've always kept everything I write, as though I imagined that there, in that diffuse mass of words, the traces of a personal voice would be preserved.

Sunday, August 3

Last night at David's house, I try to compensate for the fact that I don't visit him as often as I should.

I want to be able to write in any state of mind. Now, I'm killing time before I go with Toto to the printing press, where Issue 2 of *Los Libros* is now ready.

Monday 4

A scrap merchant with a broken voice is yelling out on the corner ("I buy old beds, I buy mattresses, rags, old newspapers. I buy aluminum, bronze, I buy glasses, bottles, clothing"). He reminds me of the old man who used to go by in his car every morning, just at the moment when I was lying down to sleep after having worked all night long.

I was walking through Buenos Aires to Plaza de Mayo, and at a corner on Florida I saw the first afternoon newspapers coming in. At Hachette I ordered *L'échec de Pavese* by Dominique Fernandez and looked at the magazines and books, then stopped by David's house, but he was not there, and I kept going without a fixed direction, and when I returned, a while later, David was back and we went to have a coffee in a bar on Corrientes.

175

Wednesday 6
Yesterday General Onganía shut down *Primera Plana*, attempting to take away the voice of a floating middle-class sector, very important for imposing a general sensibility.

Yesterday I had lunch with David and went to the bookshop with him, and everyone was arguing in the café next door: García Lupo, Mario Trejo, etc. No one gives Onganía more than two months to live. They foresee an electoral solution via Lanusse.

Wednesday 13
The announcement of a catastrophe puts my friends on the left in check. Yesterday David was very depressed and pessimistic, Alberto S. had no money (me neither), Andrés was very worried: everyone predicts the fall of Onganía and an increase in surveillance, and the effects are growing ever closer, they shut down *Ojo* (which had replaced *Primera Plana*). Today I found out that the Coordinación Federal, that is, the political police, seized books from Álvarez's place last night and summoned Jorge to come at two in the afternoon today. Friends in prison (Lucas, Ford, Fornari, Rojo), sources of work in danger. Those in opposition to the military government are affected the most.

A dream. I was talking to Barba, my teacher at the College, in a room lined with my books, and I was ashamed that he had seen them because they were covered with dirt. He berated me for having dedicated my life to literature. I made excuses: "It's my form of madness," I told him, "as soon as I can control this delirium, I'll go back to historical research." He made me look at his latest book and rejected my collection of short stories because of its title. He was flipping through the yellow, egg-colored edition, very worn out. He told me about a diary that he was about to publish. Of course, I thought, he's a professional historian and makes conventional literature in his free time between hours. "It's untitled," he said. "All books these days have titles." I looked at him, admiring the originality of that blank book, a cover with no symbol other than his own name.

Thursday 14
Series B. At long last, I have understood my schizoid way of thinking: I attribute to others the issues that I want to understand in myself. I choose a real double (Dipi, Miguel Briante, Walsh, Germán), so to speak, and through them I experience issues that I can't see with any clarity in myself. I give them the mechanism of thought that gives rise to the *fixed idea.* In this way, I split myself secretly into others and attribute ways of being (which are my own) to them, and I observe their workings. Using the scene of an external life, I think about my own ideas concerning what I am (or want to be): I use the other as a critique of my own shortcomings, seeing them clarified, more real, and can thus undertake a critique of my personality through my parallel lives. In other writers, I experience what I myself want to do. It is a more radical form of working with possible lives. My contemporaries are the test, the trial, the clear vision of the risks of living inside the imaginary. I've been doing this since adolescence, ever since I started to write these notebooks: Raúl A., Luis D., and also some women like Elena and Helena. It seems incredible to me that I have discovered it only now: friendship as a testing ground for my life. Instead of, or at the same time as, using fictional characters as models for projection, I do it in real life. A means of expanding my experience vicariously.

Friday 15
I want to write about my Halloween night on the *boîte*, in Mau Mau, the party: thirty TV screens showing different places and scenes of what is happening live. I have to find a prose that could present that collective tone, the social voice of a group.

Curious, there is no envy in tangos, there is only loss and betrayal. They narrate the fait accompli and its effects.

Monday, August 18
I cannot perceive with any clarity what some women look for in me; it has always been that way, since the beginning. Mistakes, misunderstandings. I used to escape, now I play dangerous games.

León R. stops by to say that he'll be back at 10:00 p.m., but I want to prepare for seeing Álvarez, bringing him my now well-developed projects, writing a summary of what remains to be done, and so I postpone my meeting with León. Julia gets angry, saying that I was hiding her since I didn't ask him to come in. I have to fight with Omar to get him to pay me the fifty thousand pesos per month that I settled on with Jorge, because right now he's only paying me twenty-five thousand—and always late. Then I'll go to León's house, now that he's moved to a distant neighborhood (Calle Salguero), to ask him to do an article on Althusser for *Los Libros*.

Tuesday
Yesterday I saw León, very depressed, in crisis, the same as David. Bad times: a crisis with the MLN, the free left, the form of structuralism, and he has no desire to work on his book about Freud and Marx.

Dipi came over a little while ago, tense and incoherent, telling me about the photographs of Sandro that he's going to take, the three-hundred-page novel that he says he's finished.

I see *Touch of Evil* by Orson Welles, top-quality film noir, with Welles inflated to seem even fatter in the role of the villain.

Tuesday, September 2
I'm resisting the current tendency toward writing without characters.

A visit from David at noon, wanting to move ahead with my magazine project, he suggests *Carta Abierta* for the title, with León, him, and me directing it.

"Anxiety pulverizes concentration," Norman Mailer.

Thursday 11
I see David, who goes on about the magazine project as a way to combat his feelings of being outside, marginalized. I also run into Aníbal Ford, who got out of jail, and he tells me that he identified Fiorentino as the singer who showed up at the prison tango audition, which helped him become friends with the regular prisoners.

Pasolini is right to question how far the distinction between the novel and poetry can continue to exist. But I'm not going down that road; for me, the novel must go deeper into the construction of characters.

Saturday 13
I want to separate the linguistic experimentation of the work from its plot and at the same time free myself from objective and "realist" prose. A writing in which the continuity is altered. The hero sets aside a domain of experience for himself in which he struggles to avoid the novelty of the new. The new is an incursion on temporal continuity. From there comes the sense of a time based on the petrifaction of the present, the chronological void. Fixity. The time must cease to flow.

Monday, September 15
Series A. Will I be dead at the beginning of the twenty-first century? Less melodramatically, will I manage to see the year 2000? What will I be like at age sixty? Will all my hollow ambitions have been answered?

What I wrote earlier was an effect of the insomnia that woke me and has kept me awake since three in the morning.

Wednesday
I prepare to move; a bad outlook for Tiempo Contemporáneo, pessimistic, threatening, closing down the publishing house, everything depends on the sales of *Cosas concretas*. Luna gives me two hundred dollars as an advance and I think I'll use it for my move, which I'll try to work out in the next few weeks.

Thursday 18

I find an enormous apartment on Sarmiento and Montevideo. With a phone, three rooms, good lighting, and a lease until April 1971. I left a down payment, but we'll see if the guarantees work.

Saturday

I'm reading *Heartbreak Tango* voraciously, the striking control of tension, the ruptured movement of the narration, the final perception of social relationships. Eroticized flesh as an engine for the plot. Prose that is very attentive to registers of speech. And the most innovative part is the absence of the narrator.

Suddenly, I feel nostalgia for my old knowledge of history. The reconstruction of complex structures and long spans of time.

Tuesday, September 23

For the last few days I've had anxiety, angst, difficulty working. I'm always waiting for a catastrophe that never comes. There is a waiting akin to that of a hunter in a blind, lying in wait for the prey (but I myself am the prey).

Friday 26

I leave behind my apartment on Pasaje del Carmen, the window that opens over the street, the city sounds and the daylight, all the time I've spent here, writing. We'll see if I can manage to put everything into place and organize my books.

My plans, as always:
1. Write final versions and not drafts.
2. Improve the diary.
3. Write criticism on demand.
4. Systematize my reading.
5. Don't postpone the publishing work.
6. Sleep little.
7. Go to the cinema often.

Saturday 27

I've already settled into this large and bright apartment; I set up my desk in one of the rooms, all my books in boxes, no furniture, happy with the excess of space.

Sunday 28

Good light, Faulkner's portrait on the wall, we went out to look for chairs and tables in the neighborhood shops.

Tuesday 30

Last night with David, who was back from La Rioja, where he'd gone with Olivera to scout locations for *El caudillo*, a film David wrote the script for. I went to see him to ask for ten thousand pesos, which I need to pay the library. At the magazine office I see Osvaldo L. and Oscar S., they show too much desire to astonish and be original, and I watch from a distance.

Series E. I struggle—clearly—to find a tone for these notebooks, but that's exactly what I like about them: the prose is spontaneous and swift, and therefore it's very changeable, there's no common rhetoric. The best part is the continuity, the persistence, which are the great challenges of writing. Another thing that appears is a feature of everything I do: I never concentrate on one point but rather disperse myself, letting myself be led by the impulse of the writing. The breadth comes through accumulation, not because I give time to the writing and develop a subject to its end, and motifs reappear but are not developed. Everything that I've managed to do, I've done in the pure instant, without a future; for me, the future has always been a threat.

October

Series C. A copy of *El Corno Emplumado* magazine came for me, and as always it brings up the memory of Margaret Randall, because she always used to send it to me in spite of my silences. I met her in Cuba; for me, she was the living connection to San Francisco and the Beat Generation, since she was connected to them. Close friends with Ferlinghetti. The night we walked along the beach and then stretched out on the warm sand until the next day is still very present for me, as though it were a photo, or rather a sequence of photographs. Margaret had a poetic theory about instantaneous love, free, casual: "It's like metaphors," she would say, "they're everywhere, and so is physical love. An opportunity for pure metaphor."

Always this surreal quality, as though my life were happening to someone else. Yet, for the first time, the phantoms meet the present. I devote myself to dreaming of a future that is the same as today: conservative, for once. What do I mean? A job that does not take up my time, a good place to live, enough money to deal with the inclemency of the moment, books for free, and a personal writing that moves forward, slowly but continuously.

Tuesday 7
A good time with David yesterday, he has developed facial tics due to the imminent release of his novel *Cosas concretas*; he wants Pirí to handle the publicity, he's jealous of the five thousand copies per week that Pirí sells. In the middle of all that he keeps himself in shape, we talk about the intersection between Sarmiento and Hernández (desert, blood), he recalls my article on Puig, and we go back to the intersection between sex and money.

Before, on Saturday, I have an intense argument with León R. when he reproaches me for having cut apart the bookcase that he gave me a few days ago. "I put it to the use I needed," I told him. "You should've asked me. What if I needed to use it again soon?" "Don't worry, León," I told him, "In that case I'd buy you another." The argument went off down a dangerous path: how do we connect our thoughts with our actions? No one has solved that problem.

Wednesday 8
The Cubans sent me several books and hinted at a possible invitation, although the relationship on my side has cooled following Castro's support of the Soviet invasion in Czechoslovakia.

Figures of the public writer: David Viñas, Günter Grass, and Norman Mailer.

On reading. There can be no reading without an extra-verbal situation. These situations are *a priori*; they control and organize what is read. This can be seen clearly in works with a strong existing hallmark: detective novels, classic works, melodramas. There is an existing provision that determines the way a book is used. Criticism must describe these situations: these include what we might call "the prior knowledge" with which we approach a book, and even a debut work responds to that background. It is a book that we know nothing about, and therefore we read it with an established attitude that is not the same as the one we have for a consecrated author.

Friday 10
Notes on Tolstoy (8). He writes a new Gospel (*Gospel in Brief* by Leo Tolstoy) based on uniting and synthesizing the four existing gospels. Wittgenstein: "You are living, as it were, in the dark and have not found the saving word. And if I, who am essentially so different from you, should offer some advice, it might seem asinine. However, I am going to venture it anyway. Are you acquainted with Tolstoy's *The Gospel in Brief*? At its time, this book virtually kept me alive. If you are not acquainted with it, then you cannot imagine what an effect it can have upon a person" (letter to Ficker, July 1915). Tolstoy discusses the gospels: the moment when Jesus admits to his disciples that he is the Son of God is the most extraordinary moment due to the enunciation and use of language (because he is).

Sunday, October 12
The conflicts at the magazine grew worse, arguments with Toto, Willie, etc., about attempts to reorganize the magazine and leave us out. I listened to myself as I raised furious moral diatribes that had little effect. Everything goes on in the same way, and now I'm the one who wants to detach myself (after I earn this month's salary to cover my deficit from moving).

Monday
A visit from David, caught up in one of his economic thrills that always seem attractive when he describes them. A project of starting a publishing house, starting a magazine, buying a place for a bookshop. It will all dissolve as soon as his euphoria passes. I lent him an ear with the same indifference as always.

My unexpected and "visible" memories: the projected, metallic, perfect voice of the announcer for *Cabalgata Deportiva Gillette*, announcing a boxing match with Lauro Salas, brings me back to my cousin Lili's house; she had bought a TV a few days before. It would have been in the year '53 or '54. I can see the glass of the window, the device placed on a Japanese-style table, and I can see myself sitting on the floor in front of the screen.

Tuesday 14
Yesterday, Andrés Rivera, like all the writers of his generation, brings liberal temptations with him: nostalgia for a strong CP with newspapers, publishers, jobs, positions of power in the cultural sphere. He criticizes the Tupamaros after the attack in Pando: they rented a funeral cortege and took over the town, cut the phone lines, robbed three banks and the police station, etc. A radio enthusiast gave them away: the army and the police came in with helicopters; there were three dead, six arrested, and twenty of them managed to get away. For Andrés, it is suicidal adventurism.

Wednesday 15
The books in the Serie Negra have had a very good reception and are selling well.

The "I" in narrative is no longer the singular subject of the biography, but rather the occasional experimenter. The first person can be generated by the third person, etc. Writing produces a series of transformations and disintegrations, whether it is the "I" who stages the story, or the material or experiences that are integrated into its workings.

I'm tempted to abandon Pavese as the subject of the story and to include the maladjustment of the outsider who doesn't have a good command of the language in the country where he lives.

Thursday 16
Last night too much wine after the dinner that followed the magazine meeting. Today I had to get dressed early in the morning and go out to buy aspirin to combat my headache. The little neighborhood shops were almost empty, with lone women and men wandering around at five in the morning while the garbage trucks crossed the damp streets.

Hemingway's three books of memoirs (*Death in the Afternoon, Green Hills of Africa*, and *A Moveable Feast*) are also exercises in nonfiction and anticipate many elements of what is now called "new journalism." They are also admirable examples of the open novel: several levels in the prose, rupturing of genre, direct speech, etc. The final chapter of *Death in the Afternoon* is resolved in the same way as the still unwritten "possible stories" from "Kilimanjaro."

Along these lines, the contemporary writer moves among several registers. I myself could be an example of that condition. A person who reads detective fiction "professionally" because he is in charge of a series, receiving more than three hundred books every month, out of which he selects five. A detective novel is always good for the first twenty pages because that is where the author presents the world in which the intrigue will develop: for example, let's say, the Japanese laundromats in Buenos Aires. First, that world is described, which always holds some interest, and one finds out or wonders why it is that the Japanese population in Buenos Aires opens laundromats. After that question is answered a crime appears and, from that point onward, the bad novels respond to the mystery with predictable schemes. Only the best writers are able to add something extra to the construction of the intrigue, going beyond simple suspense or simple solutions to the problem. A writer who is able to write something beyond the simple plot is one who achieves a novel that is worthy of translation.

But if I continue with this sort of anthropological vision of myself, we could say that this individual is also part of the editing committee at a cultural magazine. He participates in meetings, discusses the material, suggests topics for upcoming issues, and fills his time, as is my case, writing brief reviews—never more than five lines—of all the books that are published every month in Buenos Aires. What's more, this Argentine writer writes two newspaper pieces per week and receives a fixed salary for them; the pieces began as bibliographic reviews, but after some serendipitous event (the crime reporter is sick or was sent to cover a crime in Bajo in Buenos Aires) he also became the crime reporter. In 1965, he was sent to Montevideo to cover the police's siege on three Argentine criminals who had robbed a bank truck in San Fernando. For a week, he sent back notes about what was happening there, from when the police first came until it all ended two days later. In addition to keeping up with his correspondence (an average of two or three letters per day), reading the newspapers (habitually the morning papers), a news magazine, and subscribing to several foreign magazines, he dedicates part of the day (never more than an hour) to writing down his life's adventures in a notebook. The question is: at what point does this Argentine writer sit down to write? For the moment, there is no answer. Further, we could say that this individual is invited, often, to give courses and lectures in a variety of places.

I have recorded here a substantial though incomplete part of my daily activities, which, due to those same occupations, I can't always record in this diary.

Friday
Notes on Tolstoy (9). Tolstoy's respect for the common man, his simple and frank affection for an ordinary worker. ("More intelligent than me.")

Saturday 18

Yesterday a very good conversation with David, who started my afternoon with a phone call that sounded at once attractive and mysterious, announcing his visit. When I agreed to see him, the bastard said: "Thanks." We went to Ramos, where I had a tea and he had a café con leche, and we saw César Fernández Moreno and other friends passing down Corrientes, as though we were on the balcony of a country house, observing the movements of our neighbors in their cars. David was bitching about Félix Luna and Ayala, who ruined the script he'd written for *El caudillo*. He fantasizes about cursing them out and telling them to go to hell despite the million pesos they've given him for his work. "And about the ability to ruin them," I said. Then some ideas about the speed of consumption, "burning through" products (books, authors). With a very wise reflection, David perceives the current logic of the cultural world: circulation accelerates, and there is a consolidation of the places that decide which literary products will be published or not. We ended up at the publishing house where he's going to publish his novel *Cosas concretas*.

I read David's novel, it is in a confessional style. All the characters drift into a very personal kind of declaration and a direct and excessive sincerity. The novel is written with more monologues than dialogues. Politics is the thematic aim of his work. In that sense, the genre in which he undertakes his critique of the dominant violence is never distinguished: it can be a novel, an essay, or a film script.

Friday

Yesterday a car ride along the edge of the river with my mother, always more intelligent and entertaining than I imagine her. Yesterday her ironic discourse had to do with family relationships, with a special critical statement about abusive mothers. She knows the tiniest minutiae about the whole family: she is the youngest of twelve siblings and, in a sense, is the heiress to all of the stories that have been circulating since the beginning. She has a particular quality that I admire, one that I've learned a great deal from: she never criticizes anyone, whoever they may be or whatever crime they may have committed, as long as they belong to the family. She never judges others' conduct if they are part of her circle. In that sense, as I think I've already said before, my mother is, for me, a model of what a writer should be. Detailed, meticulous, and incapable of condemning other people's actions.

Saturday

Yesterday was the roundtable on "the new generation" at the Hebraica. Many friends and many enemies in the audience. A slight argument with De la Vega, who recited McLuhan, and some points of agreement with Jusid and Manuel Puig. I was very nervous, but I calmed down in the moment and said some amusing things.

Sunday

I'm writing a short piece about "Beckett's Nobel." He wasn't to blame, and he hid and wouldn't let himself be seen by the reporters or the Swedes who had awarded it to him. In any case, it is yet more proof that the system can incorporate what, at first glance, seems most contrary to its values and most antagonistic.

Tuesday 28

It is five in the morning and I'm working on Hemingway: reading several articles, a chronology, and several texts. I'm defending the writing in his first works, closely tied to his experiences on the front lines.

I travel to San Fernando with David to see Carlos B. and console him about his brother's death. David is grieving as though someone close to him had died, although on the way back he told me some secrets about his life (which I won't reveal) that allowed me to understand his melancholy moments.

Wednesday 5

"A symptom is formed as a substitution for something that has not been able to manifest itself externally; it is a sort of permutation," Freud.

Sunday, November 9
I spent all day Saturday in La Plata with Nicolás Rosa at Menena's house. The old, touching house where I lived for many years stood one block away. I wrote "Mata-Hari 55" there one clear October morning; I'd bought peaches and plums and chilled them in a bucket of ice and ate them throughout the day while I wrote the story. At one moment, yesterday, I went out to buy cheese to have with wine while we were waiting for Toto to finish the barbecue, and then I tried to go to the house and spy through the balcony to see what was there now, but I was afraid I would lose my way in the night and turned back.

Wednesday 12
My father's voice came through the air pocket of the stairwell, asking for me from some part of the building, searching for me, and he finally came in and sat with me to talk about his suicidal temptation and fear of death, his night terrors and anxiety. Oh life, oh pain. What can a son say to his father about the hardships of existence. The whole time, I was on the point of saying to him: "Don't tell me these things," but I contained myself and said: "There are moments of depression, losing streaks, we all have dark moments. The worst thing you can do is to think they'll never pass, but they always leave, they pass, and you forget them." He seemed relieved, not because of what I'd said, but rather because he'd been able to talk with his son, which, I think, is what he'd come to do.

"A suggestion that, like all magical practice, finds its only resources in a situation of prestige and dependency, capable of inducing the victim into significations that are foreign to him," J. B. Pontalis.

One of my first memories—not the first—is of a moment when my grandfather Antonio is carrying me on his shoulders in the garden at his house, and on the other side of a green wooden trellis is my grandmother Albina and a table with a rubber cover by the right-side wall. (Is the patio across from that wall, with the two doors leading inside and one door leading to the kitchen?) I can see a little jug for drinking maté on that table, and someone—my grandfather, I think—tells me that it's my beer jug because I'm a child. (My grandfather had a white ceramic jug for drinking beer.) I also remember his death; one of the two doors on the wall (the first, passing through the trellis) leads to the room where the casket is located. There are some women ("neighbors" I recognize without knowing who they are), and there is the body. Someone takes me by the waist and lifts me up to kiss "the deceased."

A dream. Watching the city below, in a room full of light. I want to say what I'm expected to say but can't remember the words. I see a woman's face, her bright eyes. All the while, I'm taking a leap of faith. The woman has an air like Marlene Dietrich, a clever face, keen, very bright eyes, a light on her tanned face.

Friday
All the walls I've written on, seeing nothing.

My face is burning, I feel a slight stinging on my cheek, I slide my palm over it, the burning grows. I rub brutally at my cheek, a way to bring the skin of my face back to life.

"This first account may be compared to an unnavigable river whose stream is at one moment choked by masses of rock and at another divided and lost among shallows and sandbanks," Freud, on a case of hysteria.

Series C. I thought that I was an unknown, that no one knew about me, that there was no motivation behind my activity. I had to reread what I'd written in order to remember. I had the feeling that I'd done things she never found out about; it was nothing but a metaphor for forgetting, for my death to her. That is, a way to erase loss and to combat death.

Outside, a boy is reciting aloud the multiples of two: "two times two is four, two times three is six, two times four is eight." I remember the classroom near the entrance to school no. 2, where I was trying not to cry because they were transferring me to a religious school and I was going to lose my third-grade teacher forever.

Saturday 15
Lunch with David. "You suddenly feel that everything has become naturalized for you, and you catch yourself telling time by the changing of the seasons," he said.

Series E. A central core that radiates out in multiple directions, all of my fantasies are transformed into different levels of the same story. A narrative delirium, hundreds of tiny anecdotal centers, scenes, situations, a microscope of time and memory. A diary.

Sunday 16
I'm reading Freud with the passion of all my unforgettable discoveries. "For the child, just like the adult, can only produce fantasies with material that he has acquired from somewhere; and the ways in which he might acquire it are in part closed to the child," S. Freud.

In fact, *The Interpretation of Dreams* is the first modern autobiography.

Freud speaks of the "narcissistic origin of compassion."

My current terrors are grounded upon a fear of excessive consciousness: thinking too much.

When I'm writing by hand, after a little while, after I've written a page, let's say, the pain in my wrist forces me to run through the events quickly here, to be superficial. And so I use this physical situation to explain my difficulty in "writing the truth."

All of that without forgetting the methods, that is, certain that only one who understands technique can be sincere in writing.

An interesting part of *The Interpretation of Dreams* is the abundance of perspectival changes in the writing. For example, "Through this displacement of the emphasis, this regrouping of the elements of the content, the manifest dream becomes so dissimilar from the latent dream thoughts that no one would suspect the latter behind the former . . . I am aware [that is, in the present as he writes] that this conception cannot be generally demonstrated, but I maintain that it can often be demonstrated even where one would not have suspected it, and that it cannot be generally refuted [transferring to the future an unknown that he, of course, has not resolved, but leaves the solution suspended]."

Another example: "The patient, who succumbed to the toxic effects of the drug, bore the same name as my eldest daughter. I had never thought of this until now; but now [in writing this] it seems to me almost like a retribution of fate."

A third example: "There must be some reason why I fuse the two persons into one in my dream. I remember that, in fact, I was on bad terms with both of them for similar reasons." It could be said that Freud is a detective going after himself in this book; he becomes the field of his own investigation. He shares the peripeteias and the intrigues of his slow process of recognizing the reasons—or the meanings—behind the dream, or rather, behind his own dreams. We could say that the form Freud uses in his dream analysis is the narrative monologue, recounting his discovery to someone else, following the order that the dreams took on as he was analyzing them, and that is the reason for the abundance of interrogations such as, "Am I thereby trying to make fun of Dr. M?" Another, "But what can be my motive in treating this friend so badly?" Or, "How do these . . . get into my dream?" These questions not only pause the account but rather are formulated from the position of the person whom he addresses in his writing (a reader). In fact, he asks himself the questions that an intelligent reader would ask in his place. On the other hand, in this way he dramatizes the things that he writes about.

Saturday, November 22
Series E. A diary, this series of notebooks, is made from little traces, isolated situations, nothing spectacular, a narrative imbalance for which dead time seems not to exist. This is why I feel good when I'm able to include my projects in a history, that is, in a narrative temporality, when I say, for example, "I have a week to finish the essay that I'm writing for the magazine." I tend to make the experience exist in the present and, in that way, all of the stories and all of the places convene in a single moment.

Sunday 23
Last night, we saw a film by Enrique Juárez about the events in Córdoba: high-quality documentary and journalistic material, but held back by naïve commentary, poor resolution. I still can clearly see the narrative possibilities of journalistic style in film (an agile camera, nervous rhythm, abrupt cuts). Also, the need to work with everyday realities so as not to mythologize the story or turn it into a spectacle, narrating, for example, a failed strike.

November 25
I was at *Los Libros* and saw Osvaldo L., with whom I keep up an ironic relationship based on some level of intellectual agreement. In L., one can see a very willful path toward perversion, considered as a fine art. Anyway, I'm tired of his affectation and his conspiratorial insistence that never leads anywhere.

December 1969
At noon, one Gabriel Rodríguez visits me, coming to see me in search of work. He doesn't know anyone in Buenos Aires, comes from Rosario, tells me he's an astrologer, and asks me if I think it's a profession with potential. He speaks in a very serious way, and I answer him seriously as well. Someone vaguely mentioned me to him as a way to get rid of him. I tell him that the person who can help him is David Viñas; I give him the address and send him there but also give him a little money. I expect the kid will traverse the whole city, going from one friend to

another, advised and compensated with bits of money that he hasn't asked for.

Then I meet Germán García, the only person in whom I see an intelligence that works quickly. He's now working on popular singers. I go to the magazine, which I'm running for a few days because Toto went to Córdoba. I ran into Ismael Viñas and he seemed tired, with no spark, as though defeated, mentioning his daughter every two minutes because he never sees her. The kind of parent who abandons his children; that kind of fatherhood is what I've rejected all of my life.

Tuesday, December 2
A journey amid multitudes. I met David to get lunch, then coffee with Fernando Di Giovanni, and from there to Andrés, who was back from Uruguay. I went to the magazine office and ran into Eduardo Meléndez. On my way back home, Ismael Viñas was waiting for me, and at eight Roberto Jacoby came over with a friend and they stayed until one in the morning. The conversation revolved around the usual axes—is an avant-garde politics possible? The answers were divided over whether art or society would be the site of the experimentation. Power dynamics in both spheres. But literature is a society without a State.

Wednesday 3
I am moved by Arguedas's suicide. He had announced it and postponed it. The ills of the soul; he sought to unite Andean culture with contemporary culture and died in the attempt. That's not why he killed himself (he was succeeding there). He killed himself because life is, often, unbearable. His death is also a metaphor for the hidden Latin American writer, never revealed, underground, opposite to the marquees of the Boom.

I make good progress this week with added hard work (a review of *Cosas concretas*, with the difficulties that always come with writing about a book by a friend, especially if one doesn't like the book). Hot weather and social relationships. Today Manuel Puig came over in the late afternoon, a long conversation about our mutual projects: developments in the detective tradition. Manuel uses the genre to critique the criminal relationships in the world of art and settles his debts along the way with the stupidity and despotism of cultural criticism.

Friday

At *Los Libros* I see F., a disciple of Oscar del Barco, he is circulating *Tel Quel* problematics, purism in terminology, the cult of destruction following Bataille. They seem to think that desire in literature only functions in the writers who make it explicit. The same thing happens with language. Snobbery invades Buenos Aires with the jargon of structuralism. An absurd joint article on Marechal, using Greimas's actants to analyze *Adam Buenosayres*.

Sunday

I travel to Mar del Plata, my father was hospitalized. I spend the night with him, look at him lying nearby, the intravenous tubes that immobilize him, in a room with two beds in the Central Clinic.

A very surreal feeling. Indecision about the future; I want to be here and, at the same time, I decide to travel back home in the early morning. My father in a fetal position.

"Private property in the sphere of language does not exist," Roman Jakobson.

Thursday 11

Several encounters with David, he meets me at Ramos to give me a fairly decent piece about Chacho Peñaloza to read, and he seems very nervous about the release of his novel. Then G., who goes on talking, never stopping, no matter whom he's with, always about whatever he's been reading lately. Dipi Di Paola, who, from what he told me, has stopped "using his head," and De Brasi, who gave me a short piece about Dal Masetto. I saw all of them in El Colombiano. Last is Toto, who wants to start a publishing house with the money from T., and finally, around midnight, I'm at a table on the sidewalk along Carlos Pellegrini.

I always end up getting the money I need, though that knowledge does me no good while I'm trying to get it. It's as though I were cultivating a certainty that I don't want to "earn my living," or, rather, it's as though I thought—in harmony with society—that the work I do is for free.

Tuesday, December 16
I went back to Mar del Plata to see my father. These are physical returns to the past, the streets that lead me backward, toward the time when I started thinking for myself.

I spend several hours with my ailing father, shortly after the operation. I recognize in myself, more and more, the signs of his personality, especially the need to not see reality. That is, I start to distance myself from him, seeing him as a future double and, in spite of everything, I construct the facts of my own independence.

A little summary. On Friday morning Aunt Elisa called to let me know that Dad was having an operation. Some trouble cashing the check from Jorge Álvarez (dated 12/29), and then I went to León R., who makes his own interpretations in such cases and treats the family as the center of balance in everything. Well, he suggested that I should psychoanalyze myself, something my friends often suggest these days.

In my conversation with León, I once again discovered the importance of my theory about *guarantees* in literature. Society demands some support, some foundation that guarantees the form. For León, that support is not just "talent" but also pain. He believes that with greater pain comes greater truth. At the same time, he's opposed in all of his philosophy to the Christian logic that views suffering as the path toward salvation. Rather, it is experience that functions as support in literature. Of course, I have a less direct notion of experience than León. For me, what matters is not the life lessons, but rather the memory left—in the future—by lived events.

For example, I could write a story about my experience of the trip to Mar del Plata to see my father in the hospital. The key is how the events of the journey anticipate—in the frightened gaze of the narrator—what is to come.

In that sense, it is clear that there's always a treasure hidden in each of us, which can guarantee the writing. The foundation is always the unknown, and the issue is how it passes from that dark place into the clarity of the prose.

I traveled late in the afternoon on Friday. Several stops during the night in desolate towns along the road. A woman got off with her hand luggage and listened to music that she played on a jukebox with cards changing in the case.

"Ideas that have first to be translated from their native language into a foreign language in order to circulate, in order to be exchangeable, constitute a slightly closer analogy; but the analogy here lies not in the language, but in their being in a foreign language," K. Marx.

Wednesday 17
Series E. I wake up alone at seven in the morning and go out to drink maté in the park. When I reread my spontaneous notes, I put these notebooks in crisis. I hope to adjust the tone, which frequently appears and frequently fades away. I want to maintain three or four levels in the prose: narration, reflections, irony, developments.

On Friday I saw David at Ramos, anxious, delirious because of the release of his novel. He concentrates all of his competitive ability into rivalry with Cortázar, as he did before with Sabato and before that with Walsh or Puig. Like me, he never uses his acquired momentum, the possible "certainties" acquired with his previous books, forgetting about them in favor of competitive composition. Rivalry is the key to his drive. We also talk about his work on Chacho Peñaloza, following Hernández and Sarmiento. I'm interested in his internal analyses, except for their political framing, in which I can clearly see his spontaneous tendency to schematically control a circuit with far too many levels, trying laboriously to synthesize them. He crosses Calle Montevideo to buy *Confirmado* magazine and shows me a short piece by Miguel Briante announcing his novel *Cosas concretas*.

I returned to Buenos Aires by train. An intermission in which everything is organized around consumption, a scene traced falsely from international travel, an attempt to depict the wide world in which attendants pass along the sleeping car, offering whiskey and champagne. In the middle of the night, we pass through Adrogué and Temperley, the settings of my childhood. In the dining car, I rediscover the past and classical myths. Sitting opposite me, a covert couple is traveling to a resort for a silent getaway. That unexpected proximity fosters sociability, the professional sympathy that can be found everywhere, something I've seen many writers cultivate with skill, seeming to be (or being) diplomats: Urondo, Fernández Moreno, Rodríguez Monegal.

In Mar del Plata, disorientation at first, my mother in the terminal, no one at home; Cuqui, my cousin, found out in the clinic that "a son of Sr. Renzi" had been there and thought someone was pretending to be me.

Thursday 18
A visit from Aunt Coca and Marcelo Maggi, the family myths. Marcelo took her out of a cabaret and imposed her on the family.

Series E. Setting aside recollections, writing as though I don't know how the stories will end (though I've lived through them). An absent writing, without memory: the model for these notebooks.

Friday
My mother establishes an ironic tension, an incessant and blind activity, and I've been fleeing from its fatal attraction my whole life. It is a kind of euphoric activism that leads me to passion and chaos. In the midst of that circle, to calm herself, my mother has been reading, for years, one novel every day (or nearly). Currently, the trilogy by Durrell.

My father's fears in the night when I was alone with him. My weeping (rather theatrical) when I saw him come out of the operation with the same pale face that I will see him wear in death.

Now the shrill voice on the television, the empty hours, the free time, the waiting. My mother comments on *Justine* by Durrell. "Love taken too seriously," she tells me. She is referring to the "artistic" excesses in the description of landscapes, which she dislikes.

Saturday 20
Rulfo's silence, fifteen years without publishing, is connected to his prose: restraint, rigorousness, short form, fragmentation. At the same time, Rulfo's silence is an aid to understanding his writing, allowing its true dimension to be seen.

Monday, December 22
I'm back in Buenos Aires again, writing in the semi-darkness that won't let in the sun, and I let myself go with this notebook, trying falsely to persevere in it. I walked around the motionless city at dawn, a newcomer knowing nothing, waiting for phone calls that will never come.

A terrible final night in Mar del Plata. An asthma attack, choking, terror that forced me to grab at the light and sit up in bed, as though I were about to die. Like a child, I had to sleep with the light on to shake off the ghosts and be able to breathe (the ghost of Hamlet's father, he always returns).

Late afternoon. A first walk around the city, euphoria at Tiempo Contemporáneo because they were chosen as the best publishers of the year. The Horace McCoy novel came out, volume 3 of the Serie Negra. *Cosas concretas* is selling well in its first week (four hundred copies).

Earlier a phone call from David: "Finally you came back, I missed you." The affection that he shows when he's in crisis. Now obsessed with *Último round* by Cortázar, his sole rival these days.

Tuesday 23
David called me at midnight because of a very negative review of his novel that came out in *Periscopio* (ex-*Primera Plana*). A frontal attack, according to him, from the right, a rejection of the "literature of ideas," etc. David refuses to come to my place so he won't have to face Julia and Beba, already forgetting that he himself is the only one to blame for all of that business.

Tired of my clever little pieces in the magazine, which I stop liking when I read them.

Series E. I wrote six notebooks like this one over the course of the year, and I doubt that more than twenty pages will survive, an index of failure, inadequacy, and loss. I know that literature is founded there, at least that is where the writing of this diary began for me. A true record of illusory events and promises (that I will not keep). My writing grows ever worse, unintelligible handwriting, caustic style, dry (I go around in circles, trying to find my personal style of writing). I hope that the only possible reading will be ideographic, viewed as hieroglyphics in which only the suggestive image of the words matters. The lines grow more frustrated, furious, ruining themselves and tracing the shapes of my soul . . .

A good critical response to the detective books in the Serie Negra. I insist, in vain, that we announce a hundred titles in order to maintain our advantage of novelty, before they start copying our concept in Spain.

Thursday 25
A party last night, lots of alcohol, in a country villa on the outskirts, we stayed there swimming in the pool until sunrise. Old Luna increases my salary to forty thousand pesos for my pieces in *El Mundo*, and then I see Toto, we're planning Issue 7 of the magazine, which I don't believe in.

The fundamental thing is to break through this feeling of vertigo, of being lost in a tide of incidents that I never manage to understand. What matters most remains outside tonight; I've thought about all of my past Christmases as though they were a single day.

Ismael Viñas shows a certain arrogant helplessness this morning, with his shirt open to make himself seem easygoing and free, asking when they'll pay him for his article in the magazine. I ran into David, having seen him through the window of La Paz while I was there with Oscar Steimberg. He seemed reclusive and very intelligent to me, and I thought that when I'm forty I'll cry just like he does, trying to process the very harsh reviews in *Confirmado* and other magazines, not really knowing what to do with his future, absent, not breaching the topics of digression that I offer to him like someone holding out a hand to a castaway.

Tuesday, December 30
The whole journalistic world is caught in the delirium of assessing a decade. Even I: the "decade of the sixties" brought about a myriad of divisions. The politics of the left changed. Great freedom for seeking what each person wants. Argentine literature, with my generation, managed—after Borges—to enter into a direct relationship and become contemporary with literature in any other language. We cut away the feeling of always being out of sync, behind, out of place. Today, any of us can feel connected to Peter Handke or Thomas Pynchon, that is, we have managed to become the contemporaries of our contemporaries.

Wednesday, December 31

Some facts about "maturity," which have been accumulating over the course of my life, allow me to predict a future in which some signs will be repeated, to the point that my reactions seem to be the movements of a stranger. In any case, even though I haven't finished anything that I can really feel satisfied about, I've learned to live in multiple series, like parallel lives, without worrying about how they are superimposed. I imagine that my prose is the only place where all of these paths cross. For me, the key is to think in opposition, to struggle and to live against the current. That's why I've always thought of myself as being five years behind. But with respect to what level, age, or established norm?

Confidence in my "talent" has marked all of these years, which explains the way I've worked, brilliant nights followed by long empty stretches. So far, the results have halfway confirmed my prediction. I want to change my life just as everyone does, but in my case that pretense means changing the way I write. Being more systematic and tenacious, less "inspired" and sudden. I seek a continuous brilliance, persevering in a story that lasts as long as the time I take to write it.

3

Diary 1970

Monday, March 30
Last night a meeting at home with Julia, Josefina, Nicolás, Toto, and Germán to discuss the book *Crítica y significación* by Nicolás Rosa. Oscar Masotta and a troupe—Luis G., Osvaldo L., and Oscar S.—made an unexpected appearance. Masotta went to work like a psychoanalyst and unleashed—helped to unleash—chaos, narcissism, and competitiveness. He accused Nicolás of copying his style from him and Sebreli, when in reality all three of them are translating Sartre. Then he confronted Nicolás as though the two of them were enacting the conflict between Lacan and Sartre. We fight to the death to defend these translations as our own.

Schmucler had planned two committee meetings for *Los Libros* magazine to discuss Nicolás Rosa's book and use a transcription of the debate as the bibliographic note.

A blank night, going in circles around the bars of the city with Germán García, who is somewhere between insane and abandoned, the same as me.

Thursday
X Series. Yesterday the "sudden" (as always) incursion of Roberto C., his cautious and docile air, a kind of calm that makes me nervous and sparks moralistic introspection within me.

Friday, April 10

All afternoon in La Plata in the old hall of the University Library in Plaza Rocha, as always, the same broken clock and students from Peru who sleep with their books open.

A scrap of paper and some pencil marks in a book that I read more than ten years ago, as if they were the faint traces of acts that have now been lost.

Places evoked memories as I entered the city; in this sense, a return is nothing more than a memory, one documents the distance and the difference compared with the city in which one lived, and each place shows the absence of the emotion preserved in memory.

Taking note of all the books displayed in the windows of various bookshops in Buenos Aires—seeing the genres, the authors, the nationalities, the ages, looking at what is repeated and what is differentiated—would be a way to evaluate the state of literature in the city.

Let's review: ten years ago (April 1960) I was in this same library, which I came to by crossing the diagonal avenue with blue flowers along the ground. What would I have said back then about a day like today? Or rather, what would I have said back then if I could have known what I would be now, sitting here in the same place?

Saturday

In Jorge Álvarez with David, his moustache growing bushier as though the face he always had were being drawn again. He bought gel and shaved in the little bathroom behind the bookshop, every now and then sticking his head out to argue with Germán, who was trying to defend Masotta from his combined attack: "He is a simple translator."

Artificial Respiration. I determined two things (while crossing Calle Sarmiento to buy tea) as a synthesis to respond to Celina Lacay's report for *El Día* of La Plata. It's the story of a homicide that a man commits against himself because of a woman. Two: it's a detective novel in which the narrator, the murderer, and the victim are the same person.

Sunday 12
I go around through secondhand bookshops, walk among shelves where the most outlandish books are mixed together, where literature acquires a particular coherence and shows the dislocation that it's subjected to: Bataille coexists with Bellamy, Bellow: the real order is visible, which is not that of Bataille beside Bachelard or Barthes.

Monday 13
Last night at home with Beatriz Guido and Torre Nilsson, drinking French wine with homemade empanadas and Gruyère cheese, and she was calmer for being with him. Bapsy had lain down in the leather armchair, suffering from a painful hernia. The essence of the night was confusion and surprise, somewhere between irony and "innocence," because of the fact that the film *The Knight of the Sword* has made a profit of two hundred million pesos in its first two weeks. Based on that, we revive the Fitzgeraldian world of excess. Burning through money in the Mar del Plata casino, buying a house with a pool in Punta del Este, and, at the same time, there is the underlying attraction of the young, talented, poor writer of the left with so much ahead of him. Then the exchange of information about Jorge Álvarez's self-destructive decadence. Beatriz shows interest in having me read her newly finished novel and two new stories by T. N. or, as Julia thinks, it's an attempt to offer me a position in the distribution and publishing house that Bapsy plans to start based on the structure of Contracampo. Unknown quantities that time will dispel.

On the bus a woman was saying to another in a low voice: "So she says to her mother: 'Mamá, I want you to wash me.' 'No, *hija*, no, they're going to operate on you.' 'No, Mamá, they won't operate because I'm going to die. I want you to wash me and call the priest so I can leave my body and soul clean.' She said that several times and then fell asleep: 'What a dream I had, Mamá, if only you could see what a dream, I can't describe it.' She left carrying that secret."

April 15
I spend the day at home, half of the afternoon in bed with Julia, and the evening reading Trotsky. In the middle, a conversation with Schmucler about Issue 8 of *Los Libros* magazine. The prospect of opening with a polemic based on David's article about the new generation. If that works, I'm thinking of saying that David talks about us because he's obsessed with Cortázar. At noon, I find David himself in Ramos, desperate due to his lack of money: a striking relationship between his writing and money. All of his novels are "finished" by economic deadlines.

Thursday 16
Spent the afternoon with Toto, who loaned me his tape recorder and spent an hour showing me how to use it. Finally he said goodbye, because he's going to Chile to gain the patronage of the university publishing house for the magazine. Then Ismael came, and I spent an hour with him recording the history of his life. Before leaving, I recaptured his ironic and intelligent conversation and his excellent characterizations of León and David. Now I'm waiting for Juana Bignozzi, who is going to bring money for Andrés, and it annoys me because I have a lot to get done.

Sunday
David just came over with the same destitution he has every Sunday, alone in the empty afternoon: as always, he is intelligent in understanding my reclamation of the concrete historical against the structuralists' abstract and unrestrained consumption. Then, his anguished greed when faced with the two hundred million that Tore Nilsson made.

Monday 20
Dream. Julia is about to give birth to my child, and I sit waiting in the hallway of the hospital, uncertain because I don't know what name to choose, having doubts, and my imagination is closed off. I think: "Why

did I leave this until the last minute." I go over boys' names, Luciano, Horacio, and rule out each one. Suddenly I find the name: Juan. I think Juan Renzi, I like it, but immediately I remember that it's Juan Gelman's name, and I'm estranged from him. At the same time, I'm secretly sure that it will be a girl, and I have two names to choose between: Greta or Pola. That calms me down.

Nicolás just called from Rosario: deep down, he seems slightly withdrawn. I've never gone to visit him, haven't written him the letter that I promised (the truth is that, secretly, I've always been bothered by his way of installing himself in my house every time he comes to Buenos Aires).

Yesterday a walk around the empty Sunday city with hundreds of teenagers walking arm in arm, and, after confirming in the display window of Galerna bookshop that the books from Mexico had come (Lowry, Pacheco, José Agustín), such an anxiety was unleashed that I still haven't recovered from it even now, as I write this. Julia opens the door with Lowry's *Panama*, translated by Elizondo, and tells me that Polo "stashed" the books by José Emilio Pacheco and Agustín that I'm going to look for this afternoon.

Tuesday
A heavy atmosphere, a mixture of the heat, my three-day stubble, the humidity, the exhaustion, my mute fight last night with Julia; before she went to the College she made excuses about why I shouldn't see Germán, who just called, even though I didn't have the slightest intention of meeting him.

Earlier I saw David, who's in his depressive and penniless phase; then Pancho Aricó, from the Signos publishing house, where they keep getting letters about publishing the nouvelles from the series with Onetti, Sartre, Beckett. In the midst of that, Andrés Rivera read a chapter of my novel with a careful eye, interested in the tone and the irony. I picked up Pacheco's poems and José Agustín's autobiography from Galerna and read them in one shot, together, before midnight, with great intensity.

Wednesday
All of us originate from Roberto Arlt: the first one who manages to connect him to Borges will have triumphed.

At night I talk with Carlos B., who grasps onto me to stop from sinking into delirium: fear of death after a nocturnal phone call predicting that he had the same congenital defect (of the liver) that killed his brother.

Thursday
Dinner with Jacoby last night, many different plans and projects. *Sobre* magazine and the cartoons about the illustrators' strike. At noon today I had lunch with León at the publishing house; he's reading Freud as though it were a dream of his own. Now it is three in the afternoon, and I'm dying of heat in this prolonged and humid summer, reading Scott Fitzgerald with excitement. I come back to his line: "There are no second acts in American lives," as if American writers were condemned to always be immature because they refuse to cultivate their natural talent, and their best writing is always in their first books (see Hemingway, Faulkner, Salinger).

Fitzgerald has such a natural grace that it seems calculated.

I should analyze my relationship to illusion as the creator of a desired reality. Just now, Rozenmacher asked me for information about American literature. I think: that guy is trying to flatter me. I've already told Julia about it. I think: she was at the magazine and heard the conversation; she confirmed that it was true.

Twofold hesitation: the unreal quality of the desires I've achieved and, at the same time, illusion as the realization of those desires. I should trace my relationship with literature here, as well as certain verbal anticipations of desires that are achieved because I need it.

Friday
A strange nostalgia this morning as I crossed the street to go to the market and buy milk and bread. The humidity and heat against the dark light of dawn, tired working girls returning to their homes, garbage cans lined up on the sidewalks one after another: deep within, a memory surfaces of other early mornings in the "pauses" before the action began. Dead time that always leaves its mark.

David called at noon and then stopped by here at two in the afternoon, and we spent a while dreaming up collections of writings by travelers who have passed through Latin America, "which would allow us to live for two or three years." Then I stopped by the publishing house and went to have a coffee with Rodolfo Walsh, who's going to Cuba for the jury on the new testimonial genre. We talk about the relationship between nonfiction and the novel.

Saturday
Series E. Everything had become so dark that he could have committed suicide that morning. Bound to the personal notebooks in which he hopelessly attested to what he had lost. As if he had already lived the best part of his life and only the void remained.

Sunday
Notes on Tolstoy (10). His wife, Sophia, hardly more than a girl when they married, let herself be molded according to the writer's desires, providing him with ample collaboration not only in his private life, but also in his literary work. His wife is materialistic and practical, in the style of Brecht's Mother Courage. A feminist, Sophia sets herself against her family and children. Faced with Tolstoy's ambition to become Christ, she responds: "It is not possible to save all of mankind, but you can feed a child and teach it to read. It is impossible to feed the thousands of starving human beings in Samara, the same as all poor populations. But if you yourself see or know a man or woman who has no bread, no cow, no horse, no cottage, then you must provide them immediately." She sees

him as someone who "was in Yasnaya Polyana to play Robinson Crusoe." And she adds: "If a fortunate and happy man suddenly starts to see only the bad side of life and closes his eyes to the good, he must be ill. You must get better. I say this with no ulterior motive. It seems true to me. I experience great pain because of you, and if you reflect on my words without resentment, maybe you will find a remedy for your situation. You started suffering long ago. You used to say: 'I want to commit suicide because I cannot believe.' Why then are you so wretched, now that you have faith? Did you never happen to notice before that there were sick, unhappy, perverse people in the world?" She also thinks about another moment when he fled: "If he does not return, it means he loves another woman." (The intense sexual attraction that bonds them.)

And it is she who fights for him to return to literature. "That is your salvation and happiness. That will unite us once more: it is your true work and will console you and illuminate our lives."

May 1
I remember the tradition of barbecues twenty years ago, when the whole family would get together to celebrate their continued existence (although they took advantage of the moment to retell the stories of the fallen). The trampled earth of the back patio at my grandparents' house with the cross grill driven into the ground. A confusing memory of Uncle Gustavo, a kind of conservative *caudillo*, to one side of me, listening to an argument? They were blaming him, I think; the curious thing is that I can see myself, I have an awareness of the place where I was and yet, at the same time, in that moment I'm someone watching the scene—as in a dream.

In the late afternoon David dropped in, with his habitual neuroses around the holidays, reciting his renewed fury against Cortázar, which this time came from an uncomfortable magazine cover on *Atlántida* with a caricature of Cortázar holding a baby bottle and a cigarette, announcing statements from his mother (which seem like one of Cortázar's stories with his mixture of flamboyance and "refined" commentary). After that, David went on all night about his misfortunes: he doesn't know whether to continue with his novel about the urban guerrillas (in the style of a thriller in order to exorcise his latest "obsession"), or to put together a book about the anarchists. Pulled back and forth by his need for money and his desire to publish with Barral in Spain, he exaggerates his intelligence as a way to make excuses (like all of us). He feels alone, underestimated. He tilts at windmills that keep coming back, confusing the life of a writer with that of a boxer, always attentive to rankings, always in "the news." We ended up eating pizza and drinking coffee while watching the city, which had been deserted all day, as it began to fill with people.

Saturday, May 2
I woke up alone at seven in the morning, dying of cold, worried about money, there isn't even enough for us to go to the theater today because of the mess last night with David (fifteen hundred pesos). Those dismal thoughts helped get me out of bed and steered me to the letter I have to send today by Air France. I get dressed and turn around in pirouettes to close the blinds without waking Julia, who's going to sleep all day. With these lovely domestic thoughts, I go to the kitchen and prepare maté. In *La Nación* I find out about the American invasion of Cambodia, and I look at the schedule to see when we could see *Midnight Cowboy*. I sit down at the table here in the kitchen and start writing these notes while a sharp pain in my stomach comes and goes. Immediately I think it is an ulcer, connected to the regimen of amphetamines that I use to write at night. I don't like it and promise myself that I will change my system, start writing every day in the early morning "next week." The burning in my stomach pursues me. I want to make love, but once Julia wakes up after I make coffee, she will be hurt because of our fight last night, forgetting the real causes of the conflict, sure of her indignation and my egotistical mistakes. This is my new day, an exclusion due to a physiological intermission, I sit on the toilet and then get up and fill the bucket with water to flush away my remnants since the water system isn't running well, thanks to the porter's "fix" for the water loss that we've been dealing with for a week; I'm in the midst of a recurring primitive procedure, sitting down in the bathroom, the same as every morning (and thus repeating this ritual,

undervalued, no doubt, in contemporary literature). As I sat, I read an article about Philip Roth in *La Quinzaine* and decided to copy a fragment that weaves together literary analysis and psychoanalysis, which, back in the kitchen once again, I now copy: "The patient is at once the actor and the spectator in this dramatic game of which he is the author, under the offhand but attentive gaze of the psychoanalyst" (signed Naïm Kattan). My stomach burns, and in the future I may lie (like my father) in a hospital bed, terrified of the coming operation, certain of my death.

Pavese. The model for Pavese's lover must have been Juan from *The Seducer's Diary*: "I can imagine him able to bring a girl to the point where he was sure she would sacrifice all, but when matters had come that far he left off without the slightest advance having been made on his part" (S. Kierkegaard).

A story in Italy. I would like to find a mythical structure that could work as the basis for this *nouvelle*: I don't know if Pavese will work, of course he is too modern. Anyway, he is all I have, and in order to give it weight, the best thing will be to connect it to other modern "myths" (*The Seducer's Diary*, *Othello*?). In the story, I have to write Pavese as though he were a negative hero. What if the myth were the repetition and replication?

Sunday 3
At six in the morning, the center of the city is a strange mix of night owls, young people going to mass, gentlemen buying meringues with cream. In Ramos, where I get breakfast before going to bed, there's a group of actors or, at least, a noisy group, all false happiness and gesticulations, drinking beer, shouting back and forth. There's an older platinum blonde woman with them and they all celebrate her with speeches and toasts.

Monday 4
León R. came over on Saturday night, more intelligent than he is on other days due to the analysis of Freud that he started writing that afternoon, a work that has obsessed him for around three years. Carefully, I show him

that the texts he is working on (*Moses and Monotheism*; *Group Psychology and the Analysis of the Ego*; *Totem and Taboo*) don't seem like the most representative examples, but León doesn't hear me. What I like most about him is his savant-like obsessiveness, which leads him to persist again and again with an idea when you critique it, as though he thought you didn't understand him. I also like the way he makes a symptomatic analysis of Freud's writings, reading them as though in a dream.

Tuesday

Yesterday afternoon at Beatriz Guido's house; she is "suffering" because of her latest novel, in which, like other writers of her generation, she has discovered—after the success of *Hopscotch*—experimental literature. As in David Viñas's case, she remains bound to a type of imagination (journalistic) that doesn't match her formal intentions.

Yesterday I ran into Francisco H. at El Foro and he wrote me a check for fifteen thousand pesos to pay for a story of mine that he took without telling me for one of his anthologies; even though it seems unlikely, I earned thirty-five thousand pesos this month for my works of fiction. Anyway, I haven't resolved my economic problems with this. Today I'm going to Signos to get one hundred thousand pesos (for the collection of nouvelles) to pay off my debts.

Wednesday 6

Many visits, David, Ismael, Andrés, Nicolás on Friday, which have contributed to my feverish state (it's true, I have the flu). If I could take all the time I needed to finish the *nouvelle* that I'm writing, I would feel much better. But to do that I'd have to live alone, on an island or in a town in the country, without my friends, who are asking me to publish all the time. Without having to earn my living in that way, without people imposing a rhythm of work and problems to resolve, like Toto with *Los Libros* magazine, like Carlos B. with the script, like Nicolás with his visits, like León with his Freudian ideas: that is the only thing I have to learn to do.

Tuesday 12

Maybe in Joyce's story "Grace" and his altered allusion to Dante's inferno (a drunkard who *falls*, just as Tim Finnegan falls, drunk, down the staircase to the basement) one can see the germ of Lowry's *Under the Volcano*. Coming back to *Finnegans*, which I was reading until two in the morning today, Tuesday, May 12, after rising at eight to once again sit at the desk and go on reading this impossible book.

Finnegans Wake. Is it not about incest? Written in a language that echoes the maddened language of his daughter Lucia Joyce, that disjointed style, doesn't it disguise another initial myth? In any case, beyond any interpretation, one must remember that the entire novel, ultimately, narrates a drunkard's dream.

Wednesday 13

Concoctions, comings and goings: Roberto C., Manuel Puig, Nicolás Rosa, et al. Always the same exasperation. The will to become a stranger (to myself), to move in the world with another rhythm. I know now that I will never learn how, at least not in these dark times, lit only by the lamp with its white light, with no way to shut it off except for a complicated ceremony of kneeling on the floor, going under the desk and unplugging it, a tiring effort (clearly) so that I can sit alone in the dark.

As always, I seek refuge in books, brush off my problems (this month: the rent, my economic future) and enter some walled-off enclosures where I experience the forms of my own insanity: reading from five in the afternoon until two in the morning, then from eight in the morning until two in the afternoon, the same impossible book—*Finnegans Wake*—which I resume at five in the afternoon to continue until ten at night with annoying interruptions like breathing, getting some air, changing positions, so that, having read thirty pages in two days, having understood an average of thirty lines per hour, there's a point at which I have to go out into the street, browse through bookshops, and search for another volume that I can hide behind to stave off my apathy or desperation. I play hide-and-seek, a moral game if viewed from up close; I too am writing thick volumes, behind which some pessimistic or rather contemptible young people will be able to seek refuge in the future, people who will, after confirming the monotony of that solipsistic exercise of reading, be able to move from the chair to the table, senselessly, until finally they too will come to write thick volumes, behind which other young people will hide in the future, etc. I project, then, from a history of literature as a reconstruction of the positions of the body in the moment of writing, fixed forms that have been repeated since the beginning of time: someone sitting in the solitude of a room, moving through characters marked on a page. Let us not forget the beginning of this game: someone, designated by bad luck, faces the wall with a book in his hand and reads in silence until, months later, he too begins to write . . .

I have thought that, perhaps, one path to salvation for me would be to set everything aside and dedicate the next twenty years of my life to studying Sarmiento, for example, inside libraries, filling out notecards, consulting old editions, alone and friendless, in order to reach the end of my life with hundreds and hundreds of notes and cards, to finally compile an enormous volume of a thousand pages talking about Sarmiento—and only Sarmiento—or maybe about *Facundo*—and only *Facundo*—and in that way one would remain forever outside of life, so consumed with knowing another person's life that he would come to forget his own, and, in a moment of despondency, it would be enough for him to go back to the notecards to recover his happiness, and he could even look for moments of despondency in Sarmiento to find relief and comfort. Because it always comforts us to know that someone else has lived through the same sad vicissitudes that we privately think of as unique, different, individual and idiosyncratic. Isn't that happiness?

Artificial Respiration. A novel of the pure present, because that is my natural tense and that is the tense of this diary, no remembering, no thinking, just letting the future come. That is the logic of this notebook, in which I take notes according to the present moment, without narration.

Miguel Briante just called me on the phone, a long conversation about Rulfo, whom he's going to interview in Mexico.

As before with the short stories, and before that with the books I read, and before that with jazz musicians, and before that with soccer players and before that with comic series—I write lists. Shopping lists, to-do lists, lists of friends to see, lists of friends to call, lists of cities I haven't seen, lists of chapters for the novel that I'm going to write. Lists have always calmed me, as if I could forget the world by writing them and, in some cases, as if taking notes were the same as doing the things that I imagine or promise. Happy then, as if, by jotting down the chapters, I had already written the novel. (*Artificial Respiration*. Dedication: to Ramón T. and Roberto C., for what is to come.)

David came over, angry, nervous, anxious about his conflict or his fight with Daniel Divinsky, affectionate and forever disoriented: David went looking for money and Daniel answered him with some jokes and then David, confused, told him he wasn't there for jokes and said a series of other things that he's already forgotten. Don't worry, David, I told him, Daniel will be very happy to have a story to tell.

A significant presence of politics in Joyce, Parnell, the Irish hero, arguments in the family, always implicit and allusive. Very good control of the possible awareness of the characters, never saying anything that could signify some external knowledge that the protagonists would not possess.

Monday 18
When he loses control, he has the experience of madness. Everything collapses, he lives up in the air, in pure contingency, money problems, too much sleep, not enough time to do the things that accumulate day after day, he clings to isolated moments, like an inmate who leaves the asylum to take a walk around the block.

"I am afraid we are not rid of God because we still have faith in grammar," Nietzsche.

All day spent locked in, dying of cold because the heater doesn't work, a morning wasted, an afternoon going in circles.

Yesterday, a car trip through Olivos with the family. The neighborhoods cut off from the world among the plants and the river, the old abandoned station. My mother always dreams the same dream; every night she has to rebuild the same ruined house.

On Friday, dinner with León, David, and Beba. Prognoses about actions for the intellectuals to take, we plan a dictionary, several public actions, and David as always is obsessed with having an impact, polarized about Z. Then León, whom I always argue with (when David is present): he's thinking of setting up an analysis of a revolutionary against a bourgeois. I demanded a less simplified option.

Stuck in this house, I spend a long, lonely, freezing night, reading Joyce. "Artifice is that ability to make of one's mother tongue a foreign language."

León returned after midnight, wanting to discuss his article on nationalism: lucid, with good ideas about the "private" and the real, but perhaps too tied to the problem of the subject.

Wednesday
Yesterday at noon David came to have lunch, to ask for money, and to recount his concerns about the anarchists, whom he is studying. We went to La Paz at two in the afternoon and I ran into Palazzoli, who gave me his book about Peru. From there I went on alone in the rain as far as Viamonte to see Aníbal Ford and discuss David's article about the new generation, which he published in Cuba. He uses all of us (Puig, Germán García, Néstor Sánchez, and myself) to fight with Cortázar, saying that we're all influenced by his literature; in my case, that's ridiculous because

he knows full well that I have based myself on Hemingway. It bothers him that he doesn't have literary disciples. At Signos, they assured me that on Friday I'll get the eighty thousand pesos I need to buy a bed. Things are getting back on track; Andrés brought me sixty thousand pesos from Córdoba, and the guys from Tiempo Contemporáneo gave me my salary of fifty thousand pesos. They're very enthusiastic about my project with the magazine. We'll see. Possible issues: on Borges, on style, and on violence.

Call:
Toto (Gusmán),
De Brasi (Lukács),
Altamirano (Lefèvre, Mussolino),
China book,
Boccardo.

See:
Álvarez,
Willie.

David just brought me a heater, which raised me out of the arctic climate. I told him I was thinking of starting an argument over his article about us (Puig, Sánchez, García). According to him, Cortázar invented collage and the use of beggars. "*Querido*," I said to him, "my writing is based on Hemingway and Roberto Arlt; I hope you aren't offended."

Friday
Series C. Yesterday I walked through the city with Julia, beautiful with her short hair and the boots I gave her, surprised, as always when she receives something; she was confident in her own beauty, confirming it in the windows and mirrors of the city, but can also doubt it in moments of great conflagration, when everything has been lost, and the Shadow comes toward her for any number of reasons, like when the zipper on her boot got stuck and provoked her anger, or when a tiny little red spot

appeared on her skin, behind her left ear, which, according to her, is surely an incurable cancer! And then she cries until she's sprawled out, only to get up, go to the bathroom, and touch up her eyes, becoming beautiful again as she was in the early afternoon.

Sunday
At night, Rodolfo Walsh came to record a conversation that will precede his story "A Dark Day of Justice." Dialogue with him is difficult, he's too pragmatic for my taste. He shows a cautious abstention when faced with any abstract thought, but his journalistic reflections work very well, and he confirms his intelligence several times. Politics serves as a common ground for us and, at the same time, he too can clearly see the close relationship between nonfiction stories and persuasion. He derives his ideas about the novel, if I'm not mistaken, from two places: his difficulty in finishing his novel *Juan Was Going Down the River*, despite the fact that he had dedicated more than a year of work to it, supported by the salary from Jorge Álvarez; on the other hand, his suspicion of a Borgesian root behind any story of more than twenty pages and his absolute loyalty to a very precise prose, which makes "long-distance races" seem impossible to him.

Tuesday 26
To fall (like Cacho, like Malcolm X) on account of a clock, isn't it an omen?

A visit from Aníbal Ford, who gives off a dull tension, as if the two of us were giving each other little jabs to the liver between smiles. What is it on his side? An excess of references to himself, to things he has written or is writing, and a populism that logically results in anti-intellectualism, the division between some things that can be criticized and others that cannot. An overly thematic view about issues that he should work on more closely. The ideology of the artist circles beyond his poetics. The writer places himself in the center of the world, and everyone should read him, etc. I don't run those risks. I'm too proud and too sure of my value to beg for people to pay attention to me.

Wednesday 27
Carlos Altamirano brought an article for *Clarín* and stayed over for dinner, always sharing good ideas about literature and politics, aesthetic complexity: distance and discord between the writer and the reader, who are—or are not—connected based on experiences and cultures that are different, divergent, and often antagonistic.

Friday 29
Yesterday I got up early in the morning, sat down to write at noon, and by five in the afternoon I'd finished an acceptable version of chapter 5. Then I stayed in bed with Julia, reading, listening to music on our new radio, making love, until finally we went out for a walk around the city, bought the latest novel by J. H. Chase, drank peach nectar from tall glasses while sitting on the sidewalk of Calle Corrientes opposite posters announcing a new edition of *Uncle Tom's Cabin*, a very popular novel in the nineteenth century, of course, which was published in the same year as Melville's *Moby Dick*.

At midnight, León came over to discuss his article about nationalism, full of good ideas, very critical about the idea of symbolic and invisible units like the concept of a nation-state, and we ended up eating chitterlings in Pippo and talking about David, who finished his play *Lisandro*, talking about how wonderful it will be to work in peace, writing alone at night in an empty factory. Two good ideas from León: people on the left reproach the weakness of the revolutionary parties because they take the ideal of traditional parties as a comparative model; that is where—I would say—the seduction of Peronism comes from. That can be applied to any "entryism" that resolves the issue without deepening it, always looking uncritically for the positive moment of the traditional organization: its drawing power, its real proximity to powerful forces and groups, etc.

Déjà-vu: a feeling of having already lived through a situation, a way of altering experience and erasing the restlessness of the present, turning it into something already lived through and passed.

Today I slept until mid-morning, and when I was about to eat breakfast or had just finished breakfast, David came with the manuscript for *Lisandro*, the play that he wrote in five days, excited, harried by his need for money, sustaining himself on amphetamines. He read Lisandro's long monologue in front of Bordabehere's catafalque, accentuating the words, working himself up as he read with a civilized and even romantic emphasis, a kind of local Victor Hugo talking to ghosts. I still can't talk about the work, I like the idea of the chorus transformed into a variety of characters, but I see the development as overly simplified. I went out with him and we walked together to Corrientes, at which point I continued to Viamonte and visited Aníbal Ford, who gave me back a couple of books, and then I went to the publishing office but didn't find anyone there. At the Galerna bookshop I picked up the translation of Lukács's *History and Class Consciousness* and Freud's letters to his lover. I drank a coffee and ate a ham sandwich amid the apocalyptic chaos of the publishing house, creditors and labor lawsuits. At a table in the bar, I wrote a couple of notes about the kidnapping of Aramburu; I skimmed through Lukács's book looking for connections to his ideas from *The Theory of the Novel*. Afterward I visited Signos publishing, where I collected fifty thousand pesos for the collection, although I had to wait for the office boy, who brought me the check in the late afternoon.

Saturday, May 30

I've been working on a response to Altamirano's article for *Clarín* since ten in the morning. In the middle, David came over to have lunch at my place: he's broke. His immediate predicament is contagious; he's closed off in himself, smothered under the urgency of publishing, success, competition, etc. After going out to the street and drinking a coffee, I returned home and finished the article with a thirty-eight-word paragraph in response to the question, "What is literature for?"

It is ten at night, I want to read Doris Lessing, eat grilled provolone cheese, and go to bed with Julia without thinking about the days to come, the things I have to do, or the books I want to write.

Sunday
Mid-morning today, after patiently reading the Sunday papers, filled with turmoil because of the mysterious kidnapping of General Aramburu, I ran into Nicolás Casullo and rediscovered a natural relationship with him in terms of his politics and his very grounded vision of literature, uncommon among Argentine writers these days. I appreciate Casullo's determination to organize the intellectuals and to bind them to political work. At night, Altamirano came over and took the article. I ended the day listening to Radio Colonia; I too am intrigued by Aramburu's kidnapping, was it the Peronists or the security services?

Monday, June 1
I woke up very late and had lunch at four in the afternoon. David dropped by in the middle, going around looking for money, hoping to sell his play for the Signos collection. We discussed the matter of Aramburu with little success. I stopped by the publishing house to pick up an advance of twenty-two thousand pesos. At *Los Libros* magazine, I insisted on doing the issue about American literature, which I'm putting together. Finally I ran into Battista; he sold the first issue of *Nuevos Aires* (exhibitionism, prestigious signatures in no order). Ismael was waiting for me at home, tired, out of commission: we agreed that oratory is a disappearing literary genre (just as the novel will one day disappear).

Tuesday, June 2
A letter came from Onetti, responding to my questions about his story.

Wednesday, June 3
On Calle Carlos Pellegrini I come across an old woman screaming in the door of a luggage store. She was insulting them without pause: "People walk by on the sidewalk and these bastards grab them with a hook and use their skin to make the bags." The woman had a certain haughty dignity, buried in a horrible truth that she alone knew. She repeated the insults over and over again, once again describing how they hooked the men and women, pulling the skin off their backs to make bags.

Thursday 4
Thinking about Onetti: he works with isolated situations, with no past-tense, narrating from the present. The mosaic expands as though the writing had no axis. *A Brief Life* is a deliberate growth outward from a nucleus that was already present in *The Pit* with the story of a man who invented a life for himself.

Friday 5
X Series. An attack of the liver, too much wine last night. Rubén K. came at eleven, bringing his revolutionary stories: a Huracán fan stole an umbrella painted with the Racing colors: the police arrest him for disturbing the peace but immediately blame him for a murder and torture him, and he spends two years in prison. Everyone in the yard stares at him like he's an idiot. He goes up to the bars, calls for the policeman on guard, sticks out his arm and hits him. Sent to solitary confinement, he makes a shiv out of a steel strip from his bunk, and when he returns to the yard he fights the king of the hill and takes his place. In prison he meets a militant politician from the left and becomes a revolutionary. Now he's Rubén's clandestine partner in Córdoba. Then Menena came over, suffering a reaction from some illness I don't know, and we had lunch in a Chinese restaurant to combat the power outage that's affecting all of Buenos Aires.

Sunday
Of course Onetti has his flaws; they are flaws of his tradition, I would say, as with Arlt, who is "metaphysically" explicit; his characters suddenly devolve into desperate sentimentality, and they're always thinking about suicide or murder and don't love anyone except women lost in the past or adolescent girls. No doubt Cortázar saw that with clarity and tried to escape from those "depths," but sometimes he goes too far in the other direction and everything seems like a children's game (except in *Hopscotch*).

A meeting for the next magazine that I've planned for Tiempo Contemporáneo publishing: León R., David V., Eliseo Verón, Oscar

Braun, Eduardo Menéndez, and we're also thinking about Oscar Terán. A certain tension was circulating, especially at the beginning. For a while, Verón would only talk to me, and then there was an argument about Borges, about the character of the magazine and its relationship to politics: in the end, after two hours—with León trying to drag Verón into political argument that Eliseo, always abstentious and amiable, wouldn't get into—we had agreed to put together a first issue on violence, and we'll see about the others.

Monday, June 8
I got up at seven thirty, ready to continue with the chapter about Malito and the preparations for the robbery. I'm writing a twenty-five-page outline: from the preparations until the escape.

Coup d'état: Lanusse supplants Onganía, who resists. It was Toto who came to wake me with news of the army communiqué; everything is a result of the Cordobazo.

Wednesday
Many dreams last night: in one I was a prisoner, maybe of the civil police, in a house with friendly people whom my very presence endangered. Other dreams of empty streets and an old ice box that I used as a sarcophagus or a pencil case. My father, at the end of a sidewalk that cut up crossing the train tracks, and I, maybe to his right, looking at the sky so I could see his face and tell whether he was dead and why he was walking with a limp. I woke up at midnight, filled with rage against the world, I am as sharp as a knife, though not so in reality, certain—from the outset—of the quick workings of my intelligence.

"Whether the life is criminal or not, the decision is to encourage the psychopath in oneself, to explore that domain of experience where security is boredom and therefore sickness, and one exists in the present, in that enormous present which is without past or future, memory or planned intention, the life where a man must go until he is beat, where he must gamble with his energies through all those small or large crises of courage and unforeseen situations which beset his day, where he must be with it or doomed not to swing," Norman Mailer.

Friday
If I maintain my intention to read only in service of what I'm working on, then I almost completely stop reading. I prefer to try selecting the books for themselves, forgetting about what I'm writing.

David came over in the morning: both of us are broke, and we put together what little we have to eat at Bachín. David sermonizes about historical themes, wanting to write (for Signos) a novel with Urquiza's death. Two conclusions: he always writes for money, and his project is a homage to my story "Las actas del juicio," which—in my modest understanding—exhausted the subject in ten pages. At the publishing house I find Eduardo Menéndez, and we talk about the possible future magazine. Eduardo is a very lucid anthropologist, and the two of us are thinking about the possibility of using the magazine to conduct field work. Possible subjects: libraries and their audiences, militants of the left as a tribe, a register of feminism in Argentina (its history and its present state).

Saturday, June 13
After an unexpected encounter with Gustavo F.—who came to see me, full of adolescent expectations—we went to the theater to see *Stolen Kisses*, an excellent film by Truffaut. In the late afternoon Roberto Jacoby stopped by for a little while and ended up staying until one in the morning. Very imaginative plans to use comics in political propaganda, also ideas about the work of artists and the definition of actions, the design of publications, and the "format" of leftist positions.

Sunday 14
I'm reading Deleuze's excellent work on Sacher-Masoch, a brilliant synthesis: sadists create institutions, and masochists sign contracts. I'm also reading De Micheli's book on the avant-garde.

First with David, overly eager about the possible premiere of *Lisandro* at the Liceo theater, always agitated and dependent on success. Then Manuel Puig came over, calm and collected: he worked for three years on *Betrayed by Rita Hayworth*, "writing," as he smilingly told me, "every day, except one." He started his third novel in October of 1968, and so far he has written a hundred pages (eight chapters), only 20 percent of which is salvageable; he'll have to rewrite the rest. He turns down a proposal from the Stivel clan to write an original plot for TV, he turns down Ayala's proposal to write a script for a film of *Heartbreak Tango*. He's working on a novel, he says, based "on the Dantean space of the detective genre."

Series E. The diary: a "psychotic genre," a denial of reality, a drawbridge, and a last resort.

I keep working on a novel that, inwardly, I already consider a failure, and I describe it here so that something will remain of all these months of work: a hundred-page story based on the robbery of a bank truck in San Fernando. It centers around the confinement and persecution that the criminals are subjected to as they hold out in an apartment in Montevideo, besieged by the police. Written in classic third-person, it combines their situation of being trapped (they hold out all night and die at dawn after burning the money) with the biography of a hostage they capture as they enter the building. The whole novel respects the unity of time and place and is interwoven with the monologue of the man who has been captured (a Uruguayan soccer player).

Tuesday, June 16
At Corrientes and Montevideo, a casual meeting with David who "was thinking about you." We had a coffee at La Paz, he's obsessed with theater and the next premiere. Then conversations with Andrés about some friends, Maoist militants: they sell everything (their cars, their apartments) and give the money to the party, they make eighteen thousand pesos per month when they become professional. A meeting at

Nicolás Casullo's house at eight: Dal Masetto, Germán García, Carnevale, Alba, Plaza: a good disposition toward being tied to politics, distraction and snobbery, laborious possibilities for work that will have to be organized.

Wednesday

X Series. Celina tells me that Lucas T. was uncomfortable because he couldn't tell me about having seen my book published in Havana while he was doing military training in Cuba. Political secrecy conflicts with the affectionate spontaneity of friendship. Causing hatred, promoting indifference toward acquaintances in order to protect the secret of a covert life. They live two lives, and the visible one changes and turns gray because it exists in service of protecting the other life (going around armed, pursued by the army). I remember one afternoon when Lucas came to visit me because he was near my place and, when he sat down to have some tea, I saw, though he didn't realize it, the pistol that he wore in a shoulder holster.

Monday 22

I got in line to buy kerosene because the cold had come, and it's impossible to work without the heater. The frozen, gray city seemed enveloped by a tulle fabric. The woman in front of me was talking to a man in a suit with an imperious aspect (similar to Marcelo, my uncle): "A naughty little seamstress, a low-class nothing, I wouldn't think of going to her. I take advantage of it. It works for me. You should see them, four or five men a week, married men, the most. They're only eighteen and already look old. I'm thirty-four and look like a little girl next to them. Bad living eats them up (pause). By age thirty they've seen it all, they're worn out."

Yesterday I watched the World Cup match, Brazil 4 – Italy 1, in Mexico. Six hundred million viewers on TV. Pelé and Gerson's talent. The Italians, violent, mediocre, caught off guard by the Brazilian players' "natural ability," rendering the Italians' effort and sacrifice to contend with them absurd.

Tuesday, June 23
I think I've given up on the magazine project for the publishing house, a poor meeting last night at Eliseo Verón's house. León disagreed violently with Eliseo, who opposes the magazine due to a "lack of common motivation." He added: "We can't go putting together articles just to make a sack of potatoes" (my own position previously). I said that making a magazine went beyond our "desires," it had to do with responsibility. Eliseo answered that this was political paternalism. León stayed silent. I reproached him when he left. Hard to bring a group together.

Wednesday
Notes on Tolstoy (11). *A Sportsman's Sketches* by Turgenev and *The House of the Dead* by Dostoevsky are his favorite books. He turns away from the novel. "It was probable that, as a result of these two works, a new literary form would evolve which would leave the novelist free from the usual necessity of devising a formal plot." The future of writing will not depend on the imaginary construction of a map of events, but rather a combination of autobiography, observation, and reflection.

Thursday, June 25
I ran into Manuel Puig, who mentioned his work on *Heartbreak Tango* to me: he had to work for six hours to finish half a page. From there to *Los Libros* magazine, commenting on the meeting last night at Eliseo's house. And then I gave the script to B., though I don't like it very much.

At 4:00 p.m. a call came from the Rodríguez bookshop; I went all the way across city, avoiding the corner where Pedemonte restaurant is, and came back with Ellmann's *Joyce*, eight hundred pages, and I've already read a hundred.

Friday 26
I sit down to read Ellmann's book on Joyce, trying to forget everything I have to do.

Saturday, June 27
A tribute to Emilio Jáuregui in Recoleta: we walked around among the graves, assembled, and took off running, pursued by the police. Outside, ochre explosions of fire from Molotov cocktails, the dull noise of tear gas bombs, a car tire starting to burn. The tearful faces of people walking through the empty streets with a seditious air, avoiding the police.

Monday 29
Marechal died (on Friday?), but he managed to finish his novel. According to David, no one was there. And when I die?

Let's take a look at today's itinerary: I wake up, startled as always by the open window that lets in light through the glass; it always seems like a neighbor from the upper floors is spying on me through it. I get up despite my fatigue and cross the freezing house, wrapped up in my old gray overcoat, and pick up the paper, a letter from my parents, and the magazine *Actual* with the article on Puig that I wrote two years ago. I try not to look at or read the letter because I can foresee what I'll find in it. I sit down to write at ten in the morning and "forget" about my afternoon appointments (Cozarinsky at two, Lafforgue at three). I work well until five and then go out to get kerosene at the old garage where I used to go in 1966 (when I lived on Riobamba and Paraguay). I walk through the old neighborhoods without nostalgia, thinking about what I would have said four years ago about a day like today. But they no longer sell kerosene there, so I end up walking all the way around the city, stubbornly, with my empty twenty-liter can, and end up on Lavalle and Jean Jaurès, finally taking a taxi back an hour later with the fifteen liters of fuel I need to warm up. I leave the fuel and go out again, stopping by Premier bookshop to get Camus's *Notebooks*, talking on the phone with China Ludmer (about her piece on *Heartbreak Tango*). Nicolás Casullo calls me about the meeting of young writers planned for Thursday night at nine o'clock at 1560 Gallo, and I sit down to write these notes before I resume reading the book about Joyce until midnight, when Julia will come, bringing the passion I need.

Tuesday, June 30
David dropped by at noon, as he always does when he's broke, inviting himself over to eat. He's engaged in a delirious project: he has to write three hundred pages per month to fill the seven volumes on Argentine literature that he sold to Siglo XXI for seven hundred thousand pesos, which he already received. In reality all he sold them was the index, which David usually comes up with euphorically in ten minutes: according to him, the book will be called *De Sarmiento a Cortázar*, and I don't expect he'll leave anyone unscathed. Then I went to Abril publishing to meet with Cozarisnky, the manager of the magazine's film section, who seems more intelligent every time I see him. There I ran into Osvaldo Tcherkaski, and, in the editorial office, everything was revolving around the insubordinate policeman in Rosario who occupied the headquarters demanding a raise. I found the notes I was looking for about Larry, the Chinese bartender who was murdered in Bajo (Issue 143 of *Siete Días*), and then I let go with Lafforgue, Rozenmacher, and José Speroni, a Trotskyist worker who worked with me at the *Revista de la Liberación* in 1963 and these days writes columns about himself. Editing as cynical theater: skepticism, frivolity, and coarse humor.

The Chinese bartender will be the person whom Almada kills in the detective story I'm working on; I'm going to connect the crime to the deranged woman I saw a while ago who was raving in the door of a luggage store. She will be the witness to the crime.

Wednesday, July 1
Series E. I am always confronting false dilemmas and symbols or signs and signals that justify inaction. Today I took a piece to the newspaper and then went around the English bookshops on Florida to buy the notebook I'm now writing in, here in a religious bookshop on Viamonte, where I once bought another, one afternoon in '65, having just arrived in the city, and started it, sitting in the Florida bar . . . Ridiculous rituals that mysteriously accompany life.

Julia and I had lunch at Pippo and then went out into the cold of the city. I stopped by Signos, where Aricó gave me the recording of my feature on Walsh. At *Los Libros*, Toto and I made progress on putting together an issue about American literature. I brought Updike's story collection *The Same Door*, with includes the story about a deceased champion that was the initial seed for *Rabbit, Run*. The character is there, the family, a certain squalor that adds to nostalgia for the "paradise lost" of adolescence. I want to work on stories that were the initial seeds for novels; there are several short stories by Faulkner and a couple of stories by Hemingway, and they could be used as examples of the germ of a narrative.

Suddenly I remembered Joyce writing *Finnegans*, with all of his friends trying to dissuade him so he wouldn't squander his talent with those incomprehensible obscurities. "I might easily have written this story in the traditional manner. Every novelist knows the recipe. It is not very difficult to follow a simple, chronological scheme, which the critics will understand. But I, after all, am trying to tell the story in a new way. Only I am trying to build many planes of narrative with a single aesthetic purpose . . . did you ever read Laurence Sterne?" Joyce says something along these lines in a letter to one of his friends. Chased by his debts and economic difficulties, Joyce got Miss Weaver to finance his book and continued writing it, although she quickly tried to dissuade him because she didn't understand it. We could call that a writer's drive.

A Montonero commando group occupies La Calera in Córdoba (military zone). They take over the police station, the post office, the city hall, the telephone exchange, and the bank (from which they took ten million). They communicate among themselves by radio. They force the police to sing the "Peronist March." They escape in a car, a Fiat, it won't start, so they steal another car and are pursued. They stop the car, there's gunfire and two casualties. Luis Losada smiles at the photographers, argues with the policemen who curse and kick at him. That night, forced entry. Gunfire. Several women. Two serious injuries. The army occupies the area. The colonel in command of the operation is the same one who suppressed the situation in Córdoba in 1969. (Narrate those incidents starting with him . . .)

Friday, July 3

He invents dreams of the future for himself and in their place has catastrophic landscapes. Better to forget.

I spent the afternoon at Abril publishing, where many magazines are produced, and had lunch with Tcherkaski, who works at *Siete Días*, at a restaurant in Bajo where the waiters were obsequious and welcomed him jubilantly. He gave me an interesting story to read, a sort of inferno with an ex-communist and a Polish worker in a foundry. Then long Faulknerian stories that he'd gathered in Buenos Aires: Wassermann, the owner of San Blas island, who made the police stop the traffic when he got off the *boîte*; the nineteenth-century player piano which played "The Internationale"; the French millionaire who came to nothing and got drunk on whiskey every day, alone; the old market with the story of two *guapos* who talked and then left together and were lost forever.

Saturday 4

At noon I meet Schmucler in the empty footpaths of Retiro while waiting for Nicolás Rosa. From that moment a cavalcade began: successive discussions, lunches, dinners, visits (China, Jacoby, David); sociability and friends make life possible, but I've always preferred to be alone.

Monday, July 6

I rose at seven and got in line in the fog to buy what I need to make the heater run. When I stopped working and lay down to rest a while at five in the afternoon, I thought about how, paradoxically, writing is an experience that erases all others, so that I have the feeling of an uneventful day. The most striking thing was that I discovered the ending for the story I'm writing. Rather, I thought about how there would come an afternoon—or morning—when I would see a binder containing the finished novel.

Tuesday 7
Today at Lorraine I saw Strick's film adaptation of Joyce's *Ulysses*. With the plot laid bare, the weight of the novel's prose is clearly visible. The events become blurred, ill-defined; the film is centered around Circe, that is, at the end with Molly Bloom.

Wednesday 8
In the afternoon I stopped by Jorge Álvarez; the publishing house is going downhill. Germán and David take one hundred thousand pesos worth of books, trying to stop Germán's eviction; on top of that, his wife is eight months pregnant, and we're all taking up a collection for her.

Thursday, July 9
A tenacious nightmare, with several horrible plotlines. I was coming back home, unable to find my way, and I met Kafka at a kiosk. Even in dreams I keep going in circles around literature. An indescribable relief when I woke up.

Saturday 11
Soot-black my heart (he had dreamt that phrase a few days before). Plummeting toward the deepest underworld, he wonders where a pursued man can flee.

Sunday 12
Series E. Copying a page of my notebooks from ten years ago every day, always keeping that distance, never letting it advance to the present, so that in ten years I can write a page about this page.

Literary history is always a prison sentence for one who writes in the present; in it, all books are finished and function like monuments, placed in an order as someone might walk through a plaza at night. A "true" literary history should be made for the books that have never been finished, failed works, the unpublished: that would be a way to find the truest atmosphere of an epoch and a culture.

Artificial Respiration. In what I'm writing, I would like to elevate this project, which I don't talk about, even here. For now, I keep going with the story about the deadly violence of the men trapped in Montevideo, and sometimes the story develops through dialogue alone.

Monday 13

I walk around the city, moving distractedly, and pass by the house of Aramburu, who was recently kidnapped, with photographers, police, onlookers. At night with Andrés and Carlos, their gangster stories in a new style: wearing trench coats to assault hotels, gunfire with the police, ambiguous graffiti on the walls.

Tuesday 14

I woke up at midnight thinking it was six in the morning and got up to record the story of the failed kidnapping of a notary who had acted in the Vallese case. The voice of that man recounting how he had managed to escape through the window of the apartment next door; I didn't quite know where I was.

I got in line with disappointed older women who live in misery, wanting, like me, to feed the fires in their freezing homes. I spent my last three hundred pesos on kerosene, and now I'm going to sit down and write in a lukewarm room with no money.

I've always rejected the opposition between feelings and ideas because that is the classic mode of thought held by the anti-intellectuals who abound in the cultural world. Everything that is considered external to literature seems to me to be the only interesting material: intellectual dramas, dead time, arguments, etc. Writing must be sustained on the things that everyone leaves out of a story. Showing, on the one hand, the absurdity and the rhetoric of narrative in the strictest sense and the "well-crafted" story and, conversely, strengthening the impact that can be achieved with materials considered "cold" and anti-sentimental. In that way, the narrative world opens to areas usually classified as outside of the story. That's what Joyce and Puig have done.

Desolation when I stopped by the Jorge Álvarez bookshop and saw the empty shelves, no one—except for Marita, the forty-year-old virgin with her face white as though powdered—no one in the place, the lights shut off. I remembered that afternoon in '63 when I discovered the bookshop and stopped in front of the display window, facing the newly published books.

Wednesday 15
A walk with Julia around the College of Philosophy, now located in the old neighborhood on Calle Independencia, transformed by the frivolous and intellectual presence of the students who gather in bars and pizzerias around the area.

Thursday 16
I write to Onetti, imagining the letter I'll send him when *Artificial Respiration* has been published. It makes me happy to know that this novel has made it into his hands because I know well how much of it is owed to his books.

Saturday, July 18
Through the wall of the house next door comes the voice of a TV presenter narrating Aramburu's funeral. That is how the news of history must come.

As always, I feel distant from the writers of my generation, as though I were living in a time prior to theirs. I think about this while writing the essay on contemporary American narrative for the magazine. I see the most advanced work coming from writers who have set aside their confidence in literature.

"Sense of inner opposition to friends and enemies; no desire to be either here or anywhere else while still complaining of being rejected both here and everywhere else," R. Musil, *Diaries*, 1939.

"The story of this novel amounts to this, that the story that ought to be told in it, is not told," Musil II.

In Joyce, I'm interested in the change of technique with each chapter, as well as the form; in Borges, the rupturing of genre, the scattered and persistent use of the detective; the treacherous use of the conventions of reading.

Tuesday 21
All day yesterday in La Plata, Calle 7 in the sun, the trees beginning to flower, the places from my childhood. Perhaps, then, this crisis is the beginning of a repetition in which the awareness of my "lost past," nostalgia for myself ten years ago in the same place, was bursting with grand ambitions, founded on the future tense.

All modern novels (since surrealism) tend toward poetry; see Cortázar, Néstor Sánchez, Sarduy, Saer. For my part, like Macedonio or Musil, I see the path toward renovation in the essay; that is, I aspire to an approach that coheres several styles, articulated in a novelistic manner, even if they don't come from narrative forms.

At his house, David did a reading of *Lisandro*, his play, in front of Cossa, Rozenmacher, Talesnik, Halac, Somigliana. Very good, written in five days, great verbal register and technique, excellent control of tension. The device of the chorus gives it a great freedom and synthesis. A declaratory theater, tied to the current situation, very demagogic and dramatic.

Wednesday 22
I come and go through the Bajo area, down Calle Florida, down Viamonte, and stop at the Biblioteca Lincoln to take notes for my essay on American narrative. Yesterday was the end of Jorge Álvarez publishing; the legal team shut down the bookshop. The same as the feeling I had when I went to Elena's house and she no longer lived there. The house was abandoned, and I thought about all of the feelings I had left inside it.

Friday 24
Andrés has a theory that Guevara tried to incite an American invasion in Bolivia and thereby start a new Vietnam. It could be. The curious thing, for me, is that the Cubans didn't rescue him alive.

At the publishing office, I receive several books of American narrative: Pynchon, Barth, Barthelme, Vonnegut. At Signos with Toto and Pancho Aricó, news about Borges's divorce (?). It seems he left without saying goodbye, helped by his lawyer.

Saturday, July 25
I'm interested in the microscopic plots that proliferate in the novel (the same as in this diary).

Personal translations of miniature stories. "The lover doth polish the face of his beloved until he produces a skull," John Updike.

"I came down the stairs with my usual innocence and pain right smack into her silence which is the sign that she has a weapon," J. P. Donleavy.

X Series. At night with Roberto C.; he's spending his vacation with us. He came yesterday, along with his beautiful wife, the heiress to a famous restaurant in the city. Anyway, he's doing well despite the suspicions (?) that he inspires in me. Revolutionaries are simple men who conceal shady actions, in the face of which we all feel, in some sense, intimidated. He went into the room next door and left the pistol and leather shoulder holster that he wore under his overcoat in there. Throughout the conversation, without any mention of the weapon, the words seemed charged with a dark weight.

Sunday 26
First outline of the American novel. William Burroughs, technical hell. Comic delirium, LeRoi Jones. Revolution and violence, the Black Panthers.

We went out to dinner and stopped to find David. Tension about seeing his daughter (from his first marriage?), who doesn't seem right in the head, and there was also an elderly, "long-suffering" woman present, who was missing her front teeth (it was his ex-wife). In the restaurant we made ideas spin, happily, at top speed. David was raving about a magazine (another one): monthly, not many pages, provocatory. Not a bad idea, a magazine that circulates from hand to hand like a pamphlet.

Tuesday 28

It is early morning, I spent the infinite night working with several books at the same time, like that night in 1964 in La Plata, in an attic, writing about Goodis and Jim Thompson.

Wednesday 29

Insomnia last night, as in my best times. It's rare for me, it comes every now and then and, since it isn't frequent, I have a feeling of being sick, delusional, my eyes open, one of the living dead, breathing and trying to sleep.

Lucas T. at Jacoby's house. Roberto always very lucid, he shook people up at the Di Tella, proposed the dematerialization of art and also an artistic use of the media. Now he looks at political revolution through his artist's eyes. He critiques the left's tendency to see the State's information services as being behind any political event that they can't—or don't want to—undertake. Aramburu's death, for example. The night show, Sabina (?), the woman whose mother is a judge who spoke without parentheses, with histrionic determination, maybe so as to hide her beauty, deliberately degraded by her "display."

Thursday 30

I get up after noon and accompany Julia to Congreso, she's going to La Plata. On the way back, I ran into Osvaldo L., he spends eight hours selling books for a salary of forty thousand pesos. He complains ironically and always seems to be the only artist in the area and therefore the only one who needs economic advice and help.

Friday 31
It is five in the morning; I write little and read poorly, sustaining myself on infinite circles, turning over pieces of paper where I write down lost ideas. The heater warms the room, and Julia sleeps in the room next door while I, unable to sleep, pace from side to side in this room, passing two hours.

Saturday, August 1
Series E. I dreamed that the notebooks in which I write day after day were finished; I had just turned thirty, which coincided with "the beginning of the dictatorship," that of age thirty, I guess. Sitting in a bookshop, I was waiting for someone, who looked very much like Portantiero, to finish convincing the salesman to give him one of the rubber-covered notebooks. The salesman refused. I think I had the thought: "If he manages to convince him then I've lost, he won't want to give in again."

I distance myself from the narrative tradition of the young writers "of my generation," seeking a type of story that is at once more deliberate and more violent.

Sunday, August 2
At four in the morning I made some passes at the art of the essay and at noon David stopped by; we went out to walk around the city, and I (affectionately) disagreed with the way he tackles the entire history of Argentine literature with excessive certainty. Historical thought that only historicizes a confusing assemblage of relationships, attributing a single meaning to them. When I returned, as a result of that conversation, I euphorically wrote a brief panorama of contemporary American narrative (1960–1970) in a couple of hours.

Monday
Reading the weekly papers reveals a schematic coherence, created for cultural consumption. With three or four items or names, they also summarize what they call "the present," the now, what emerges from within the ephemerality of cultural circulation.

What things would have changed if I'd lost my typewriter in 1966? "Mata-Hari 55," maybe the whole book. I'd taken it to get cleaned when robbers broke into my room in the hotel on Calle Riobamba, stealing a suit and Cacho's leather jacket. They didn't find the typewriter, which was exactly what they'd come looking for.

As always, the immanence of working all night immediately provokes a feeling of joy within me. The darkness is a parenthesis, and reality lies waiting until the next morning.

Wednesday 5
I visit David this afternoon; he's in a bad mood because the essay he's writing "isn't working," but it seems to me that he's trying to move on to Latin American literature and is confronting the difficulty of working with his method of drastic synthesis. Basically, it's because he doesn't know that culture or those writers in the way that he thinks he knows—and certainly does know—the Argentine tradition. David does a kind of micro, close reading, that is, he reads a few pages or dedications, or sometimes even a few book titles, and on that basis, he builds up theories that approach the context.

Thursday, August 6
This afternoon Rubén K. came over, proposing that I take part in the editing committee for *Cuadernos Rojos*, where I would be in charge of special issues. He's very interested in my theories about new nonfiction literature, the Soviets' *literatura fakta*, the possibility of recording the life stories of people usually outside of written culture. It's a way to keep myself close to politics without getting too involved, working based on what I know or am familiar with.

I never let politics have a direct impact on what I write. I collaborate with my friends on magazines and newspapers. I keep literature separate. I try to convince them to leave fictional prose in peace, instead using testimony and the tape recorder as outlets for the attempt to politicize writing.

Friday, August 7

Maybe one day I'll have to confront the phantoms that sometimes come upon me: fixed ideas, psychotic ceremonies, and at the center of the circle there is only the figure of Steve, walking away in his white bomber jacket; I see him from behind and know that it's the last time, that he's going to kill himself. I didn't know it in the moment, but what would I have done if I had? I wasn't capable of saving anyone at that age. For me, it isn't about guilt but rather shame, a different and more noble feeling. Not being up to the task, or not saying what I would have said now. Steve's memory comes and goes without my looking for it. I haven't made up my mind whether to write about him, and the things I note down here have to do with me and not him . . .

A difficult time, Raúl Sendic was imprisoned. The Tupamaros abducted an American this morning. The police confronted them in Malvín and seventeen fell, among them B., the military commander.

Saturday 8

I finished writing the article about American narrative. In a sense, I used Burroughs's cut-up method by interspersing phrases and sayings from other writers in the essay, trying, for the first time, to use collage form.

Monday 10

I was up all night and don't intend to go to bed now because I'm trying to recover my sleep schedule and catch up on the day. I just finished revising the article on the United States and am confident that I can soon return to the novel waiting for me in green binders.

Wednesday 12

I am writing this at a table in La Paz at seven, after determining to change my hours of sleep. Yesterday I went to see Umberto Eco with Jacoby. Jacoby brought him the magazine *Sobre*, and Eco was surprised. He couldn't understand the "publication," which consisted of a brown paper envelope that could be bought in any bookshop, containing, in no order, comics, stories, interviews, and political manifestos. Eco looked at us without quite understanding, and we (or Roberto at any rate) understood, yet again, that we could do some things that were ahead of the official avant-garde. Eco, superficial, a tourist.

Friday 14

Jacoby, Schmucler, Funes, and I recorded a conversation with Eco for the magazine. We went back to discussing McLuhan's theory with him, as well as his book about those who deny the mass media and those who extol it. Is there a third way? For us, it's about uniting one sphere with another. What Jacoby calls "the art of the media."

Saturday 15

A meeting with Haroldo Conti after not seeing each other for months. He finished his novel *En vida*; he always has that melancholy air, the same dull strain while writing his personal stories of spies, English sailors, voyages to Antarctica. He gives me back Lajolo's book on Pavese, which I had lent to Daniel Moyano. On that afternoon, I went up to the room in the boarding house on Medrano and Rivadavia with him, looking for the book in the cardboard box under the bed with piles of magazines and books. Haroldo showed me a copy of *Los oficios terrestres* in which Walsh had written an inscription when he gave him the book: "Haroldo, between you and me we're going to do this thing." That is, we're going to define the future of Argentine literature. The same thing Briante and I said to one another, one afternoon five or six years ago, with the same anger at what we had been given and the same confidence.

Monday 17

There's a tension between the short form and the novel that I want to confront, that is, bringing the swiftness and precision of short story prose to the novel, trying to work with multiple micro-stories that combine and expand over the course of the book. Creating a style based on digression.

Tuesday 18
I stopped by the magazine and found Germán García and Toto; we made up the same proposals as usual, all of us attached to projects that languish with no clear resolution. Then I stopped by Luna's place, picked up sixty-four thousand pesos, and went to eat with Julia at Churrasquita. There were two beautiful and sophisticated women, wearing large hats, fine furs; the waiter, acting as a guide for two rather stupid Americans, spoke to them in a monosyllabic English, fascinated by his international customers. A typical scene from a film about colonial tourism.

Sunday 23
In *Brodie's Report*, Borges's latest book, there's a certain loss of words that affects the prose and turns the style into a kind of previous version. Borges no longer writes because he can't read, so he dictates, and his texts suffer from the lack of the complexity that has always brought such a convincing tone to his fiction. This book is good, but one is nostalgic for his short stories from the forties.

Tuesday 25
Jacoby and I worked on his article about the Di Tella for *Los Libros*. The large old house with its high roof, empty, the bed unmade, the past coming and going, and Roberto trying to smuggle Peronist versions of the Cordobazo.

The meeting with the new generation of writers who run the magazine *Uno más uno* reminds me of my own juvenile years. Impunity, radicalism, abstract theories. Was I any different six or seven years ago?

Wednesday, August 26
Suddenly, I think that I'd like to live in Paris, in an apartment, in a loft, not knowing anyone, shut in and alone, dedicated to writing. Living on what? I still didn't think about that. Between the hours, the long walks along the street, among people who speak another language, secure in myself, not thinking about validation, and publishing my books—or

a single book—under a pseudonym. To be dead to everyone except for me. Tied to that, I should see why I've stopped showing my friends what I'm writing.

Thursday 27
The Beatles are playing on Boccardo's tape player. In a flash, I remember hearing them for the first time in La Plata in '60 or '61.

I do complicated but amusing things after I finish working, trying to distract myself so that my temptation toward bad thinking isn't realized. And I remain in a placid state of mind in which I'm like a seventy-year-old man, without a future, empty, yet still not wanting the day to pass so as not to come closer to the end.

I go down to buy a paper on the corner of Corrientes and Montevideo and find out that they killed José Alonso this morning. When I find out about these things, before I make any political analysis, I always think: who did it? But I can imagine it, and then ask: are the Peronist union leaders the ones who must be confronted? I don't think so.

I'm reading the newspaper *No transar*, which Elías brought me. Immediately I notice: future tense and potential verbs used for the working-class sections. The present tense for quotes and axioms (Mao *says*, the working class *knows*). The past tense for the bourgeoisie (the evacuation *started* on June 4), which lives in the past. Lots of apocalyptic descriptions (*rotten, suffocating, dirty, monstrosity, deadly* swamp, *savagely*) directed at the enemy. And, at the same time, angelic descriptions (*magnificent* treasure, *flourishing* communist jungle, *happily* receives) for the working class, which in this way is depoliticized by moralistic writing and blind optimism. Another key element is the kind of exhortative writing (*we must rebel, compañeros*, and then *we call, we organize, we act*). This style, then, is composed of an excess of verbs in future tense for predictions, corresponding to exhortation, appealing to the present of a future awareness that they alone can decipher (the working class *knows*). I should make an analysis and write an essay about the political language of the left, looking at the clichés, the style of translation (*workers of the world, unite*), the proliferation of quotes from sacred texts, which are never relevant.

Friday 28

I stopped by *Siete Días* and went to lunch with Osvaldo Tcherkaski; he gave me a book of short stories that has good moments and flowing writing. Then with Andrés, who has just come from Uruguay, where, according to him, the Tupamaros number seven thousand. I ended the day in the publishing house talking to Alberto, who complains about the economic situation and can see no way out for the publications. At home, Edgardo F. pays me a visit. I take note of all this in order to leave a record showing the fatigue of social life, which is the cause of the stylistic weakness of this fragment. As though I couldn't narrate my encounter yesterday with Osvaldo at the restaurant in Bajo, the waiters who obsequiously recognize magazine editors. Then a greeting from Mario B., who comes over to me, "moved," and transfers his awkwardness onto me, so I distance myself ironically and talk to him about his beard (you look like Melville). Then Gusmán, at a table with Rozenmacher.

And so he tries not to succumb, holding on to the remains of a sharp and free-flowing intelligence, squandered by distraction, because he can clearly see that he has few chances left and that, if he has decided to bet everything on a single hand, he has to lay down the cards without a shudder. He had to return to the values of that fast and easygoing young man, always disparaging the value of effort and tenacity. Bursts of clarity that came in my moments of deepest confidence, so sure of myself (thinking about his life in third-person).

Sunday 30

The murder of Alonso provokes reactions that are worth analyzing. On the left, the event seems too "well done and efficient" not to be attributed to the right (it's the army services, they say), as though the right were the only ones capable of a true control of reality. The right doesn't suffer from the break between words and actions that the left berates itself for repeatedly. What's more, "coldly killing" isn't a pardonable offense for those who attempt to be respected as "serious" politicians.

X Series. As Rubén K. said the other day, the point is not to heroically contemplate the smoke as our own ships burn, but to be able to jump into the sea and get onto another ship. He meant that he wasn't just trying to change his thinking, tied to the past, but rather that he was trying, by changing his life, to gain access to the thinking of those in the avant-garde.

Series E. Perhaps, when I transcribe these notebooks and type up copies, I'll have to say something about the gap produced in 1962 and so tell the story of how I burned a notebook on the floor of the hotel in the winter of 1967; a spectacular, empty gesture that erased several months of my life.

Eduardo came to see me, along with his inseparable friend; the two are married and seem like well-integrated heterosexuals, yet some gestures and words show the true reality of his desire. Like the atmosphere of James Purdy's stories. Remember, for example, the accident when the two friends who are together all the time fall asleep in a car and wake up in the middle of the country, having crashed into a pole.

The little red notebook holds the truth, only numbers and days of the week; I started taking notes of my actual working hours so that I don't delude myself. Calculating my hours every month, I get an average of 50 hours, less than two hours per day. That explains why the novel is going along so slowly. Over twenty days in July I worked 53 hours, and so far, I've done 53 hours in fifteen days in August. The least I can allow myself is 90 hours per month, that is, three hours per day, so I have to try for an average of 20 per week. Let's say I worked for 14 hours this week . . .

Monday, August 31
Last night, not knowing why, we picked a restaurant that we never go to and there was Helena, sitting at one of the tables at the end. It was very

painful for me to remember her (despite how much I once loved her). We each went our own way after eating, without saying hello.

I see sickness growing within me as happiness grows in others. Trapped in my own delirium, I spend the days bound to diversions dictated by the fever in my soul, not worrying about the consequences that this disease may bring in the future.

A visit from Roberto Jacoby, unforeseen, in the middle of the afternoon; he wants us to work together on the review of the play *El avión negro* by Cossa, Rozenmacher, and others. The idea doesn't attract me because we would establish ourselves in—or from—different areas. For me, it's an effect of populism; for him, a critique of Peronism. Then Boccardo arrived and David came at midnight, and we all ate dinner amid the tensions, very entertained.

Today with David, we viewed Trotsky as a myth, a tragic character of Shakespearean stature. By contrast, Pavese is a failed hero for me, a lonely man who can't solve his passion for women.

When I think nostalgically about the past, I should recall that conversation with Pochi F. on a bench beneath the trees on Calle 51, near the start of the summer of '63, killing time before going to eat at the university dining hall. At the time, F. was full of righteousness due to the piece of knowledge he was showing off (he was the first to tell me about Sciarretta's courses and private lessons in philosophy and logic). When I ran into him the other day, F. looked at me skeptically, completely detached from my literary predicament, more interested in getting into the university dining hall with my ID card than anything else. Now he is working at *La Prensa* and *Confirmado* at the same time, where he will doubtless be successful. I write in these notebooks because I trust that, one day, it will make sense to type them up and have them published, because my work will have justified the reading of these daily personal notes.

7:30 a.m. I get up.

8:00 a.m. At La Paz, I read the newspapers and write in this
notebook.

9:00 a.m. I work on the novel.

2:00 p.m. I have lunch.

4:00 p.m. Tiempo Contemporáneo, *Los Libros*, Luna, work.

8:00 p.m. I go back home, varied readings.

11:00 p.m. I eat dinner at Claudio.

12:00 a.m. I go to bed.

September 1

I go for a coffee at La Paz to read the papers and clear my head. I sit down at a table by the window over the corner of Corrientes and Montevideo and watch as the city changes, in a manifold process, according to the time of day. Once again, as often happens to me these days, I think about the life that I could have lived but lost, something inside myself that I've killed in order to become who I am ("If it is true that I am someone"). Little imperceptible choices, sometimes making me think that my laziness has taken precedence over the conscious decision to construct a particular way of life. I return home along the walkway through the market, avoiding people of my own age who lift boxes of fruit, their hands in gloves. I enter a shop that opens onto the street, stop in front of the counter—which is a cooler—and buy bread, milk, and Chubut cheese to eat at noon without having to interrupt my work.

Wednesday, September 2

I spent two hours with Roberto C. transcribing the recording, slow verbal work. The tape reel rotates and so does the language; you have to know how to scan what you hear, capturing the style and power of the testimony. The usual misunderstandings with Luna, we agree but are speaking different languages. I often see him nodding at what I say with a stunned look on his face, not understanding a word. Two friends who work together at a newspaper and talk to each other every day for years, never understanding what the other is saying. Finally, at the magazine, the artificial euphoria of F., too conscious of his extreme passion for professional transgression (via Del Barco); Artaud is Allah and a number of people from Córdoba are his prophets.

In Turin. The character doesn't flee or take flight; he breaks apart. Like *The Golden Bowl* and Fitzgerald's china plate. I've cracked, he says. It means "I'm cut up" (broken), and he shows the scars on his chest (he opens his shirt, a theatrical and ironic gesture). Possible title for the story: *Rajado* or *El rajado*.

"In my early days I was too demanding with the form, I would write sentence by sentence and correct those sentences again and again until they satisfied me. Now I work in a different way. For while I think about everything, then I write about it almost any way I can, and finally I correct it," J. L. Borges.

Thursday, September 3
Yesterday at Tiempo Contemporáneo they rejected Andrés's book (which I had presented to them) "because the stories won't sell." On my way out, Andrés was sitting in a chair against the wall, in a suit and tie, waiting. A sympathetic meeting with Schmucler, who is seeking "legal counsel" because police from the Coordinación Federal "visit" him. At Signos, José Aricó, a great publisher, uses his information to put together excellent books, very useful works of dissemination in the cultural conversation. Proof of this is the *Cuaderno de Pasado y Presente*, dedicated to Trotsky, which I read a hundred pages of in one sitting yesterday. I try to convince him to approve a volume dedicated to Brecht, but he smiles, it doesn't excite him, he doesn't want to dedicate his publications to literature.

At times, I fear that the amphetamines are ruining my mind, that I'm becoming an addict, that I can't think without their help. Fifteen-year-old kids these days take LSD and other stimulants like candy. At least we've broken out of repression in that area and use the drugs to move forward.

I write fifty pages of a story that I call *Soundtrack*, which is an oral account that I attribute to a recording. An effect of truth in the process more than in the content or referent. It is real given that—as I stated—I've recorded and transcribed it; within that frame, I can say anything, and it will always be read as truth. I call this "textual realism."

Friday 4

In B., I see approaching dangers that I avoid without realizing it: cynicism, fatigue, the conviction that only one's talent matters, no need for substantiation. His juvenile hopes slowly fall away, and meanwhile he dedicates himself to earning five hundred thousand pesos per month, buying a large apartment, getting married and having kids. Because he views me as what he was when he was young, it's only with me that he dreams up ideas for films he wants to make, talking about nothing else. Apart from that, his sensational book covers (for example, one for the Serie Negra, envisioned as a screen showing a violent scene) show his quality, his skill, but being an illustrator doesn't seem like much to him; luckily, he's preparing an exhibition of his sculptures, envisioned not as objects but as crystallized narrative situations, that is, installations connected to cinema, storyboards with volume that exist in space. It isn't a bad idea, a sculptor as a failed filmmaker who creates films fragmented into "sculptural" scenes. I make a note of this because he's a friend and also because, like me, he experiences the difficulties of being an artist (pardon the word) in these times, in this country.

Strange, forgetfulness erases a sentence from my mind just at the point when I'm about to write it. In place of that lost line comes another phrase that I can't recall or recognize. Absent writing.

David stops by at three, comes and stands in the doorway with a guilty and theatrical air, pulls me deep into his projects and obsessions. I take him to La Paz in order to get away, and there (after talking about Trotsky, fighting with a guy who talked too loudly, criticizing Jitrik, and watching as Murena walked past and sat down at a table in the back to write and drink 7 Up) he tells me about Miguel Briante, his face disfigured by a car accident. I inevitably return to my ideas about fragmented and fractured destinies, which makes me think, yet again, about the life I could have lived. David can't be anyone else, and he ends up acting as a *partenaire* to his invented public persona. "David," I tell him, "shave off your moustache and change places, that's the way you'll find new paths for your literature." He looks at me in surprise and defends himself with his Sartrean theory of authenticity (he's been reading it for so long that it's become incarnated so that he thinks he came up with it himself).

Saturday, September 5
Allende's victory in Chile ("the first Marxist in the West to take power through an election," according to the papers) suggests several interpretations: on the one hand, the communist parties' traditional stance on taking power through peaceful means has triumphed; on the other hand, a warning light has gone off on the right. Since they don't pay attention to whether the socialist government's new position was won by guns or votes, they're going to attack it and try to eliminate it without fair play, through—no doubt—the use of weapons. Che's death and Fidel's support of the Soviet operation in Czechoslovakia frame the situation. In Chile, reformism is a politics of the masses and the left may perhaps gain what they really sought with the vote. The armed forces' line appears to be discredited in this situation, strengthening Peronism's negotiating position in Argentina (it also supports itself on the masses and unions).

Sunday 6
The meeting at Alberto S's house had a merit other than wine, whiskey, and food. As always happens in social encounters, I split into two and see myself acting, always at a distance. Arguments with the girl who came with Casullo, stupefaction at the political analyses made by the comfortable young people of the left. Whenever I go to those places I swear that I won't ever go back, but I do. I came and left with León, who lost interest when he entered because there were no single women there, but he had five brilliant minutes, which confirms for me that

he's the most intelligent one in the whole gang. Then he withdrew, as he always does, and dozed off for a while, maybe thinking nostalgically about how he could have accepted the invitation to travel to Chile for Allende's inauguration.

Series E. In rereading my notebooks, the continuity from 1958 to 1967 appears clear; that part would be Volume I of my written life. The solidification of a young aesthete who comes back down to reality, lives alone, earns his living, and begins to publish. The second volume starts in 1968 and is still in progress.

Monday, September 7
I'm writing at the table on the street corner, in La Paz, facing the city, the fragment of the city where I live; a cat circles its territory, marks out the place where it goes to hunt for news of the outside world. I'm doing a translation of Fanon for *Cuadernos Rojos*. When is violence legitimate? That is the current question. Since no one now believes that the masses will act for themselves alone, Fanon associates violence with the individual actions of a new subject, who often functions suicidally.

Tuesday 8
An absurd discussion of literature and politics at *Los Libros* with Funes, Germán G., Toto, and David; how can we get out of the merely testimonial position of writers, only displaying their agreement with good causes. For me, it must begin with a renovation of artistic technique, putting art in service of action; first and foremost, it means changing or expanding the concept of art itself.

Wednesday 9
Working on implicit poetics, not what is said about literature but rather how it is made. The avant-garde refuses to enter the circulation as it is and seeks to open new channels for the diffusion of the art; it must invent a new territory in the same way that the political avant-garde must abandon the parliamentary struggle and find different forms of expression.

I work on the lecture that I'm going to give in Rosario. Thinking about examples for my argument.

Thursday 10
The wooden table, painted yellow, that Uncle Luciano and I carried on a bicycle, turning like a ship. The rubber mat of the kitchen table at the house in Bolívar with lines intersecting each other as on a map and a hole on one side that I opened without being noticed. The time I was going to my room and saw my cousin Lili naked, walking (she covered her breasts with both hands).

Friday 11
Close to noon, I ran into David, who wavers between seduction and madness. I spoke with Willie Schavelzon about a collection of writers' essays and got him to give me a check for five thousand pesos as an advance for the article I'm writing for *Los Libros*. David picked up a package from the bookshop with copies of his novel *The Owners of the Land*, which was just republished, and he went to the bookshop opposite Dávalos, on Calle Corrientes, to sell them himself, trying to fish for a bit of money. "They're the author's books," he tells me, smiling, "they give me ten copies to give out as gifts and then I get rid of them at the cover price." I stopped by Tiempo Contemporáneo, a variety of conversations with Casullo; when I got back home, Ismael Viñas was there and then my brother came over. When I finally went to bed, I felt like the day had begun a month before.

Saturday 12
A true story. The siblings of Natalio W.'s father tried to move from Poland to Russia after the revolution. The group attempted to cross the border but ran into the police. Only the guide, a deaf-mute, made it back, and he used signs to communicate that they'd all been murdered, all except for a woman with very long hair (he spreads his hands behind his head and moves them down to his waist), it was Sara, the youngest sister, her aunt, her father's twin.

Polish Jews can't get onto the trains full of fleeing people, so they go down onto the tracks, slowing them down enough that they can jump onto the running boards and make it to Warsaw.

The Red Army, the soldiers dying of hunger, ragged, passing through the town and singing "Warszawianka."

Series E. I keep looking for a structure with which to publish the diary. The material will be real, but the form of its presentation must have a tone that allows it to be read as an autonomous story, that is, with its own laws.

Later, David came to see me and we talked about his book of essays on Argentine literature (which I don't like). Then Dipi Di Paola came over and we walked around the city until mid-afternoon.

Sunday, September 13
My decision to involve thinking (still not thought out) and narration creates multiple problems for me. The tenuous solution that I have at hand is to argue with examples, that is, with stories, or rather with plotlines. The concept must be made narratively visible without having to be uttered. I call that conceptual writing.

Visual artists are closer to reality than writers. They don't face the—miraculous—hindrance of language. They can use what they find and turn it into a work, and they can erase the artist and turn him into a figure that could be confused with anyone. At seven in the afternoon Roberto Jacoby came over, long and violent political arguments about possible characterizations of the Montoneros group. They've all become Peronists now.

Monday 14
In "Strange Comfort Afforded by the Profession," Malcolm Lowry works on the construction of an imaginary writer. It's about Sigbjorn Wilderness; in the story, he visits Keats's house in Rome and recalls his encounter

with Poe's grave. "What is it to be a writer?" is the question of the story. Alcohol is one of the answers and, in the story, the fictional writer drinks five glasses of grappa, taking them as if they were water. And that seems to be his natural talent.

The character of the writer lies at the center of a web of stories. "Besetting fear, as a writer taking notes, of being taken for a spy," writes S. W. in his diaries ("Through the Panama"): you have to remember that the consul in *Under the Volcano* is killed because he is accused of being a spy. The figure of the writer as a spy in enemy territory was Benjamin's definition of Baudelaire as a bad poet who refused the morality of capitalism.

In the series of novels and stories that have Sigbjorn Wilderness as their protagonist, the issue is twofold. On the one hand, he finds himself "in the middle of the street with a notebook in his hand" and fears that he will be taken for a spy because of that. On the other hand, the issue is that the things he's written in his novels come to pass in his life. Fiction is an oracle that determines his experience. Alcohol is there to support that double punishment.

In my eyes, David is an imaginary writer. I think about him as a kind of Silvio Astier in the midst of life. His uncomfortable—for him—and inauthentic dedication to literature gives him a sort of handicap, as though he were a martyr who is entitled to everything, and so he calls on the phone, begging, tempting, and if I refuse to see him he drags Julia off to a bar, forcing her to listen to his obsessions, imposing his problems as though he were the center of the world. I see in this an attitude, not to call it a pose, that I often find exhibited in stories with imaginary writers as their protagonists. Thus, I see David as an actor who is playing a writer, but at the same time he hates that figure, believing him to be a fraud who must be criticized by the action, that is, by the empirics that wipes away all illusions. There's also something of that in Walsh, who feels uncomfortable about his literature (because it's also very hard for him to write) and decides to become a political militant.

So, I'll try to make a survey—or an encyclopedia—of the figures and figurations of the author in contemporary culture. Not an artist but a witness, a chronicler, whose life—real or imaginary—is an attempt to justify—or understand—why one would dedicate oneself to literature. Meaning that, in this era, literature is not justified for itself alone and must be legitimized.

Tuesday 15
Another image survives and comes to me from my past self, seeking some meaning that I can't decipher (because I don't know or can't remember what comes before that scene). Mom carries me in her arms along the path at my grandparents' house (which will later be ours), along the hedge with white flowers and round leaves (and edible fruits, I think). She cries and moans, asking me if I'm not sad about Uncle Eugenio who was just killed in an accident. Then, in that moment, as an effect of my mother's crying, I sense the presence of a truck parked at the entry door, loaded with bricks in a kind of pyramid, where he fell. Much later, I understood that he was an alcoholic and died because he was drunk.

They're holding a wake for my mother's father, my grandfather Antonio, I'm playing soccer in the street, and my father comes out of the house, calling me and reprimanding me for my lack of seriousness. Then I see everyone dressed in black, in mourning, and I'm ashamed about my colorful tie. I am, if I remember right, thirteen or fourteen years old.

That German restaurant with cane chairs on Calle Rivadavia, one summer in Mar del Plata, we ate sausages with fries and drank beer (which woman was I with?), we saw Dipi and acquaintances from La Plata, and, sitting at one of the tables by the window, we talked about Braudel and longevity. What is it that lasts and survives? Or rather, what will it be? Braudel talks about geographical spaces (valleys, rivers) that change so slowly that there hasn't been time to think about their presence in history. What will longevity mean in literature? The gesture of drawing signs for an unknown recipient. The pose survives, the good hand is used to write.

In reading Barthes's "The Discourse of History," I confirm the truth—or the true path that opened that realization—of my insight in 1963, in the apartment I shared with Oscar C. on Calle 1 in La Plata, while I was studying American History: viewing history as narrative, studying the methods, the techniques, etc.

Series E. Julia takes refuge in La Plata and I, alone, sit down at Pippo on Calle Paraná to read the paper and eat a steak with salad. I think about the grand theme of my life: the solitary man (what he sees, what he can see, how he thinks, etc.) is the basis and condition of the writing of this diary. Thus the hope to discover an individual form and a private language. That style—if it exists—has no recipient, and therefore nothing that is known needs to be stated. The prose tends toward the present tense and toward description, a radical exteriority of the person writing—the imaginary subject, or rather, the conceptual writer—in his relationship to language as his own material. An object that tends toward the unsaid, toward psychotic laconicism (that's how the prose appears) and toward hermetic non-communication.

Thursday
Notes on Tolstoy (12). A deal with the devil. (Faust.) Chekhov perceives it. He writes to Suvorin in the spring of 1895: "The devil take the philosophy of the great ones of this world! All the great sages are as despotic as generals, and as ignorant and as indelicate as generals, because they feel certain that they can't be touched. Diogenes spat in people's faces, knowing that he would not suffer for it. Tolstoy abuses doctors as scoundrels, and displays his ignorance in great questions because he's just such a Diogenes who won't be locked up or abused in the newspapers. And so to the devil with the philosophy of all the great ones of this world!"

Friday, September 18
In the late afternoon Néstor G. comes over, back from France, the same as always. He saw, he tells me, *Muriel* by A. Resnais, he went with Diana Guerrero, who gave a simplistic and damning analysis of Arlt. I went to

the magazine and found David, euphoric about his conversations with D. Stivel, who proposed that he write something for his TV program *Historia de jóvenes*. A writer like him feels accomplished if he can imagine a massive audience.

My strange behavior in Havana in January two years ago, affected by my encounter with Virgilio Piñera. I brought him a letter from Pepe Bianco. V. P. came to see me in the hotel; he was a lean, lucid man, someone I admire very much. He said to me: "Let's go to the garden, there are microphones everywhere in here." Out in the open air, he quickly told me that he was being harassed by the political police, they had isolated him, he had no work, they were spying on him, etc. A fragile person, amiable and very sophisticated, he was only interested in literature but happily accepted the revolution and didn't go into exile. Why is he being pursued? "Because I'm invested," he said with a smile, appealing to an old-school term. Invested, inverted, a person turned around. They see him as a political danger, a delusion generated by those who believe that history has imbued them with political truth. Then, at Casa de las Américas, I asked for G. Cabrera Infante's story collection *In Peace as in War*. There was vacillation, some detours, but they must have preferred to avoid the scandal that could have come if they'd refused me access to a book published by the Revolution. We went down an endless staircase that sank into the bowels of the earth and finally, down below, they found the book and gave it to me with a discreet and reproving look. In the Casa de las Américas library there was a notebook with a pencil attached, hanging from a cabinet. You had to leave your name and information there if you wanted to read *Three Trapped Tigers*, G. C. I.'s novel, published in Spain in 1967. Many readers ran the risk of showing their faces in order to read a novel they admired. Apart from the discussions and meetings, I imagine that all of that brought me to a state of great nervous excitement that lasted until the end of my stay in Cuba. It had to do with the brutal presence of a reality that I wasn't prepared for. *Me caí de la mata*, the penny dropped, as the Cubans say.

Saturday 19
A visit from David; Stivel rejected his proposal to do a self-critique as a condition for staging *Lisandro*. Then Rubén K., who defends the linear novel and hates intellectuals out of pure anger toward himself. The anti-intellectualism of the left replicates the position of the mass media. Mistrusting any analysis or position that poses complex questions, they think that everything is simple, that the people don't understand them because they lack social consciousness. Dramatic and sad.

Later, I went to the magazine, the issue with my long article on American literature came out. Extreme positions that help me survive. I pretend I'm invisible. I go to León's course on Marze to air out some of the heavy feeling of recent days. We read *Pre-capitalist Economic Formations*. Asian means of production tied to Eastern despotism. León quotes Hegel from memory.

Sunday, September 27
A summary of my excursion that began on Friday and ended early today. I took the train to Rosario at seven in the morning, an experience of simultaneity; I heard Beat music, in the railroad car, I heard a group of furious people talking about money without pause, and I mentally tried, as if I were someone else, to explain the term *bibliotherapy* to someone by transmitting my thoughts, saying to myself: it is healing through reading. I was going to a conference of librarians, I imagined, and everything discussed there would reveal the truth of a particular reading. At the same time, through the little window, the city ended abruptly and the country began, a barren, flat land, and in the background, against the horizon, I saw a little village, the last populations, and then, in the desert, a shanty town. "A Pampa Indian camp," I thought, that's how one would see the tents and huts of the nomads on the plain, leaving the fortified positions "of civilization." I thought: "The height where I am, sitting by the window of the train, is the same as the perspective a man on horseback would have." What can be seen is at once distant and near, silhouettes sketched out from afar, looming in the void.

In Rosario the cavalcade began; Nicolás was waiting for me and immediately filled my hands with his writings, hopefully I'll be able to practice my obligatory reading, but I react in opposition and can't read in these cases. Articles and papers from many origins and with no "personal" interest, institutionalized, neutral writing. "On top of that," he made it clear to me that he too was working on the problem of translation, which for me, I told him, wasn't important because we all write the way we see fit. His response was to not leave me alone, even for a moment, as though he were monitoring me or following me. I found, then, that mixture of arrogance, perversion, and provincialism, ways of differentiating oneself in bureaucratic spaces.

At night I gave my lecture, very lucid, but in a bad place even at the best moments. I took Borges as an example of double enunciation, or rather, of the double text. Quotation, plagiarism, and translation, examples of one writing inside another, which is implicit. An outside text is read in writing, and the appropriation can be legal (quotation), illegal (plagiarism), or neutral (translation). Borges uses his personal mode of translation to appropriate all of the texts he quotes or plagiarizes: his "unmistakable" style turns everything he writes into his possession. He also uses erroneous, outrageous, and manifold attributions with great skill: he habitually attributes his own lines to others but also takes others' phrases as his own.

Throughout the entire talk I was distracted by an open door to the right of the stage where I sat speaking to that clever audience: I thought that the listeners weren't following me because they were waiting for someone to arrive (and that was why they had left the door open). Who could be coming? Whose specter? And, while trying to work it out, I "heard" myself talking. When I was about to give some explanations, applause and praise broke out, following me into the next day.

Novel. The point isn't to try to turn the document into fiction or to explain where the truth is in what I'm writing, it's to define fiction in the way real materials are enunciated. For me, fiction is defined by the formula "the person speaking does not exist," even if he says that his name is Napoleón Bonaparte and everything he says or relates is the truth. The readers' beliefs are in play, they decide whether to receive the story as true or false or, rather, as real or imaginary.

Curious behavior during the lecture: first in the office, while I was waiting, I felt an emptiness in the air as if I was no longer there: I imagined myself—saw myself—losing my thread. As soon as I sat down and began to talk, my attention was displaced toward the right, toward the door that led to the patio. There were silhouettes in front of me, empty faces, and my words sounded hollow, I felt I was moving too quickly.

That night in the vast and empty restaurant with an open-air patio in the middle of the room, everyone—except for me—ordered pork chops. Sitting next to me, Juan Pablo Renzi talked to me ceaselessly, half drunk, and asked me if we were relatives. He had seen the name in a detective anthology that came out, signed and translated by someone who had the same last name. "We're nothing," I told him.

Monday 28
Notes on Tolstoy (13). Art as temptation. While writing *What is Art?*, he takes notes in his diary. "I do not cease to reflect upon art and upon every form of temptation which obscures the spirit: art is certainly one, but I do not know how to express my thoughts."

Tuesday 29
I feel like I'm living in a house without walls.

Successive visits and meetings. At *Los Libros*, a plan to attend a conference in Córdoba. I refuse to go, which causes a great disturbance. We'll see; if I do go I'll have to travel on Friday. They offer me tickets, lodging, etc. Yesterday I saw Beatriz Guido and Leopoldo Torre Nilsson; I found them frivolous, ingenuous, a bit cynical, with the certainty that comes with money. She was worried about the publication of her novel *Escándalos y soledades*. Lots of exposure, articles in all of the magazines. She gives me the manuscript to read: I'm the young one, a prodigy, and I'm on the left, so she expects me to write the review of her book in the magazine. While Nilsson stays apart, he shows a childish eagerness when talking about "his literature." He gives me two stories to read and tries to steer the conversation toward his writing. I like what he does, a certain criminal tone, a spoken prose that isn't bad, fairly personal. Meanwhile, he's putting together his next movie, another historical one, based on the life of Güemes and his gauchos, who defended the northern frontier from the Spanish. He talks and describes the millions he made with his movie about San Martín. He has an incredible certainty that the triumph of socialism in Argentina is imminent, and he tries to be as close as possible to people like me, imagining that we can protect him from being killed and give him time to go into exile. During that historical-political-artistic-personal conversation, we drank Scotch whiskey and French wine, and we ate delicious empanadas, cooked by the maid from Corrientes.

A single man cut down the familes of the manager and two treasurers of a bank, passing himself off as a member of an urban guerrilla group. The thief made them travel in a van from one end of the city to another while he waited for them in the bank watching television. Using only his intelligence and the power of collective fear, he made off with eight million pesos after five hours of work.

A long discussion last night with Schmucler about their interview with me in *Uno por uno*; I immediately move toward an extreme position (the same I took in the interview) while he, intelligent and sensible, argues scientifically (repeating Roland Barthes without quoting him), he defends "writing," non-representation, and even hermeticism as cultural alternatives, and I—in line with Tretyakov, Brecht, Benjamin—defend nonfiction, writing that doesn't depend on the book form and circulates socially, and thus deny the possibility of committing fiction in an impactful way.

Only if we write parables and fables with morals, in the Chinese style or with the form of allegorical stories from the Bible, can we use fiction as propaganda. We were crossing Calle Paraná, arguing about the avant-garde and unrest, when a car almost crashed into us.

Wednesday 30
Ismael Viñas cut my afternoon short, we concocted an apocryphal political inquiry that sparked his voracious sense of competition with his "intellectual friends." All disguised with lines about the communists, but based on conservative positions. Then David dropped in, insecure and ridiculous in the eyes of his brother, who always sparks theatrical behavior in him. They joined forces to insult Perón; they're still liberals on the left, psychologizing history just like the most obstinate populists, making Perón the axis of political reality for the last twenty years (something which is true). I feigned a compromise to get rid of them; we walked down Corrientes (empty, with the shops shut down because of the census) and then I got on the subway at Uruguay, got off at the first station and left via Callao, making a large circle around Riobamba and Sarmiento so as not to be seen. A thief protecting "the treasures" of his private thoughts.

Thursday, October 1
In the afternoon I watch Godard's *Weekend*, a loose adaptation of Cortázar's "The Southern Thruway" that turns into a tribal journey on the road with catastrophes, cannibalism, and delirium. I work with some ideas from Tretyakov's position for my statement at the conference in Córdoba on the avant-garde and politics. Then I started reading and the calls began. Luna also wants to travel to Córdoba and offers me collusion and money. I already see the dubious reactions that David, León, and Toto will provoke in him. I'm "his friend," and he will want to prove it constantly. He offered to get my ticket so that we could travel together, pay for my lodging, and extend our stay. Then León also offered to pay for my transportation so he wouldn't have to travel alone, followed by David, who wanted to invite us to dinner. Their persistence eliminated my desire to travel.

Friday, October 2
I reread my notebooks from 1968, an aggressive and solitary character throwing punches in the air and fighting blindly against reality. Those were the days when I was working on the story about the trip to Italy with Pavese's diary and the obsession over a lost woman.

Monday 5
A weekend in Córdoba, open discussion on Saturday afternoon and all day Sunday with Oscar del Barco and his acolytes (Marimón, Dámaso Martínez, Giordano, etc.); in the line of Bataille, they defend a version of the autonomy of literature with its function explicitly tied to the poetics "of desire" and transgression. A kind of politicized mauditism, very French. For my part, I went back to insisting that a political literature must go beyond the book as object and circulate as an open practice of manifestos, photocopied stories, life stories, based above all in nonfiction. In the midst of that aside, numerous assemblies, posters with Che's photo, slogans, speeches by radical workers from the factories of Córdoba. No one talked with anyone else, there were only firm positions, declarations that never intersected one another. On the way back, David came over to rationalize his silence in Córdoba. In reality, neither Del Barco nor I kept David's theory of commitment or his social novels in mind. We commented on Toto's letter to Cortázar with reproval and praise.

Sunday 11
I lock myself away in my writing like the hero of the novel I'm writing. Any idea scrapes against my skin, I'm raw as though suffering the consequences of a fire. It costs me something to write in these notebooks because my work is going well, but in the diary I'm always the other person, the one who writes in order to survive. All I have to do is turn on the light or plug in my phone to have everybody straining to come inside.

The narrator returns to the places of his childhood to reveal himself to his new woman.

Everyone takes me for a human until I start to talk. My head floats like a balloon in the air.

Saturday, October 17
A decision, let's call it, to get rid of my beard and enter age twenty-nine next month "with another face." I see condemnation in age.

Sunday 18
A party at Alicia's house, an argument with Sciarretta and Malamud that leaves me feeling bad. On one hand, it repeats my argument with Del Barco (impossibility of a critique of literature), and in that sense I'm sure of being right. But, at the same time, I once again encounter the use of a culture that comes up more and more with these almost lumpenproletariat intellectuals who aggressively exhibit a closed-off knowledge that they've settled themselves in. On that side I have a feeling of competition, my own desire to seek the support of a theory that can be recited confidently and yet, at the same time, I'm certain that refusing to be a passive consumer, a repeater, is the only way to produce a "work."

Monday, October 19
Series E. The stylistic effects in these "diaries" derive from one fact: I'm trying to explicitly reproduce my hidden life. Which would that be? Not so much the events that lie behind the most visible things, but rather the bond that unites people and places. I must narrate the nexus even though I can't perceive it now. I write in a more representative prose in which the threads are missing; I deliberately move away from interpretation and approach pure description. I seek a writing that has value in itself and that accurately reflects my current state (fear of *surmenage*).

Wednesday 21.
Schmucler talks to me about the letter that Del Barco is thinking of sending to *Los Libros* discussing my article on American literature, to which I will have to respond. Dinner at Ramón Alcalde's house, boring and with no explanation or motive.

In reality, the polemic with Del Barco began in Córdoba. He lives under the delusion that a dead language is the fabric of literature: a language "without society," without ways of life, empty. It concerns a rhetoric of perversion as creative force: thus, there is a monotony and repetition of methods in the writers who respond to that logic. For example, Osvaldo Lamborghini, or Del Barco's good story "La Señorita Z." On the other hand, in *El Escarabajo de Oro* Liliana Heker critiques my statement in *Uno por uno*. I am, as I might wish, at the center of the storm: Castillo, conservative in literature, and Del Barco, the marginal, join together to discuss my attempts to find a way out of the debate of realism vs. delirium. An old settling of scores, but of course I won't get into an explicit polemic, I'll answer in passing, we'll see.

Wednesday 28
Despite the psychosis that I experience after doing something purely for the money, I managed to put together the storyline for Hugo K.'s script. A media tycoon, the president of a soccer team, who also manages a TV channel, is threatened with death. They want to kill him, he doesn't know who or how. A descent into hell; he feels himself pursued, feels there was something in his past that got him involved, but he can't recall or doesn't know what it is (that is key: he did something but has managed to forget it completely). Everyone, especially his bodyguard, thinks he is delusional; they show him that there's no danger. The viewer has to believe the same thing, that is, that he's having an attack of paranoia. He convinces himself and organizes a party to show that he isn't afraid and that the signs that made him think they were going to kill him were just bad thoughts. Then, on the night of the party, they kill him.

The history he has forgotten: a group of adolescents, one of them finds his father's revolver. One night they go out and head to the Parque Japonés in Retiro, and on the way back they get on *la vuelta al mundo* (a large Ferris wheel that revolves high above the amusement park), and up there, sheltered by the darkness and the mass noise of fireworks and raucous music, they fire randomly into the crowd. Panic, running, no one notices the middle-class kids who move calmly through the place after killing a stranger. She has two children who decide to take revenge. Hugo K. gave me twenty-five thousand pesos in advance for this plot.

Saturday
A feeling that I've made it very far by leaving things along the way: a person who never pauses, who cannot pause, who advances into the darkness because he doesn't want to think. Above all, he doesn't want to know or find out (and that preoccupation is abstract, not knowing what it is that he mustn't know, the pure and empty form of a pursuit of ideas and thoughts).

I make a balance sheet for this month as it is ending. Liquidation and balance are the formulas of the neighborhood shops, especially at the end of the year. I'll use this method in my personal life. I quite like the verb *to liquidate*; it means, of course, to sell for cheap, but also to kill. I've written sixty pages of the "true" novel based on real events, with the escape to Montevideo and the subsequent trap into which the "lowlifes," as they say, fall. (We're all lowlifes, he said.) Moreover, along those lines, separate from that plot, is the story of the magnate who threw a great party to defy his pursuers, who of course kill him (for Hugo K.'s script). Echoes of my new positions on the political role of literature (excluding fiction): a long piece about the Black Panthers' writing in response to William Burroughs's reflection: painters have left the canvas, but when will literature be able to leave the page? I investigate in that area: fragmented writings, often recorded, life stories, pamphlets, poems, complaints that circulate from hand to hand, outside of the commercial circuit of books, publishers, booksellers, critics. A world of great freedom opens, a prose tied to what the Russian avant-garde called "social demand." It advances along those lines during the debates of the left in Córdoba. I posed the example of Walsh's stories of denunciation and nonfiction, as opposed to the idea of taking an existing form like the novel and changing its content. It is the form, the fiction, which must be reformulated: it has its own mediated system of reception, and we must seek an immediate and urgent prose that disputes the endless cycle of news on radio and television, inventing the news, as Walsh says. Documentary prose liberates fiction and allows for experimentation and private writing.

The reactions and criticism prove that I'm moving in the right direction. At the same time, financed writing: here too is a direct and unveiled relationship between writing and money. The hundred thousand pesos that I'll make for inventing a plot. Everything is going well, I can say. My fantasies from ten years ago are being realized. We'll see how far I can go.

Tuesday, November 3
In the French bookshop Galatea, the salesman, so dapper and elegant, who cultivates a James Mason look, thought I'd stolen a book and checked my hands, and—since I wasn't taking anything today—I could insult him, making him step back and beg forgiveness.

Using lines from tangos as referents for the narrator.

Lunch with Vicente Battista, who publishes *Nuevos Aires*, a magazine; I try to convince him not to include an article about Sabato as a kitsch writer.

Saturday 7
Once again—for the second time, from what I remember—I refuse fatherhood; once again, literature is my substitute. Maybe that was why I caught myself writing words with the letters out of order, an elegant and incomprehensible prose. Disjointed, I'm a broken mirror, the sun shines in every direction, and it's impossible to reflect the reality (of this room).

Pavese is connected to certain women's writing. I never realized it before. What defines that touch? Extreme sensitivity for detail and atmosphere, anecdotes always announced but never narrated. I see him as connected to Silvina Ocampo, Katherine Anne Porter.

Series E. The only way to save these notebooks is to trust in the pure surface of the prose: not trying to record my life, but rather creating a homologous space that serves as a mirror.

A true story. Caught after an anonymous tip just as they were about to rob a pharmacy, Guillermo P., 22 years old, and Miguel R., 18, together are charged with assault, attempted forced entry, etc. R. had been the winner of a contest organized by the Club Alsina in Villa Urquiza after having stayed awake with no rest for one hundred seventy (170) hours, a performance that he almost followed in another contest at the Club Cabral in Villa Adelina with one hundred hours awake. Both events were reflected on television and in the papers. He was acting on drugs. His partner, for his part, who also competed in the first event, took such a disproportionate amount of those marathon drugs that he suddenly suffered an attack of madness and tried to throw himself off of the balcony of the club's second floor, for which reason he had to be detained (*La Razón*, 11/6/1970).

Monday 9
The powerful distributor of newspapers and magazines, who runs the stand where the papers are distributed and controls all the kiosks in the city, makes millions and receives his payment in bills and petty cash, protecting himself with a team of bodyguards. He's so used to handling money that he leaves a package with two hundred thousand pesos on the roof of his car, where he had put it down to free his hands and open the door of the car. The money flies like confetti down Calle Corrientes.

Tuesday 10
A strong feeling of failure at times, as though the novel were lost and I were insisting (without any real conviction) on making it survive. I hold myself up on writing to save myself from drowning.

Thursday
Today a general strike. In Tucumán, the students took control of the city for two days in a row. David comes over in the afternoon, just back from

Chile, euphoric, thinking that Buenos Aires "smells like shit"; he blames the city after checking that the smell isn't coming from his armpits or his shoes (he's only wearing socks, and he bends down in his chair to smell his feet), now he has to write a book about Chile for Galerna; they already paid him the advance.

Friday 13

Unexpected arrival of Jacoby, who's excited about mobilizing a group of artists to create images and cartoons in support of the workers on strike. In some way, I take this year to be finished and thus my lack of enthusiasm, insensibility before a critical date: I'm going to turn twenty-nine years old. Dead time, as though I were on the eve of a great journey. I live ahead of myself, not giving myself time, hurried.

Sunday 15

Yesterday the FAL liquidated the deputy chief of the Coordinación Federal; he was a torturer. It takes effort to criticize them, but I, knowing them, criticize them. Recalling the strategies of masses to argue with small elitist groups of visionary guerrillas.

Monday 16

"Why repeat the awful custom of considering people who wear elegant clothing to be cultured, instead of considering the ones capable of making that clothing to be cultured?"

Tuesday 17

Cortázar has been around Buenos Aires for the past week without showing himself. Rather, only showing himself to his bodyguard, eschewing any kind of literary and/or political discussion. David V., by contrast, desperate, euphoric because he got money for something that he promised to write after he'd gone two days without eating. He invited me to dinner to fight off his ghosts (among them, Cortázar's fame).

More and more, I need less money and more free time.

Wednesday 18
To discuss Peronism is to discuss union structure, which is, by definition, based on negotiation and only mobilizes itself and fights as a last resort, for concrete reasons. Therefore, attempts to create strike groups that designate themselves as revolutionary Peronists, an expression that sounds like an oxymoron to me, seem illusory.

"We cannot leave unobserved, in the first place, that the citation and installation of foreign pages in a proper context is common in Brecht," Paolo Chiarini.

My bedazzlement with Brecht or, put better, with Brecht's prose, is growing. A perception as well founded as the knowledge of Pavese, Hemingway, Borges, or Joyce.

Thursday 19
I continue passionately with Brecht, I find my intuitions confirmed, the work that I've called "double discourse," for example, putting one text inside another, not through allusion, but through double inscription of what is written. Essays must also be seen according to their second meanings: attempts, experiments with forms of argumentation.

Saturday 21
I decided to set aside the novel and finish the script and the stories that I have in progress. A confusing time with no pauses, vertigo that doesn't end, no chance to sit still and think (for me "stopping to think" comes before knowing what to think about).

I go to the cinema and see a retrospective of Argentine film. *Deliciously Amoral* by Julio Porter, with a script co-written by César Tiempo, starring Libertad Leblanc. The mother, obsessed with Gardel, goes to the theater every day to see him singing in his old films that play as reruns in a theater in Almagro. The father destroys himself because he wants to sleep with the daughter, dedicating incestuous songs to her.

Sunday, November 22
Everything comes from the fact that I don't recognize this other person who lives within me, the fear that he will betray me and prevent me from reaching the place I want to go. Mistrust between him and me, many surprises at once, doubts about what I'm looking for. A whole life to live.

Tuesday, November 24
I enter the age of reason, slightly sentimental, like an amateur who avoids all social responsibility and knows less about himself than he does about any other close friend.

Thursday 26
Yukio Mishima, a very good writer (*Confessions of a Mask*), committed hara-kiri screaming "long live the Emperor" and was broadcast on television. Modern society turns medieval rites into happenings and spectacles.

In the afternoon I run into Bernardo Kordon, and he proposes a trip to China next year. The idea amuses me, but I don't take his proposal seriously. Then I see Beatriz Guido and Leopoldo Torre Nilsson at their house, agreements and differences.

Friday 27
I meet Walsh at Tiempo Contemporáneo. I've put him in charge of the translation of Chandler's stories. We shoot the breeze, which always happens to me with him, too aloof and populist (and anti-intellectual). He isn't above trying to sell me his old *Antología del cuento extraño* for ETC. He tells me: "This is one of only two anthologies that cites Roger Callois." A pause. Then in a low voice: "The other is Borges's." I smiled: "Of course, they're the only two."

It is clear that I don't want to go to China now, I'm not "prepared," it would be like going to the moon, plus I want to finish the novel. Always the same surreal feeling, I watch myself from the outside as though it were happening to a stranger.

A pair of scissors on the desk causes a pain in my throat: it's as though someone were pulling them from my body after sinking them deep inside. A damp, hollow sound, like a basin draining.

Saturday 5

I finish the script of *Cinematógrafo* for Hugo K., forty pages to tell the story of the mogul holding a party where he will be killed. I have fifteen days to rewrite and adjust B.'s script. I'll see if I can take some vacation days and then return to the novel.

Sunday 6

Let's say that with too much free time I go astray: I sleep too much, ship-wrecked among the little details—I have to go out to buy maté, have to pick up my clothes from the dry-cleaners . . .

To escape the feeling of being an amateur, I should systematically study the books of essays by the writers I admire (Brecht, Pound, Pavese). I will look to ideas as a means to break free of the idiocy of literature.

4

Diary 1971

For years, Bianco was our Rulfo. He wrote two short masterpieces (or two masterful short pieces), and then kept silent for close to thirty years. One of those masterpieces is, of course, *The Rats*. Aside from the pleasure derived from reading the smooth quality of his prose, elegant but never affected (never affected by the deliberate elegance of those who have copied him, trying to exhibit the features of great literature), there are different ways to read this book: we can read it in the context in which it was written, and also in the space of the present.

One must recall that, when *The Rats* was published (in 1943), it was Borges who paved the way for Argentine literature: the short stories he had started publishing in 1940, which he later assembled in *Fictions*, had caused a domino effect, the clearest example of course being *The Invention of Morel*, a Borges novel, we would say today, a novel that Borges "wrote" in poor prose, in Bioy's prose. For his part, Bianco, very close to Borges, took a different turn (as Onetti did years later): he sought the great path to the renovation of contemporary narrative in the psychological novel, a genre despised by Borges. And so the point was not a novel with a rigid plot, bound to a genre, as the writers whom Borges called his masters had taught (Chesterton, Kipling), but rather the other great path of renovation, started by Henry James, which had continued with Julien Green, E. M. Forster, and Ford Madox Ford. A very subtle kind of work with an abnormality on the part of the narrator, an abnormality tied to the terror and awe generated by an unstable world. That narrator saw reality as an

275

impenetrable fog. Read today, Bianco's book is enriched by the development of some contemporary literature: Nabokov, Auster. "Every time I sit down to write," Bianco said with an ironic gleam in his eye, "I feel like Borges is watching over my shoulder." Today, however, there are many who think it is Bianco who should be looking over Borges's shoulder.

February
Yesterday morning I worked with B. on adjusting the script; at night, Carlos Altamirano came over with a plan for an interdisciplinary work group centered on research into the colonial situation, seeking its relationship to literature. He suggests beginning with a discussion of my work on translation. (I'm not interested in that interdisciplinary horror or any issue as abstract as THE colonial or neocolonial situation.)

Praise for the Serie Negra in *Panorama* magazine, I can't stand my own photo, I see my face and think: that isn't me (and neither am I).

Tuesday, February 2
Last night in class I talked about Brecht but also about Karl Korsch, Walter Benjamin, and Lukács's *The Theory of the Novel*. I see a line of continuity, there, of leftist criticism using the conjectures of the Russian avant-garde (particularly Eisenstein, Tynyanov, and Tretyakov).

I meet with Hugo K., who is interested, to my surprise, in the plot that I wrote yesterday in exactly ten minutes. They are flashes, done for the book, which I'm so far removed from that I can't even remember the plot and will have to takes notes on what they tell me about the text so that I don't lose it completely.

Thursday 4
A long conversation last night with Manuel Puig, multiple coincidences; he possesses what you could call a technical clarity, profound knowledge of the narrative art. He insists on his need for obsessive concentration and the rejection of everything that disrupts his writing; there is an iron

will in Manuel to correct and to start over every time it is necessary. Total overlap in that area; of course, in my view of things, he's too attentive to what happens to his books after he publishes them (public relations, controlling the reviews, working on the translations).

Miguel Briante called me under a trivial pretext as though he wanted to make sure of my admiring reading of his book *Hombre en la orilla*. We met at La Paz and I once again felt the ironic mutual understanding that has been with us since we were twenty years old. His book is extraordinary, and I published it at Estuario because Pirí Lugones rejected it at Jorge Álvarez when I recommended it, saying that they weren't interested in rural stories. Blind to literature, just like her grandfather. Miguel grows bitter because he sees the incredible number of morons who are applauded while he sails adrift in loneliness and alcohol.

A time of confusion and dispersion, I try to complete the script I'm writing for money, the article for *Pasado y Presente* magazine, and above all there is my constant temptation to read everything that comes out to stay current. There's nothing more ridiculous than that pretense, but in my case, it's tied to my work at the magazine, where I have to review *all* of the books that are published in the month. The work that I earn my living from, reading, inevitably turns me into someone who is "informed" and can talk to any idiot about the literary news.

Friday 5
I work on adjusting the dialogue in the script. It is strange, but I have to find an effect of reality that can only be had by moving away from the visible hallmarks of speech. Because of that, the criminals in this story speak in an invented language, unconnected to immediate reality, and in that way it's possible for their words to be believable. In film, in contrast to what is believed, everything becomes artificial.

Still under pressure from the lesson in professional rigor that Puig gave me—without thinking—the other night. He traveled from Italy to

New York to settle himself down in peace and work on *Betrayed by Rita Hayworth* for three years in isolation. Unknown and unsupported, he sustained himself on his own obstinacy. Along with that, he is "unable" to read, which allows him to base any knowledge on what he is writing. "I can't read novels, because I correct them," an excellent definition of a writer's way of reading, he reads every book as though it were his own, still unfinished.

Saturday, February 6
I see *The Brothers Karamazov* at the theater (director I. Pyryev): the figure of Smerdyakov, who "hated all of Russia," and the line from Ivan: "Who has never wanted to see his father dead?" (I too have wanted to see my father dead, and I too have hated my country).

Wednesday 10
In a couple of hours today I wrote a chapter of the novel that doesn't displease me: the woman in the room of the Hotel Majestic. It's been a while since I've felt this good, confidence in the book after some months of uncertainty.

Yesterday at the publishing house I received a letter from Sartre: incredible. Addressed to me with compassion, he authorizes me to publish two of his essays and a long interview about literature in a book. With a private sense of irony, I imagine Sartre buying the paper he used to write to me. Obviously, of course, this letter didn't come by way of the holy one himself but rather through his secretary.

Thursday 11
I end the day by seeing *The Wild Bunch* by S. Peckinpah in the 95-cent theater, where lonely men and women of the night go to sleep, to rest from the fatigue of the city, sheltered in the air conditioning.

I remember the carnival costumes from Casa Lamota: the Lion of Damascus, the Old-Fashioned Woman, the Pirate, the Zorro, precarious but brilliant fantasies. We chose our costumes from the illustrated page in *Billiken* magazine.

The empty city, beautiful in summer with a warm wind coming in from the river. I stand on the sidewalk outside the bar on Carlos Pellegrini as night falls, outlining the silhouettes of the buildings among the trees. A woman of uncertain age with pale eyes is talking to herself in the street, never moving from the wide sidewalks, and has a shouting match with a younger woman in a shiny dress who leads a bulldog puppy and a boy dressed in yellow. The older one wanted to kick the dog off the grass and was defending the pigeons. The woman in the shiny dress insisted on continuing the argument as though there were some logic to the delirious back and forth of the two among the flowerbeds.

X Series. At night, Elías and his family are going to Córdoba; they possess a quiet certainty and resolve in certain political convictions that I too would like to believe in. Memories of his stay in Tucumán: Don Arias couldn't get any work and wanted to sell kisses "at night," when his wife wouldn't see him. Or the convicts sentenced to life for killing their wives, going out to work and coming back at night to sleep in the prison. The guy who sold ice cream because he didn't have a job and took a taxi back home every time he earned a bit of money.

Monday, March 1
A meeting with León R. who comes over to eat, happy with his electric typewriter, but always devastated by periods of dark insecurity.

Tuesday, March 2
Roberto Fernández Retamar sends me a letter via Walsh, an invitation from Casa de las Américas to be part of the drafting committee for the magazine. It's strange and comes at the wrong time; as they know, I'm less and less in agreement with the Cubans' cultural politics, and for me everything has cooled down since Fidel Castro's support of the Soviet invasion in Czechoslovakia. I write a cordial but distant letter to him,

asking for details about the formation of this Extended Committee, and send it to him by way of Toto, who is traveling to Madrid. I find him in the afternoon, and he thinks Retamar's sudden decision is strange as well. I talk with Aricó, who is overseeing the publication of the next issue of *Pasado y Presente*, and he tells me I don't need to rush my article on translation, which he had asked for by the middle of this month.

Wednesday 3
At night Roberto Jacoby comes over, amusing himself with outrageous stories about J. Posadas, the Trotskyist director of *Voz Proletaria*: his infinite texts in all languages about all subjects. Roberto insists that J. Posadas is a working collective, which Borges surely must be involved with, and you too, he says to me. Aren't you? According to him, everything that's written in Argentina winds up in the writings of J. Posadas.

Thursday 4
As soon as I lower the drawbridge David calls and comes to see me: anxious and doing badly, no house, no work, trying to get accommodation in the tower on Cangallo and Rodríguez Peña.

Series C. At night, while waiting for Julia to return from the College so we can go to dinner together, I reread my notebooks from the year '65. At times my conviction has been psychotic. A character who gets tangled up in his own thoughts, drowning himself in a web of fixed ideas until he is completely paralyzed, face up on the bed, struggling to breathe.

Friday, March 5
The city destroyed, cracks and trenches in the street. We walked in single file along the wooden walkway that serves as a bridge over the deep wells that have been dug into Calle Florida, "unrepaired." The humid sun, hot gas jetting from the exhaust of a little tractor that went along the sidewalk at walking speed, piling up hundreds of pedestrians behind it in a long line.

Saturday

I meet Ricardo Nudelman and the Chilean guy who sang boleros in the bar on Viamonte and Maipú. The Chilean uses saccharin to sweeten his coffee, a little white device that reminds me of the round containers of DDT they used to spray anthills when I was a boy. We travel all around the city by bus: he talks about playing a duet with Gregorio Barrios. Later, in a house in Belgrano, we spend three hours talking about the situation in Chile and about the world in general. A strong impression. Instant camaraderie, encounters that always seem to occur among friends who've known each other for years.

Tuesday, March 16

In the reading room of the library of La Plata. Difficulty writing with a new tip on my pen. I'm reading several works on Meyerhold.

I skirt around the plaza to get a malted milk at a kiosk that sells sandwiches to students; opposite, the diagonal street with blue flowers on the ground that I used to walk down to my boarding house on 17th and 57th.

"The aesthetics of our times will be seen forced to accept norms manufactured in other media of society. Our art is nevertheless something different to the art of any prior era," Meyerhold.

Wednesday 24

I shut myself in, close the door, turn off my phone, ready to write all day. I go to the kitchen to make tea for myself, and the phone and the doorbell start ringing at the same time. I stay in the kitchen, in the dark, and the bell rings several times. After that it starts to ring every five minutes, but I don't pay attention to it, determined to seize the day all the same, although I feel a strange, indefinable sensation that I'm making a fool of myself. Of course, literature is my excuse: what I'm seeking—the only things I'm seeking—are these flights from reality. Locked in, all of the blinds closed, with artificial light, it's as though I were absent. Hence the impression caused by the weak ringing of the phone: as though I were besieged by an enemy tribe, trying to break through my defenses and enter. The funny thing—other than the anecdote itself—is that, while I'm hidden away, political reality continues its course: when I go out into the street, I find out that one military president has been supplanted by another.

Friday
The afternoon with Julia in La Plata, rowing in the lake among the woods and then pedaling some strange velocipedes that move like marine motorcycles.

Saturday
Notes on Tolstoy (14). Leo Tolstoy was the first writer to use the new invention of the typewriter, in 1855. "The Death of Ivan Ilyich" (1886) and his great final works were written in that way. "The Kreutzer Sonata" (1889), "Father Sergius" (1891), and "Hadji Murat" (1904) took his narrative capacity to its limit; formally, these nouvelles are very different from his novels, complex, direct, almost without description. He also allowed his daughter Alexandra to learn how to use it, and in time he dictated his works and correspondence to her, so that Tolstoy's daughter became the first typist in Europe.

Tuesday, March 30
Nostalgia just from glimpsing vague silhouettes in the streets of the city where I was, remembering a hazy past, missing what I imagine I have experienced; an inversion of Borges's line, which I will use in my novel: only what one never had can be lost.

I spent all morning finishing my delayed work: I wrote a review and several pieces about the books we're going to publish; the usual stops in the afternoon, Galerna, Tiempo Contemporáneo, meetings with David, who is still obsessed with Cortázar, and then an interview about the publishing house with a stupid journalist for *Siete Días* magazine.

On Monday I meet León R. in the bar on Tucumán and Uruguay, a long conversation that veers toward León's opinions about David, his compulsion that forces him to write one book after another at top speed, his rationalizations to compensate. You have to take León's version with a grain of salt, in any case. Behind us, a girl who was reading Marechal said to the boy who was with her: "Normal people bore me."

Wednesday, March 31
Series E. I feel certain that my entire life is a learning process, the rehearsal for a role I will never perform. The bench on Avenida 51 where I sat with Pochi F. one evening in 1963, waiting for the university dining hall to open, saying that it was essential to study for ten hours every day. A bench that I return to with Julia on Sunday, telling her that I sat in the same place ten years ago, talking with Pochi F., etc. This notebook is proof of the precarious nature of my attention: I take notes of confused feelings, writing them as I experience them in the context of the present; when I read them some time later, they must hold value for themselves and act beyond the circumstances they originally referred to. In that sense, a diary is a laboratory for literature, but in this case the writer is putting himself to the test.

A confusing, exasperating month, buried in ridiculous worries. I'm doing good work on the novel, which is now around a hundred pages. The same lesson as always: if I shut myself in and isolate myself, the novel moves forward, but if I get sidetracked, my progress halts.

Thursday, April 1
X Series. Ricardo N. recounts the years he lived in a slum, his own political choice. The smell that comes up from septic tanks in the summer, getting up at five in the morning in order to get to the factory at six, the cold, the journey by crowded bus. A need to converse with neighbors but an inability to read or write. To me, it seems like the experience of an ethnographer trying to assimilate into the culture he is studying and making it his own.

Thursday, April 8
I extended my rental contract for another year, so I'll keep working in this apartment full of books for forty thousand pesos per month (one hundred dollars) until April of 1972.

Saturday
Today David appeared, surprised at the news he read in the paper announcing my course at the Universidad de La Plata; he thought I'd gotten a professorship and projected his own desires and fears for the future. Who, at his age, still goes to the theater to stave off his loneliness and writes a weekly installment about the people's struggles at full throttle? Always obsessed with Peronism.

A good meeting in the afternoon with Elías, his ironic intelligence, his wisdom helping me to assess a proposal on social demand by Osip Brik, of the Russian avant-garde.

Monday 12
I spend half of the afternoon with the apartment's landlord copying the rental contract for the next year, and his show of compassion and declarations of affection don't prevent him from making me pay for the photocopies and the stamps, raising the deposit, etc. Meanwhile he talks to his wife, nervous, very sensitive. Reason: her father killed himself in front of her. He sends her to the United States to calm her, but as soon as she arrives, she endures an earthquake in Los Angeles; she returns the next day.

Wednesday 14
A strange time, an astronaut floating through space in his capsule.

Sunday 18
In the cold early morning on Monday I read Haroldo's novel, *En vida*, which has an American tone, so to speak, written in present tense like Updike's *Rabbit, Run*. Rather, the conquered hero, the loser, narrated in

Conti's "naïve," spoken, and lyrical style, although he has grown tired of his overly "natural" form. I was with him all morning yesterday and he told me about his trip to Cuba, about Álvar Núñez Cabeza de Vaca, about the daughter of the philosopher V.; he's going out with her and talks about her with "masculine" detachment.

Saturday 24
In these uncertain days, when things happen to me even though I don't seek them, I visit polite English literary agents in a large Victorian house in Belgrano R. to negotiate the translation rights for several American novels.

Penniless, pressed by need, I decide to write some essays and set the novel aside for a while. As a way to distract myself, I read a novel by Mary McCarthy in one sitting, drawn to her narrative mode, intelligent, traditional, in a fast and enticing third-person. The novel is called *A Charmed Life*.

Monday 26
I go to see León but first repeat my old tricks; penniless, I count coins before I go out into the street; these tricks are old because I have aged and have nothing to lose.

Tuesday 27
At home, Luna brings money after five days of destitution. Vague news from Córdoba, including the honoraria for my courses and plans for teaching there again in the future. We end up drinking whiskey at Ramos; I haven't eaten anything since the day before, and I order some cheese, but the whiskey still makes me float away.

Thursday 29
An overcrowded dinner to inaugurate the main office of Siglo XXI in Argentina. Orfila Reynal was forced to step down from the Fondo de Cultura for having published *The Children of Sanchez* by Oscar Lewis,

considered to be anti-Mexican; he immediately organized a new publishing house with great international support and headquarters in Mexico: a great catalogue that starts with *The Order of Things* by Foucault and the novel *José Trigo* by Fernando del Paso, highly praised by Rulfo. Bad food and many speeches at the dinner. Varied and fleeting meetings: Briante, Jitrik, Altamirano, Mario Benedetti, et al. A myriad of circulation, ending up with several friends at La Paz bar, Schmucler, Tandeter. On the way out, Federico Luppi praises my script about the criminals' standoff.

Friday, April 30
At noon walking around the city with Nicolás C., bound to the past, trying to get me excited about a new meeting of leftist intellectuals . . .

Saturday, May 1
A visit from David, this time because of the Peronists' review of the movies he made with Fernando Ayala in *Envido* magazine; he reacts like a liberal, but he's intelligent and is working on anarchist texts now.

Series B. Earlier with Carlos B. He goes back and forth about the movie, wants to wait until January of next year so that he can make the film with Luppi. Sitting at the beautiful bar on Corrientes and Callao, La Ópera, which I've only just discovered: vast, empty, and bright, ideal for meeting friends or sitting down to read.

Monday 3
A series of calls makes me get out of bed, dead tired, freezing, to hear about my friends' outrage at Fidel Castro's speech against the intellectuals. The Padilla affair is at the center of it, and Fidel's use of description (rats, etc.) is in the classic Soviet tradition. Everyone knows the model, an administrative dictatorship tries to impose a single type of thinking, eliminating any possibility of criticism.

Dinner at the house of Juan M., a poet and tango pianist. An old apartment, elegant, with a patio and an entryway with large art deco doors.

M. reads me a strange story with an algebraic logic of the absurd, with surrealist devices and pornographic images. It is articulated in an archaic voice, propped up on alcohol. At times, while I listened to him reading it amid the suspicious and offended indifference of the others (his wife, his brother), I thought that he reminded me of Malcolm Lowry and that his text had the visible mark of Kafka. He is one of those men who goes onward with his work with a stubborn will, in spite of everything, as though he could do nothing else. In M.'s case, I find out that he has three novels, a book of short stories, two works of theater, and a book of poems. All unpublished. Where does he draw the conviction from to keep writing those paralyzed stories, outside of any accepted conventions, abstract, symbolic? On the other hand, he is a recognized tango pianist who has played with great orchestras, has enjoyed the Buenos Aires nightlife, and is now the pianist in the Sexteto Mayor, playing special concerts in Buenos Aires and traveling around the world. Always half-drunk, loquacious and charming, dressed with an old-fashioned elegance (he wore a velvet *robe de chambre*), yet the only thing that mattered to him was finding a reader for his secret work, which no one around him has any interest in.

Tuesday 4

Various sources of distress among the intellectuals on the left, faced with Padilla's ridiculous Stalinist self-criticism and Fidel Castro's police speech. The convention that the Cuban leaders use to justify themselves is based on the idea that intellectuals must have no privilege, but one thinks straight away that, if they treated a poet who posed as a dissident as they did, it's easy to imagine what will happen to opponents of common origin. Or should we think that they don't exist, that Padilla is just a solitary madman imagining critiques of the system? On the other hand, the working of the criticism is, in itself, proof of Soviet influence: the conscience that Padilla seems to have acquired while in prison (solitude, isolation, introspection, police pressure) is totally opposite to what we might imagine socialist democracy to be; that is, no one from his field argues with him, only the police, and they convince him and take him to the stand so that he can play the role of the repentant clown, telling off and questioning the writers present, as though he were now an example. In fact, the administrative methods of the Cuban leadership are visible: they never open the discussion until the issue is closed, and then everyone can be in agreement with the decision they've made in secret. Otherwise, the content of the self-criticism that I read today in *Marcha*, while drinking a coffee at a bar on Viamonte and Uruguay, is shameful: anyway, the worst part isn't the content of what Padilla says, but rather what we on the left call the conditions of production of his little discourse (which seems to have been edited by the political police).

Wednesday 5

Decrepitude of old texts from the sixties, magazines, statements, news pieces that were alive in those days and caused argumentation and suspicion. Today, for forty pesos, I bought an issue of *Eco Contemporáneo*, a magazine in a complaintive style: "lyrical" sadness, depoliticization, and "poetry" of experience. Its greatest merit was that it dedicated an issue to old Gombrowicz.

I came and went along the streets, swept by the freezing wind, crossing the city to Fausto on Santa Fe in search of the diary of Ernst Jünger. On the way back along Callao, pausing on every corner, disoriented as in old times.

A gray-haired man in Pippo restaurant was giving cigarettes, medallions, and foreign coins to a platinum blonde in hot pants. She was provocative and had come accompanied by a young man; the gray-haired man—dressed in a buckskin jacket, seemingly friends with the two—was getting hot with the woman and started to touch her skin, gave her a pack of Camels. She touched up her makeup in her little hand mirror and showed off her breasts squeezed into her sweater. When the young man went to the bathroom, the gray-haired man moved his hands to his neck, detached a little gold chain with a cross, and handed it to the woman. She shook her head, the gold chain in her right hand, maintaining the same hard and cold expression. When the young man who was with her came back, he made her stop resisting and she accepted the little chain, put it around her neck, and buried the silver cross between her breasts, under the sweater.

Thursday 6

I will never be able to help Julia with her fears (a brutal summary: the daughter of an unknown man, Julia herself abandoned her own newborn daughter for the father to take care of). I can't come up with any real solutions (find her father, whom there are some traces of, recover her daughter, who is now three years old). Instead of these possible actions, all I do is embrace her and console her, uselessly. Then, in my despicable style, I rationalize, give definitions, talk about codes, talk about Kant, trying to cover up her mantra.

New rituals, I go out at dawn (five or six in the morning) and walk down Montevideo to Corrientes to buy *La Opinión* (*Le Monde*, translated). The frozen city gray under the white lights, and in bars, in restaurants, nocturnal people crowding in to survive, trying not to lose the night.

Friday 7

I am alone (Julia is still in La Plata), I get up at three in the afternoon, my mouth dry from working all night, and write these notes. Then I cross the gray city in the light rain, go to the publishing office, find Eduardo Menéndez and Eliseo Verón, and we talk about books in translation, collections, and new projects.

I try to free myself from the stupor of last night's alcohol and work on the article about Brecht.

Saturday 8

I am at home, it is raining outside, an invisible chill in the early morning (six thirty). I reread my notes and old notebooks, in which I envisioned glorious futures.

In a veiled way, he schemed faint suicides, letting himself fall, coming undone. Murder inside me, he said.

Monday 10

I go to sleep at seven in the morning on Sunday, worried about my lack of money, after feeling my way forward with the essay. In the middle of that Roberto Jacoby visits me, conversations about the possible influence of *La Opinión* on the culture of the left. Will it come to have the influence that *Primera Plana* had in the sixties? The avant-garde today defines itself as an alternative to the media; it infiltrates them, criticizes them, and ignores them.

I want to see whether, by sleeping very little (today I got up at eleven, after four hours of sleep), I can "reverse" time and start to work during the day.

Tuesday 11

An hour and a half waiting to negotiate a ("universal") loan that I need in order to make it through the year without economic problems. The episode has the effect of plunging me into reality (which I always deny), making me see the weight of money. As I say, so as to put my aristocratic relationships—and wasteful spending—in jeopardy, it will be enough, with the money I make.

Thursday, May 13

My reading in the last few months (especially Joyce and Brecht) confirms to me that I am (at least) five years "behind" with respect to the rest of my generation. I'm always reading out of sync, and that reading is more productive; I always work on books out of context, in different relationships tied to my own rhythm and not to the atmosphere of the times. For example, with Brecht I'm interested in the essays and not the theater, and in Joyce I look for his classical forms and want nothing to do with the stream-of-consciousness writing that wreaks havoc among my contemporaries. Being at the vanguard is being outside of time, in a present that is not everyone's present.

Saturday, May 15
I've already wasted the night, it is four in the morning on Saturday, and I have been working uselessly on an essay that seems to have no end: I accumulate notes, outlines, scattered ideas, trusting in my ability to structure them later.

I don't manage to "flip the day around." I start working at ten at night, and dawn is already coming by the time I realize it.

Wednesday 19
A roundtable about literary criticism for the cultural section of *Clarín*: Jitrik, Romano, Horacio Salas, Schmucler, and me. I talked about criticism as the writer's way of reading, using the example of Brecht the Marxist and—for provocation—Pound the Peronist: both are anti-liberal and therefore readers of the avant-garde, etc. Paradoxically, the discussion "organized" itself: Romano and Salas vs. Schmucler and me. Noé Jitrik in the middle.

Sunday 23
X Series. Rubén came over, always the same contagious and gentle conviction. A curious simplicity that lets him elucidate the most complex issues and, at the same time, ferociously defend his political, voluntaristic, and minoritarian line. His group seems to be the only one that opposes Peronism while still being populist and that criticizes the militantism of the guerrilla groups while also defending some revolutionary violence (of the masses). I talk with them, listen to them, collaborate on their clandestine publications under a pseudonym, and stop there. Rubén and Elías laugh at me a little: I'm a theorist who never reaches practical reality. But what they see as a flaw, I cultivate as my finest quality. It rains ceaselessly. It is four thirty on Monday morning, and I listen to the latest news on Radio Mitre.

Monday, May 24
Exhausted, dead tired, he is surrounded by sinister ideas, moods of escape: locked up in this house with the windows shuttered, he sleeps badly, sits

down at the table at eight in the evening, and the fatigue makes him suspicious of everything, himself most of all. He prepares for the classes he will teach at the College in La Plata, writing notes, making summaries, diagrams, etc. Such is his life in this dull time, working without pause or happiness. He envisions glorious futures, just as gray as this afternoon, and he is breathless yet again.

Friday 28

All of the intellectuals on the left are stuck on the Padilla affair. A meeting at Walsh's house to discuss a possible statement. There are the liberals, horrified at the Stalinist violence against human dignity. "So, life is better under capitalism" (Rozitchner). The anti-intellectual populists with their opportunism, pragmatism, fetishization of strength. "The one in power is always more legitimate than any political legitimacy that isn't in power or has no power" (Walsh). Viñas stays in sullen silence the whole time. Urondo yields to Walsh's position. For my part, I argue that politics is leaving its own sphere and that we, as writers, must therefore politicize ourselves: the incarceration and subsequent self-criticism of a poet—whose poems we all value—is something we must use to think about our relationship to the Cuban leadership, speaking generally about all of the problems, taking positions on any issue that doesn't follow the path we consider correct. We have to start from what we know and, in this case, we have a fairly clear idea of what happens in the literary sphere in Cuba and so can talk about that. It seems impossible to criticize the liberalism of intellectuals, who want to be the protagonists of history, and the Cuban revolutionary leadership at the same time.

I met Heberto Padilla in Havana at a bar in El Vedado with tables on the terrace. He recited fragments of a novel by Mallea to me, as though he admired him or was making fun of him and laughing at Argentine literature in passing. There are those who make history and those who suffer it, he said with a smile. A friend of Cabrera Infante, he published a laudatory essay on *Three Trapped Tigers* in which he made fun of Lisandro

Otero and his novel *Urbino's Passion*, but Otero is an official writer, and so an obscene letter threatening Padilla appeared in *Verde Olivo*, the army's magazine, signed with a pseudonym but surely written, according to Padilla, by Otero himself. Literary enmity under socialism turns into a State matter (remember Pasternak's reaction to Mandelstam's imprisonment).

I listen to music, Schumann, Mozart, Schubert . . . in the night. It is four thirty in the morning.

Saturday 29
Classes in La Plata, a divided audience: my old friends (Sazbón, García Canclini, Schmucler, etc.) and the young professors of letters, poorly trained and very attentive. I established some good relationships between Tynyanov, Tretyakov, Brecht, and Benjamin via Asja Lācis.

Once more I found the city where I had lived for five years just the same— sophisticated, welcoming a legion of students from all over the country every season. I remembered that day in 1959, shortly after arriving, with Alvarado, happy to be starting a life far away from everything.

On Thursday, eating dinner in a strange restaurant with a family room, I see Pola again, now foolish, a beautiful and decadent actress in the style of T. Williams's heroines. Who ever changes?

Sunday, May 30
Maybe I should bring this notebook to a close by saying that, today, I have an almost absolute certainty that the novel I've been writing for three years isn't working. We'll see what I do.

Consecutive and undifferentiated nightmares. I wake up at dawn with a clear feeling of horror, my body sweaty as though I'd been swimming in contaminated waters.

Tuesday, June 1

I load myself down with books (Bryce Echenique, Mailer, Beckett), something done thoughtlessly amid a series of distractions set off by the four-class course I taught in La Plata on Marxism and literary criticism for the series organized by Néstor García Canclini (in which Nicolás Rosa talked about psychoanalysis and literary criticism and Menena Nethol about linguistics, etc.). Preparing the course took me two months, and everything was centered around Brecht and Benjamin's essays and their polemics with Lukács. In Marx, the most interesting thing is his concept of art as unproductive labor for capitalism (it doesn't produce surplus value). Benjamin and Brecht developed the consequences of this opposition.

I see Marta Lynch at La Paz; strangely, she arranges to meet me for no clear reasons, and I see she is afraid of not being involved with the possible statement we are making about the Padilla affair. Dressed in gray, aging but attractive, as soon as she sits down she tells me about her ovaries getting inflamed because of her appendix. I look at her with a resigned expression.

Wednesday, June 2

I slept for twelve hours straight.

Thursday 3

I stopped working at night. I got up at ten in the morning and revised the article on the situation in Chile with Lucas. Then David came over, still vacillating: a letter to Fernández Retamar about the Padilla affair, centrist and ambiguous. We already know, as Barthes said, that the neither-nor is the key to middle-class thought; he called it *thought scales*. David has always been the opposite, although he does like binary oppositions too much; but, in this case, he's clouded by the possibility of making things bad with the Cubans or with us.

Saturday 5

In a room at Signos publishing, we recorded a roundtable in which Aricó, Altamirano, Schmucler, and I discussed the Padilla affair. The problem is the self-critical confession that sounds, on the one hand, like something forced by the police and, on the other hand, like a parody deliberately carried out by Padilla himself to take all of the seriousness out of the situation. But that would be a cynical reading because the truth is that it makes no sense to take a poet prisoner, not because he is a poet, but rather because it is supposed that literature has no political potency. And so there are two possibilities: either the Cubans have become fanatics of the potency of poetry, or they are using Padilla in order to attack tendencies or groups opposed to the government's politics.

León R. calls me at midnight and then comes over, desolate and sad, to have a glass of wine, "tormented" because his opinions on Borges in the newspaper *La Opinión* were unclear and because of his article on the Soviet Union in the UNESCO magazine.

Imaginary economy. Yesterday, after León left, I went down to the street at three in the morning in a bad mood to buy *La Opinión* and look at his article about Borges, and on the way back I found five thousand pesos (almost a hundred dollars) in the entry door. Delight, a strange feeling of a trick or a crime: I took the stairs so they wouldn't see that the elevator stopped on my floor and be able to find me. I turned out the lights to make it seem like I was sleeping, and then I thought the bills were counterfeit or had been stolen and were marked. Only tonight, when I paid for my dinner, could I believe that the cash was real. Actually, I perceived the fetishistic relationship between the money found in the street, as though it were just paper, and real value; it was "trash" and not money while it lay on the ground, and if it was money, it was only there to make me dirty and compromise me. All of these delusions because it's irrational that five thousand pesos could be thrown on the floor, in reach of my hand.

Wednesday, June 9
Standing on Corrientes and Talcahuano with Luis Gusmán: I'm looking for a biology book for Julia, and we talk about his book, which I'll take

to read. A couple approaches us; she is bleached-blonde, he wears tight pants and has a book. He bends forward and speaks with excessive humility: "Could you give us any change, we have no money to travel." I give him what I have in my pocket and they leave. Then I think about the two of them in some kind of boarding house, counting the coins. A way of life that must surely organize their relationship in a "singular" manner.

Thursday 10
Yesterday I met with Haroldo Conti, who experiences winning the Barral prize in Spain "as though it were happening to someone else," just as depressed and insecure. We had lunch together at a greasy bar on Lavalle where he works on a "Latin American" script with Sarquís (in the style of Glauber Rocha).

Lots of vacillation over the Padilla affair. First discussions about the matter with Schmucler and Aricó. A decision not to push forward any statements, to let things run. Then David, who is just as euphoric as he is every time he has money (fifty thousand pesos for *Lisandro*); I argue with him, forcefully, about his letter to Cuba (liberal, hesitant, etc.).

Friday 11
In the morning I write the introduction to the article on Chile for *Cuadernos Rojos*, which I sign as Juan Erdosain.

Saturday 12
At night at home with Páez, a delegate from the combative labor unions of SITRAC. The usual amazement, especially for me, of being rapidly implicated by "others" in a special situation that I generally haven't chosen, as though I were dragged in by the circumstances themselves. And so today, Páez from SITRAC, one of the leaders in the Cordobazo. He sat down on the sofa with his bare feet on the table, the center of attention all night. "A seducer," I thought, "this guy is a seducer." It had to do with something else, but that's the way I think about situations that are foreign to my world. The problem, according to him, is motivating the unions

individually by factory so as to oppose the bureaucratic centralization of the Peronist unions. Of course, that weakens the popular sector's ability to negotiate.

Monday
I go in circles around the city, which I no longer yearn for as I did in the old days, when I had my life ahead of me and a clear sense that justice would prevail for me. (Who will make their voices heard in this deserted city?) Now, by contrast, I perceive what can never be had.

At *Los Libros* I meet Viñas, Germán García, Casullo, et al. Many projects: a press conference tomorrow at Philosophy and Letters with the people from SITRAC, which we prepare for with (excessive) enthusiasm.

Among the books that I receive to review for the magazine, one is an anthology, *Nuevos narradores argentinos*, which Néstor Sánchez put together for Monte Ávila in Venezuela (it includes "La honda," a story I wrote ten years ago).

Tuesday, June 15
I crossed the city in the warm June night to attend the SITRAC press conference at the Núñez University campus. I remembered an assembly at the College in La Plata (how long ago?), which I didn't attend because it was raining. Luis Alonso's face in the doorway, unable to believe it.

Friday 18
I walk down Corrientes, pass through the bookshops, spend a long time looking over used books in Moro. I run into Luis Gusmán at Martín Fierro and we talk about Lacan, or rather he talks about Lacan while I think about something else: I have to let Haroldo Conti know that the second edition of *A Moveable Feast* came out. Then I go back, buy sausages at the market, cook them up, and eat them with salad; I think I'll have the whole afternoon to work in peace. Now I'm going to make some maté.

Tuesday 22

I'm reading Macedonio: extraordinary narrative positions about the possibilities for writing a novel. Analogy: Macedonio is to Borges what Pound is to Hemingway.

Wednesday

Luna came from Córdoba unexpectedly, the same stories as always. That bastard Montes, who betrayed Fiat in exchange for four hundred thousand pesos so he could pay off his debts. After that, he "fled" to Buenos Aires like a criminal.

Friday

I decide to take a walk, to distract myself for a bit; I run into David and go to El Foro with him. He smothers me with his current obsession: the magazine *La Comuna*. We discuss the inclusion of a poem by Gelman. Opportunism, I don't agree with it (Gelman directs the literary section of *La Opinión*). David knows I'm right, so he gets angry. He just came from seeing Aricó, which reminds me about my article for *Pasado y Presente*. I keep going and walk alone down Calle Corrientes toward Air France, where I ask if a ticket to Paris came for me from the Cubans. As I walk around the city, ideas circulate around my head at top speed: better to write at night, to detach, to see no one. But, since I always wake up at sundown if I work until sunrise, because I go down to have breakfast and buy the papers, it's better to work in the morning . . .

All that time going in and out of bookshops on Corrientes, Florida, Viamonte, absurdly looking for a book of short stories by Raúl Dorra, and when I leave Ateneo I hesitate between going back toward Viamonte and Florida or continuing along Reconquista to Paraguay. I do the latter. I enter Harrods and go to the bookshop where Lecuona is. I am awkward and brusque, but in spite of everything I confirm that Dorra's book is in Tres Américas, number 1300 on Chile. I go out and come across Miguel Briante on Paraguay, but I barely wave to him and then keep going at a distance even though he stops, wanting to speak to me, and I turn halfway around and get into a taxi. (We have decided to save up and not spend more than a thousand pesos—two dollars—per day to make it to the end of the month without debt.) I spend four hundred pesos on a book that I'll likely never read.

Saturday, June 26

It is three in the afternoon. I just ate a couple of sandwiches for lunch with a glass of milk, an apple, and a double espresso in the bar on the corner, and now I'm at home alone with the door locked, the phone covered with blankets to muffle the ringing. It is cold, the afternoon is gray, my freezing hands make it hard for me to write, and I am happy.

Sunday

Series E. The Pavesian part of me is mythical resonance, and so these notebooks must be "open," with stray information and moral centers.

July

Satisfied with the roundtable in *Clarín:* a certain obsessive repetition of the same idea (to write is to think) gives some coherence to my remarks.

I run into Horacio. I used to play with him as a child, and now he has a Citroën, two children, a profession, and lives in the house where he was born; he is who I would be if I had stayed in Adrogué. We wander around the city in the sun and eat lunch by the river. Everything that I "have," I have gained by "losing" what he has, and vice versa.

I am reading Kafka.

Friday 2

The matter of a pair of shoes: Julia buys them for me because, in my flight from reality, I won't even do that for myself. She brings them over and I think the salesman gave her the wrong ones, these shoes aren't size 40. They feel too big (especially in the right foot), so I vacillate between going to exchange them or not, wasting the afternoon on that, and now (having decided to keep them because I can't deal with showing up in front of the salesman with the box) I feel my foot is too loose in the right shoe, as though enveloped by some void.

I ended up at the theater to make myself forget the wasted day: *Metello* by Bolognini, based on Pratolini, old stories that I admired in my adolescence.

Saturday 3
A good afternoon's work on the novel, sometimes I think I have a "great" book in my hands. Earlier I saw David on Montevideo as I went out, furtively, to buy milk and ham for breakfast. He "hangs" on me once again, conspiratorial after our recent distance. He came back from Córdoba, where he had fled to get away from a new emotional crisis. As always, he creates ideologies to compensate: he leaves without warning and disappears for a week so that everyone will think he committed suicide or is in prison, and he chooses Córdoba as a place of refuge because he can justify himself when he returns by talking about politics, the need to see what's going on there, etc. Typical.

Monday, July 5
X Series. Rubén K. in a blue suit, handsome, because he came to say goodbye to his father, who is going to Europe. He brings a record by Viglietti, and "interprets" the lyrics while he listens to it, humming, etc. He is able to be many people at the same time, which is all of a politician's allure. He talks about the difficulty of working in Córdoba, where they concentrate on SITRAC without paying attention to the rest of the country. Stubbornness, optimism that must be renewed every day.

Earlier with Schmucler. Worried about the difficulties of making *Los Libros* work without support from Galerna. We prepare for the trip to Córdoba in August. I get some books and am content (Henry James, Hammett, etc.).

Tuesday

At night with Edgardo F. and Eduardo M. A woman follows Eduardo and gets onto the train to Mar del Plata after him. "Her makeup deformed her face, don't you think it's strange that a woman would have so much makeup on at eight in the morning?" The fatal coherence of the paranoiac: a great subject. Then at midnight in La Paz, with Dipi Di Paola describing his journey to Robinson Crusoe island. He makes himself call at the magazine (*Panorama*) where he spends his afternoons, even though he has no interest in the work, writing a book review every week for five thousand pesos.

Wednesday

I travel to La Plata with Roberto Jacoby to participate in a conversation with García Canclini in Fine Arts, and we discuss the role of the union bureaucracy. Roberto thinks that breaking up the workers' movement into unions by factory weakens the struggle; you have to be attentive to real politics. He is a Trotskyist, but also half Peronist. A packed room in La Plata, one hundred "artists" who don't understand a single word. We talk—especially Roberto—about art as a social practice that includes circulation as a part of the work. Then an assembly, and a kid with Bulgarian features defends the Ninth Symphony . . .

Friday, July 9

I went down to the city at midnight, populated by strange groups, young people with manes of dark hair, half-naked women. I walked alone along Corrientes as I had before, five, six, or seven years ago, barely sustained by my excessive hopes and grand fantasies. The lights, the passers-by, the music in the shops. I know of no more perfect solitude.

I am reading Virginia Woolf's diary.

Sunday 11

I spend the morning at a table in La Paz reading newspapers and magazines, and then I take a walk through San Telmo and come back along

Carlos Pellegrini to avoid the wreckage caused by the lengthening of the avenue, admiring the profile of the city that seemed to grow against the ruins.

X Series. Yesterday Lucas and I ate lunch together at Pippo after walking down Avenida de Mayo, and we ended up having a coffee at Ramos (he found a hundred pesos on the sidewalk, so we could pay for it). We grew closer to one another, sizing each other up with the help of irony: his fictitious self-appreciation, brusque shyness, resentment for his failure in the great omnipotent projects from age twenty. More than anything else, these things unite us. Politics is what coincidentally comes afterward, something we throw away because it hinders the fluid circulation of intelligence. He was a prisoner after Taco Ralo, and that experience radicalized him even further. He is always armed.

Monday, July 12
I go to León R.'s course. An agitated argument about mythology in Greek art according to Marx. León sees in mythology something previous to ideology; I find him religious, Hegelian, but of course I cannot prove it. Anyway, I drag the ensemble of people attending the class behind me. "But then *everything* is ideology to you," León rages, and we start all over.

At night I go to the theater and see *The Gospel According to St. Matthew* by Pasolini. There can be no more beautiful story: all of them come from there, from Shakespeare to Faulkner. I'm moved by incessant monologues, always aimed at proving something: sermons, parables, prayers, speeches, there is no other word. All it accomplishes is to give the word of Christ a delirious and obsessive dimension. A good way to create a character: on one hand, everything he says is "significant" and, at the same time, that very expressivity serves to create him as a character. Thus, he is the "bearer of a message" and at the same time a delusional character who only speaks of God, of heaven, of hell and, faced with any action, question, or situation that takes place in front of him, responds with sermons and stories. Thus his relationship to Don Quixote. Both are "naïve" because their word is preexisting, already written (in the books of chivalry or the Holy Scriptures), and both are slightly ridiculous because they always seem to be talking about "something else."

Tuesday 13
Near the end of a good afternoon's work, Juan Carlos Martini calls me on the phone: "I'm recording," he says. "What's your opinion on Proust?" After that I splutter and say foolish things like someone caught off guard in an uncomfortable situation—climbing over a wire fence, let's say—who is asked to recite "Ode on a Grecian Urn" by Keats. When the interview comes out in *Confirmado*, I'll die.

David came over at noon; more and more time goes by when we don't see each other, but there's always the same sympathy as a result of our agreements and (my) concessions. He grumbles about the PCR cadres, following him at half speed on his project for *La Comuna*. He discovers the same schematization, the same foolish resolutions that are traditional for militant politicians. Distance from the most flexible leaders and, along with that, the personal obsessions that he turns into ideology, against which (the politicians) must fight. He wants to write a theater piece about Manuelita Rosas, etc. Euphoric about the success of his work *Lisandro*, which has given him enough money so that he is absent from the places he frequented when he was poor (that's why I see him less than before). My situation with him: deep down, I seem "cold" and not very sincere to him; he says that I'm his best friend, and at same time he demonstrates a way of being—excessively explicit and self-centered—that is my antithesis. He keeps getting stuck on certain writers, Manuel Puig, Conti, Borges, Cortázar, or Bioy, who are, according to David, carrying out a project for the right. I argued this point very determinedly with him, saying that he talks like that because he doesn't read books, just builds his theories based on arbitrary and very intelligent readings that center around the figure of the writer. At the end of the argument, I offer the example of Walsh, who has written ten short stories in ten years of work and now directs the newspaper of the CGT.

Wednesday, July 14

Series E. I spend the morning rereading these notebooks, and with this one I have reached number forty-eight: a thousand pages written, and I hope two hundred can be salvaged. Maybe 25 percent? I'm getting sick of all these numbers.

Thursday, July 15

If no one knew anything about him, he would be happy. To live in secret, to walk through the city, forgotten, convinced of his future glory. That's all he needs these days: today, for example, a long process at the publishing office to get his salary check so he can pay the rent. I'll be at peace until the middle of August at least, with no need to think about money, he said, disillusioned.

Friday 16

I run into David on Corrientes at noon today when I go out to have a coffee at La Paz and read the newspaper. Instantly we turn to Peronism: he criticizes *La Opinión*, which plays the game of the current way of living with Perón. It's almost a personal matter to him. It feels like David and I are patrolling the area (from Corrientes and Callao to 9 de Julio), two solitary wolves in the city, and that's why we meet each other so often in the street. Before that, I had spent half of the morning with Vicente Battista and Goloboff, who are writing an editorial about Padilla for the magazine *Nuevos Aires*. They critique the politicians' harshness toward literature and defend the autonomy of art (as if that were the issue).

Last night I meet Manuel Puig, anxious around each translation of one of his books, as though he were always writing them for the first time in another language. Very wise, with a fine professional awareness and a great sense for detecting "what" is a good piece of writing: he critiques the monotony of Conti's style, "always the same for any subject," the sloppiness of Mailer, "who doesn't write anything well." His knowledge is very instrumental, as a writer's training must be:

he has a great ability to find what he needs quickly. For example, he tells me: "I looked over Joyce's *Ulysses* a little, saw that every chapter was written with a different style and technique, and that spoke to me." When I asked him how his relationship with Spanish had survived, given that he had lived in New York for many years immersed in another language, he answered me with a smile: "Spanish, for me, was my language in bed." All of his grace and charm are mixed in with the drama of his personal life: tempestuous love with a Brazilian journalist, unexpected and casual romance with a taxi driver who picks him up on the corner when he's on his way to spend the night in the underbelly of Palermo. A strange and very friendly relationship with me: he is suspicious of my "merits" for reasons inversely proportional to my suspicions of his own.

What is the cause of this winning streak I am sinking into? Invitations to give lectures, offers for anthologies, magazines, theater projects. Of course it doesn't mean anything, but where is it coming from?

Monday, August 2
Julia studies for whole nights, preparing for three subjects in turn. I use the day to wander around the city, visiting bars and bookshops, and end up at the cocktail party at Siglo XXI, where I find Sazbón, with his usual irony, and some other inhabitants of the world. Among them B., who insists on having me work with him on a documentary about the student movement. At one point I am cornered among books, armchairs, and the wall, and I drink whiskey ceaselessly while simultaneously talking with Eliseo Verón, José Sazbón, Luis Gusmán, and Manuel Puig, who in his turn comes with a professor from Yale: I talk to everyone at the same time about different things.

Tuesday 3
I work for a couple of hours and then go to the theater to see *Little Big Man* by Arthur Penn, and when it ends I go for a pizza at Los Inmortales.

Friday 6

I am writing at six in the afternoon when I find out on the radio about the death of Germán Rozenmacher, a great friend and companion whom I met at the beginning of everything, in 1962, when we, along with Miguel Briante, won a short story competition in *El Escarabajo de Oro*. He was in Mar del Plata, spending a few days with his wife and son, and died because of a gas leak from the heater. I remember that night in the bar on Córdoba and Reconquista, or the last time in the bar on Córdoba and Callao; I was sitting out on the sidewalk, and he stopped to say hello.

Sunday 8

Yesterday I went to the funeral service for G. R., in which each of us saw our own death.

Wednesday 11

A meeting at Pirí's house with Walsh, Briante, and Conti to discuss the political situation and to see how we can participate in everything that is happening. No clear conclusion, Rodolfo thinks it would be best for us to all collaborate on the CGT newspaper, but I'm not a Peronist and don't like to pretend such things.

I find David in the early morning in the bar on Cangallo and Rodríguez Peña; he wants to write a novel, which he has started to outline, about anarchists and the attack against Ramón Falcón. So far, the best part seems to be the real police report that he's thinking of inserting into the book.

Friday 20

X Series. Lucas is still despairing because of the death of his friend Emilio Jáuregui; he was his supervisor at the time of the action in Plaza Once, and he shouldn't have let him carry a weapon, shouldn't have let him go alone. The police ambushed him and killed him. After six months, Lucas slept with Ana, the widow, and signed his notes as Emilio Vázquez. A year later he is alone again, stunned by the pain; today, he stayed over with us because it was raining, and he told Julia about his desolation. Ana lives with a painter, and he has to move on from one day to the next. What makes the story most tragic is his idiotic need to deny the legitimacy of that pain.

All afternoon I read Carlos Baker's biography of Hemingway.

Tuesday 24
Last night a dinner at Osvaldo T.'s house with him and his wife, listening to their stories: the guys from the Fuerzas Armadas Revolucionarias, who leave him a message in the hotel when they find out that he's in Córdoba to write a piece about the death of the chief of police. They call him on the phone, and when he crosses the hall to answer, a stranger appears: "Just answer, then come with me." On the phone a woman calms him down, tells him to follow the stranger to her room. There they do the interview, right in the middle of the city, and they show him the cartridge used to kill the policeman while all of the security forces are looking for it.

Friday, August 27
I decide to tell my friends that I'm traveling but then actually stay in Buenos Aires, shut in at home for three days, to see what happens. I was sitting at the table from ten in the morning until nightfall. Doubtless this too is a kind of "artificial respiration"; I invent my father's illness in order to justify my absence and so find, in a way, a chance for happiness, shut up in this dark and silent house, reading and writing as though I were a survivor.

Saturday 28
I am now writing on the round table that Julia painted orange; I've sequestered myself at my desk, calm in my second day of total seclusion (with three more days of not leaving the house ahead of me), isolation that promotes a dubious peace, some confidence in my personal future (despite all of the omens). I work according to my plan, finishing chapter two and getting the third ready.

A second day of seclusion that I withstand very well, a certain torpor, a vague sensation of strain and a slight dizziness that causes me to look at the walls that box me in. Besides that, a certain restlessness comes over me when I think about how I keep gaining weight by staying shut in here, nourishing myself with cheese, potatoes, and bread, a lack of exercise to such a point that I sometimes get cramps in my feet. And so, except for the miserable thoughts that make me think I'm going to become "un gordo," the rest is fine.

Sunday, August 29

Third day of seclusion. As long as I keep filling my time with work on the novel, I don't think I can write anything worthwhile in these notebooks. Especially if I try to narrate my reclusive state.

Monday 30

I get up from the table to celebrate these days of isolation, during which I saw no one and was as happy as I am capable of being these days. I go out to the street and have the feeling that everyone is moving at a speed unknown to me, the cars shine too much under the lights and the noise bothers me. And so I turn down Paraná and enter the restaurant on the corner of Sarmiento. The spacious place, the tables with white tablecloths, the mirrors on the wooden walls, and the motionless waiters in the back calm me down at once.

I have ventured into the street after eighty hours of voluntary reclusion, so I immediately prepare a story about my father, who is "doing badly." Earlier, Julia, whom I let come in, cut my hair too short, causing a certain dark unease within me, strange ideas regarding my face, as though it had transformed in my solitude; I also realize the weight I've "gained" in my stasis while being shut in. This feeling of bodily failure "helps" me to achieve a sufficient tragic atmosphere and theoretical air necessary to make my father's sickness seem realistic. And so I go around the city, repeating my habitual circuit: Los Libros, Galerna, Tiempo Contemporáneo, and a long walk to the Galería del Este and the Di Tella, down marginal streets of the city. The curious thing is this: my story awakens an instantaneous solidarity in the others. Natalio, Luis, Alberto, and Toto tell me about some personal tragedy of their own, conflicts with their wives, their parents, to maintain the climate of sincere tragedy that I have established by talking about my father, hospitalized and ill. In this way, the fiction guarantees me a friendly relationship with everyone after a week's solitude.

September 1

Today is already the next day, but I don't want to leave this notebook without having recorded my current situation: I am waiting for Luna, who arrived this morning and is bringing the money that I need for this month (we have less than three hundred pesos, and I haven't even been able to buy the next notebook). I have to move with great caution to prevent Luna from encroaching on and destroying my plans. He comes with the intention of accompanying me back to Córdoba, but if I don't travel with him he will no doubt change his mind. These details matter little, at least until he arrives in the next hour, when I can better understand his intentions and so prepare "my version."

At noon, while having coffee at La Paz and reading *Libre* magazine, someone tapped on the glass of the window on the corner; it was S., whom I've known since '62. That year when we went with Miguel Briante to read texts by Avellaneda in *Vuelo* magazine, and S. told me that Rozenmacher repeated Rulfo's atmospheres, and I was amazed because I'd never thought of that before. Now he sat down with me and went into the megalomania that is familiar to me; he talks about himself as though there were no other subject. He tells me about some short stories he has written, novels he is about to write, with the certainty and confidence needed for him to believe everything he says.

Luna came, bringing me the money for my classes in Córdoba. He was invited to Vietnam, and he will leave in October and return at the end of January. All of my friends are traveling: Osvaldo T. is traveling to Madrid to interview Perón, León R. is going to Paris, Eliseo V. is traveling to the United States; immediately I think: "Everyone is leaving except for me."

My economic situation has improved. Along with the sixty thousand pesos that Andrés brought for me, I can add the fifty thousand from Tiempo Contemporáneo publishing: with these I'll have the next two months secured.

Julia stopped by Tiempo Contemporáneo to get the check for fifty thousand pesos and also brought a letter from José Giovanni. He is a writer who works on detective films and is also the author of *Le Trou* and *Le Deuxième Souffle*, which I've admired for years. He used the genre to construct an epic based on honor among the marginalized.

Thursday, September 2
I see David; he calls me on the phone, and we meet at La Paz. Worried, he tells me that he was at my house, ringing the bell, knocking on the door. "The bucket and the newspaper were there, I thought something had happened." Just like Andrés, that afternoon when I met him in the hall and he thought I'd committed suicide. David tells me about his project, writing a piece about Dorrego's executions (in plural, the story repeats itself). He sees Dorrego as fat, expansive, demagogic (similar to him), dressed in white, showing his face on the balcony and moving to and fro, swinging around to receive the applause.

Friday, September 3
Perón has received Eva's body. I listen to the story of the events on Radio Belgrano transmitted from Madrid. "The cadaver presents some marks and bruises on the face. Except for that, the body is found to be in perfect condition." I think about Perón, who opens the coffin and—sixteen years later—"finds himself" with the image of Eva and her body before him. "One of the witnesses of the burial ceremony stated this morning that, at the moment the coffin was opened, the ex-president looked for a while at the woman who was his wife and said: 'Eva . . . ,

Eva.' Perón was very moved, and his face was cut up with tears." The remains of lady Eva Perón were transported inside a coffin of dark wood in a van with an Italian license plate. In order to guarantee discretion and the secrecy of her passage through Italy and Spain, the van was switched three times.

In that story, there appears a side character who could be the basis for a novel: Colonel Héctor Cabanillas, head of the Secretariat of Intelligence under Aramburu, who was tasked with taking the body to Europe in 1956 and, five years later, was the only one traveling in the van. Finally, of course, the body of Eva Perón herself: most reviled by the bourgeoisie, who were the least accepting of her (calling her a "whore," an ambitious second-rate actress, viewed as amoral). She was an axis and a symbol with her social ascent and her union with Perón. She is redeemed and exists as the mythical figure who returns in a kind of "journey of the dead," something that is present in all cultures, which she embodies as a new metamorphosis of her brilliant presence. Eva crosses the ocean and has her most consistent enemy as a deluded guardian for sixteen years (given that the colonel was the one tasked with making her disappear). "Colonel Cabanillas silently carried out his mission to deliver Eva Perón's remains in Madrid (just as, before, he had discretely carried out the mission of shutting her in an anonymous tomb in Rome with a plaque bearing another name)." He, who had been tasked with making her disappear; he, who was the only one who knew the key to unlock the secret that the whole nation pursued. His whereabouts are unknown. What became of him, after having kept the very symbol of the working class as his charge? A condemned man, it's enough to think about how he was never promoted in the last sixteen years.

Saturday, September 4
Series C. Suddenly, without any prior warning, the sensation of being absent from life returns, and he moves like a ghost, uncertain. Everything he touches dissolves and is lost, and he no longer has confidence in what he writes, and he thinks it makes no sense to create literature without

conviction. Certainty precedes writing, it is its condition. He is at the nerve center of the story of his life, which has turned into an initiation story. When Murray comes in while Greta is naked, all of his poetics of subtle atmospheres and elliptical prose fall down.

Friday 10
Last night we met M., who goes to the plaza every week to give music classes at Fine Arts and walks lost through the city. With him was F., who seems like another man after having been imprisoned and tortured; he seems nervous, brusquely deciding that we should go to the bar, where we had a few drinks (Llave gin). He recounted his experience in prison with humor (and despair), how he went ten days without eating, "the grill" (the metallic bed where they tied him naked and applied electric shocks with a prod), the commissioner who cocked his .38, a non-regulation caliber, and threatened to kill him and throw him into the Plata river since no one knew he was a prisoner. An extreme experience that you can notice slightly in certain abrupt gestures, the eager way he lights one cigarette after another. Otherwise, Eduardo M., half mute, hiding his terror, his paranoia, which has been building for months, with people who follow him and friends who betray him.

I read the short stories by Baldwin that I'm going to publish at Tiempo Contemporáneo and the stories by Bruce J. Friedman that I will have translated and published by Fausto. I am with Julia in Mar del Plata, a quick visit. Forgotten images awaken me. Now the sun is shining in this frozen city.

We return by train, having café con leche and croissants in the almost empty dining car, illuminated by the sun and the always-lit lamps with glass shades. Earlier, in the afternoon, we saw two Billy Wilder movies for one hundred pesos.

"I am not a realist, I am a materialist . . . I get away from realism by going to reality," S. Eisenstein.

In B. Brecht, it is understood that the opposition between thinking and feeling, or between intelligence and the heart, or between rationality and emotion, leads toward a very dynamic tension between the unconscious and the fictitious self; there is no equilibrium between those two fields, which are present in all practice (even in pure theory and in politics). Brecht changed the axis of the discussion on creativity by accepting that this overlooked force is the key to the artistic worldview.

Sunday, September 12
I am in Buenos Aires once again after a couple of "family" days during which I neither read nor write: I go to the theater, watch television, wander around the city, and stop in front of the sea (empty as an empty oyster shell), struggling with the conflict between my childhood memories and reality, which shows my inability to control the situation. We drove in the rain to the Balcarce space center, where inscrutable white cones receive and transmit images from satellites: an oneiric landscape. The route passes among the dark hills, which delight Julia. Halfway there I leaned back in my seat and slept for half an hour, not dreaming, my mind a blank.

Monday 13
Yesterday on the journey, the sun in my face, the train stopping in towns buried in the plain. The empty station, locals hanging around to watch the train pass. Julia was annoyed because there was no room in the dining car, and the little window wouldn't stay open, and the sun was in her eyes, so she closed in on herself, seeing the failure of her hopes to make the journey an adventure. Meanwhile, I read Friedman's short stories, many very good ones, his ironic handling of black humor and the absurd.

As soon as I get up in the morning the phone starts ringing to announce the visits: Szichman, Marta Lynch. Aníbal Ford, David, Schmucler. I enter the state of vertigo that both attracts and frightens me. With David, an entertaining talk at La Paz; he was euphoric, as intelligent as in his finest moments. I walked down Corrientes, trying to figure out the political situation from the headlines on copies of *La Nación* hanging from clips under the roof of a kiosk, burning up in the noonday sun in the aching suburbs, and David smiled at me through the window over the sidewalk, seeing my "neurotic expression." Then, with him, the same old refrain: Perón, Getino, Solanas, Jitrik, Cortázar, his phantom rivals who manage to renew themselves without leaving the threatening circle that, according to him, condemns him to being forgotten, and at the same time he is euphoric about the periodical *La Comuna*, which he is managing, excited about its third issue.

Some news from Schmucler. He proposes (after an intimist prologue about how he needs to write and use his time better) that I co-direct *Los Libros* with him, and I suggest that he add Carlos Altamirano as a third director. The proposal is attractive to me because of the new political image of the magazine, which participates while still remaining centered in cultural life, and also because I have a desire to fight (reasons: arguments with my friends from Vanguardia Comunista, new references to the opinions that I raised in *El Escarabajo de Oro*, they can't deal with the fact that I raised them and have followed my own path without needing to protect myself in the progressive cave they've courteously constructed, and also my polemics with Walsh, Urondo, and other new Peronists. Although I'm worried about losing my rhythm of working on the novel, scattering myself, etc.).

Finally, at night, I go to the theater with Julia and Ricardo N. to see an excellent adaptation of Musil's *The Confusions of Young Törless*: the violence of the future Nazi officials, who are, in the novel, young pupils in a military academy, also showing the viewpoint of a Nietzschean philosopher who seeks to reconcile mathematical precision and practical efficacy. A beautiful ending, with Törless expelled and leaving in a car, "he considered the faint whiff of scent that rose from his mother's corseted waist."

Tuesday 14
I spend the day putting away the books that covered the floor of my study. New shelves on the wall open up the space I need to settle myself in.

I walk through the city carrying a lamp with a metal stand on my shoulder. I try to go back to the Pavese story, seeking the syntax and tone. Two hours after I start, David comes over, and from that moment I can no longer concentrate. Ideas of escaping to the Río Tigre, to an island, to the country, to a provincial town, to a hotel, to an anonymous room in the center of the city, and spending one or two weeks isolated, with no interruptions, writing.

Wednesday 15
X Series. Ricardo furiously tells me the story of the revolutionaries (Peronists) who are seduced by Guevarism, opposed to those who, like him, are trying (reluctantly and without much conviction) to raise up the line of the masses, laborious, gray, and humble (nothing epic). The girl from his political group who breaks contact with her ex-compatriots because it's becoming "tedious," and whom he finds at a showing of *The Hour of the Furnaces* in a very elegant apartment in Barrio Norte. Or the guy with a mane of red hair who pontificates about revolutionary violence while dressed in imported designer jeans with leather sandals, disguised, Ricardo says, as a revolutionary mystic.

A little while after noon David visits me and I listen to him without enthusiasm, lost in my own haze. A curious sensation of seeing my body floating in the air and hearing my voice coming from an unexpected place, as though it were being transmitted from a tape player.

Thursday 16
Notes on Tolstoy (15). Relationship between language and ways of life. *Big Typescript 213* (1933). In the chapter "Philosophy" (86:2), Wittgenstein reflects on Tolstoy's opinion, according to which the significance of an artistic object lies in its general comprehensibility. Tolstoy reflects in *What Is Art?*, an extraordinary text that must be reread in order to understand some of Wittgenstein's positions. Tied to the issue of private-esoteric language (as anti-Tolstoy). Wittgenstein says that the slow movement of Brahms's String Quartet no. 3 has brought him to

the brink of suicide twice. What happens with this quartet? Can we use it to kill our enemies? Mandelstam said that an artist thinks about the meaning of events and not about their consequences. Philosophy is an activity and not a doctrine, and its primary sphere of application is language. Tolstoy maintained a direct relationship with his literary work, but he took it one step further; he sought not an ideal, but a pure language (direct and sincere), faithful to events. A language in its uncorrupted form, capable of representing the world as it truly is (in its implicit and simple purity). Tolstoy imagined that it was possible to find that language (which would serve as the foundation and starting point and opening for the creation of an ideal world: not an Esperanto, but rather a simple tongue). In this sense, Tolstoy's conversion signifies the abandonment of literature in favor of a more advanced form of verbal practice. At some point, he understood that the form and content of "pure" language were ineffable. The gospels he wrote are proof of his attempt to use a new language (he studied Aramaic, Greek, and Hebrew and wrote them in Russian). Tolstoy was in search of a perfect language and considered literature (Shakespeare included) to be a corrupted version of that attempt. From some indications in his *Diaries*, it is possible to confirm that Tolstoy was in search of an impossible language (a "never-never-language"), an absolutely hypothetical language. A language as removed from what we use to write as was the simple and uncorrupted life (a "never-never-land") from the corrupt society in which he was fated to live. In that way, a line could be established between the first and second Tolstoy, between *ostranenie* and engagement. Abandoning literature was an extraordinary sacrifice ("To write is easy, to not write is what is difficult," Tolstoy said), but he had still not reached the level of sacrifice that he must achieve. In that way, Tolstoy's works propose the theory that pure language postulates a reality (does not only refer to it), and therefore it can be claimed that the world this language must represent is an ideal world, postulated, which language can create. And what language is that? (prayer). And what world is that? (the peasant world). He sought, then, a language in a natural state (a natural state of language), and he sought it beneath the stunning mask of ordinary language. It lay in some place deep beneath the surface of everyday language, but he never found it. And he reached the conclusion that it was not there where he could find it. He thought, first, that a natural way of living was necessary, that pure language would spring forth from that way of life.

Friday, September 17
Series E. I am writing here now because I am disoriented, and these notes are like a map that I sketch, trying to follow the most direct route to an unknown place. Bad or good, with my usual slowness, I am writing the novel with energy, at the very limit of my abilities, settled into what I call the "psychological frontier of society." I send back messages and news from that place but also suffer the consequences of a prolonged stay in an inhospitable no-man's-land. I don't know whether the effort of my search for concentration is justified. If the story advances toward the void and opens new paths to me, I can't even consider the possibility of failure to be a loss.

To the dissatisfaction born of unaccomplished plans, of unachieved expectations, must be added social demands. For example, my newly realized participation in the leadership of *Los Libros*, which means both a political gamble and an agreement to travel to Córdoba, which I can no longer postpone. I could trust in my capacity for work, in my good economic situation, and think: I have many projects (as a publisher and director of a magazine) that I can carry out without neglecting my personal work. Being in the action, inside of reality, is one of the many things I have always sought. In summary, I earn my living by reading and am present in the world without being forced to publish according to the publishing market's rhythms of visibility. My intellectual situation demands rigor and effort. My passion for literature makes me think that, in effect, I am in no position to withstand so much exposure.

"Money turns the lives of men into fate," Karl Marx. This line gives a good definition of the pathos of the detective novel.

Tuesday, September 21

I return home, where Manuel Puig is waiting for me; he's about to go to Europe, obsessed with the translations of his books, which are untranslatable because of his oral style and the effects of David's thesis on "the generation of '66" (Viñas names it that after the year of Onganía's dictatorship, since he divides literature into periods with sequences directly defined by political events), which he characterizes as depoliticized (a trivial cliché that has been taken up in Spain and France to characterize the new Argentine writers), also worried because the mafia of the Boom forgets about Manuel and raises up Bryce Echenique. Anyway, he has his novel number III almost ready (a detective story about the artistic world of Buenos Aires in the era of Di Tella and the legitimizing power of *Primera Plana*). His position as a writer transforms him, for me, into another one of my "body doubles" (as they call the anonymous actors who replace the stars in dangerous movie scenes, inserting their bodies without recognition), and he provokes deep worry and envy in me.

Wednesday 22

I go back to the idea of writing a family novel based on the stories and myths that circulate in my house. Many characters and many plots, I have to find an ironic tone to tell that epic. Curiously, when I am making some notes, I can't remember the name of Luisa, one of my mother's sisters who was married to Gustavo, a failure of a man, close to the conservative *caudillos*. Among the women who told stories in my house she was the only one who died whose funeral I didn't attend. Perhaps I should set aside everything I'm doing to write the family saga, my own, with the stories I know better than anyone else.

Those stories are the material of my dreams and have settled into the depths of my life. They are rumors, clear situations, unforgettable characters that I've buried in my subconscious with its melodramatic structure of great passions and great crises. "I know no better advisor in art than the subconscious," says Puig.

Thursday 23
A failed meeting with Haroldo Conti, who arrives late, by which point I had set up an appointment with Osvaldo Tcherkaski. Anyway, Haroldo takes the time to tell me the storyline of his next novel with the Príncipe Patagón, ailing León, and Raymundo writing letters to his dear Lu. As always, Haroldo has a great feeling for telling stories about underdogs, common people who resist and always have some illusion that sustains them, but now I fear that he may have added to it the tyrannical lyricism of magical realism, García Márquez's rhetoric of using poetic situations as a manipulated escape to a new reality in the rural world. Then I have dinner with Osvaldo, who tells me about his trip to Madrid to interview Perón while insisting on talking about my novel as though it were already written.

Thursday 30
Meetings with Luna, who talks about Córdoba and the fluctuations of his ever-changing enthusiasm. Discussions at Tiempo Contemporáneo about the project of publishing Sartre's *Flaubert*, hundreds and hundreds of pages of turbulent prose that require readers who are either addicted or condemned to read that book.

Summary of a short season in hell. My pessimism: doubts about the novel I've been working on for years, still stuck on the situation of the confinement of the criminals, surrounded by the police in an apartment in the center of Montevideo. I'm unable to maintain the tone because the structure leads to nothing more than a long short story. I'll have to open up the story to what happens beforehand: the plan for the robbery, the attack on the bank truck, the violent escape, how they break their agreement with the police and escape to Uruguay with all of the money. A casual incident with a policeman forces them to flee, and they lose the contact who was going to guarantee them passage into Brazil. They get an apartment with the help of a streetwalker one of them picks up. But the place is burned, and the police surround it. I don't like what I've written so far; it is disorganized and confusing.

Friday, October 1

Fantasies of escape, of spending the summer on Haroldo Conti's island in the Río Tigre and finishing the novel there, as though my problem were geographical, and I only had to change locations.

Let's take a look at yesterday. I got up at ten in the morning, as I always do these days, had a cup of black coffee, and sat down to work. I ate lunch alone because Julia had gone to the College, fried myself a steak and ate it with a salad that was already prepared. When Julia came back I went to *Los Libros*, where I found Carlos and Marcelo arguing about Borges. At Tiempo Contemporáneo we made progress on the project of publishing Sartre's *Flaubert*; we're going to entrust Patricio Canto with the translation. I went back to *Los Libros* to look for Schmucler. We had a coffee, talking about television and its effects, always digressing, and then we walked to La Paz together, where Gusmán was waiting for me, hoping to see a short story published in Casa de las Américas, and we talked about Conti, who has grown stagnant and has been repeating himself since *Southeaster*, about Díaz G.'s project, how he won't publish his volume of short stories and is dropping the story he's been working on (more than fifty pages) because he doesn't like it. He wants to make some money before he goes back to writing. Later, at home, I met Andrés and ate dinner with him and Graciela and Ricardo N. I insisted on the plan to rent Haroldo's island in the Tigre. And we didn't go to the theater because Julia has a damn midterm to study for.

Analyzing Guerrero Marthineitz's very influential radio program: dialogism, folklore, politics in support of Lanusse in the specifics, proof of a new form of politics based on journalists as shapers of opinion (replacing the intellectuals).

Thursday, October 7

Last night a new catastrophe, a violent (recorded) argument with Kaplan, Jitrik, León, and others. They all set themselves against me as soon as I questioned the autonomy of literature, or rather, the illusion of autonomy in literature. The classic premature reaction of the liberal left, which considers culture as a neutral field of abstract positions. Any discussion of the concrete conditions of intellectual work makes them unite in defense of their personal smallholdings. They're accustomed to arguing with Peronists and defending high culture, but they're not prepared to face an avant-garde strategy that seeks to intervene on art's relationship to society (and not the reverse: the way in which society is viewed in art), or rather, the function of art in society.

Short Stories
1. Suicides: the father who fails.
2. Pavese: the woman who refuses to see him.
3. The jeweler: he carries a revolver.
4. Mousy Benítez, told as a reconstruction.

Friday 8
I excitedly come across my thesis and notes on Borges. All the same, I'm still in the gray area, an effect of yesterday's argument with the group of intellectuals from the left in *Nuevos Aires*. I separate myself from them in the same way that I separate and distance myself from the writers of my generation. My way of defining the public figure of the writer leaves me alone (proof that I'm right), but I'm still stuck on yesterday's argument, which was very violent. Some sentences come back to me, situations, I come up with answers that I should have given. Distance between what I want to do and what I really can do.

X Series. I see Elías S., always intelligent, similar to José Sazbón, with several simultaneous conflicts against reality; he tells me about his fantasy to sell books door-to-door in Córdoba. The discord of political practice, militancy is always difficult for an intellectual.

I know of no other heroes than these anonymous friends who change their ways of life and put themselves at the service of the revolution.

Saturday 9
I go in circles around the empty house. Julia is in La Plata with her daughter, and I go down the street, as far as Corrientes, people walk from one side to the other, it is Saturday night, they are enjoying themselves. I am alone in the world, I think. I need to go into a bookshop to confirm which books are there and that there are readers who buy them; you can flip through them, always the same titles, reviewed twenty times in a week. They are real objects, and so it's possible to think that it makes sense for you to waste your life on them. And so I go into the grand used bookshops, Dávalos or Hernández, where you can always hear protest songs and there are crowds of young people from the left. A single glance is enough to check whether any new books have come in from Spain or Mexico, the only ones that can surprise me. Then I go back home and heat up some coffee.

Monday, October 11
I've been alone since Friday, Julia is in La Plata, she comes back tonight, perhaps that is the reason for this melancholy, a sadness without substance. I go to *Los Libros*, meet Carlos Altamirano and Mario Szichman, come back, and walk around the city like a ghost.

Saturday 16
X Series. I continue my research into revolutionary politicians' ways of life. They are professionals; the group decides how much money they will receive every month, which is always a small amount and works as a moral example. They carry out covert activities and divide their lives between a visible surface and a hidden area, about which there is conflicting information. Roberto tries to deny in me what exists in him, for example—and most of all—the will to create a personal work. He pays tribute to the intelligentsia. We talk about my letter with advice about cultural work. According to him, I use irony to keep myself at a distance. In the middle of that, Juan Carlos M. dropped by, so I followed him to his house to get away, and he brought me the Salinger stories I'd loaned him.

Lucas had stopped by earlier, another professional revolutionary who comes to see me in order to recover something of his previous life. He also has plans to rent a house on the Tigre and spend the summer near me. I'm always on the point of asking him if he's killed anyone, but it is never the appropriate moment. He talks to me about the past and the future but says nothing about the present, "for security reasons," I can't know anything that might place him in danger. He lives with a mixture of ironic skepticism and naïve weakness, fantasizing about a woman who lives two thousand kilometers away, whom he has barely seen once. She is a clandestine militant, and he doesn't know her name but spent a night with her after a meeting of his organization's political leadership. He thinks she's the widow of a dead man, a hero. With force and candor, he builds up a myth of impossible love and, after looking for the weapon he'd hidden under a seat cushion when he came in, he tells me: "I want a dominating woman. To love her, I need to be afraid of leaving her for someone else."

Yesterday morning I came to the bar to read the papers and found Beatriz Guido, miserable, dressed in red, recovering from the failure of her novel *Escándalos y soledades*. "We're professional writers, not authors of a single book." She made me think about how it's true that the great writers that one admires are authors of a single book, that other novelists incessantly produce works that are immediately forgotten, yet they make a living on them. Authors of a single work (even if they have written many others) lie outside the economic circuit. That's the difference between authors from the nineteenth century (Balzac, Dickens) and those from the twentieth century (Joyce or Musil). Beatriz is the same as always, harried, funny, always gracious to me. She asks me about my novel, and I tell her it's almost ready.

Series E. It costs me more and more effort to narrate events and situations in these notebooks; there is a tendency to think before acting, to forget the body and its displacement. And so, what I want to do here is to describe the mental state and history of a captive soul (caught in the nets of language). I have already filled fifty notebooks, in which I have written the series of my encounters with reality.

Monday, October 18
David stops by and doesn't find me. I set a time with him on the phone, and we go for a coffee at the bar on the corner of Tucumán and Uruguay. He was too euphoric when I saw him arrive, greeting Roberto, who joked that he'd gotten fatter. In the bar, I realized that euphoria is David's way of covering up his angst, a kind of excited theatrical performance in which he plays a character with comedic aspects. A crisis because they rejected the script about Juan Moreira that he'd written for Ayala, fear that they might back out and not produce his play about Lisandro de la Torre. He put aside three million pesos, which gives him a feeling of vertigo. He keeps himself going as best he can, setting himself against Jitrik, clinging to the memory of a lecture that he gave in Bahía Blanca, which was attended by five hundred students. He thinks about his father, a judge in Patagonia, who turned down all bribes. And, conversely, he talks about his age and fears for the future. While he was at my house, he left me a book with a touching inscription and "wellsprings of weakness."

I argue with León on the way out of a meeting. First, he tries to make excuses for Jitrik to me. Straight away I try to make him see his own vacillation. "Fear of thinking," I tell him, and he accepts it. He accepts everything and talks about misunderstandings or recalls that our friendship only progresses because he takes the initiative. I am, according to him, categorical, aggressive, and see no nuance. I'm pleased, I tell him.

Wednesday 20
Always arguing with Roberto, who accepts criticism, and we generally agree. The issue is thinking about the place of the culture of the left in politics, rather than thinking about the place of politics in the culture of the left.

The side entrance—on Calle 50, I think—to the post office in the Galería Rocha, in La Plata. I had to go up a staircase that led to the telephone office, from where I sent out telegrams notifying students that they had passed and giving them their grades (which were almost all tens).

Thursday 21

Restlessness pursues me as though I could never overcome it. It is "that damned feeling of anguish" that Roberto Arlt speaks of, a dangerous relationship with the future and its alternatives. Within me we are many (though the expression may seem strange): there is one who covers himself up like a thief in order to seize any certainty. Someone I can't overcome, an enemy who shows me the fragility of my certainties and erases the force of reason, which is one of the last allies on which I place my trust.

Again, I talk to Haroldo on the phone; I've created the myth of my journey to the island. Everyone treats me as though I were going to go to Havana. I think: that's why they call me. I think: I have to write to Retamar and make my position on Cuba clear. I also think: I don't want to go; I'd rather not go. Stay and finish the novel I'm writing once and for all.

Sunday 24

Only Brecht's prose saves me from the tension of this unease inside, a sort of restless catalepsy. Maybe that's what is hell for me: paralyzed, unable to move, but not peaceful and calm, instead uneasy, anxious, always on the point of leaping to one side. I cling to some Brechtian maxims (the way Alonso Quijano would cling to the novel of chivalry to forget reality), for example: "Do not bind yourself to the good times past but to the bad times present," Brecht says, and I add: "Nor to the bad times yet to come."

Subject. A short story about the history of Blanco, married to the daughter of the mayor of the city, and R., married to the daughter of the president of the republic. Both are handsome, fair-faced, rather similar physically, blond, refined, artists of the left and nationalists respectively. The upstart who ascends by seducing the daughter of a powerful man. A Stendhal atmosphere. Here, the hero—a kind of Julien Sorel and Fabrizio del Dongo—was not fascinated by Napoleon as a model for audacity but rather by Perón as an astute negotiator. Stories that will end badly, if my novelistic intuition is working well.

Wednesday 27
Lots of news. The main thing was the intervention of the leftist unions of SITRAC-SITRAM, in Córdoba, the city occupied by the army. David brings me a document to sign. Amid the series of political events, I try to return to the novel. I have a fantasy of escaping to the Tigre and spending the whole summer on Haroldo's island.

Julia's birthday; we go to the woods of Palermo, walk in the sunlight, eat chorizo sandwiches beneath the trees arranged in a grid beside the river. We take photos together next to the lake with a street photographer who has an old box camera. I read a book about Salinger, sitting on the grass, my back against a tree.

Sunday, October 31
Several meetings with David, who is obsessed with Ricardo Monti's play at the Payró. "A populist avalanche," he calls it.

Wednesday, November 3
The story of Nacha, Julia's friend. Rather schizophrenic, she attempts suicide twice, unsuccessfully, but putting herself at risk. She wanted to go back to her first husband, whom she has been separated from for years. Before that she had broken up with her boyfriend, who hit her and broke her nose on the night she left. She is in the hospital with her face disfigured and bandaged, aching and under the effects of ether. He ex-husband looks after her and then literally rapes her in the hospital bed that morning. Days later, a sort of intellectual working-class guy with a goatee "picks her up." He invades her house, which is "luxurious" (Nacha's father is a general and has a lot of family wealth), along with his minions. Julia finds them there on Sunday: all gather, they talk about the objects, the paintings and decorations of the place while drinking whiskey. Julia leaves, and Nacha finishes telling the story of that night. She goes down to buy a bottle of whiskey, and "the one who broke her nose" sees her, the one she left because he was inflexible, jealous, and he starts calling her on the phone. Eventually the ex-husband stands guard

outside, and, when someone opens the downstairs door to leave, he goes up and finds her in the apartment with the whole working-class gang. It seems like a *nouvelle* by Salinger.

Many discussions at *Los Libros*, the positions will have to be imposed by force.

Friday 5
I set out for the house on the Tigre with Haroldo, we drive to the boat station and then, at the rowing club, Haroldo rents a boat and we go along the river together to his place on the island. He shows me a copy of his novel *En vida* published by Seix Barral. An impression of being in another world, the Delta has a magic of its own. I prepare to spend the night on the island.

Saturday 6
I get up very early and walk around the place. The shop owned by Tito, a rower who won the Olympic medal for double sculls with Tranquilo Capozzo; the shop has photos on the walls showing his victories and pages from the newspapers celebrating him. He had rowed on the Tigre ever since he was a boy and naturally became a great rower. "It's natural," he told me, "country people know how to ride on horseback, and we islanders learn to row before we know how to walk."

Little by little I grow accustomed to the place. The swelling of the river isolates us, and we can no longer get to Tito's shop. I settle myself calmly into the house with many windows through which the sun comes in, mixing with the foliage of the plants that surround the park.

Sunday 7
The beating from the motors of boats that cross the river, at the far end among the trees, last night. Early this morning I went downstairs and prepared myself a Nescafé, adding a spray of whipped cream. Now I sit in the open air on the veranda of the house. Yesterday afternoon, on the

balcony with a view over the Rama Negra, some slight ideas about what I want to write.

The language of technicians has always fascinated me. The way they talk about the tides and the river's changes, the crewmen who live on the Tigre with their little motor boats that carry them to the sand barges on which they cross over to Punta Lara, or the fisherman who give detailed accounts of how they put bait on the hooks and the way the pole should be cast (half squatting to get the buoy to reach near the middle of the river). There's a certain practical ability in the way they verbalize the action.

Unfortunately I'm a city man, tired of the Tigre, the mud and mosquitos, and tomorrow I'll go back home.

Monday 8
At noon we literally fled from the island covered with bugs. Tito brought us a rowboat and we crossed the muddy rivers with him to return to the city by train.

I rediscover all of the problems that prevent me from thinking.

Thursday, November 11
Each day I'm further removed from these notebooks and from myself. On top of that, I meet with David, obsessed with Peronism and Sabato. The next day, after thinking about writing a note on the book as a short piece for *Los Libros*, I was sitting at La Paz reading Steiner's book on Dostoevsky and Tolstoy when I saw Sabato passing. I had to come and go many times because, even though I gave him time, I found him yet again on my way back home, looking in the shop window on Plaza and Janés. I turned back and crossed. This morning, David was also particularly obsessed with Machi, who presents him with versions of his play *Lisandro*, which he hopes to premiere at the theater in January.

Saturday, November 13
Otherwise, this morning, I'm certain that I've failed with the novel I've been working on uselessly for four years and am tempted to throw in the trash. A mountain of papers written and rewritten over and over again.

Completely immersed in Flannery O'Connor's short stories, I come back to my ideas about writing my family stories.

Tuesday 16
I meet David at La Paz and he gives me a copy of *Lisandro*, his play that just came out. We walk toward the Congreso post office, great agreements in the sunlight, while I send a letter to my mother.

Thursday 18
I get lunch with Altamirano and David at the restaurant on the corner and we talk about the possibility of the military government led by Lanusse. David is as obsessed as ever with Perón. Then I find Eduardo Menéndez at *Los Libros*; I like the calm way he handles his anthropology studies, avoiding, to all appearances, any of the competitive turmoil of academia. I go to *Gente* magazine with Alberto to offer an advance for José Giovanni, and, after half an hour waiting in a dark room with beautiful women waiting for their turn to be photographed, we leave, fed up. Finally, Francisco tells me about his misfortunes, discouraged at age thirty-two, all of his hopes have died. In the end, he unexpectedly presents me with the book *Claves de la Internacional*; surprised, I get flustered and don't know how to respond.

Saturday 20
While I am reading and taking erratic notes at a table in La Paz, David appears, standing at the ice-cream shop across from Ramos on Corrientes and Montevideo: he starts to wave at me, dying of laughter, while the cars pass on the street, and he gesticulates, gesturing to himself and pointing at me, happy about the piece on Sabato in *La Opinión* in which Carlos Tarsitano defended David.

A while later, drinking a coffee, I tell David my idea to extract a one-hundred-page novella from my unfinished manuscript that I've been working on for years. Unexpectedly, he reaffirms the seriousness of my work, one's right to take time, and talks to me about *Ulysses* and *Adam Buenosayres*, and so I embark once again on a project without end.

Wednesday, November 24
He turns thirty years old. The virtue of hitting rock bottom and being alone, so far down, with no discomfort other than a shortness of breath. Lost, he walks through the city at the start of summer, dubious, learning to recognize his own limits. I am dead, he says, nothing of me now remains. What has become of his old delusions and blind confidence in the future? Defeated, he has nothing to say; it has all been said before.

I went out for a walk in the afternoon and saw Inés on Lavalle, near Florida. Nothing there, we are two strangers. Of course, she doesn't remember that today is my birthday. I remembered "The Sojourner" by Carson McCullers. Sad, etc. LSD, gold from Peru, living in France.

It is midnight, I am listening to Duke Ellington, I am broken up, I no longer believe, and I expect the worst. A name that echoes inside me. Penny Post, Fournier, Eva.

Saturday
Rubén K. comes over, the professional revolutionary, always skillful, always convincing. We have a drink at Ramos and go to the movie theater: *Easy Rider*, the world of the Beat Generation, the road, rock music, powerful motorcycles crossing the country from east to west.

Tuesday, November 30
A stupid joke: the guy from downstairs, who lives on the third floor, complained to the porter because I write on my typewriter at night. That can't be, I tell him, I don't write anymore, I wrong. The porter looks at me

to see if I'm messing with him, and then I give him two hundred pesos and ask him to tell the downstairs tenant to come see me, if he wants.

Friday 3
I spend the afternoon going through the process of renewing my credit so that I can buy an air circulator to let me work at night with the window closed in spite of the neighbor, nervous and idiotic.

Saturday 4
My true discovery this year has been Bertolt Brecht. I'm very interested in his prose, the way he thinks narratively and constructs plots to deal with multiple issues. He has a "Confucian" side: he likes parables, epigrams, allegories.

Sunday, December 5
The strategic discussion today revolves around one issue: is there popular support for the armed struggle? The ones who think so are the armed groups, who above all denounce the State's repression of popular forces. But the problem is that the political organization of those who act is defined by Peronism, and it's a delusion to think that Peronism has revolutionary tendencies.

In La Paz, an effusive guy with a Mephistophelean goatee who shouts out about the virtues of living in the country. He is a photographer and shows landscapes of the province of Buenos Aires to the waiter, who listens to him indifferently. A striking older woman with a hallucinatory look gets hooked on the photographer's monologue and the two get caught up in a "conversation," shouting from one table to the other, full of erotic connotations. I, he says, spend three thousand pesos per day, I go to Victoria Plaza, which is the best hotel in Salta, and drink two pitchers of beer.

Thursday 9
I run into David at La Paz; he is thankful and supportive, with a knowing reading of my participation in the roundtable about intellectuals and

revolution, which came out last night in *Nuevos Aires*. I fight with everyone, according to him, and that's a good thing. "An Argentine fighter." Touched, he thanks me for having referenced him because he feels excluded, etc. For my part, I look at my participation in that roundtable with irony and suspicion. All of them quickly united in defense of a liberal position while I argued energetically but very much on my own.

Later I go to *Análisis* magazine for an article about the publication of Sartre's *Flaubert*. The journalist is Osvaldo Seiguerman, whom I know by name because of having read him in *Gaceta Literaria* and other leftist magazines ten years ago. I tell him that Sartre wrote a series of works about the writer as someone who dedicates his life to the imaginary world. He tries to understand the decision that would lead a person to live under the delusions he believes in. He has done the same thing with himself in *The Words*. Flaubert is the central figure in the creation of literature as a religion.

Friday 10

I go thirty-six hours without sleeping. I write all night long, very engaged and happy, once again trying to salvage what I've written. When I go to bed at dawn, I still can't sleep, so I get up and go down to the street and walk in circles around the city. I could base the novel on that sleepless night. At any rate, in the end, I find Gusmán and Francisco Herrera, who receive me as though they were waiting for me, with great euphoria. I never really figure out what they're proposing to me or what they want us to do together. In order to record reality, I will say that all I've consumed in the whole day and night are three hard-boiled eggs and two glasses of milk. But when I ran into those friends in the bar, I broke the rule and had two whiskeys.

Saturday, December 11

I work on my article about the combative unions attached to the left in Córdoba. I recorded the interviews and life stories when I spent a few days there and was connected with the workers at Fiat. The question is:

how was the internal commission that directed the struggle defeated? Or rather: why was it defeated? On that point, the testimonies function as statements before a courtroom, and the question takes the form of an interrogation. Thus, the tension must come from the endless circulation of arguments. It has to do with one case, an exemplum in the classical sense, but what concerns me is that we're always recording defeat. There's nothing but defeat on the horizon, which is interesting from the epic point of view, but devastating from the political point of view. The idea of organizing unions by factory would allow the left to direct the movement, but it also isolates combative unionism and that makes it easy to defeat. Peronism is very strong at a union level because it defends rights with the force that comes from a national organization (the CGT).

A quote from Brecht: "The tension did not come from the plot but rather from the excitement caused by the abstract logical demonstration, augmented by pressure of the concrete political events."

The nonfiction story must have the tension of an ongoing trial, determining who is responsible for the defeat, not the guilty party—which is the leadership—but rather the ethical stance of a group of worker leaders who prefer defeat to negotiation.

On the other hand, fate here is manifested precisely in the dialogue among the workers and the "bosses," working as an oracle. First, the temptations that the activists are subjected to, with the company offering one million two hundred thousand pesos as "compensation" for the layoffs as long as they consent to sign an agreement admitting that the layoffs were fair. There we have the tragic dilemma. Workers marked by their union activism lose their work and are condemned to unemployment because no one will hire them in any factory in the country. The blacklists circulate in the newspapers. In debt following a strike during which they don't receive their salary, pressured by their family situations, and at the same time considered heroes of the great worker struggles. But what is a hero good for if he can't survive? Heroism is an ethics reserved for wealthy gentlemen who can make drastic decisions without major risk. The subordinate classes have another notion of success. For the better, the situation is given in a context of retreat and escape, with the SITRAC cornered and defeated. I'm thinking about a choral book without a narrator, only the voices of the protagonists discussing and recounting the experience. Style of Peter Weiss or Alexander Kluge.

The combative workers, especially the leaders, don't have the ability that Martín Fierro had to go off and live with the Pampa Indians, to take refuge in the desert . . .

Thursday 16
I pass the days walking around the city, dying of hunger, fatigue, and exhaustion, with no excitement about anything. I should be careful of obsessing over the stories of failure too much; one is also immersed in the world he narrates.

In the midst of that Shakespearean drama, anonymous heroes fight against the management and against the Peronist union bureaucracy. They have no allies; the left has no politics of alliance, and the activists remain alone with no one supporting them other than morally.

I spend the afternoons in La Paz reading Brecht and see David V. every day; he is doing badly, as though absent, shaken by the rise of populism and by the lessening awareness of his literature among young people. He too feels defeated. To gain some balance, he makes omnipotent plans, novels that take place in seven cities, historical dramas.

On the other hand, yesterday I saw Haroldo Conti at La Paz. He was nominated for the Guggenheim fellowship, nine million pesos that he's decided to accept in spite of his vacillations and qualms. Evidence that he has triumphed, the Premio Seix Barral, good reviews, etc., yet he is consumed by his family conflicts.

Friday, December 24
I spend Christmas Eve alone, reading. I buy myself grilled chicken and a bottle of white wine. I read Fanger's book about Dostoevsky for hours.

In the early morning I went out to walk through the empty city, the bars all closed, not knowing where to go. I end up sitting in La Paz. I imagine points of escape and make plans on a notepad, drawing paths and exits, escape routes.

Wednesday, December 29
Very hot weather these days as I let the year come to an end. I have lunch at *Los Libros*. I rediscover friendships that are forced upon me, leaping over the fence I've built up around my life. Schmucler, Aricó, Altamirano, Marcelo Díaz. The same with the dinner with León's study group, saying goodbye to the year, which I'm added to as a special guest, so to speak. Always from the outside, pursued by my own ideas. Calls from Haroldo, from Tcherkaski, from Boccardo, which I receive indifferently. I'm inside a glass box.

Thursday 30
I visit David in his new apartment with many rooms on Calle Cangallo, very big, new furniture, a pedestal fan. I'm impressed by David's ability to rebuild his life. He destroys himself, sells everything, is left alone in the world, lives in cheap motels, is lost in the city with no money and, suddenly, a few days later, he's settled down in a home with his books once again. Perhaps that is his greatest talent. We talk about his play, *Lisandro*; he is obsessed with it, needing it to be a success in order to validate his continued existence. Yet again, he bets everything on a single hand.

I walk through the scorching city. Today I went to San Martín, to the movie theater, seeking refuge in the air-conditioned room. I watch Boorman's *Excalibur* and plan to meet Ricardo at Ramos. I change my gray pants for another pair of the same kind, drop off an article at the newspaper, and pack my suitcase to travel to Mar del Plata. In the late afternoon I meet Julia, beautiful after spending the day in the pool.

Nothing remains, not even the illusions I had ten years ago. Or rather, nothing remains because the illusions no longer remain.

Let us end with a line from Brecht: "All of the morality of the system is founded on this issue of the means of life: anyone without money is guilty."

5

Diary 1972

Monday, January 3
Julia and I sit on the terrace of a bar over Calle Independencia in Mar del Plata. I listen to myself talking to her without any conviction in what I'm saying. The cold air filters in through the sliding glass and plywood window. The waiter is missing the thumb on his right hand. A strange sensation, as though there were an insect moving around the table.

January 4
The end-of-year family party, a tribal, cannibalistic reunion. Roberto is the circumstantial narrator, with the clan as a narrative system. Several recurring archetypes, the gambling uncle, the crazy sister, the drunk cousin, the suicidal sister-in-law. Then he adds nuance to the story: Susana and Agustín, who have been fighting for forty years, only married out of necessity (she was pregnant); they barely speak at all now, except to argue. In the end she threatens to leave him and to go work as a maid, but he warns her: "As long as it's not in Adrogué . . . "

Political cartoons. Investigate the first worker organizations, the typographers' assembly, the early socialist groups (1900). The minutes record that a worker arrived at the meeting three hours late because his wife was in labor. "I want to let my comrades know that I've given my daughter the name Revolutionary Socialist." Make a propaganda comic strip, setting aside the pamphlets and illegible newspapers.

January 5
Series E. The only solution to the problem of style in these notebooks is to determine their tone, nothing to do with interiority. Set aside the illusion of writing. At this point, I should already know that it's useless to transcribe a life. I could only construct a fiction based on certain real facts, but then, why write novels? I can't rule out finding plots and anecdotes in these diaries that I can use in the future.

Marcos, my brother, left for Buenos Aires last night, determined to get married and find a job after a year of going in circles. At home, this is experienced like a crisis. Encounters with loneliness and old age, children being lost just like life.

Monday 10
Last night I found Juan Ñ. in a German bar downtown. The usual unraveling conversations, not overly intelligent, out of tune. He, as an intellectual, is my antithesis, the type to secure their social status first, making thought secondary to that position.

Monday, January 17
Everything is suddenly unleashed. On Friday there is an army search operation in the building. They don't enter my apartment. "They're looking for a young couple," on the fifth or sixth floor. A week later, on Friday the 14th, six guys from the Coordinación Federal appear in the entryway, machine guns in hand; they wake up the porter and ask about me and someone named Bordabehere. After I hear about this, the chaos begins, and I pick up all of my papers, the apartment in disarray, make three trips, take out some clothing, the novel, the typewriter, the notebooks, and leave everything in the house of Tristana, Julia's friend.

I have to move everything, the library, the clothing, the furniture. I transport suitcases, trying not to look at the books I abandon. I gather clothes, papers, come and go several times, look for a taxi, calm in the face of what cannot be changed. Later that night in Tristana's house, conversations.

Tuesday 18
I see the attorneys, who offer opposite versions of the future (to move or to come back?), but both agree that it's best to disappear until the end of the month.

I go back to working in bars the way I did when I'd just moved to the city. Dejected about my library and about being unable to continue with the novel.

Discussions about poetry with Tristana and her sister. They give me a hilarious retelling of the story of a taxi escape, or rather, the taxi driver's escape; he goes off at top speed after a crash, chased by everyone, and then crashes three more times.

Wednesday
A conversation with Andrés and Lucas in a beautiful house on a street lined with trees. We sleep here after a day spent traveling around the city amid the heat and cracked streets. I'm reading Pound and Joyce.

Saturday 22
I start to work slowly, bit by bit. We keep moving around the city, but at least I have a place now. On Thursday night I ran into Benjamín and came to this ramshackle house in Boedo with him. I remember my houses as a student, the lights that never worked, the broken furniture.

Wednesday 26
I have dinner with Enrique. We talk about Borges. He is capable of a careful disparagement of the Socialist countries, which guarantees him work at *La Opinión*. Meanwhile, he's making progress on a story about Aramburu's death. An excellent style but still weak, not much clarity as a writer.

I spend the night with Tristana and her stories, how she traveled to Europe with her family in the middle of the war.

Thursday 27
Tristana is helpless, clinging on to anyone who will listen to her. She tells her suicide stories. "When I was born, my mother left me behind to go to Europe." Her husband, caring for her in the hospital.

The same as always at *Los Libros* magazine. Fatal boredom, news of expanding the committee that catches me off guard.

Sunday 30
Since I moved to this house, with a Spanish patio full of trees, things have become organized. Every morning I go to Benjamín's place and work on the novel for four or five hours there. I feel like I'm "on vacation," as though Buenos Aires were a city I've only just gotten to know, an effect of simultaneous changes of residence that force me to travel around different neighborhoods.

These "reality checks" have always helped me in one way or another. They force me to adapt quickly and yet dis-adapt with the same speed, like a traveler unpacking his luggage at every stop and then repacking it the next morning. For example, the afternoon walk south to that house where I shut myself in to write, alone.

Monday 31
The waiter sees me reading about the ERP robbery of the Banco de Desarrollo in the newspaper *Crónica*, when they took five hundred thousand dollars, and he starts talking to me about his life with almost no segue. An orphan since age six, he is raised by an aunt and uncle who make him live in an attic where they pile suitcases, old furniture, things they don't need. He doesn't even have a table, and he has to sit on the floor to do his assignments for school. "Even so, I managed to make it a quarter of a fiscal year before I had to leave for reasons out of my control." He talks to me about books: "And what good does it do me if I read? What do I look like to you? Wearing my white jacket, working as a waiter." He complains about the political situation.

340

News, people from the Coordinación Federal visit my apartment two more times. Impossible to go back, etc. A feeling of relief, as though I'd been hoping for that. No idea what to do, really, but anyway I'll be able to find somewhere for myself for the month. We'll see in a while.

At midnight I go to visit León, who phoned looking for me at the magazine office and rebuked me for not having visited him. His beautiful apartment on the 17th floor, a great high-intellectual atmosphere. He finished writing his book on Freud and Marx and hopes to submit it this month. Social conversation, and then he recites part of his book for a while. Of course, I ironically recount my own odyssey, etc.

February
Conversations with Rubén, who criticizes me for not putting my ideas on agitprop into practice. He's right about that, I'm now too bound to my obsession with literature (which I never plan to abandon). The example of Walsh hangs in the air; he abandoned fiction to direct the CGTA newspaper. Walsh had called on me to join the project, but I declined. The rest of the discussion is difficult because of his demagogy around me. Accepts everything, etc.

Later I go to *Los Libros*, a great commotion. Carlos A., Marcelo, Germán, and Toto are there, talking about David's psychotic outburst. He came in and asked who published Alejandra Pizarnik's book of poems at Siglo XXI and why, saying that the book is a piece of trash, that whoever published it doesn't understand anything, that she's an illiterate. The matter grows worse, Toto barely defends himself, David becomes furious. He comes right up to Toto, takes off his glasses as if he's about to fight him, and abuses him: "Fuck you, your mother and your grandmother, I'd punch you if you didn't have your glasses on." A spell of madness and, at the same time, a demonstration of David's dangerous spontaneity, so competitive. Why did he go after Alejandra Pizarnik? No way to know, although maybe, I now suspect, it's because she's one of Cortázar's protégés.

Friday, February 4

I am in my new apartment now, a spacious environment with a large picture window, the city eleven stories below. Nervous about possible dangers in this place (the phone being tapped by the people from the ERP). I try to write or, rather, try to get myself going. I discover what a sedative complete solitude is for me, and I plan to rent a studio and live there alone.

Sunday

I can't find myself inside this luxurious, empty apartment, floating in the terrible world of the city. At three in the morning last night, I stood in the corner with my briefcase, ready to leave. Lunch with José Sazbón, we talk about the translation of Sartre's *Flaubert*, which he edited. José, lucid and shy, is humble despite his brilliant potential. A doctoral fellowship in Paris, a guaranteed career as a researcher, etc., free to study for his whole life. By contrast, I see myself up in the air, without a future. Let's imagine a person who goes along making choices and suddenly suspects he has taken the wrong path, but he doesn't know how to turn back or where to go.

Detective genre. Anonymous craftsmen who habitually write under pseudonyms, acutely aware of the market and the price they are paid per written word. Their stories first circulate in cheap magazines and then in books at kiosks. Demand that is not very diversified and undergoes sudden jumps: from the mystery novel to the thriller to the spy series. Often the same writer will write books in a variety of registers under different names, J. H. Chase for example.

At night in the publishing office, we have a conversation about the complications of publishing Sartre's monumental *Flaubert*. We will get it done, but there's a great deal of difficulty with the translation.

Monday 7

A beautiful landscape, the city in light rain, the river in the background. Airplanes taking off from the airfield nearby. The only color that of posters for 7 Up.

Wednesday 9

Julia to has started to separate herself from me. She sustains herself as best she can in the midst of this absurd chaos.

Yet another move, and now I'm in Tristana's house, closer to civilization.

Yesterday David signals me from a bar across from San Martín as I am passing on the way to meet Ricardo at El Foro. Overblown greetings and promises to meet soon. Ricardo and I have lunch on Calle Paraná and walk around the whole city, the French bookshops, Hachette, all of the books double the price of a year ago. At the end, there was a drunk who insulted the waiter, and then he got punched and cried in humiliation.

Later with David, who has finished the first draft of his work about Dorrego. He leads me off to a room with a view over the rooftops and talks to me, downcast, about his psychotic outburst with Schmucler, blaming himself without conviction.

Thursday 10

Well, last night was the end with Julia. I meet her in Galerna and we walk to El Toboso, have dinner, and say goodbye as though we didn't know each other.

No one has ever been as alone as a lover saying goodbye forever to the woman he has lived with for five years.

I sustain myself in the void, not even dreaming of writing or reading. My friends are charitable, and I affect a stoic pose. I meet Ricardo and wait a half hour for him, stunned, dead. I rediscover the exercises that I learned in my youth for how not to think; I hadn't practiced them in six years. In a while, the predictable conversation continues. The kind of lines like "all relationships end, etc." Almost without a word, he brings me to his clandestine house, where I have lunch with him and we talk about the political future. Finally we hug, somber.

I have nowhere to work except for friends' houses. I have no idea what I can do to get my books without having a run-in with the police.

Thinking about what is to come weakens me so much that I can only cling to the moment. If I want to avoid spectacle, complaints, it will be best for me to stay shut in alone, waiting for sorrow to pass and become dulled.

Friday 11
Aside from matters of passion, I was with Szichman and Germán García yesterday. Germán says that I'm the hinge between Marxism and the avant-garde in Argentina. David reiterated to him that I'm the best essayist of my generation.

Sunday 13
I try to erase last night's dream: the police were in my house and destroyed everything, I regret not having left during carnival. Why are they looking for me? There's always a motive.

Wednesday 23
Series C. Maybe I must ask myself why I've stopped writing here in recent days, so full of events, but maybe that is the reason. Maybe I don't want to "see them" as they are. Last night, for example, with T. until five in the morning, the games I lost. We had dinner in Taormina and, after having a whiskey at El Blasón, sat down in the plaza of Las Heras and then walked through the empty city until dawn, making it to the large house with a thousand rooms on Calle Arenales, where we listened to Schumann and continued drinking alcohol under the Flemish tapestries; I didn't know what I could do to cut the night short without sleeping with her or at least trying. Today I am still overwhelmed, and I call her and cannot reach her.

Earlier, dinners and walks with the gang from *Los Libros*, Germán, Marcelo, and David.

I'm trying to figure out how to get into the apartment on Calle Sarmiento. At night, or would it be better in the middle of the day?

Julia and I come and go, carried by the wind. Resolution to live separately. Days without seeing each other and then she appears, beautiful as a stranger, subdued by herself.

Thursday
What a time this is, solitary as a cat and lost in strange houses. Surprisingly, waiting on a woman I never would have reconciled with three months ago.

March 4
I should have at least tried to record this frenetic period of time day by day: I wrote an article on Brecht in ten days, without my library, lost in this house on Calle Uriburu where the sun hits my face at seven in the morning; along with that, my affair with T., born amid the chaos while Julia was leaving, has started to grow and is now another unresolved issue.

We went out together several nights in a row to eat dinner, to drink whiskey until four in the morning. Feeling my way around in the darkness, fascinated more and more by her way of being. Finally, on Saturday, February 26, I am lonely and feel so bad that I tell Ricardo about it, having gone to the theater with him, and then I call T.'s house and Julia is there. The three of us playing this ridiculous game. I go out again the next day and stay the night with her until eight in the morning. I accept that the issue revolves around the axis of whether to "tell Julia or not," as she is her friend. I see T. again the following afternoon, and she actually insists that we continue. At noon on the 27th I run into Julia in Pippo and play her and T.'s game of being "sincere." But as soon as I say that I've been with T. for the last few days, Julia runs out of the restaurant. I try to talk to T., but all of the public phones on Corrientes are out of order.

I meet David in Ramos at three in the afternoon and then Julia appears, along with T. I go to the Politeama theater and tell T. that I'm going to call her. She can't look at me and lowers her eyes. "What for?" she asks me. She backs out, will not take it any further, in fact has chosen Julia.

On March 1 I had a hellish night. "Goodbye" from T. and also distance from Julia; in the morning I go back to Ramos, where Julia has plans to meet David. She comes and tells me that I can't be with "her friend," but yes with another woman, etc.

And so, I kept my distance at Ricardo's house today; yesterday I met T., who respects the decision and is beginning to understand.

I walk home along an empty Calle Santa Fe at around four in the morning, with no transportation because of the strike, and suddenly a block of cars shoots around the end of the avenue. When they get closer, I can make out a patroller and two army trucks chasing a Torino: on the corner of Suipacha, twenty meters away from me, they cross in front of the escaping car, forcing it to stop. Men in civilian clothes and soldiers with machine guns step out and make three young people get out with their hands up, vulnerable. I cross toward Charcas trying not get myself involved in the matter and return to the empty house, tangled up in all of my catastrophes.

As has happened to me at other points in my life, I find Julia's handwriting when I open this notebook. *I want a word*, she has written. *You knew I would be your first reader, but you didn't know how astounded I would be when I realized that, in a few years, you would reread the notebook and would really believe what it says, and it's this astonishment that drives me to the sacrilege of writing in your notebook so that, one day, I will be something more than a vague presence that structures your story. A strange case, this novel in which a character who has been killed off comes back to life and talks back to the author, telling him he didn't understand how to read my signals, and saying that this dead man was an absurd Dostoevskian who talked about "fantasy," meaning reunions of those distant adolescent friendships he once cultivated. Maybe one day you'll begin to remember that, the way I was, I was always too brutal for little emotions, because (with you!) I never wanted to use big words. That's why I'm trying now to make you understand what you did wrong, that, to me, your relationship with Tristana was too commonplace. For my part, I haven't been with anyone and, if I had chosen anyone, I would have chosen your brother, or maybe even your father, something a bit more unthinkable because, as you know, that would fit my style better. The rest was as miserable and shameful as your interest in that poor, crazy little millionaire who found a chance to be reborn with the man who had been with her friend. A sad little bourgeois girl whom I helped you to invent because, to stand up in front of you (terrible and brutal child), I needed to exploit someone who believed she was with me. My style lies in actions that are terrible, beautiful, cruel, but a bit more generous.*

March 25

Finally I return, and for the first time am writing in an apartment on Canning and Santa Fe that I managed to rent a few days ago.

It's impossible to write in these tumultuous times. As I read what Julia had written, I once again understood that no one ever says what they should, that everything is a disastrous misunderstanding.

And yet I still moved forward with the things in my life. I wrote two political articles for *Desacuerdo*, but I couldn't write an assessment of these two eternal months when my life changed its course. Where will it go?

Moving was the hardest thing, a fantasy of the police coming to my hideout; the day before, baskets to carry my books, papers, a chaos that mirrored my soul: old notebooks, photos, shoes, letters. A new chronology. Sitting on the floor, surrounded by all of the objects I've managed to accumulate. The next day the electricity in the apartment was shut off, and I lit candles at six in the morning. The incredible feeling of being forced to abandon a place where I've been happy. Then, the landlord, who understands the clandestine nature of my move, charges me twenty-five thousand pesos (instead of the fifteen we had agreed on), insinuating that he has to sort things out with the police.

A feeling that I am moving in leaps, here now in this empty place where I will bring abandoned remnants and settle myself in to survive.

Tuesday, March 28
I saw Andrés yesterday, his book has been seized. He hopes to be able to shut himself in for the winter.

Go back over these impossible months. See what I am capable of.

March 29
A meeting for the newspaper *Desacuerdo*, nothing but good intentions. Oscar proposes that I direct it, but I decline with the politest firmness possible. I listen uncomfortably to the conversational discussions about my merits for the position. In short, I'm unable to accept what I myself have chosen. This legal newspaper, which comes out in the kiosks and discusses the politics of the dictatorship, is my chosen political work, but I can't devote all of my time to it because all I am is a friend of my friends who have dedicated their lives to politics.

I see Andrés, ceremonious, weak underneath his aggressive exterior. With each of my friends, there's always something that separates us.

There is little to be said about me at the moment, three packages tied up with sisal twine holding my notebooks. I untie them, again find what is written here, and avoid talking about saying goodbye to T.

A man who finds himself cornered, his face to the wall, realizing that the wall is a mirror.

April
I have discovered Charles Ives. A good time to come across this music.

I've been built by certain readings; let's remember Pavese's puritanical voluntarism, it's as though I found in that the written prophesy of my life.

At night I listen to Ives under the lamp that silhouettes me in a circle of light, alone with this perverse feeling of estrangement that I always confuse with loneliness.

"What the subject seeks in a prostitute is the phallus of all the other men; it's the phallus as such, the anonymous phallus," J. Lacan.

Tuesday, April 4
Perhaps I've made a mistake yet again (it's always the same, we always come back to the same place) in choosing solitude as a way of breaking ties. An effect, but of what? Arguing with León, watching television are only weak consolations. I never could escape this obsession in which I live. What I mean is that my absurd argument last night with León left me disoriented because, as always happens in such cases, I've discovered some incompetence, weak in a way that no one knows better than I.

"The style of sentiments is the Baroque," G. Rosolato.

None of what I've written in the last five years is working; I just reread drafts of my novel with a fatal indifference. It tells the story of a gang of criminals who attack a bank truck in collusion with the police and then escape to Montevideo, breaking their agreement. A few days later, because of a betrayal, they are traced to a downtown apartment. They decide to hold out until morning even though they know it will be impossible for them to make it out alive if they don't give in earlier. They make this heroic, unexpected decision, which in fact turns them—at least for me—into tragic heroes. To complete the circle, at dawn, when they can no longer defend themselves, they decide to burn the five hundred thousand dollars from the robbery. I've put together the story here so that something will survive of a novel that I'm going to throw out the window (if I can bring myself to do it).

Now I'm listening to Alban Berg; musicians are doing the same thing as Joyce. I'm sitting in a leather armchair, facing the window with a view over the river, in a curious state of mind, euphoric to realize that I've managed to find a place to live in spite of everything. A feeling of unexpected faithfulness to decisions made at age eighteen, which are also being validated in this dark time as I test my limits.

Saturday, April 8
Arguments at the newspaper *Desacuerdo*, casual meetings with friends at the Galerna bookshop, and I went to *Los Libros*; the magazine just came out on Monday. I came back home, worked on the notes for *Desacuerdo*, dropped them in the mailbox, walked around Plaza Lavalle, and ended up having dinner alone at Dorá.

Sunday 9
Opening the package with original versions of the novel I've been working on for three years is enough to make me feel a sort of deadly chill. I think about setting it aside, doing something else, or starting it over.

Wednesday 12
I sleep for ten hours, the same as in my best times. Before that I walked around the city all day trying to get some air and ended up watching *Murmur of the Heart* by Louis Malle in the theater.

Police sirens while I write. The ERP killed Sallustro, the director of Fiat, when he was discovered by the police. An ERP-FAR unit killed General J. C. Sánchez, Lanusse's second-in-command in the Gran Acuerdo political plan. He was the strategist for the anti-guerrilla struggle.

Saturday 15
I'm reading biographies (C. Baker on Hemingway, E. Jones on Freud) the way people read escapist novels as an attempt to get out of their own heads.

Yesterday I visit David and find him doing well, tense at the prospect of the *Lisandro* premiere and yet calm, as though he found a way to relax himself. The possibility of economically securing this year and the next calms him. Germán is with him and we argue about Peronism, amicably. They say Perón is going to establish himself in Europe in order to confront the United States. A kind of pro-free trade version of the struggle against monopolies. For his part, David is very attracted to populism and, presented with the fait accompli, thinks with the same mechanism of fascination. Realistic criteria; what is present and visible forces him to fantasize about a reality that the left is far from attaining. Later, Germán and I walk around the city, he wants to work on "the institution" of psychoanalysis because the Mannonis spent a week talking about it during their tour through Buenos Aires.

Wednesday 19
X Series. I meet with Rubén K., intelligent, wise. With him there is no need to insist on my confidence, which vanishes as soon as he leaves anyway.

"Theatre takes place all the time wherever one is and art simply facilitates persuading one this is the case," John Cage.

A meeting for the magazine; Schmucler goes on about Perón, I grow bored.

April 24
Both here and everywhere else I'm writing less and less. Some incidents happened in the last few days. David, for his part, premiered *Lisandro* on Friday to quite a mixed audience. We're all there, everyone on the cultural left and the liberal right are also there. A kind of internal X-ray of David. The *mise-en-scène* is good, adding to the outrageous "sacramental" quality, and for what it loses in political potency, it gains in rhythm and sculptural quality. Applause at the end, and David goes on stage to receive the gratification he needs. .

Political conflicts in the meantime, disagreement that advances amid Andrés's deviations. Rubén stays over for the night and gives me his version: Andrés is being pressured by Susana I., some resentment. León visits me on Saturday in the middle of all that, and I have a good time with him after months of veiled tension.

Tuesday, 25
I'm working, answering letters for the publishing house, writing articles, jacket copy and introductions (Uwe Johnson, LeRoi Jones, etc.).

Sunday 30
David stops by to see me, euphoric about the success of *Lisandro*, an opening week with five hundred audience members every day, and his newspaper and television adventures: he denounces Jozami's kidnapping live and direct on Channel 9.

Thursday 4
The first issue of *Desacuerdo* comes out, made out of what we have. We reversed the slogans: against the dictatorship's Gran Acuerdo Nacional. Intense days, meetings, success by the priest Longoni, Rubén's driving force, and a variety of other events that I observe with unpleasant irony.

I write in these notebooks because it is no trivial thing to accumulate facts or implications that will be erased for everyone. Today, for example, I'm about to start the prologue for Chandler, and Aurora is on her way, coming to occupy the apartment while I go to the meeting for *Los Libros*.

Monday 15
David visits me, euphoric about the success of his work, great impact. He accumulates projects like a madman.

Tuesday 16
Diary of the young man who made an attempt to kill Wallace, the governor of Alabama. The pages tell the story of a lonely and confused boy. Some

passages say: "Happiness is hearing George Wallace sing the national anthem or having him arrested for a hit-and-run traffic accident." "I am part of the world . . . I am one three billionth of the world's history today . . . " "If I live tomorrow . . . it will be a long time." "I'm playing the game of life to win." He had been living in his apartment since November; the neighbors say he was a recluse and they only saw him a few times, and they even said that his mother came to see him, and, though she knocked on the door and heard noises inside, there was no response.

Wednesday 17
Last night David invites us over to dinner. On the way out, Germán, Osvaldo Lamborghini, and Luis Gusmán, whom I had actually been planning to meet, are talking on the corner. I go have a coffee with them to break the tension, primarily caused by David. Plans to organize an anonymous literary group, to publish a pamphlet against the channels of literary distribution. I continue wandering around the city with David, euphoric, paranoid, until three in the morning.

Earlier with Mario S., naïve to the point of the grotesque. He comes to me with a story of his romance a few days before with a blonde coworker. He finally asks her out on a date on Friday, arrives in La Paz at six in the afternoon and gives her a box of chocolates with a card declaring his love. All of this, of course, said with all seriousness. She backs out kindly, etc.

I'm reading *Eve* by Chase. Striking, I'm going to publish it. Later, a book by Mailer with an autobiographical story written in third person.

Also excited about the idea of incorporating family history into *Artificial Respiration*.

Sunday 21
I travel to Córdoba with Boccardo and Ricardo. Six hours recording life stories in a church. On Saturday a dance for the political prisoners, a

record player alone on the stage, the empty paddle ball court, a false happiness. At the end, everyone sings "La balada de Sacco y Vanzetti" with fists raised in the air.

Wednesday, May 24

In the morning David comes over with a suitcase, escaping from the hotel where he was, and everything seems to be halfway done. David is raving more and more, hiding his weakness behind exasperation. He argues with Somigliana-Cossa and Halac-Talesnik: he shouts at them that *Lisandro* is the finest work in Argentine theater. The kind of outburst that he needs to believe more than anyone else.

I go around *Los Libros* with Beatriz S., we agree that David suggests a nineteenth-century literary model along the lines of Sarmiento, and *Lisandro*, settled into that project, finds a passive, comfortable audience.

Thursday 23

I spend five hours listening to the tape recorded in Córdoba, good at certain moments. Eventually, Andrés and Rubén and I go out for dinner at Pepito. "Overjoyed," Andrés tells me about David's fit, how he threw himself at Cossa, Halac, etc., challenging them to outdo *Lisandro*. In the restaurant, Julia, who has reappeared in my life, very dazzling, corners Rubén, arguing about the place of women in politics.

Friday 26

Altamirano came to see me so that I'd go to the first meeting. When I get back, David drops in, going on about his obsessions. He wants me to be witness to an argument with León in the next three or four months, planning to accuse him as a false friend.

Saturday, May 27

I woke up at six in the afternoon, having fallen asleep at noon after writing several letters and going out to buy envelopes in the freezing morning. I read until seven thirty. Then David came and we went to have dinner on Paraná and Sarmiento, and I went to the theater with him: sold out, with bourgeois ladies and gentlemen applauding at the least expected moments.

Monday, May 29
I go downtown and find Marcelo with Ismael and Tula. Trotsky's books found in the used bookshop for three hundred pesos, Ismael will go to see David's play with assistance from Soriano, since "my brother didn't send me tickets." Then I meet Néstor García Canclini, misfortune in La Plata after the Peronist invasion at the College.

A meeting at home with Rubén, Ricardo, and Carlos. Rubén gives a very dense account of the source of the funds, the relationship between money and politics, "donations" and austerity. Julia and I went out to get empanadas; she finally signed the lease for an apartment on Cangallo. Each of us will live on our own.

June 1
I go to the Lorraine theater to see *Made in USA* by Godard again, the shadow of David Goodis. The room cold, its paint peeling. The group of cinephiles—four or five—watch the film passionately, and the rest of the spectators—some twenty—just watch pictures to kill time. I am a synthesis of these two behaviors.

That fit of paranoia when we spent a few days at Alicia's house, having left the apartment on Calle Sarmiento after it was broken into by the army. I was writing some notes on the living room table (white, oval shaped) and, in a surprising episode that summarized the tension caused by the events, I went down to the street, certain that the house had been "burned" and that the police had tapped the phone.

Busy all morning yesterday with the semi-covert move. I can't carry the sofa bed and the cupboard that I'm giving Julia; the moving-van driver— an old Italian man with a light and comical air—complains bitterly and, in the end, hires a worker. Even so, they leave the cupboard on the second floor and I have to hire another two men to carry it up.

I finish my works in progress: the introduction for an article on street theater for *Desacuerdo* and a piece on Uwe Johnson for his book at the publishing house. I stop by the magazine office and see Carlos Altamirano, who reminds me about the roundtable with several intellectuals (Viñas, Rozitchner, Aricó, Sciarretta, etc.), which I am the only one to attend. I travel around the whole city by bus as far as Núñez before finding "Farolito" in the bar on the corner, the redheaded guy who instigated student struggles among the young people. He seems to have inflated, besides the little moustache that gives him the look of a villain in a Hungarian film. Along the way I'm uncomfortable because I couldn't get myself free. In the College of Architecture, students are painting posters, talking with ironic gravity about everyone who is absent, and I stand firm, not admitting I was the only one to show up. With an admirable motion, Gutiérrez—student leader who was expelled from the university and moves among the students like a fish in water—invents a varied series of arguments to prove why, in fact, instead of the scheduled action on Vietnam, the best strategy is an inflammatory assembly for the students imprisoned in the mobilizaton on May 29. Carlos reads a proclamation that we'd prepared, and the students listen apathetically, yelling at him every now and then to speak louder. We leave, going down alleyways covered with posters and writings, and go to the little plaza from which the buses depart: a beautiful image of white lights from the buildings of the University campus, glass and wood in a sort of Mondrianesque abstract structure. Carlos and I come back, commenting on the state of the left among intellectuals, discussing whether specific work in that field is appropriate (as I believe), or whether the matter is an area (as Carlos insists) that must be determined "from the outside" through political struggle. Some jokes, too, after an incident that takes place while we were waiting for the matter to be established: one of Carlos's student friends approaches. Straight away I don't like the guy (the idiot is studying architecture and sociology); he goes around with a sort of snobbish superiority made out of current references: the situation with Portaniero's professorship, Sciarretta's courses. On top of that, he seems obsessed with Oscar Landi, whom he quotes, paraphrases, praises, and traces in every magazine or class he can get his hands on. After his praise for Landi, he talks about the *Nuevos Aires* roundtable and says: "The one I don't understand is Renzi, too avant-garde." Conspiratorial looks with Carlos, and he explains it to the guy, who is immediately embarrassed. I smiled at him, understanding, and a while later recall a line from Brecht: "It is good when one who has taken up an extreme position is overtaken by a reactionary period."

A meeting for *Los Libros* in the afternoon; Germán, Carlos, and I argue with Toto, who is fascinated by the success of Peronism among intellectuals. Hard times are in store for this land, there is no doubt that they have the hegemony and will leave no room for us. Toto is a symptom, they control the media (newspapers, magazines, film, consensus) and can do whatever they want; and, since they employ certain phraseology that seems similar to ours, it appears that they're able to impose a line, not because of that but because of their own political ability. By contrast, we always seem ineffectual and abstract, detached from practice. In this regard, Viñas should be analyzed as a populist who separates himself from them faster than anyone, not just because of that, but because he is anti-Peronist.

David comes over and we have dinner together, then he takes me to see his new apartment on Corrientes and Paraná, very high up. Above the city. He stands fearfully on the balcony and looks at the lights of the city as though they were the signs of some personal triumph. He's very wise when he talks about literature, seeking his place and continuously reconstructing the history of Argentine literature. "Sicardi, for example," he says to me during dinner. "You know what's present in *El libro extraño*, there's all of the grotesque, Arlt is there already."

357

June 3

I get up late and go walking from Callao to Santa Fe, and on Córdoba and Callao someone walks parallel to me: "Documents," he says. It's the porter from Pasaje del Carmen. Desolate, he tells me about how they kicked him out. He talks without stopping, bearded, his teeth chipped and stained, furious, almost cornered. He won't leave the apartment, threatening to kill someone. He can't get work. Expelled from the Communist Party, close to the PCR, the administrator kicked him out. And he says: "I have dignity, it's not pride, it's dignity. A porter isn't a doormat." He trusts that they will help him. "My comrades won't abandon me." He was a metalworker, laid off in the strikes of '62, and he moved around the city like a shadow about which we—the intellectuals of the left—make up theories. "Want to get a coffee?" he asks me. "No," I say, "I'm in a hurry, you know." We say goodbye, I can't remember his last name at that moment and smile, trying to seem optimistic about his future. "No," he says. "The whole thing's fucked up." I go into the subway entrance, kill some time leaning there in the staircase, and then furtively go out again and cross Córdoba in the middle of the street, trying not to let Merlo see me.

Sunday, June 4

Julia tells me a comical story about David trying to seduce a girl, and then she makes up a ridiculous theory, he always falls into a kind of theatrical mauditism (he offers to take the girl to Europe, to buy her fine clothes), and she immediately starts to interpret him ideologically to her credit with quotes from Marcuse and others. Ultimately, it reminds me of a series of writers who think that their writing warrants any behavior in the world, like Oscar D. for example, who always has a Bataille quote at hand. On the other hand, the economic success of David's play has made him turn out worse; his work is much better when he thinks like a failure.

Monday 5

I wake up at nine thirty, read the paper in bed, then take a shower, tidy the apartment, make toast and drink café con leche. I'm reading the original of *Red Wind* by Chandler to decide the subject for the cover image and the introduction. Walsh's translation is very good, he captures Chandler's tone just right, a sort of ironic distance that creates a twofold plot: the view of the narrator on one hand and the series of events on the other. In his best moments, Chandler is as perfect as Borges; he narrates violence well (or rather, the effects of violence) and is a master of the incidental details that create an atmosphere of reality in stories that are always a bit far-fetched. The detective gets mixed up with murderers, femmes fatales, police, cadavers, and junkies as though he were in a space suit; none of these dramas belong to him, and he watches them from the outside, looking for clues without emotion, sustained by a cynical sarcasm. Detached, the narrator, who is the hero, attends to events as though he were watching a film at the same time. His story is constructed like commentary on events that have already transpired, a sort of comic critique. On the one hand, the "romantic" effect that underlies Chandler comes from an uncertainty: at times, the detective who narrates is touched, is implicated in the events; on the other hand, he does everything for money and is a loser, and yet he has lonely and sentimental rituals (the rite of coffee, chess games against no one). When the two planes intersect, Chandler's best work appears: the ceremony of the gimlet, etc. That double bind is concentrated around Linda Loring, a deadly blonde, attractive and romantic, who is also a millionaire. In essence, one of the core elements of Marlowe is the fluctuation between economic profit and stoic morality, which also defines the tone of the story.

As with many great writers, Borges first of all, there is a contradiction in Chandler that is never resolved: an attraction to aspects of life that most traditional writers end up resolving by choosing one of the two (for example, in Chase only the cynical side is valued), whereas the greats always struggle against two symmetrical temptations.

Tuesday 6
At noon I went over to Pocho P.'s place. He's a likeable gangster who works on the black market: an automatic elevator to the 14th floor, where you

have to say the name of the confidant who recommended you to the person spying from behind the electronic peephole. Inside is a carpeted and very luxurious office: international travelers, servants in white jackets, high-class women clutching their purses to their chests. No gangster looks like a gangster here, they're all gentlemen who've learned their manners and style from *Playboy*. A certain nervous anxiety breathes through this rather abstract office with its view over a long stretch of the Río de la Plata. Inside, constant activity, elegant men coming and going, employees, numbers, prices dictated by the movement of the black market. The dollar may change its value at any moment, rising and falling to create a sort of theatrical metaphor here for money as fate within capitalism. Maybe a satire could be written with this setting: the characters feel, suffer, and become happy according to the fluctuations of the global market, as if their bodies were connected directly to the international circulation of capital. P., gray-haired, well-mannered, attends to everyone, resolving several issues at the same time, going in and out of different offices. "I'll send Willie for you," he tells me. "Here's another," and he indicates Marcelo Díaz, who, with his murderous appearance—he's letting his beard grow and his face is shadowed as though stained or dirty—is trying to find out, in the finest tradition of the detective genre, who stole the five hundred dollars that the University of Mexico sent as payment for the magazine advertising. I go back with Marcelo and together we stop in at Martín Fierro to see Gusmán, who's anxious about publishing his novel. There I run into Puig, who has returned from Europe.

At five in the afternoon I meet with Néstor, who always seems frightened, and in a while the students from Universidad de la Plata show up, proposing a course for me on literature and the avant-garde.

Wednesday 7
Series E. In my case, it is a difficult and slow road to what Pavese calls "maturity," meaning autonomy and passion as a territory that must be earned each day. I don't like the work, but I don't want to practice the juvenile rhetoric of the writers in my generation either. I've been writing

a diary for fifteen years and that should be the proof that I'm trying to transform some things in my life.

I go to the publishing office and spend several hours reading and answering letters, sorting through reading reports and magazines with international information about books and translations. Then I stop in Galerna to look at books and kill time, and Sebreli comes in; we study each other cautiously, and finally he approaches. His book about the Anchorenas is about to come out, and he talks about it emphatically, but at the same time he gives off an impression like he's just gotten out of jail or is about to go back there. He talks about the Trotskyists, the political essayists. "Milcíades Peña plagiarized everything from Nahuel Moreno," he says. "Nahuel Moreno is sensational, but he doesn't write anything: he, Ismael Viñas, El Gordo Cooke, and Abelardo Ramos are the only political essayists in this country." Then, a while later, he talks about Peronism: "The students are always wrong. They were wrong in '45 and they're wrong now. Back then they compared Perón to Hitler and now they're comparing him to Mao Zedong."

Earlier I had written a letter to Andrés; if I'm clear about the people I converse with and know what they expect of me, I can be a very effective writer. Virtue or calamity? First of all: knowing the audience and yet not knowing it at the same time. Friends are writer's audience; beyond that circle, there is darkness.

David turns up at my place depressed, apocalyptic, as in his best times. He is hung up about a critic from Entre Ríos who accused him in the newspaper *El Litoral* of being a totalitarian because of his essays. He is also hung up with himself because he has to set up his apartment again after having just organized the one in Cangallo. Loneliness, no doubt, lies at the root of everything. She finds him in the street, tells him that she's in love with someone else, and he knows he can't go after her again and feels lost. As he is leaving, he asks me for a thousand pesos even though he's making a million and a half per month from his play. A clear metaphor, taking something from me since I wouldn't have dinner with him, like a boy stealing an apple at the fair.

Thursday 8

A dream. An altercation with a social democrat taxi driver, we argue, actually there are several of us traveling in the car but I'm the one who confronts him. I feel that I haven't made it to the root of the argument but, nevertheless, they take me to court a few hours later. Everyone accuses me, even the people who were traveling with me. Someone, a fat guy, says "he's the one," and he points at me, saying "both of us are just as fat." Everything takes place in a courtroom, and I'm convinced that they're going to sentence me, and then the dream is in color (it's the first time in my life that I have dreamed in color, at least that I can remember). On the sea, crossing the Mediterranean, there is a party. From one of the boats that have gathered in the place, I see three or four sailors coming toward me, pushing a globe of many colors as they swim. "This is the festival of the cross," they tell me, "you have to celebrate, it's like losing your virginity."

I stop by Galerna to use the telephone and find Vicente Battista, who now has a beard, and who, as always, laughs uproariously when he has nothing to say. He tells me about a roundtable organized for *Nuevos Aires* about popular culture and populism. With Getino, Villarreal, Puiggrós, and China Ludmer: monologues, indecision. This makes me remember China so I go over to see her; she's working on a good project about Onetti and tells me her version of the roundtable, sharing her idea to attempt a dialogue with the Peronists instead of always confronting them at the table in the way that David or Villarreal do. I have to think more about this and decide a strategy. We agree about confrontations and immediate definitions.

Monday 12

I write to Andrés and prepare the jacket copy for the Chandler book. In La Plata, they've offered me twenty-five hundred pesos for the course to talk once per week for a month. I work at home and David comes over in the middle, furious about Granica. As for me, I go to the publishing office and Centro Editor and manage to get seventy thousand pesos for a variety of work and then get "stuck" with Germán García, over dinner, talking about Lacan and his followers.

Saturday 17
I spend two hours at the College of Architecture, first contact between "artists" and writers. The distinction is clear, the difference is that we— the so-called writers—have language as our material. That is the only thing that unites us. The artists are a more varied gang that also includes architects, which is no bad thing. We discussed commitment and practice. This argument is always the same; for me, politics is internal to artistic activity, while most of them think about politics as something toward which they must go. Basically, for the majority of those who were there, the point was to talk constantly about torture and repression, subjects that seem to guarantee an art of denunciation. For my part, I tried to recall some experiences from the avant-garde that were closely connected to determining a specific language for the left's slogans, newspapers, manifestos, and declarations. We came back by train at four in the morning when today's papers were being distributed in Retiro. I go to Pippo before sunrise and watch the nocturnal people celebrating, up all night.

Monday, June 19
David stops by at eleven in the morning looking for me and makes me get out of bed. I make him come up, he whistles on the balcony while I get dressed, and then he takes a book from the shelf and finally we go down to have breakfast together. We walk down Santa Fe to Coronel Díaz and, in Tolón, after the basics, David asks me: "What are you up to?" I give him a drowsy version of the state of the novel I'm writing and tell him that I'll probably end up throwing the whole thing in the trash. "You know," he says after some hesitation, seemingly touched, "from a competitive standpoint, it made me feel satisfied to see that you have

limits; I on the other hand am omnipotent." I saw red and, after that, after a few exchanges of words, I said to him: "Look, old man, let's leave things here and talk again in ten years. Remember what I've said this morning, and pay attention to how each of us has turned out then." We each went our own way, and I had the feeling that my friendship with David was in danger, at least from my angle.

Tuesday 20
Ricardo comes over, and we go to see Boccardo and get tickets to go to the movies tonight. Throughout all of that I show no enthusiasm. I eat a steak at Pippo in front of them while they try to turn back to the subject of the script. On the way back we run into Viñas, tension between him and me. He greets everyone ceremoniously while I stare down to the end of the street, and he talks without pause, trying to find some way out. "Give me a call," he says to me in an aside as he leaves, trying to affect the pose of a beggar. "Stop by and see me," I say in my best indifferent tone.

Some writers who are "politically" reactionary, so to speak, are at the vanguard in everything else, as though their archaic political position afforded them a critical view of the modern world. Examples: Borges, Céline, Pound, and along the same lines but in an opposite political spectrum Brecht and Benjamin. One outlier case is Gombrowicz; I particularly like this quote of his: "Everyone is a writer. The writer does not exist, everyone in the world is a writer, everyone knows how to write. When one writes a letter to his girlfriend, that too is literature. I would go even further: when one converses, when one tells an anecdote, one creates literature, it is always the same thing."

Series E. In reality, these diaries should be used in order to search, in the monotonous plot of days, for the turning points, the differences, things that are not repeated, things that persist in themselves beyond habit and are unique, novel, personal. Do such things exist? That is the question of literature.

Saturday 24

Tied up with a series of projects. A prologue for Luis Gusmán's book *El frasquito*. I have to reread the book so that I can think about what I'm going to write (starting this weekend). A report about the meeting of artists and writers at the College of Architecture to submit to *Desacuerdo* on Wednesday. A meeting with Germán García to put together the survey on criticism for the special issue of *Los Libros*; I have to write the introduction. Script for B., for the film *El atraco*, which must be finished before the end of the month. A class for the group of psychoanalysts this coming Thursday about negation in Freud. Starting the course on Borges at the University of La Plata, four classes that begin the day after tomorrow (give them the syllabus). Otherwise, various projects for the publishing house: notes, copy, reading reports, a prologue for Chandler. I make lists because it lets me delude myself, thinking that by making them the things will get done, when in reality all I'm doing is enumerating them.

Sunday 25

I meet Julia, taking notes on Gusmán's book while I wait for her at her house. I eat with her at Pippo, and she tells me about her encounter with David, who seeks her out so that he can cry about our schism.

Monday 26

Andrés drags me out of bed in the morning; we have lunch and say goodbye to each other in the mid-afternoon in front of Tribunales. He reads me an excellent story, lyrical, epic, with a Faulknerian tone, long (at some points, we might say, it's a bit too rhetorical and literary in the bad sense). Then a meeting at the publishing office with the habitual misunderstandings; the Serie Negra is selling twenty-five hundred copies on average and, in spite of that, they're resistant to expanding it.

I meet with the group from La Plata, we put together the classes on Borges in exchange for twenty-five thousand pesos. Then I say goodbye to León R. with a certain nostalgia. I meet with Héctor, a good conversation about theater; he's planning a show in a circus, and I suggest an adaptation of the novel *Hormiga Negra* by Gutiérrez. After leaving Pippo we go for a coffee at Ramos. David comes in with Daniel Open. Tension, furtive glances. On the way out, I pass in front of him: "*Salud*, David," I say, and he looks at my face, solemnly, and stretches out a hand to me. A ceremonial, "significant" handshake. We turn down Corrientes toward Callao, they tease me a couple times. It is Julia, coming from Sciarretta's class. Next to her, more present than my denial would have given credit for, also bearded, was Pepe. Introductions, greetings. I insist on having a coffee with them, but they refuse because they're on the way to dinner. "I'll see you tomorrow," I say. A situation in a tedious atmosphere that overwhelms me.

Wednesday 28

Just now, at four in the morning, with the gas burners lit to stave off the cold, I'm starting to write about Gusmán. First notes center around organizing the "excess" of meaning that the story brings. Everything is stated, and if it seems strange to some, it's because they lack the context on which it was based.

All of the difficulty with the prologue for *El frasquito* lies in the fact that I don't want to write a "Freudian essay" but rather organize the excess of meaning, showing what literary writing is there.

Friday, June 30

Suddenly a clear vision, an epiphany, an unexpected, photographic memory: I see the street, or rather, the sidewalk parallel to the plaza by the cathedral in La Plata. A wall with concrete balconies, a portal with an inner door, trees, the empty plaza on the other side, to my left, and, most unsettling of all, I see myself from behind, walking toward Calle 7. Every time I see myself clearly in a memory, something has happened that I can't remember, but the image, without saying anything, points to the existence of an event. In the memory, I am concurrently the person recounting the event and its protagonist.

July 1
I spend a while working on Borges for the course on Monday and then meet Julia, and chaos is unleashed. Always the same turmoil when she's there. I head home and run into Juan De Brasi on the way, and I spend three hours with him, none of which I remember. I get home at midnight, and it's impossible to work, impossible to sleep either. I go out, take the bus, go to Julia's apartment. She isn't there. I stare into the void until five in the morning, but she doesn't come home, so I go back down to the street and return here.

Sunday 2
After my Dostoevskian attack last night, I am calmer. I don't really know what I'm looking for, since I was the one who separated from her. The illusion of a woman who's always there when I go looking for her. For reasons like these, Raskolnikov kills the money-lender.

Monday 3
I find Sazbón and Marcelo Díaz in Galerna; the crisis at *Los Libros* because of Carlos Altamirano's article continues. A violent argument on Thursday, Toto travels to La Plata with me, taking precautions in the face of Carlos's dogmatism. The issue remains unresolved.

Melancholia on the diagonals of the city. I teach my class, and everything turns out alright. Then we all have a coffee together in the bar at the station. I come back, like so many times before, on the dark bus, an hour and a half of thinking in the same way as ten years ago.

Tuesday 4
After some back and forth I write the prologue for Gusmán. A six-page draft titled "El relato fuera de la ley."

Saturday 8
On Thursday an argument about the composition of *Los Libros* until three in the morning, first at Germán's house, then at my place. Schmucler

decided that Altamirano's article won't go out. His "passage" toward Peronism is not explicit and the debate is circular, elliptical. What space does the magazine occupy? The issue remains unresolved; in Peronism, Toto seems to have found the same path as many other intellectuals close to him, basically the group from *Pasado y Presente*. The general turn toward Peronism is growing immeasurably, and anyone who opposes it is isolated. It would seem that Toto wants the magazine to follow that path.

On Friday a meeting for *Desacuerdo* with Roberto C. Maybe I'm too sensitive, but I see traces of political pedantry, and I react. I don't believe politics should be the thing that directs all spheres of reality. Let's recall Roberto C.'s behavior at the roundtable of politicians at Philosophy and Letters. The issue has not been resolved and everything stays the way it is at *Los Libros*, up in the air.

Sunday 9

In the afternoon Beatriz comes over and we work on publishing the magazine, pessimistically, sure of failure. Some fantasies about Nené on my part, but who could blame me in the middle of this situation? She suffers from a mimetic impulse, she saw *Hiroshima mon amour* and got married to a Japanese architect. Then she enrolled herself in a speed-reading course; such is the critic who writes.

Tuesday 11

Nothing can happen to me at three in the morning, alone in the city, like a sleepwalker who is losing everything he has, struggling to gain freedom of movement as though he were on another planet.

Wednesday 12

I sleep for four hours and then at noon walk in the freezing wind to pay the electricity bill at a bank with a very high ceiling. Then I have lunch at Hermann, alone in the empty room. I live like someone who is carrying out a delicate and secret mission in a foreign country. Unknown, lost among the people, expecting nothing from anyone, learning to survive on his own resources, with no contact with the country that has assigned him the mission, and with the sole objective of carrying out a plan that he only half understands. The life of a spy in enemy territory. That has been my identity—or my conviction in the world—from the beginning, and the signs are here in these notebooks, written in a coded language whose real meaning I alone can understand. Since 1958, so many years ago now, I have persisted in my attempt to build for myself what is usually called a "normal" life. If I resist, that is, if I manage to remember my reflections from those years, I will be able to break free; in the meantime, I'm on a road with no exit.

"The position of the artist is not wagered on the materials made use of, but on the process of elaboration of those materials," Sergio Tretyakov. I find this quote in the excellent issue of *VH 101* dedicated to the Soviet avant-garde. I find a photo of Tretyakov there, and I take apart the frame that held a photo of Hemingway and put it in on top, a sign of my changes.

Subject. A gang of superstitious gauchos, gathered around a medicine man who claims to be the son of God, sent by the eternal father to Buenos Aires province; they decide to steal the Virgin of Luján to establish a sanctuary and collect donations. They enter the Basilica at night, take it from the altar, put it in the car and drive to the country, and in a forest they take one look at it and then kneel, spellbound. (It would be interesting if the Virgin performed a miracle—for example, stopping the car from starting.)

Friday 14
Series E. For almost fifteen years I've pursued a writing that I hardly understand sometimes, letting myself be guided by a certain impulse, talking about myself in notebooks with black rubber covers, not really knowing the meaning of what I'm trying to capture. In order to better understand what I'm saying, it's best for me to try to explain what was (what is), for me, this thing we've agreed to call literature.

Tuesday 25

At night I return home, and Roberto Jacoby comes over soon after; he's intelligent, funny, and the conversation flows as it always does when I'm with him. Then I walk around the neighborhood to find a mailbox where I can drop off the letters I've written. At home, the electric doorbell rings: David Viñas, aged, white-haired, weighed down, but after some tension, we go back to our cyclical conversations. David tells me about his project of a novel (*Pueblada*) with a tone like Payró: a soldier in a country town who has a "great love" with a gay barber, and at the end a popular revolution arises. Then he describes his argument with a kid who criticized him for his liberalism during a lecture. As he is leaving, I say: "We have to talk." He smiles, nods his head: "Didn't I come?"

Sunday 30

Yesterday Héctor came over, hurried, excited. He's planning to take theater into the street, expropriate the setting, make an enclosure, he seeks me out and it is effort for me to think with him.

Thursday, August 3

I work amid interruptions, but at least I organize a presentation on philosophy for the group on Mondays. I find some core ideas: negation, speech acts, the situation of utterance. I want to make the psychoanalysts think about the grammar and thought of analytic philosophy. Oscar Landi suggests that we take over a professorship in Philosophy. I'm not sure if we can work as peacefully if we enter the academic structure.

Then a meeting for *Los Libros*. In the middle of the conversation, I see the shadow of a woman through the beveled glass of the door, a patch of red, and suddenly Vicky appears, timid, and I follow her out into the hallway. She has come from La Plata. "I wanted to chat," she says. We spend the night together, all the way into Friday afternoon.

Monday 7
Vicky waits for me in the station, making plans, and as always, I look at her from a distance, sitting with her in the noisy bar among people who come and go.

Tuesday 8
A fantasy of escape, going to a hotel in some country town, bringing a draft of my novel and staying there until I finish it. Working at night, eating in the hotel dining room, taking an afternoon walk through the town and returning to work, over and over, until I finish the book.

Friday 11
Some traces of "insanity" lately, which make me see possible fates. Vicky comes over, we had dinner at Hermann last night, and I look at her with surprise, some uncertainty that she doesn't seem to perceive. The next day—today—things improve. Just like last time, it's necessary to promise something, some fictional trap that appears of its own accord. And so, today, my certainty that the "matter" wasn't working: an explanation of my present state (breakup with Julia, desire to finish the novel), a pretext to leave everything as it stands, not see each other, etc.

Anyway, the best part came just afterward. We go down to the street, I with the intention to accompany her to the bus station and then be alone. We walk down Santa Fe to Coronel Díaz. There, we decide to take the train at nine, but as soon as we step on, I realize that the prologue for Gusmán's book isn't in my briefcase. I think I've lost it, don't have a copy, etc. I get off the bus at the first corner and walk down Santa Fe, clinging to the idea that I've left it in the apartment, but it isn't there. I go back out to the street, and then something incredible happens: on the corner of Canning and Santa Fe, on the pavement, in front of the store, I see a sheet of paper. It's page nine of my prologue, carried off by the wind; among the cars, I find another six pages. From there, I go on amid traffic from all four sides, trying to guess the direction of the wind. I go in circles, from one side to the other. At some point Vicky signals to me; in the gutter, in the middle of the block, on Santa Fe, I find all of the pages except one floating in the water, about to sink in. As has happened a few other times, this shows me how far my current "insanity" can go.

Wednesday, August 16
X Series. A meeting for the newspaper. An absurd discussion about the actions of the ERP; they freed Santucho, as well as other guerrilla leaders, after taking over Rawson prison and Trelew airport, where they got a plane to take him to Chile. Elías and Rubén criticize the adventurism of the guerrilla groups, putting political work in danger.

Friday 18
I bring the prologue for Gusmán to the Martín Fierro bookshop. Some wavering from Gusmán, influenced by O. Lamborghini, who, angry that I didn't mention him, wants Luis to redo the prologue. Of course, I tell him he has every right not to publish it if it's causing problems with his spiritual leaders.

Sunday 27
I meet with David, who receives my call very cordially and gets past my criticism. He shows up in Ramos, now bearded, and we let ourselves be carried away by our old mutual understanding. We get dinner together in the restaurant on Paraná and go over David's old obsessions (Peronism, Cortázar), and finally he pushes me on with everything and gets excited to have me write a plotline on the subject of the theft of the Luján virgin. "I think it's sensational, it has to come out in the theater," he says. We end up in the bar with the balcony where I saw him having coffee with Jorge Álvarez one afternoon many years ago, and now we drink coffee again and talk about our "old issues." He apologizes without feeling, and we change the subject. Finally we go to his place, he lends me one of the books from the Coloquio de Cluny, we talk about his project of writing about Túpac Amaru; the city below is filled with lights, and I return home, in the end, without great expectations.

Thursday, August 31

A dream. I was dying behind a garden wall in a vast park, a woman was trying to lift me into a wooden stroller. "Can't you see I'm dead?" I ask her. I woke up with a start, trying uselessly to remember whether I saw myself dead or whether, as happens in dreams, I just knew I was dead and accepted it naturally. Dreams are an example of how a story can be told as long as the reader knows the subtext and believes in it. A dream has the peculiarity of joining the narrator, spectator, and hero of the story in a single image; you are simultaneously inside the scene of the dream and watching yourself while the events transpire. Of course, it also you who is telling the story.

September

In reality—as I learned from Brecht—emotions that reconcile and console in the common ground of "profound" feeling (extreme misery, abandoned childhood) are always the visible extremes of a shameful reality; they are easy to access, real illusions that enchant beautiful souls. The Trelew massacre allows everyone to talk about their impressions instead of seeking an answer and finding something *useful* beyond the explanation.

Saturday, September 2

I miss an appointment at night when I leave the theater after seeing the excellent film *Deep End*. I lose my way in the city, on Saturday night, and waver between whether to eat at some restaurant on Corrientes or go back home; finally I make up my mind but just miss the train at Callao station and stand under the light on the empty platform, looking at posters, and Marcelo Díaz appears at the far end, almost hidden in shadows. I latch on to him (as others who were alone used to latch on to me), and we have dinner together at El Ciervo.

Tuesday

I call C., a psychologist recommended to me by Oscar Masotta. An appointment on Monday, October 2 at 6:15 p.m. in a clinic on Calle Díaz Vélez.

At the movie theater again, *We Are All in Temporary Liberty*, a premonitory title. Afterward I leave to meet B. at Colombiano. Someone touches my shoulder, it's Lola Estrada, excited, staring at me, mischievous and shy. "I saw you the other day," she says, "with Rivera at La Paz." I tell her I'm going to call her, that we'll get a meal together. Both of us know that I know she told Marcelo she wanted to sleep with me. I "don't want trouble" (I don't want to go back to my promiscuous life of 1962–63). Anyway, it amuses me that she would remember having seen me, as though, in these gloomy days, I'm affected by a woman noticing me.

Tuesday
Some symptoms last night. I see Nené at Galerna, she tells me she wants to stop by my place tonight to pick up *Brodie's Report* (as if she couldn't get it anywhere else). I tell her I can't today. "And tomorrow night?" she asks. I can't do that either. It's clear that she came to the bookshop at five in the afternoon because she knows she can always find me there at that time. Quickly I decide that I'm not interested in getting dinner with her or sleeping with her. I prefer to make a date with Ana despite the fact that I no longer have any interest. I teach the class at the Institute and call Ana on the way out, but she can't see me, and now here I am with the empty night, so I stay downtown and go out to dinner alone. I have a few glasses of wine and suddenly decide to call Lola. It's eleven at night and I apologize like a phantom; she can't either, she's finishing a project, why don't I call tomorrow?

Monday, October 2
First session with C. Some restlessness during the half hour before. I have a coffee at La Paz to kill time and then get a taxi on Lavalle. Calle Díaz Vélez reminds me of the boarding house on Medrano, the bridge that crosses the tracks near Rivadavia. The waiting room is just a garage, there's a heater, and I'm by myself. Leather armchairs, a painting. After a while, a short, scrawny guy with a boyish face comes in, looks around, greets me with a powerful voice and climbs the staircase in leaps. He

isn't wearing a jacket, carries books under his arm, seems intelligent; I later confirm that he is C. Now I'm thinking that he only came for me, that he had no patients, that he spent five minutes studying my information. A woman comes in after a while, then two more. Some guys with intellectual faces peek over the banister of the staircase, call for them, and they go up. Once 6:15 has passed, I think I was supposed to confirm the appointment by phone, I try to make up a pretense, "I didn't call because I wanted to postpone." But if I had called, he would've thought I was compulsive. I'm going to say that I just came back from traveling. But couldn't I have called five minutes before? At that point it occurs to me to leave, find a telephone, and call. I don't know what I can do to let him know I'm here. A short while later a young girl dressed in a pink smock appears. "For Doctor C." she says. I follow her. We go down a hallway with several side doors, and I'm again reminded of a hotel (with appointments?), a boarding house (something squalid). To the left there's a little room with a dim light, a couch (Giacovate?) with a plastic cover, a desk. Behind it sits C.; on a corner of the table, against the wall and next to the table lamp, is a stack of books. Then he opens a drawer and several five hundred-peso bills are visible. I look at the couch, at the wall with a painting hanging on it, and I try to imagine what it will feel like to lie there, where he will sit, what part of the wall I will see. (Today, I dreamed I was lying down in the other direction, so that I was facing the painting and he was in front of me. Except I sit down in this chair, that is, I use it because the other is behind the desk and the couch can't be moved.) As always, I work *a priori*. He isn't going to talk, I have to get to the essence, etc. I talk about my separation from Julia, my work conflicts. In general, he keeps himself out of it, and I don't look at him. He intervenes two or three times, nothing spectacular, more affective, you could say, than intelligent. He tells me that the basis of my work seems solid to him, that it has positive results and gratifies me, but that I should be able to accept that there's no contradiction between going to therapy to break from certain molds that impede my progress and fearing that therapy will dismantle my relationship with the work. In the end we talk about money; he's very expensive, and I set my limits (between thirty and forty thousand pesos per month). He extricates himself, asking for another session on Friday. After I leave, I wander a bit around the neighborhood, which I can't place (somewhere near Almagro?). I think: "What a sense of time, he knew it was time to stop after fifty minutes without glancing at the clock." I think: "Money and time lie behind everything."

Monday, October 9
Monologue (1). When I first came here, I told him, I thought I'd have to decide what the first sentence of my psychoanalysis would be. Where to begin?, etc.

Series C. The circulation of telephone calls and staggered appointments, just now calling Julia to see her today, Lola to see her tomorrow, all governed by the vertigo I live with. I can't pay full attention to anything, and the girls imaginarily accompany me in the confusion. There will always be someone who's there when I call her.

Thursday 26
Yesterday another goodbye with Julia. I meet her in El Foro, across from the building where David lives, which is being cleared out because there's danger of a collapse. She starts analyzing, and says we have to stop seeing each other; after much reminiscing, I tell her I'm about to travel to Europe. Two minutes later we leave the restaurant. I find Perrone at a table, he holds me back; out in the street, Julia is already gone. I walk alone through Paraná, alone in the night, doggedly. Almost two hours of walking takes me to the end of the city, past the rails of Palermo, where the low houses begin, and I take a taxi there and return home.

A meeting for the magazine; Toto doesn't come, Germán doesn't come, the others come but without enthusiasm. We decide to face the matter head on next Thursday (a different magazine?). At La Moncloa, everything for me revolves around Nené's signals, a certain mutual understanding. We leave together. We make a date for Saturday. Then I go to Lola's place, everything goes well with her as always, casual. We walk around the house, look at Russian posters, have dinner at the Salguero restaurant, spend the night together.

Friday, October 27
I meet Beatriz at El Foro and we go looking for Gregorich to go to the roundtable in Morón, and there begins one of the most delirious and mixed-up nights I can remember. We go across the city to Retiro, take a train with Susana Zanetti and Nené, get off at Morón. Throughout the trip, many jokes with Beatriz about the cultural progressiveness of the West. On the podium, little white folders and a ceramic jug. My participation goes well, more or less. Going last, Beatriz is nervous, imprecise, academic, running over her time. We have dinner at a typical restaurant and I argue unenthusiastically with G. about Borges. Finally the train back, we arrive at Once, I get in a taxi with Nené, we go to her new house in San Telmo, she doesn't have the keys. Two drowsy friends appear and let us in. We finally get in, a desolate place. Once we're alone, everything continues with the same tone. Nené is frightened by the place where she's going to live, she insists that she doesn't want anyone to protect her, doesn't want dependent relationships. "You want to sleep with me," she says. "Of course, that's why I came." Nené sits down on the staircase leading upstairs. I left in a taxi, thinking it was all a kind of creole circus, very funny.

Thursday 2
X Series. Rubén K. stops by looking for me and we go to Constitución for lunch with Chiche P., two working professionals. Lives that intrigue me; there's something bureaucratic in the succession of meetings and something epic in how they dedicate their lives to the political struggle.

A meeting of the discussion group with Landi, which is going along very well. The violence and political circumstances as a field of experimentation for discursive reality. How do a series of newspapers, tasked with describing the political world, refer to the situation?

At *Los Libros* we begin the political discussion, seeing what will become of the magazine. We can't continue with the way things are. The core of the matter is Peronism, but I also insist that we must go back and define our specific objective and plan.

In the meeting Nené is beautiful, childish. Very melancholy right away, and we exchange a couple of glances. She arrived late, and I left early. That's how things are for me.

Earlier on the phone with Lola. I stopped by to see her at night. Things went well, and neither of us wanted to stretch out the matter any further. We exchanged compliments, comforted each other, and I left, trusting there would be no dramatic farewells.

My upcoming trip to China is a point of escape for me. On the one hand, I'm explicitly retreating from areas of conflict in my current life. On the other hand, it's like going to the moon for me, a place that I imagine because I've seen it in the imaginary nights of the culture of the left. I hope the time to leave comes soon.

Saturday
In the morning at the College of Engineering, an empty labyrinth at this hour, the slow elevators and at last a group of students very similar to what I was at the age they are now. They are quick, intelligent, connect well, have initiative. Discussions about the Russian avant-garde, Proletkult, and the art of propaganda.

Walking along Paseo Colón to Plaza de Mayo, I go down the avenue, feel the loneliness of the city without affection. Then I call Tristana, make a date with her, and we eat together; I cling to that woman as I would do with any other who showed me care and affection. We plan to meet at her house at night, while I finalize the trip to Córdoba.

This woman helped me through these difficult months, and now I think I'm alone and have no one to turn to, he said, everything is distant, socialized, and false.

During the trip to Córdoba, Héctor, onto whom I project my old delusions from the sixties, tells me a story about a Spaniard who takes some people to his attic and proudly shows them a letter he received from Cuba ("from Fidel") in response to his own, which he had written because he listens to Radio Havana in the night.

Sunday, November 5 in Córdoba
X Series. The cafeteria on the terrace at the terminal, the city under the sun. I have lunch at Rubén K.'s house. He makes the food in a didactic style while they organize the working plan and discuss relationships with other Maoist organizations. Rubén, serene, wise, firm, knows how to listen.

Monday 6
I spend the morning in Córdoba talking about Brecht, facing the young people, once again feeling like a veteran in front of them. In the mid-afternoon, an informal chat with a group of Architecture students. After that I decide to be alone and walk around the city, mentally preparing the evening's talk, and I go from one end to the other without leaving Avenida Vélez Sarsfield. Finally, I return to the Department of Architecture and, in the Great Hall, pose a series of hypotheses on the relationship between the aesthetic avant-garde and the political avant-garde.

Tuesday
A second talk, equally improvised, which culminates in a night staying up with Héctor and Greco at an architect's house. Then Roberto C. comes

over with his usual tone, sententious and long-winded, a type of thinking that I recognize and want nothing to do with.

Wednesday

I'm still in Córdoba amid meetings, projects, and talks. Sometimes I have a need to isolate myself, to be alone. Finally I return to Buenos Aires, traveling all night without sleeping, looking at the open country and the lighted towns through the little window, imagining how the other journey will be, the one through which I hope to lose the burden that I carry with me. I arrive in Buenos Aires and am met with an unexpected festival commemorating one hundred years since the publication of *Martín Fierro*, and I make several calls but don't reach anyone. Things put themselves back together while I drink a glass of wine at El Olmo, Beatriz turns up for the magazine meeting, and then a while later so do the others. Straight away, Toto proposes that we shut it down and hold the funeral rites; the discussion seems unnecessary to him because we all know our own positions. We try to determine the situation, and I make him see the need to discuss alternatives as well. We know that the core of the debate is Peronism, which Toto has enrolled himself in, and of which we're all critics. At the end, Beatriz invites me to have a coffee and get dinner. In Pepito, we talk calmly and in a friendly tone, of another time, about Perón's return. Then she leaves, and I stop by Martín Fierro where I have an appointment with Gelman.

Saturday 11

I spend the night with Lola until early morning. We see Esther Ferrán dance at La Potra, get dinner at a restaurant on Calle Viamonte, and go back to her place.

Monday 13

It would seem that there's always a way out. Today, after spending the night with Lola, I find a letter from Amanda and everything is organized. I feel better, calmer.

Tuesday 14

In the morning another letter from Amanda, written prior to the one that came yesterday, and more explicit, always passionate and seductive. "In these hard times, it's easier to give your life than your heart."

Wednesday

Lola comes and stays with me, beautiful in her striped pants and black sweater, dressed like a child.

Friday 17

On TV, I watch Perón's return in the rain after so many years in exile. Surrounded by soldiers with weapons guarding him; the military officers didn't think his desire to return was real.

Tuesday, November 21

My brother comes, and we exchange impressions about family. There isn't much difference between the things we've lived through, beyond the ten years of distance that separate us from one another.

Wednesday 22

Beatriz leaves word for me in Galerna to call her. "I want us to talk about the situation with the magazine before the meeting tomorrow on Thursday."

After the meeting for *Desacuerdo*, I thought I had written down Héctor's address but it's actually Horacio's. I cross the city on the 59 bus, get off at Núñez, look for a phone, dial and then realize that this isn't it, that I'm lost and don't know where to go. I go in circles trying to find the house by chance, uselessly. In the end I return home alone.

Thursday

In the meeting for *Los Libros*, it's clear that Carlos, Beatriz, and Marcelo are working together in the PCR line and take the issue to be resolved; I am marginalized.

Saturday 25
I waited for a letter from Amanda that did not come. The dark city in Plaza de Mayo, damp and gloomy at nightfall.

Wednesday
A letter from Amanda. "At the end of December, once the theater performances are over, I'm coming to Buenos Aires. And I'll be there to stay."

Thursday 30
A meeting for *Los Libros*, Schmucler renounces the magazine that he himself founded. Paradoxes in the culture of the left. Toto's political evolution created tensions over the course of time, until finally he decided to step away.

I'm in La Moncloa, meeting with Germán, Carlos, Beatriz, et al. David appears, shy, with a humble air, he's come looking for me, and I plan to meet him at La Paz two hours later. We sit down at a table by the window and chaos soon erupts. David starts complaining because the actors groveled in front of him to get work, and from there we move on to the criteria he uses for his selections, if indeed he can select the cast. The argument grows and scatters and becomes chaotic. David chides me several times, saying he's the one who always comes looking for me, that I play hard to get, that I judge him from above, etc. Finally we leave, and, on the corner over Montevideo, David starts to cry. During our argument, he'd called me by his son's name several times. I feel bad, etc., etc.

Friday, December 1
Héctor comes over, impassioned, affected by a woman who lives in his building, whom he "loves," terrified by her ex-husband, a fascist from the Guardia de Hierro who hits her and threatens her. After that, some confusion (between Héctor and me) about childhood and the images that rise from the past while we have maté with cookies and advance clumsily in one of my typical friendships: I am the father, the "mature

one," while the other one takes everything from me, and I'm trapped (other examples, B., S., etc.).

I prepare for tomorrow's course, and in the middle Lola appears, excited, thankful for my telegram, always lost in the thousands of projects she has to do, crazy friends, surprise in the face of events. Later, at night, I was alone and started to work, without any need to go out into the street, to escape into the city.

Monologue (20). He tries to understand a certain coldness that characterizes this time, the end with Julia and the arbitrary quality in which affection—with no real bearing on the object or the moment—suddenly emerges (with Lola, with Tristana). Being cold, distant, tough against a certain nebulous area that bewilders him, one which he can scarcely name; language that is confusing, too abstract to "explain." He weeps unexpectedly in front of a painting by Morandi, violating the passage from reason to feeling, but where did this crack begin? He acts out of necessity: being with a woman, having friends, being intelligent, but what he really wants never appears: when it does appear, he grows confused and so starts to babble.

Tuesday 5
In order to be unforgettable, you must first have lost yourself, and then you are remembered because of that. The same virtue as immortality (which is reserved for the dead).

Wednesday 6
Monologue (21). One who wants, can. He said that and thought that affection was something given (which no one can steal), yet there is a certain unease because he cannot repay it, and when affection is missing, or when he doubts whether it really can exist and be given to him, he shields himself in the shield of forgetting; modesty in an ability to be melodramatic. For him, to be intelligent is to forget affection, because he cannot think if feelings enter. Thus, intelligence serves to make himself

wanted, it is the only thing—he thinks—that allows him to be wanted, but his aggressive tendencies reveal a "tough guy" who doesn't need anything and tries to straighten things out by himself. His intelligence and also his literature are gambled on those fluctuations. In order to break through his limits, he must act by surprise, like a hunter waiting for an unexpected opportunity: the short story that he wrote about Urquiza without really trying. It's as though he thinks that, if he makes it that far, he'll lose everything. One who says is one who is.

Friday 8
A dream. Several people in a room, just like in La Plata during the student meetings. Suddenly, I start reading a poem, the title: "Tristana Tejera Transita Thames." In the dream I remember and recite the whole poem. Is it a sonnet? The skill lies in the handwriting; I can clearly see the control of the T and the S because at a certain point the poem makes a lisp, and I think that this spoken first-person is something unusual: a return? I write a comment in the black notebook (where I know I write down all of my dreams).

Saturday
I teach my class, go out for a walk, the city always strange at that hour of night.

I go to see a play by Brecht at the Embassy with staging by Onofre Lovero. I escape in the middle, overwhelmed by the progressive stupidity.

Sunday
Monologue (22). He had thought that, in fact, excision was a way of being and at the same time a façade; he hadn't taken the real moment into account, and his thoughts therefore tended toward mythology.

Monday 11
I meet Beatriz, who returns the folder with pictures of the Soviets in the twenties.

Tuesday
I correct Gusmán's prologue, which is being published soon. Dinner with Boccardo, then we go to La Paz.

Thursday
A *dream*. I'm in a circular tower, a terrace on top of a column, I feel vertigo, I'm lying face up on the floor.

Saturday 16
I spend the day on the Tigre in Alberto's boat. A meeting of single men: León, Altamirano, and Boccardo.

I return late at night. Sitting in darkness by the picture window, I look at the city, the lights, and cannot think about the future.

Sunday 17
I spend the weekend with Lola. In the middle of the afternoon the doorbell rings, and it is Amanda, shy but commanding. She comes from the past. The three of us sitting around the table. "Do I have to leave now?" Amanda asked. "I knew I had to leave as soon as I came." I made a date with her for tomorrow and left her in the elevator. As always, the events decide for me; things hurry along, and I let the days flow by. We have dinner at Costanera underneath the trees.

Monday 18
Series C. I meet Amanda at Ramos, her yellow dress, her tan skin. "I told every man I've lived with that everything would go well unless E. R. appeared." I stood up to make the waiter come over. She moved between languor and energy, very erotic, not wearing a bra, and then she drank the double gin as if it was a shot. She insisted on paying. "I pay for my men." We went out to the city and walked along Corrientes to Córdoba and Carlos Pellegrini to get the bottle of pisco and the gift books that were at her sister's house. We stopped by Lafinur and I showed her the bar where I come every day, across from the Botanical Garden. We went

home and then had dinner at Hermann, and I got up to talk to Julia on the phone. We came back and went to bed. "I'll stay with you forever, let's not be apart any longer."

In the morning I run into Beatriz Guido, who hands me the things for the passport. She has her usual chaos, this time organized around her obsession with Peronism, the drugs, her brother's suicide attempt. We have a coffee at Alvear, she takes out some cash while the girl (Marieta) waits patiently for her to leave the money for the day's expenses. Always kind, charming, very intelligent.

Monologue (27). He started talking about his distance from things, the glass that separates him and traps him in an uninhabitable place. He looks at everything as though it had to do with someone else and, at the same time, events lead him from one place to another without his choosing. The coming journey, which he cannot experience as real. In that dark center, the corpses were then being arranged, as though he were in a locked room now, with no windows, with the air from the fan circulating as though it were alive. Someone takes note of what I think and writes it down. Women imposing on him, or the stories he would tell of women imposing on him. All in the midst of a great sadness.

Tuesday
I miss a date with Julia, angry because I haven't seen her in days. Then I go to give my classes at MONA, which I bring to a close. Later I see Lola, happy with her flowers. She's worried about me, and I, in turn, am worried about her. She'd stopped in at *La Prensa* to buy a copy of the speech by the Commander in Chief of the Army from 1969.

Wednesday 20
Let's look at what just happened: I talk with Beatriz Guido's secretary, she gives me the name of an officer, I go to the Central Police Department. "He's in a meeting," they tell me. I return home, worried about the delays. I write my pieces for the newspaper. I decide to go out, call

Lola, stop by to see her. I change clothes and suddenly freeze: I've lost my ID card. I look in my pockets, in the desk. I reconstruct everything I did with her. I took it out of the little booklet where I keep it, I had it in my hand when I entered the Police Station, I didn't put it back in its place, I think: I lost it in the taxi! Vertigo, self-pity, certainty that I caused the catastrophe myself. Everything is ruined, I won't have time to get the ID too. I go around in circles, stunned, for close to an hour. I go down to talk with Lola, but she isn't there. I come back. I throw myself into a chair. I decide to go out, meet Amanda. "In this state of mind, everything's going to be ruined." I go to the bathroom for no reason, open the medicine cabinet, and there, behind the mirror, was the ID. As though I had hidden it there myself. Do I feel good about this tragedy? Dazed, I let go. For the moment, I create real situations based on an element that has a particular charge for me. What will happen on the day when there isn't a real lost object (the ID, the prologue for *Frasquito*, the notebook that I gave to Vicky by mistake), but rather a void that, of course, I will never be able to find? Faced with a chaos that chills my blood and the detailed descriptions that await me if that is so, I pass the days.

Moved by Amanda this time, in a way no woman has affected me in a while. Passionate in the certainty of her love for me, she has been after me, she says, for years.

I stopped by the ramshackle house in Córdoba looking for her, and a stranger opened the door for me. I thought: it's her sister. It was her, however, with her hair wet, wearing striped pants. We had lunch in the pub on Carlos Pellegrini and then I bought her a ring to replace the one she wore. I like her: she's neither calm nor serious, she's beguiling. She holds me while I wait for the taxi: "The man tells me stories," she says, when I tell her about the past.

We go out for dinner at Costanera. Long stories, especially mine, the same ones as always. She listens to them, fascinated, and I feel that everything is false. On her part, a "crazy" love, fantasized about for ten years. It isn't me, just her remembering a past that we never lived.

Thursday 21
We argue (Altamirano, Beatriz, and I) with Germán and Miriam, distrust of "politics."

Friday 22
Difficulties with the "mandatory" work: the classes, the notes, the reviews, the reading reports. In reality, these are the things I do to earn my living. It would seem that there's something less clear, less visible in this matter. It isn't the kind of work that worries me, but rather the concrete result. I try to put together money for the trip to Europe; I have fourteen hundred dollars and many expenses ahead of me.

Lola comes bearing gifts (towels, a shower curtain). "I wouldn't have known what to buy for you." We spend the night together after having dinner and walking around the city. Early in the morning she leaves for Rosario, some repetition of my own goodbyes when I go traveling.

Sitting in La Paz, killing time before the movie. He had stopped by the large house on Calle Córdoba looking for her along the hallways with facing mirrors. He always had a slight terror of her excesses; Amanda had insisted on telling his future by reading the grounds from the coffee they drank. By then they'd gone over to the table by the window with a view over the street and had watched the city in the rain. He had a secret, perverse inkling of being seen by Julia, as though he guessed that she would also be in the theater, watching the Melville film they were going to see later.

Two older women have a conversation in the entryway of Amanda's building while I wait for her. They look at the gales of wind that heighten the rain, obsessing over the subject of accidental death. "Remember Christmas in '50?" one asks, her hair wrapped up in cellophane paper. "The roofs were flying off, remember how they flew? I was in San Fernando, and we watched the roofs flying through the air. What a wind," she said, with a wicked gleam. "Because wind is the worst thing, it brings fire, brings water," she added. "Yes," the other said, with the same biblical style. "But I'm more worried about cornices, I'm always walking along in front of brick buildings, and the cornices can fall off and kill a person at the drop of a hat." She looked at her friend with frightened eyes. "Anyway, in the year two thousand we'll all be walking around in gas masks because of the smog," the first one said, excited. "Of course, in the year two thousand we'll be dead." Then they started to develop a meticulous strategy for crossing the emptiness of Carlos Pellegrini, along which the city opens, without the wind making them fly away like the rooftops from the Christmas of '50.

A little old man lives next to Amanda's place and asks people to visit him every day because he's afraid of dying in his empty apartment without anyone noticing.

Series E. Maybe the best way to use these notebooks would be to successively transcribe notes from the same day over the course of twenty years, without explicitly providing the context or variations.

Sunday 24
I spend Christmas Eve with my parents at a Chinese restaurant; I'm grateful for their gesture in coming here to be with me, but at midnight I say goodbye and go for a walk around the city, alone, as I have always wanted.

Monday 25
Amanda and I spend the day at home and see Fellini's *Roma* at night.

Tuesday 26
I go out to dinner with Carlos and Oscar Landi at Bachín, and we talk about the Chilean rugby players whose plane crashed in the mountains; they survived for almost a month until one of them finally decided to head out over the peaks and managed to find a local guide, who rescued them. Of course, they ate the flesh of their dead companions, and that

cannibalism has led them to a sort of mysticism that allows them to move past the taboo they transgressed.

I wake up in the middle of the night with a terrible nightmare. In a barren place, a partially devoured human silhouette, the face half-eaten, visible holes and the texture of the face. An effect of the conversation about cannibals and corpses.

Wednesday 27
I spend the day with Amanda, we have lunch at Pippo, go out in the city, end up going through Bajo to Plaza de Mayo, and then to Dorá. Scenes of the past. One night she came up to my room in the attic, in the boarding house in La Plata; we slept together, and in the morning she wanted to take something, a sheet of paper. I gave her a little flat white stone and she still has it and always carries it with her. She found me once on the street, on a diagonal; I showed her a piece of paper with everything I had to do, and she was fascinated by someone trying to organize his life. Another day I found her on her way to take an exam at the College. She was wearing a hairband. "You look like an Egyptian sphinx," I told her, and then I write down the dialogue on a piece of paper. "What is it?" I asked. "Don't you see I take notes of everything?" She stayed at the College waiting for me to leave. I invited her to get a glass of something at Don Julio, the bar around back of the University, and once again I'm fascinated by this woman who gets drunk every day.

During our walk she tells me about her descents into madness, into alcohol, her suicide attempts, her phobias. She speaks about it with some pain, afraid, she tells me, that I will stop loving her. Sitting on a bench in Plaza de Mayo, facing the palm tree that divides the flower beds, Amanda passionately reads my story "Tierna es la noche" and, of course, recognizes the character of Luciana, who is, in a sense, inspired by her. Beautiful, she ties a shawl around her head to make me compliment her and talks about me, "certain of this love." For my part, I am afraid, but of what? Of her insanity (or mine?).

I was in bed with Amanda when the doorbell rang, and I silently turned down the volume of the record player. It was Lola, who slid a beautiful print under the door for me showing Don Quixote overcome by his readings. A lovely note with references to my dream archive, with a sorrowful goodbye for her absence. A reversed reprise of the first day, when Amanda came over and found herself with Lola. A predilection for love triangles.

Thursday
We stay together until noon, then she leaves quickly, fleetingly, to see her friends lost in the past, chased. I finally manage to finish the passport process and go back to pick it up. Then I have a meeting for *Los Libros*. She comes with me. We go out to buy cookies and maté, she talks ironically about us while I call and make a date with Lola for tonight. A strange certainty, at times, that I'm going to be with Amanda for years to come.

Friday 29
Series C. I meet Julia, who had called me yesterday at the magazine. Beautiful, more beautiful than anyone else, and at the same time, as always, intelligent, wary, able to guess what I'm thinking. We have lunch together at Pepito, very nice, in the best style. Promises of love with her as well; she will wait for me, she can come and live with me today. I'm going to leave her the apartment, and when I return we'll see what happens. I meet Lola and everything becomes complicated. She tells me that I'm growing distant, that she feels left out and that I'm going to abandon her when I go on my travels. She had a dream that I had another woman, and in the dream she thought: "But how can he do this to me now, just when he's about to leave." Will I ever find a way to make up my mind and speak clearly? From there I went to see Amanda. I stayed with her all day, sad because she was leaving for Mar del Plata at midnight. At home, around the city, planning the future, she's jealous of Julia. "Couldn't she just die?" We go out and have Gancia vermouth with cheese at the bar on Lafinur, and then we go back to listen to music

and be together. Finally I stop by to see Ricardo Nudelman and bring her with me, proud of this beautiful woman who sparks interest and suspicion in the men who keep coming in for some meeting, celebrating something I never figure out. We leave there in desperation because she's going to miss the train and stop by her house; she's slightly drunk, and the house is in disorder. Her sister is showering, we have to wrap up [*illegible*], and we bring some bottles of Chilean wine, but they fall in the street, and I have to pick up the wine-soaked package. At the station, we sit down on the wood floor of platform 14, and then "the girls" arrive, her girlfriends, running, hurried, at the last minute. I walk over to the train with her and she embraces me, not wanting to get on. She had stumbled earlier, drunk, and hit her knee. Standing on the running board, she looks at me in a way I will never forget. The alarm went off, signaling the departure of the train, and I was already on the phone talking to Lola. I was scheming about what I had to do to stop by her place and sleep with her, considering the time. If today isn't a symptom of madness, wrongdoing, desolation, stupidity, then I never will accept that I'm insane, wrong, stupid, or desolate.

Monologue (30). He cannot stop thinking about a nightmare from the other night, with a woman who was devoured. Her face was eaten away; it seems that, when he isn't isolated and "shut in," terror rises up and actions disorient him and are fractured. He also recalls the Chileans who ate human flesh. Society protects these "gentlemen," he thinks, they're heroes able to practice what is forbidden.

Saturday 30
I spend the night with Lola after having dinner at a table by the window in Munich, the restaurant on Carlos Pellegrini. She too will wait for me "because she loves me." Three months will go by quickly, etc.

Monologue (31). He has started to navigate among three women, seeming to love them all at the same time. He cannot "detach" himself and, therefore, he cannot choose. Things seem to be given, so that no one can alter them. For that reason, he is surprised by his own violence. He scorns A. when she puts her hand on his sex while he is sleeping. B. tells him how she feels because he's growing distant and the trip frightens her, and he falls asleep while she's talking. Finally, with C., the arrival of X when they're in a bar draws a third person into the game and violence breaks out. Because it is unexpected, anything that comes from outside, whether benign or malicious, shakes up the system in which everything could be anticipated. Then his tendency to create catastrophes and tragedies is exacerbated, making conflicts and difficulties worse, creating a void, although the void really did exist before, he now thinks.

Dream. My mother is ironing clothes and there's a cord that goes from wall to wall. Pieces of transparent cloth hang like dirty clothing.

Sunday, December 31
León R. comes to see me in the mid-afternoon like a shadow of the person I may come to be in the future. Desolate and sad, "he doesn't know what to do with his life," feels he has "failed" with his book on Freud that "no one is reading," unable to be in a relationship and maintain it. Fixated as he is on Isabel, who rejects him and refuses him. My own traits appear in him, so we understand each other very well. This promiscuity will only cease if I fall in love, because loving is the hardest thing. For the years I lived with Inés, and then with Julia, I was monogamous, didn't even notice other women, but when I have no anchor, my life is chaos. I can't focus my desire and so am transforming into a desperate scoundrel, indifferent to everything.

Lola comes over and we spend a night at home, looking at the lights of the city from the balcony. We'd bought food and champagne and listened to the Jimi Hendrix records that she brought. On the balcony, we looked at the city, the pieces of paper that fell from a window like yellow snow-flakes. The downstairs neighbors hit a pot, adding to the general noise. The bathroom lamp exploded, the next-door neighbors are partying in the hallway, I poked my head out to watch them. I peed while Lola was in the shower. I felt a temptation to throw champagne on the bald head of a neighbor downstairs. I don't remember anything else. In the morning, she had to tell me what I had experienced, though I didn't want to remember. Traces of conversations. "There is less and less that can help me."

This has been my passage from one year to another, from one place to another, but to what end?

6

Diary 1973

Monday

Series C. When we started, Amanda was studying theater with Agustín Alezzo. I went to Rosario for three days to give some lectures, returned late on Saturday night, and she wasn't there. She came back early in the morning. She'd gotten work performing a show at the Bambú cabaret on Carlos Pellegrini, near Lavalle. I went to see her yesterday. A kind of dirty striptease, dressed as a man. I sit watching her from a special table next to the dance floor. Then she comes over and sits down with me, kisses, smiles. The waiters in the place talk to me with great respect. The owner, a Uruguayan man with the air of a dandy, his hair dyed brown, says to me: "This is a high-class place, only tourists and wealthy people from the country. Good people." On the way out, she hangs on my arm. "Go on, Emilio," she says, "don't be stupid, the two of us can live off what I make." "Thank you," I say, "but I'm not Erdosain." "More like the Melancholy Thug," she shoots back. She wants to act, but there is no work in the theater . . . The artistic vocation . . . Of course, she works as a bartender and goes out with the customers.

Thursday

Last night I thought about Amanda. "She's there now," I thought. She has a dressing room, the Uruguayan man said. "I don't practice," she tells me. "I get dressed and go out there." It's a joke among actors who study Stanislavski's method. They went to see Pedro López Lagar, a Spanish actor who lived in Buenos Aires; he was doing *A View from the Bridge* by Arthur Miller that season. "And how do you prepare yourself to act, Don Pedro?" "Well, I put on my hat and go out there." The same for Amanda. Dressed as a nurse or in a schoolgirl outfit or dressed as a little kid. *I get dressed and go out there.*

She took all of her things, they fit in a single suitcase; she went to live with her sister. "I only write these things," I tell her, "I'm not interested in living through them." "You're missing an experience," she says. "I have experiences to spare." "So long, *precioso*," she said, and she rode the elevator away. Now she talks to me as if I were a customer.

On the wall, she left the photo that shows her with me in the doorway of Radio Provincia, in La Plata, in '64? Very beautiful, skinny, black sweater, long hair, air of Juliette Gréco. We met in *Once varas*, Julio Bogado's cultural audition. I don't look at the notebooks from that time, but I can well remember the night when she came up to my room, without warning, half drunk. "No, don't, don't turn on the light," she said. She reappeared in Peru a few months ago and sent me a letter via José Sazbón, saying to meet her in the movie theater. In time she came to live in Buenos Aires and stayed with me.

I try not to go out at night so that I won't go looking for her.

I work until sunrise on an essay about the novel. A very wise observation by Brecht about Kafka. He is convinced that Kafka would never have found his own form without the passage from *The Brothers Karamazov* when the corpse of Zosima, the holy starets, begins to stink. Everyone is waiting for the manifestation of transcendence. The holy man is not going to decay. Then, after a while, a monk goes and opens the window. The smell of death. No one understands what is happening. The natural thing was the miracle. An excellent observation that points to the history of technique, to a writer's kind of utilitarian reading, and also to a very precise knowledge of Kafka's work; the key in his stories is the inability to understand what is happening, centered around longing for a transcendence that fails to come. Kafka's hero seeks meaning and does not compromise or reconcile.

Tuesday

I wake up at noon, go out, and eat two empanadas with a glass of orange juice and a double espresso at the pizzeria on Santa Fe and Canning, and I read *Crónica*. A Hungarian chess player committed suicide in Mendoza when the police managed to surround him, two days after he had abducted a girl because she looked like his little sister, killed in the war. He was gentle in how he spoke to her and treated her—from what she said—and he wanted to teach her to play chess. In the act of abducting her, he killed one of the young girl's friends, who tried to stop him. He thought about fleeing to Chile, crossing the mountain range on foot. I go out and make a call from the public phone in the dry goods store on the corner opposite. Tomorrow a meeting for *Los Libros* magazine.

Passion prevents you from seeing details. For example, I remembered just now that Amanda didn't take off the little chain with the aquamarine stone, which I gave her when she came here from Lima. She also wore it when she was naked on the stage, the same as when she was with me. Imagination is the art of *linking* the same blue stone worn by two women who are—or seem to be—different. The image transmits the emotion and opens a path into the heart (a pain on the left side). You have to be calm in order to narrate a feeling that has already passed.

Thursday

Detached—detached, cut loose—he looks at reality with the astonishment of an outsider who doesn't know where he is and must learn each gesture, and every word, without taking anything "for granted." An unexpected change in the world—in the universe, in the cosmos—that forces him to be alert—in order to adapt—in order to survive. ("Don't exaggerate, *precioso*," she said.)

Let's also recall that afternoon in La Plata, ten years ago, on the corner of 7 and 50, when I told Dipi Di Paola about a novel describing the life of a man separated from the world . . . *The Wayward*, it would be called. What I don't write, I live.

Tuesday

There was a woman who wrote down her name and phone number in the men's bathrooms in bars. She went in very early in the morning, when she was unlikely to be caught. She received three or four calls per day.

There was a woman who wrote anonymous letters to her husband in which she told him the truth of her life. The amazing thing is that the husband never mentioned to her that he received that confidential information.

There was a woman who spent half of her family's wealth paying, out of her own pocket, to publish an open letter in every newspaper in the country, in which she expressed her surprise at the homages and demonstrations of appreciation and affection that all manner of people had sent her on the occasion of her husband's death; he had been a scientist who came close to winning the Nobel Prize three times. In the letter, the woman said that she finally felt free from the terror she had suffered over the course of almost thirty years of forced cohabitation with a madman, a mythomaniac, and a psychopath. As an example of the husband's true personality, she described how the scientist kept an archive of photographs with every rival or possible rival or future rival scientist, and he poked out their eyes with little platinum needles that he himself made in his laboratory at night, his aim being to paralyze them in their research, to wound them, blind them, or prevent them from overtaking him in his struggle to win the Nobel Prize in Physics.

Monday

Sitting with David for three hours in a bar to combat loneliness (and hunger). He is improved by having no money: indiscriminately—and

398

intensely—his capacity for passion is unleashed. He immediately brings his fixed ideas to the stage; today he went on about the ambiguity of *Los Libros* magazine, about the Cubans' obsession with success, about Cortázar's political opportunism. He uses colorful language, with diminutives (*hermanito*), archaic expressions (*sonaste, Maneco*), unusual applications of words (*you have to put on a passe-partout*); he employs pet words, enigmatic expressions, tending toward idiolect, toward private language. He is much better than his books: he uses a coarse rhetoric when he writes, a simplified syntax; when he speaks face-to-face, whatever he says seems like a confession, always overly sincere and risky—as though he were walking on a tightrope—and protected by a net of subtexts and beliefs, a series of allusions charged with a closed-minded certainty that is never put into question. He refers to the world as though recounting a personal secret (and in that respect, he is very Sartrean): suddenly he is obsessed with the city, because Buenos Aires is no longer the same, it is populated with strangers, with Italians, with austere and gray people. And where do they come from? he wonders, pointing through the window at the people walking along the sidewalk, what do they do? He can't bear the multitude, the others, who seem to him like inert objects, without desire, disconnected from true life. He sold his library once again; he incessantly detaches himself from everything, over and over. He comes home with me so I can lend him a hundred pesos, which I gather meagerly (in coins!), and I give him a first edition of *El idioma de los argentinos*—which he had given me years before—for him to sell. While we perform these transactions, there is no explanation and no justification ("Let's not make a bar scene," he says). We count coins on the table in piles of ten pesos while continuing to talk about politics ("Cámpora's going to fold, he's a dentist with a face like a washing machine"), about literature, he really doesn't like that I'm reading Mailer ("Novels, old man, there's no time!"), about Amanda, whom he met, although he looks at the photo very closely, with the scrutiny of a collector ("She's too skinny for me," he laughs). He is very generous, very funny, very wise, very original, but he talks to himself (as though trying to convince himself).

Economic exchange—among friends—is not distinguished from intellectual exchange: it is the same thing, and if one studies one level, one
understands the other. Brecht with Fritz Lang.

Monday
I tell Junior about Dumézil's great theory on the origins of symbolic
forms. For Dumézil, there really once existed an Indo-European people
that extended itself militarily around the whole world until it disappeared, becoming identified in the network of the defeated, the
only remnants of which are the common roots of all languages and
the symbolic structure of the trinity; it seems fascinating to me as an
historical example of a hypothetical case. Just as fascinating as Bohr's
theory of concentric worlds. No one has ever seen the Indo-European
people, and there is no trace of their existence, no archeological remains,
no documents. All that exists, isolated in different parts of the Earth
from India to the north of Europe, are a few characteristics that allow
the inference of a common circumstance. These pieces of information,
incidentally, are abstract: certain language roots, certain structures
of symbolic construction. These traces allow the reconstruction of a
group of people, situating them in the plateaus of central Asia, imagining that they invented the wheel and created the first chariots of
war and an army so powerful that they came to dominate the entire
world in little more than a century. Like all conquerors, they were
assimilated by the defeated and disappeared in the network of their
victims until no trace of their existence remained. It must be thought
that, before their disappearance, the Indo-Europeans reigned in every
culture that repeats a common morphology in language roots and
a hierarchical vision of the universe that is, according to Dumézil,
always divided into a triangle comprising those who command, those
who pray, and those who labor. That trinity was only a royal political
form, an institution of the State, for that phantom people; for the
rest, it turned into a mental structure. Junior calls that hypothetical
evidence.

Friday
Dinner with Eduardo and Juan Mazzadi, the charm of musicians. Eduardo tells of how Bach, a conductor in a country church, was "forced" to write one mass per day. He was there for four years, and "only" two hundred eighty of them have survived. He had to write one Passion per year, two of which have been lost.

Juan—an unpublished poet and tango pianist—can play five different arrangements of *El Marne* by Arolas. Once the piano was incorporated into the tango—with Roberto Firpo in the twenties—the typical orchestra came to be. He praises Goñi, Troilo's pianist, with the same admiring and compassionate tone that his brother used when talking about Bach (or Steve when talking about Malcolm Lowry).

Melancholy for the past, but no memory. In 1990 I will turn fifty, consumed by nostalgia for this time, which I won't remember any better. The anti-Proust: no involuntary memory. I live in the past but do not remember it.

Monday
A patrol car has its windshield shattered by a rock that fell "accidentally" from a construction site on Reconquista and Sarmiento. The police get out with their guns and look up into the sky, surly, furious, while the workers go on working, their yellow helmets against the noonday sun.

In 1926 Eisenstein began to develop a theory of a conceptual cinema, that is, a cinematographic language able to transmit not only emotions and feelings but also reflections and ways of thinking—through images.

Thursday
A quick trip to Mar del Plata to empty the family house, which we already sold. I use my father's address book to call his friends, his coworkers, his acquaintances. The group comes in, they talk about him, praise him, and leave, taking everything there is: they try on clothing in front of the

mirror, wrap the cups in newspaper, put the freezer on a luggage trolley. They are old, uncomfortable, they measure the soles of their shoes against my father's, they are Peronists, nurses, ex-patients, girls from the cabaret on Avenida Colón, poker players from the Club Vasco, and many gate-crashers taking advantage. May I? says a very well-dressed blonde woman, and she takes the blue vase that my mother bought in Mexico. May I? The consulting room is empty, but in the drawers there are free samples of medicine. The strangers enter and exit, the house is emptying as if in a dream. In the end there is nothing, the little lamps have no shades, the walls now have no pictures; I'm alone, looking through the rooms, and finally I go to the upstairs rooms, which were once mine, and find a fat man ("I'm El Gordo Miguel," he says) smoking in the window over the street. "I was already leaving," he says, "I'm taking the doctor's stethoscope as a memento." Then I notice it hanging around his neck. "Your father," he says, "was a great guy. A great guy," he repeats . . . He goes down the stairs slowly, and I watch him from above as he crosses the street and turns down Belgrano. He wobbles a little when he walks, and on the corner the light catches the shiny metal circle my father would apply to the naked chests of his patients to listen to their breathing. I stay there a while, leaning in the open window and observing, as I always have, the branches of the jacaranda tree planted in the sidewalk before I was born. Then I close the windows, turn off the lights, and leave.

Saturday

A dialogue between two kids traveling in the seat behind me on the bus, describing their first adventures. One laughs, the two play around and entertain each other. "My first time with a man, I was afraid I'd get pregnant."

Sunday

Pola comes from La Plata and we wander around the city, eat dinner at Dorá. She doesn't really know what to do with herself, and I almost always grow tired and separate myself quickly in bed as though trying to pretend she wasn't there.

Monday

I walk through Palermo with Pola and, standing by the lake, try to find the softest words to get rid of her, but she clings, talking with the old language that always makes me laugh: "We have to use up the experience." I watch the water of the lake running among the weeds.

The two of us go to La Plata, where I finish the course on Borges. An argument with Graciela Reyes who's a Peronist and doesn't want to learn anything. A symptom, at any rate, of the conflicts that must be endured. She reduces everything to politics, leaving no room for any specific reflection.

At midnight I leave Pola in the bus station, which looks like a market, and travel back here, trying to make sense of these difficult times.

On Constitución an unexpected meeting with Eduardo M., who emerges from the fog that envelops the plaza. He's a bit drunk, stained with the purple sediment of wine. He tells me about his misfortunes during his trips to Bahía Blanca that leave him scattered. He can't read, can't compose; he experiences music—he tells me—like a journey by train, crossing the plains toward the south. When I tell him I'm living alone, separated from Julia, he shows a glimmer of his old intelligence: "So you think you're moving forward, living like that. Be careful that you don't keep moving forward and end up back in childhood, living with your mom—like me." We argue about the magazine, which he finds esoteric, sophisticated; in the end, we go out into the city again after having a coffee in a tiny and squalid bar. The mist has not let up. He is carrying a newspaper in his right hand and walks furtively, and I think "He only came to Constitución at this hour to pick somebody up."

Tuesday

I write to Andrés: Around here things are going, let's say, well. I cultivate nostalgia the way Robinson grew tobacco; I have nostalgia because, in my case, it's the one thing that lingers even before I've realized things have already gone. Sometimes, at night, I have bad dreams, the kind in which you see the faces of certain people you love as though they were strangers, but a strong cup of coffee helps me forget them and there are no other faces, no sign until the next morning. In the midst of these nocturnal ceremonies I am able to write more peacefully than at other times, as though I've discovered that the best thing you can do in such matters is give yourself time.

Thursday

I meet Manuel Puig at El Foro, and he complains because I never call. He isn't planning to publish this year. He's working on his detective novel. Much warmth and a friendly conversation, so he loosens up, makes jokes, laughs and talks like a girl, and tells me the amusing story of the idiots who punched him in the Cervantes movie theater, "which you shouldn't go to."

At night I have dinner with Viñas in the restaurant on Calle Uruguay, and he tells me about his adventures at the Police Department. He was detained when he went to get his passport. Levels of language and pressure. The office with the ex-employee, visiting his son Gastón, whom everyone is celebrating. The car with the fat policemen, the Police Department where they treat him like "furniture" and, finally, the Federal Chamber where Judge Ure lends him his complicity. Going in circles around the city we talk about the same things we've talked about since we first met: Peronism, success and failure, Urondo and his enemies, film, politics. Later, he tells me that a girl we passed on Corrientes "propositioned" him. She sleeps with writers, and they pay her expenses. Then Pola appears after David leaves, and I look at her like a stranger or, rather, like a stone.

Saturday

Suspended, shut indoors, while the rain pours outside, I am healing from the pain in my throat, the fever, and bury myself in Ford Madox Ford's excellent *The Good Soldier*. I've gone back to 1958, at least to the texts I discovered back then, which have a central importance for me: *Gatsby*, *Heart of Darkness*, Pavese's *The House on the Hill*, a measured, distant, and agile first person. Ford's narrator doesn't entirely understand the things he's narrating.

I reacted violently against Carlos Altamirano yesterday, at *Los Libros*, when he accused me of having excluded Perón from the discourse of the dominant classes "like an opportunist." I was furious. Perón doesn't interest me much, but I would never consider him an enemy; he negotiates with the dominant classes because he's a populist, but he isn't part of the bloc of power. Carlos makes himself out to be a man of principle, but his principles change every season.

Sunday
I work in the bar on Lafinur and Las Heras; Macedonio Fernández once lived upstairs.

Tuesday
He often falls back into the melodrama that he detests: just now, he leaned out of the balcony, saw the street a hundred meters below, and thought about how everything would end if he threw himself off. He thought about his mother, thought about how they would go through his papers, would read these notebooks, would look in his desk drawer and find the color condoms that a man at a kiosk recommended to him insistently: they would know who he really was, and so killing himself wouldn't have accomplished anything. Finally, he thought: if I don't throw myself off, in ten or twenty years I'll be able to see whether the things I've managed to do would have justified throwing myself from the balcony or not.

Wednesday
A walk last night on Avenida de Mayo and lunch at Dorá, in Bajo, with B. He tells me, with a certain perverse happiness and some skepticism, that he has discovered that Juana, his wife, cheated on him "once or twice." He's obsessed, realizing that if she lied to him once, everything might be a lie.

Pola comes looking for me, so good and so foolish that I can't deal with her, and we have dinner at Hermann. She's blonde and beautiful, and she talks to me about Freud, about Lacan, as though they were men who appeared in fashion magazines.

Saturday

In the afternoon Héctor comes over, fascinating me with his romantic desire to live "freely," trying to get excited about a project that is impossible to define. Later, at his apartment, he reads me some texts, puts on a Charlie Parker record, and I give in, tentatively.

At night I'm with Pola, who always has a clear feeling and a certain acuity when she talks about me, clearly seeing what she calls "my radical oppositions." "You're this kind of gentleman or that kind." "That may be," I answer her, "but either way I'm not a gentleman."

Sunday

A country house in Martínez. Otto Vargas talks about his trip to China. I see Costantini, Viñas, Luppi, phantoms mixed in with militant young people; the talk is at a low level but has a good tone. "Political progress," El Gallego asserts, looking like a Russian revolutionary. I end the day alone on a train back to Retiro, watching the city at sunset.

Monday

In the morning I listen, indifferently, to Andrés Rivera's praise for the chapter of my novel about Almada. I doubt I'll ever be able to write, let alone read with standards.

Tuesday

All day in the street, I can't bear to be at home (for the past week). I have lunch with Haroldo Conti, always the same even though it's been close to five months since I've seen him. He's also obsessing because he's about to get separated from his wife and is thinking about "the children," leaving to live with a woman who will doubtless make him suffer. He can't write either.

Friday

I meet Ricardo Nudelman and El Gallego. We travel to Córdoba together. There is a meeting of the *antiacuerdista* revolutionary force in a desolate boxing club where we spend the day, discussions of VC/PCR, not many people, I can't see a good way out.

Sunday

X Series. In Rubén's house all day, eating barbecue, listening to his everyday life, a "worker's" tone (dignified hardship . . .), great warmth. A certain madness lies behind everything. Coldly, I observe the way they disguise themselves from what they are; the least comfortable in his role is Ricardo N. Finally, Roberto C. gets there; he stages his role as Lenin and carries it out with dedication and efficacy. And Andrés, who never really knows where to stop.

Embedded among revolutionary politicians for two days, these are my conclusions: as obsessive as any of us, they support themselves on each other, and there are large gaps—conflicts and doubts—that they see quickly and exploit: "surprising" schisms, friends who abandon the cause. They are heroic in a microscopic dimension, but they have an incalculable enemy facing them.

Tuesday

Great novels are like cities: everyday places where extraordinary events take place. All possible lives overlap and intersect in their streets, and a city is a fabric of stories.

Leopoldo Marechal accomplished something that had been an implicit desire in Argentine narrative ever since Sarmiento: to write the great novel of Buenos Aires. The beats of the neighborhoods and rhythms of the streets, the overlapping worlds and secret characters, and above all the tones and styles of the city's voices, make this novel one of the great literary events in our language. Marechal has followed Joyce's example, conspicuously defining the time and the place of the story.

The city determines the sphere of the events, and the temporal limits of the story are established (the action lasts a day and a half, from when the hero awakens until he dies). Within that frame, it is possible for a vast web of themes and motives to unfold. In that sense, *Adam Buenosayres* is connected to another of the great novels of the century: *Under the Volcano*. Each begins with a protagonist who has already died and reconstructs one day of his life. Very creative heirs to Joyce's *Ulysses*, published almost at the same time, they are twins in more than one sense. They are absolute masterworks of the narrative of the second half of the twentieth century. In a certain sense, they were "outcast" books and had to endure incomprehension. Lowry's letter and Marechal's explanation to Prieto are examples of high literary awareness. They are classical artists, founded on Virgil. The only books that can be placed next to the great projects of the twenties (*Ulysses*, *The Seven Madmen*). Their relationships with Joyce are central. Preoccupation with Dante for example. An extreme awareness of what is being done. The journey through the city. The city as a novel's subject. A coded novel. Autobiography is one of the keys. Adam incarnates a certain metaphysical journey made by the author. Literary atmosphere (Bernini). The mousetrap of vulgar life. Transcendence. The hero's destiny. Adam's metaphysical awakening. Marechal and the tradition of Catholic nationalism. *Sol y Luna* magazine, 1947. Adam is a modern Ulysses who follows in the footsteps of the Homeric hero. Others are also inverted counterparts, as Tesler is to Achilles (not only because of his kimono-shield, but because of his pride). Ruth is Circe, seduction in kitchen garb. Parody and grotesque exaggeration. The walking traveler whose fate is paralysis. A journey of initiation toward the cross. The story of a conversion.

Adam Buenosayres is perhaps the most ambitious novel in Argentine literature. Like all great novelists, Marechal was conscious of that challenge and worked using the material of his life. It would be difficult to find a project in contemporary literature as ambitious and as well realized as that of this novel.

Saturday, May 5, 1973
Once again a dream with the beggar and his son. Now in the stall where they sell food. The son makes theatrical gestures as though he were an actor in Japanese Noh.

Tuesday 8
At night León R. comes over and we lament our mutual misfortunes. Especially him, unable to continue relationships with women and yet not wanting to lose them. Then a fragmented reading of his project about Freud. In the middle of the conversation, we begin to hear some whispers, which quickly turn into moans and sighs and voices intoning the old songs of love, and the bed in the apartment next door creaks with metallic groans. Then León moves closer to the dividing wall and puts his ear up to it, to better hear the neighbors making love. A great Freudian scene.

Saturday
Maybe I'll put together a book of short stories: the woman on her own in the city, the couple with the dead mother, the caretaker who kills a visitor, the forced marriage of Adriana, a soundtrack going against the lived events, the suicide of the father, the adolescent in love with someone else's girlfriend, the redhead.

Rereading Faulkner.

I meet Rodolfo Walsh, who rationalizes his inability to finish a novel "politically" (how should he write in order to have readers?); we talk about Borges, who was attacked for his political ideas, "and whom no one considers for his literature."

May 25
Cámpora took office. We reached the Plaza when people were starting to decentralize. They were marching down Avenida de Mayo in columns, going in the opposite direction as us. Hegemonic presence of the Juventud

Peronista, armed groups jumping to the surface: posters and slogans from the FAR and the Montoneros, the walls of the city suddenly covered with guerrilla graffiti. A direct relationship is noticeable between the JP and these groups. They didn't allow William Rogers to approach the Casa Rosada and forced him to seek refuge in the American embassy; by contrast, they opened the way for Dorticós's car, letting him go without a guard. They obstructed the military parade and forced the marching band from the Naval School of Mechanics to flee, and some from the JP took the musical instruments and started playing in the middle of the plaza; they painted guerrilla writings on the tanks and obstructed the grenadiers from going to say goodbye to Lanusse. Alongside all this was the Peronist circus: people selling stamps with Eva Perón, some in costume, a street music atmosphere created by the bass drums. The popular tradition appears, theatrically "enacted" by the activists.

Then an unforgettable night in front of the Villa Devoto prison, the crowd managed to liberate the political prisoners. Politics determined everything there; fifty thousand demonstrators were there with torches and posters, remembering the people killed under repression, and on the other side the political prisoners spoke from the flag-lined windows of the prison (they used sheets to make their signs). The mobilization forced Cámpora to sign the pardon. A slow march of the crowd toward the door began following the news. There was talk of an attempt to take over the penitentiary to rescue the thirty prisoners who were left. Suppression, gunshots, gas; we scattered, but there were three lying dead in the street.

Friday, June 7
I'm traveling to China for five months; the return is delayed since I'm staying in Europe. Air France flight 090, leaving from Buenos Aires on Monday 25 at 3:30 p.m., arriving in Orly on Tuesday 26 at 12:45 p.m.; I receive a letter from José Sazbón offering me his house in Paris.

"For the members of the Gestapo, it was permitted to kill prisoners but not to rob them; instead, they forced the prisoners to sell their belongings and 'present' the money obtained to a formation of the Gestapo," Bruno Bettelheim.

Last night Pabst's adaptation of *The Threepenny Opera* by Brecht. The film's dialogue and text in German do not diminish the pleasure of a story that is always slightly excessive and frenzied.

I meet Haroldo Conti, who feels free—according to him—after his separation; he wrote a novel in seven months, which—from what he told me—runs the risk of emphasizing his populist tics.

In each of the three works in progress that people have told me about recently (Rivera, Conti, Szichman), García Márquez's influence is visible: magical realism, narcissistic nihilism.

Saturday, June 23
I see Iris, a bit of a crush. She tells me that she consulted a fortune-teller who predicted that a recluse was coming toward her. "That's me," I tell her, "wait for me to go to China and come back." Laughter and kisses. She separated from her persistent husband, got rid of the perverted Argentine professional.

Sunday, June 24
Yesterday I spent the day entombing my old manuscripts in two boxes (the novel about the gang of Argentine criminals in Montevideo, the diaries, the old short stories), which I will send to my cousin Roberto at his house in Mar del Plata.

7

Diary 1974

In Paris I get an old issue of *Les Temps Modernes* (1952) with an essay by Étiemble on Borges that has amusing allusions to China and Maoism. I take it to Guo Moruo, the great writer, whom I visit at the end of my trip.

He receives me at his house in Peking, dressed in an impeccable, dark charcoal Mao suit, his face soft, with deep wrinkles and very pale eyes. He is deaf and uses hearing aids, stumbling when he walks, faltering from age. We greet each other, shake hands and walk over to the armchairs together. "How is your health," I ask him, and he smiles as he tells me his is not very well, he feels some dizziness. Then he begins to talk, and in some places he gets lost searching for the right words. He speaks of China's enemies, who have always come from the north. "Before, we built the wall, and now we dig tunnels," he says, laughing at his own witticisms, his hands floating in the air. "The Chinese character *wen* simultaneously means characteristics, the grain of stone or wood, birds' footprints, tattoos, the designs on turtle shells, but also literature," he says, as though awakening. Several assistants sit surrounding him, offering him the words he can't come up with; they lean close and shout to him, and they write down everything he says along with the things I say. "They tell me you're a writer and a scholar," he says to me. "And you expect to get to know China only as a point of reference, because the real matter is to know your own country better." I nod and smile, "I know a bit about Argentine literature, but I don't know Chinese literature, though your poems have

413

been translated in Buenos Aires." "Oh no," he says, "no good, no good." He goes on talking to me about getting to know Argentina, and he doesn't give the translator enough time when he speaks, not hearing him. Tien shouts back my words to him and he smiles and waves his hands. He shows me a quote that Mao said to the Japanese intellectuals who had visited him: "When you go back to Japan forget everything you have learned here in China." Where it says Japan, he inserts Argentina and laughs.

This ancient man is the most famous Chinese writer after Lu Xun, but the honors and recognition began to cool down after 1966, when the most extreme sectors in the Cultural Revolution cast harsh accusations at him due to his supposed "ideological deviations." The translator anticipates him, saying that Lin Biao was responsible for those actions. Then he tells me that, after several months of ostracism and a rather forced self-criticism, he stopped writing and has dedicated himself only to writing Mao's poems in calligraphy ever since. "A prison sentence," I say. "On the contrary, a gift, calligraphy is an art as valuable as poetry or painting." He has calligraphed the poems by Mao that can be seen in the city, and they are beautiful. "I prefer to be a calligrapher," he says. Straight away someone approaches with a blue book of Mao's poems, beautifully calligraphed by Guo Moruo. "I will write you an inscription," he tells me, "how does that sound?" More mobilizations of assistants, who bring him paint brushes, Chinese ink, and a placard with my name written in Chinese. He writes shakily, apologizes, "I can't control my hand any more, how old are you?" "Thirty," I tell him, and he looks to the side as though surprised a person could be that age. "Oh," he says, "you can still do many things, learn what you want, even Chinese. I'm fifty-three years older than you," and he smiles again as he holds out the book for me. Then I give him the copy of *Les Temps Modernes*. "There's a beautiful essay by Étiemble," I tell him, "it might interest you." He thanks me enthusiastically. "I learned French in Paris in the twenties." Suddenly the movement of his assistants shows me that it's time for me to say goodbye. I say a few words, he stretches out his hands to me with weak friendliness, and I rest a hand on his shoulder. "I wish you a hundred years of life," he says, and walks a few steps with me toward the exit amid a circle of assistants, who bump into each other when I try to guess who I should pay my respects to first. A feeling that I have encountered a poet waiting for death when he quotes Mao Zedong with a certain ironic resignation.

March
Friday 15
I amuse myself by thinking about some "destiny" that I have altered for no apparent reason, or rather one sustained on old fantasies, but where do they come from? I make my living on literature, have all the cards on my side, and yet there is a dark certainty that has led me to who I am now. Just as the future dissolves, the feeling of uncertainty grows worse. It is no accident that I take refuge in nostalgia, choosing thoughtlessly at every crossroads, certain that I will achieve what I have sought. These days, the decisions seem to come from outside me. For example, I could have dedicated myself to history, pursued a university career, gone that way. Now it seems that everything is gambled on one hand. I can envision my life only six months into the future, I foresee nothing beyond that.

Outside, the city is gray, heavy, as after the rain. I am reading Carson McCullers once again, always rediscovering that reflexive writing interrupts the story and arranges the exaggerated atmosphere into a "natural" and spontaneous plot.

I went back to work on "Mousy Benítez" all day; it's already written, and I am only trying to clean up the style, adjust the plotline to make it better. Some doubts with respect to the ending, which seems to come too quickly. I am careful, anyway, not to explain it too much.

Last night, in a bar on Corrientes, a discussion of the film script with B. and Daniel S. From my first reading of the book, I think the structure is too loose, reiterative, lacking a dramatic crescendo. I propose some modifications, narrating the preparations for the attack on the journalist, making Murena's defeat worse so that in the end, when he must go into exile, his wife abandons him. This week I have to write six scenes about that odd separation.

Saturday 16
A strange peace, all day on Alberto's boat, navigating the tranquil waters of the Delta, lying in the sun, swimming. A needed parenthesis or pause.

Sunday 17
I have been working on "Benítez" since noon, having trouble welding the passages together, sometimes it seems overwritten to me.

Monday 18
Julia comes to see me, startling me once again, and absurdly I repress my desire to tell her I love her, fearing that she will want to start things over again.

I am preparing the syllabus for the course with the psychoanalysts. Philosophy, but nothing by Freud; if anything, I will present some of his texts as "misread": seeking the form and methods by which he presents the cases and, above all, seeing how he narrates dreams. In philosophy, we'll discuss versions of analysis (B. Russell, L. Wittgenstein): what happens if one reads psychoanalysis as a linguistic game?

I leave notes, search for what can't be found because the meeting is canceled. The dark hallway. The call that comes right afterward. And yet, as always, I cannot leave.

Tuesday 19
In the morning Andrés comes over. I am starting to distance myself from him. I read him "Mousy Benítez," which works well read aloud.

Friday 22
I have made decisions. I have set aside the reality I have been denying, first of all because it associates me with debts, with squalor. From this

side, my difficulties seem to strengthen my work. All of my expectations are concentrated.

A desire to leave the novel and write short stories. Then work on the book based on these diaries. Couldn't I find a better way there? The point would, in a sense, be to write a portrait of the artist using the techniques of dream interpretation. I'd have to start work on that book now while writing some stories to include in the reprint of *La invasión*.

Short stories: The Father's Suicide, The Man Who Met Roberto Arlt, The Accident, Sentimental Education, in addition to Mousy Benítez, The Swimmer, El Joyero, and Desagravio.

Start to put together material, maybe determine the essence before I read the notebooks. I can't worry about the coherence of anecdotes before I have some central concept that I can develop. Working, then, with the first seeds. It would be best to finish some stories in the next two months so I can begin writing the book based on my diary in June. I don't think I can start until April. Meanwhile, I'll try to organize my situation a bit and get the course ready so that I can ensure the money I need.

Separations, again and again. Always final, never entirely wanted. The worst part is the emptiness. A dead man who can do nothing but think.

Saturday 23
A slow, interminable month. I have, at least, realized that there is nothing worse for me than this paralysis.

Wednesday 27
Series C. Except for some doubts that unexpectedly assault me, there is hope of finding a note or being called; I could say that I've managed to temper my emotional misadventures, clinging to the idea that with Iris I can find the peace I've lost. At the same time, tension mounts because

I know the past cannot be changed; in love, the person you play games with never matters. In the meantime, I hope to write the book based on these diaries, as though I could change the present by going backward and reading what I have lived through.

Yesterday I took "Mousy Benítez" to *La Opinión*. A good metaphor for the position I've accepted, the sophistry of sending in a story I wrote in 1968.

A slight malaise, certain ideas that draw me into reconstructing reality. I'm with Iris, but I'm thinking about Julia; and when I'm with Julia, I think about Iris.

Thursday 28
Last night, in a bar on Santa Fe and before that in El Toboso, Julia carries out her rituals. I have to publish a novel, she says, so I buy a watch, since she lost hers.

Monday, April 1
I'm with Iris, and I feel good when I'm with her, but then slight storms begin. I should learn my lesson. And yet I play Julia's card and hope for a call from Amanda.

The illusion of unconditional women. That certainty is lost, and only emptiness remains.

Tuesday 2
León comes over, I keep seeing him as a future mirror of myself. Always full of doubts, always seeking what he does not have.

I meet Julia and chaos ensues. She leaves, like so many times before, compulsive, furious. I get up and call Amanda, who isn't at home. Then I meet Iris and we spend a beautiful night together, dedication, fantasies and long memories.

Sunday, April 7
I go to the hospital to see Melina, who is slowly getting better but still throwing up. The room at the end, her bed in a corner, a baby, the IV in her arm, her exhausted expression.

Sunday 14
I have spent several days with Iris, everything is going well. I'm falling for this tranquil, dazzling woman.

Wednesday 17
At *Crisis* magazine with Galeano and Aníbal Ford, many different projects.

Good economic prospects. Fifty thousand pesos for the selection of letters by Pavese. A project to write an introduction for Brecht.

Some discontinuity in my relationship with Iris. Really, I'm alone most of the time. There is no way to make everyday life work by being together. Some restlessness makes me get up with a start. Slightly bothered this morning, restless without precise reasons.

Friday 19
I work on the course for the psychoanalysts and on an article project for the magazine. A relatively easy income, I could potentially make two hundred thousand pesos this month.

Saturday, April 20
I go out to eat a sandwich in the Botanical Garden, among the old and dying.

Monday 22
Nostalgia for that fiction I create for myself with certain women, the myth of unconditionality, which is illusory but helps me to forget the cracks. To choose to be alone is to start to see reality without a veil.

Tuesday 23
Meeting for the magazine, we are organizing the next volume.

News from Manuel Puig, who has installed himself in Mexico and proposes a variety of options for me to come spend some time there. According to Puig, Mexico is "his first love."

Thursday 25
My course with the psychoanalysts is off to a good start. We read a few pages of Wittgenstein. One of them says to me: "With this class, I'll be able to work for five years."

Tuesday, April 30
I make progress on the article for the magazine. I spend several days with Iris. Everything is going well.

Wednesday, May 1
While working on the essay, I listen to Perón's speech: frontal attack of the Peronist left ("idiots," "immature"), defense of the union movement. The left is leaving its position. It is unclear why the Montoneros call themselves Peronists and then want to question Perón's leadership.

Friday 3
Today is Iris's birthday, we go out to eat and then go to the Unión bar and listen to tangos sung by Edmundo Rivero.

Sunday 26
I'm writing a piece on Hemingway. León appears at the end of the day and stays with me until three in the morning, chatting and recalling the past.

Wednesday 29
I say to Andrés: "Don't worry about my silence, it goes back a long way. I spend weeks mentally composing paragraphs, and then I forget them just as slowly."

An action in Plaza Flores. Anniversary of the Cordobazo. Few people. Police provocation, gunshots, gas bombs, scattering. Another regrouping. I see many friends.

Saturday, June 1
I see sinister shadows, leeching on my heart. Drifting, delirium, despotic dissidence. Dangerous alliterations, he said. Once more he thinks about killing himself, jumping over the balcony railing.

Monday 3
At the publishing office I find B., who has spent the weekend imprisoned, accused of psychological violence by his ex-wife. She is surely right. The women are fighting back against masculine disrespect. Anyway, I offer him advice. You have to live alone, my brother," I say, as though in a tango song.

Tuesday, June 4
I make good progress with the essay on Borges. I received the money for the course, seventy-five thousand pesos.

Friday 7
At the theater with Iris, a play by Lorenzo Quinteros at the Payró.

Wednesday 12
I go to Plaza de Mayo. Perón convenes an event to combat the crisis and the pressure from the military. Few people there.

Thursday 13
Last night, before I fall asleep, some ideas like daydreams, maybe write the story of Pavese's history. A dialogue between the narrator and a stranger on a train throughout the plot.

Friday 14
I go to Sudamericana publishing, the prologue for *Mad Toy* will not come out this year. I take a walk through San Telmo and, in a bar,

plan a book of essays: *Trabajo Crítico*, including Manuel Puig, Borges, Bioy: the detective stories, Onetti: "A Dream Come True"; Roa Bastos: the telling of history; Mansilla-Arlt: chronicles. Working with criticism as narrative. Making arguments using examples and cases (the false case).

Sunday 16
I fell asleep at seven in the morning after having breakfast and reading the papers. I enjoy the city at that time of day, shifting between people who have spent the night awake and people who rise early, opposing figures; the ones who haven't slept seem more awake.

I'm in a sort of strange inert state, maybe I'm waiting for someone I don't know to appear or for something to change. Amanda is being erased, fading away, persisting in a weak nostalgia with no certain object.

I get up at three thirty in the morning and go down to eat a sandwich (oh, these repetitions).

Saturday 22
I go to Galerna, Issue 35 of *Los Libros* still has not come out, several times delayed. I eat lunch alone at Pippo, predicting meetings that do not occur.

"I work toward my own ruin," I tell Iris. "Get out, don't tease," she says, "that pathos doesn't work anymore." That woman's irony instantly clears my mind.

Wednesday 26
I sleep in until noon, my essay on Borges is almost ready. A persistent nightmare in the night, there was a man who was the president and his eyes, respectively, were the black sun and the alchemists. Then some women on a round wooden stage, they danced and played castanets, instantly hallucinating that they were already dead.

A book of only short story analysis. The impossibility of writing: "Failed Writer" and "Pierre Menard." The lost scene: "A Dream Come True" and "Instructions for John Howell."

Sunday 30
Money in Arlt. Money and desire. Money as means of circulation: displacement, metonymy. Money as measure of value, metaphor, condensation. Money as universal equivalent, "fictitious," conventional, a generalized convention, imaginary. Treasure. Credit. Debt: temporality, promise, belief, postponement. Gold: standard of value (absent), its "shine," aesthetic quality. Exchanges, transactions. Robbery, ability, gift. Money, counterfeit currency. Infinite power of money, can be transformed into any living or dead object. Chance quality of exchanges, uncertain destiny. Savings, luxury, inheritance. "Pathological" effect of money: covetousness, avarice, fetishism. Frenzy—unruled and restrained—for accumulation.

Subjects for the course. Money in "Rat Man." Money in the facility, economy among patients in an asylum: inflation. A cigarette is worth one peso in the morning and two hundred pesos at night. Delirium and fortune. Money in the psychoanalytical contract. Money in Freud's life.

Series E. Stylistic analysis of these notebooks. The essence of the method, the key to what is written here: their function is to relieve life of its absurd and incoherent appearance, converting it into a sort of "comprehensible" event. Imaginary coherence, with dates: a diary is a diary because it follows a chronological, temporal, formal logic (and only that logic). One day and then another day and then another. Thus, the possible importance of my book based on the diary.

I meet Miguel Briante, cordial conversations, measuring ourselves against each other like two fighting cocks. We go from bar to bar, getting more and more drunk, always stating the same truth in the same way, first in a whisper, then in a low voice, and finally in a shout. In him

423

there is the myth of natural talent. "There's no need to say that," I tell him, "it's taken for granted." "Talent," he tells me, "is always shocking." I tell him I agree, but you have to be careful with bumper cars. In his desperation, he incarnates the myth of the creator. That specter, asking him for vengeance, is the ghost of Onetti. He thinks that at age thirty Onetti was just like him, but by then he had already—or nearly—written *A Brief Life*.

Monday, July 1

Let's begin with the death of Perón. On Monday, after alternate versions, stories, improvements. A meeting at home in the morning with Rubén and Boccardo, delusions with Sadovsky and other gentlemen who have discovered Lenin (what? Lenin?) because of his "prestigious names." The melancholy as Perón lay dying, at least while the story of his death emerged, which I remained ignorant of until after four in the afternoon, when I left home and started to grow worried about the lines in front of the shops (I thought: "I have oil," I thought: "The lines are coming, just like in Chile") and about the Galerna library being closed. In the bar I find out about the death of King Lear: general astonishment at my ignorance of the news that had moved everyone in the world. "Where were you?" etc. Even worse, I find out from Saúl Sosnowsky, a depoliticized escapee who lives in the United States, whom I meet to give him a chapter of my essay on Arlt for his magazine *Hispamérica*. The city is quiet, people piled up at Congreso, at nightfall, waiting for the line to begin so they can see the dead man.

I visit David, furious about the telegram from the PCR with condolences for Isabelita.

Tuesday 2

I get up at two in the afternoon. An unexpected appearance from Amanda, who comes with Anita Larronde (Luppi's wife), bringing me a novel by Pavese that, according to her, I had lent her. Trivial conversation, no great tension, a pleasant ending: I give her a copy of *Los Libros* magazine. Ana says: "There's an excellent article in here." She looks for it, it's mine, and she is amazed. "I'm going to tell Federico I've been around important people." That's what we call displacement, saying one thing in place of another.

I move through the rainy city, the endless funeral lines, and no one seems to want the goodbyes to end, no one wants to go home; I remember wakes in my childhood that lasted all night and continued on after noon, but now they are expanded, crowded, with serious gestures that are repeated on every street. Some have waited for thirty hours to see the dead man, the venerated man, one last time.

Wednesday 3
I walk through the empty city, street openings blocked off, people wandering with a sorrowful air, and I end up on Carlos Pellegrini, where (without seeing it) I feel the effects of the funeral procession that crosses Avenida de Mayo carrying the corpse. Men cry, I see a policeman with his face damp from weeping, the soldiers in procession cry as well. Sorrow weighs down upon the city like a shadow. The Montoneros sing out their slogans. I lose myself in the multitude and make it to Congreso. On the way back I pass down endless streets, skirting along a persistent row of men and women lined up to see the corpse. The long procession continues along Carlos Pellegrini until Retiro. The people's pain.

I return home and observe the city in darkness from high above. The lines go on in spite of the rain.

León R. comes over and makes history personal, saying: "What has this man done to us." It isn't a question, it's a complaint, as though he were referring to the ghost of Hamlet's father. León's personal view refers everything to himself and his own feelings. That is his philosophical viewpoint. What does the world mean for me? More deep-seated and extreme than Descartes: the subject is the truth of reality.

Iris talks about the relationships between life and writing—between living and writing—with the same words I have used for years: "Leave everything behind. Live to write."

Thursday

Perón's death has erased all meaning, the despotic signifier has vanished; the mourning is endless and stories proliferate. I register some of them as I walk through the streets: "A regiment from La Tablada rose up" (they say on the first day). Or rather: Perón is dead, the officers are making their comeback. Cámpora appears to be the only political figure from Peronism who has some backing and support. The right sees him as an enemy and wants him to disappear. And so, news has been circulating all day about an attempt on Cámpora's life. Balbín is the only one who can unify the dominant classes: he is the lower-ranked, imaginary substitute for Perón. In front of the coffin in the incandescent chapel, the empty speeches went on until the Chinese man with round eyeglasses appeared, standing beside the dead man, and said, inspired with a high Latin rhetoric: "Today, an old adversary comes to say goodbye to a friend." Everyone cried except for him; proud and serene, he spoke for the first time as an equal to the Man (as my father and all of the Peronists called him during the Resistance years) who had defeated him and imprisoned him and humiliated him. I remembered the unmatched tone of Quevedo's prose after the murder of Julius Caesar: "Marcus Brutus was a severe man, a man who reproached other's vices with his own virtue, not with words. He had an eloquent silence, his intellect keen." Epic emotion lies in a man's praise for the rival who has defeated him, or whom he has conquered. It takes the form of a challenge, transforming anger into admiration. The heartfelt requiem uttered by the defeated, now free of hate. All of the politicians and the whole of the public pointed to Balbín as the dead man's heir.

Friday 5

I am reading Marthe Robert's book on the Freudian family romance as a fundamental root in the history of the origins of modern storytelling.

426

She studies Robinson Crusoe as the figure who negates his father and invents a lineage and a territory of his own.

Julia calls me on the phone, I meet her at Tolón and immediately my peace is gone. She has lost her handbag with her glasses in it—now she can't see (does she know who I am?)—and her documents. She is broke, alone, and lost, and she weighs me down with everything. (She also fantasizes about getting together with David, who will be alone on Wednesday once Beba goes to Europe after a Chilean man.) Of course I have nothing to say to her, and I tell her as much and give her a thousand pesos to get back home . . . Oh, those lost loves. It's like a waning light. The woman we once loved is a stranger, speaking to us and chiding us as though she knew us. She seems insane, talking nonsense. That is how I see her now; love makes people better, and when it ends, oh, it is too late for tears.

Saturday, July 6
On the bus, a chain of associations, the criminal always tells his tale as though it belonged to someone else. He can kill, but he cannot say, "I have killed." It works the same way as dreaming, where the intensity of the experience cannot be transmitted with words: in order to say it, the killer has to kill again. A grammatical reasoning behind the serial killer: he can only speak through the bodies of others. And who can read his message carved into the corpses, as words written in sand? He cannot say it and so repeats the act.

I go to dinner with Iris at América. León calls after I come back, a melancholy encounter. He speaks from another planet: he analyzes Perón's death solely through his perspective, as though Argentine history were part of his life. It is the left's problem with Perón. He has stayed with the working class as though he had abducted them. That's the issue with León and David. Peronism is seen as a scheme, a tyrannical means of using the subordinate classes through deceit and lies. The personalization of politics viewed as a psychological trap. What has this man done to me, he who governed the country for years and then died without having been condemned? Everything is experienced in first person. Politics as a private drama. That is the merit of impassioned thought and also its self-referential closure.

Sunday 7

A peaceful and happy day. I watch the World Cup finals on television: Germany–Netherlands. Soccer is like life, as my father would say: the better one never wins. Iris and I walk around the city, marked by the absence of the Man. Iris laughs, "he was always controlled by women. First Eva and then Isabelita. The best thing," she adds, "is that he always got married to fallen women." *Cuarteleras*, barracks girls, as military jargon calls the female soldiers who accompany men to war.

Andrés comes over: his oldest son is dying of cancer. The whole succession of catastrophes, no work, his ex-wife living with Juan Gelman, his ex-best friend—he needs to move. Weighed down, at his limit, he raves a bit and I follow, raving along with him. "Is it possible to kill and not be caught?" We speak calmly, analyzing several alternatives.

Tuesday 9

One could say I spent the whole day sleeping. I got up at ten, and Carlos came to visit me. I went to lunch at the tavern on Calle Serrano. I went back to sleep until three in the afternoon. Now I imagine I will go out into the street like a sleepwalker, looking for a woman.

Friday 12

I receive a beautiful letter from Tristana. She announces a delivery of rock for the man with the golden arm. Once more the fantasies are reborn in a corner, what can I say to a woman (married, with two children) in a letter. A Stendhalian theme.

I spend the day at Iris's house, very good. We go out for dinner in the rain, under the pale lights.

Sunday 14

I listen to Mozart, make myself some tea and prepare to write "The Two Lineages" of Borges. I act as copyist, going over and over the initial pages of the essay. Three pages that barely suggest the tone. An essay depends on the conviction transmitted by the prose.

Tuesday 23

What can be said of a man like me? A simple letter from Tristana was enough to cause the dull anxiety that follows me. Uncertainty brought by the flight of birds; I see symbols of fate in the slightest traces of wind among the trees. Reading those signs takes up all of my time and strength. Her letter, on the other hand, reopened a wound in another part of my body. Everything can form part of the novel that I'm writing. The novel and my life, always the same schism. It would be better to say: "the novel of a life."

A feeling that I'm bound to the barrenness of the times. I see David, who calls me to meet in La Moncloa. A meeting for *Los Libros*. We have Issue 36 ready. An excellent article on Althusser by Altamirano. Several articles about urbanism. What dangers disquiet me? More than danger it is a discontentment, facing the inadequacy of my life.

The mistake seems to lie in the delusion of expecting validation in the present. Don't conjugate verbs in past tenses. Forget about the future. This present vision of the future never seems to have been given except perhaps before, in another time. I tell myself once more: "Do not bind yourself to the good times passed, but to the bad times yet to come."

The essay could be called "Ideology and Fiction in Borges." Meaning proliferates, the point is to reconstruct the fiction from the origin. The ways writers imagine the material conditions that make their work possible. Sometimes I can't stand combinatorial analysis, I need some distance, so I go out to smoke a cigarette.

Wednesday

I meet her, anyway, and as always there was no party. Even more lost than I am, nostalgic and alone, she says: "She really does want to see you and meet you because, according to her friends, you're the man of her life, and she wants to be at your wedding ceremony." Amanda, like me, talks about herself in the third person when she is emotional.

Saturday 27

A peaceful, beautiful day. Iris wakes me up at noon, and I spend the afternoon at home with her. At night we see Brecht's *The Days of the Commune* at the Payró.

Publications:
August: "Roberto Arlt and the Fiction of Money" (*Hispamérica*).
October: "Ideology and Fiction in Borges" (*Los Libros*).
Deliver these works to Nicolás Rosa, José Sazbón, David, León, Noé.

Today I woke up at noon, went down to have lunch at the grill on Serrano, and then walked through the Botanical Garden, sitting in the sun beside the plants, feeling some happiness or, rather, the vision of a life come true . . .

Friday 2

An unexpected appearance of the beautiful Kitty (Amanda's friend), a mysterious request about some materials I might receive. Amanda talks about me to her friends, and they want to meet me and, often, sleep with me. She will call me on Monday.

Sunday 4

Last night I waited for the papers to come out and read them at dawn after I had gone to the shop on Canning to eat some pizza among the drunks and other lonely people. Then I went up to bed and had a dream. Lucio Mansilla appeared, speaking—brilliantly, convincingly—so that I would recognize my mother, who was also there, seduced. That's all I remember of the dream. I think: I should write—sometime—a book that would at the same time be the story of Mansilla and a history of literary language. Mansilla, the fluidity of a kind of writing that reveals the state of a language still safe from the changes that I expect. The angelic Señora Aurora is coming to clean the apartment soon, so I'll go down to walk for a little while in the hopes of forgetting my worries.

Tuesday 6
Maybe once I've written the book based on these diaries, I'll be able to write a novel.

Yesterday I saw Iris as she approached me, beautiful, on the corner of Anchorena and Corrientes, like a cat in her pale overcoat.

Friday 9
I go over the transcript of the talk I gave in Philosophy and Letters about my trip to China. The key is to ask what kind of vision (or truth) the solitary man has of the world. That was my position: amid the unsuspecting multitudes, mixed in with the Chinese masses that all seemed to be moving in the same direction, I had paused in the middle of the road to change a car tire (like in the poem by Brecht). What does the solitary man see in the middle of the street? He sees nothing, or only sees what is written on the maps. In any case, my version has the virtue of being a personal viewpoint. Everything is social; in China there is always talk of social class, and when someone is individualized, it is because that subject is an enemy. Subjectivity is seen as deviation. The only valuable thinking is the kind that expresses the sense of the multitude, the feeling of the social classes, and yet the amusing thing is that it is difficult to guess the difference in China: everyone dresses in the same style, they laugh at the same time, shout out the same slogans, and express the same sentiments. Therefore, the difference between classes is not perceived (or does not exist), but political thought is nevertheless defined by its ability to identify class content in the midst of sameness.

I might easily be able to put together an article with the last part of my lecture on culture in China, to publish in *Los Libros*. Here, there is nothing other than the avant-garde, everything that is not moving ahead is retrograde and reactionary. The illusion of an avant-garde composed of millions of people (who faithfully follow the thought of Mao Zedong).

An example. My visit to a secondary school. The director, a man with an intellectual air, frameless glasses, his hair gray, no more than forty years of age, introspective, draws on a paper. The geography professor uses Mao's poem about the Yellow River. While one student recites it from memory, another points out the endless line of the river on a map. The English professor waits for us at the front of the classroom, looking at the clock, nervous, insecure, overactive. The lesson is centered on the Vietnam war: "The Indo-Chinese region is composed of Laos, Cambodia, and Vietnam," she explains in English, indicating the sentence written on the board. "The American imperialists are soulless killers." In the Chinese language class, an anonymous poem from the seventeenth century: the old coal merchant with a sooty face and white hair, freezing to death in his cabin in the heartless winter. The professor shows the contradiction between the old man's desire for respite from the cold and his need for cold weather so that he can continue to sell coal. In China everything is direct and allegorical.

Saturday 9
Fiction (disguise) acts with the play of bodies and above all creates displacements and substitutions. "One man in place of another" is the secret logic of the detective story. Thus is a metaphorical system of substitution defined, and also the workings of psychotic equivalency. Money is the sole measure of value.

Tired, I went down to the street to call Iris from the public telephone in the shop: I could barely hear her, she's sick, there with her son, and I want her. I walked again along the sidewalks that border the Botanical

Garden and then returned home. And here I am, looking at the city through the window and writing this in a notebook.

Sunday, August 11
I got up at noon, read the papers, made lunch for myself and sat down to work. It is now seven in the evening and I will leave everything as it is to go over to Iris's place and get by somehow.

Wednesday 14
Series C. Once again the feeling that I am living like a dead man, passionless. Suddenly, amid the silence and delirium, I start to cry. Why does the crying man cry? Perhaps the crisis alludes to Amanda's presence in recent dreams. As a result, sympathy mixed with a sense of ridiculousness (it is sad to cry alone). I go to the publishing office and find a message from Kitty (who has left it the way someone would leave a photograph). I come home without energy and lie down to sleep. Julia wakes me up; she has come to blame me because, she says, I didn't lend her twenty thousand pesos. It's her right, she says, because she lived with me for six years. And that's what worried me: how I could have lived with a woman like her for six years. Once more the disturbing equivalencies: six years in exchange for twenty thousand pesos. "That's what they're worth," perhaps.

A useless pretense, two minutes after I started reading I am already "somewhere else." Where? A curious state of anxiety and fear. I give up on preparing tonight's talk, maybe I won't go, won't have to face the people. Apart from that, how can I fill the void of the three hours left until 10? The best thing would be to lie down, let myself go. Books surround me, drown me. I am thirty-three, the age of Christ. I am alone in the city. I will be alone tonight and all of my life.

Then, the way someone might change clothes, I left home, walked to the Institute in Plaza Italia and spoke for two hours about the metaphorical economy that governs literature. A theory about those disturbing equivalencies (bodies for money, words for experiences).

I sustain myself on fantasies, a letter from Tristana, a secret rendezvous with Kitty.

Thursday, August 15
Luna comes to see me in the morning; he got some work at *El Cronista* and his dubious morals are strengthened. A reactionary, he practices a sort of tautological speculation. He describes what he sees with cynicism but imagines that his conformist vision derives from his political radicalism (he holds himself up in an imaginary elite, self-defined aristocracy). The people in the ERP are fascists, the left can't even put together five lunatics, the SMATA factory can only put together two thousand men for an action. This perception is a result of his fear of being questioned. Connected to that is his fawning to the bosses of the newspaper, his disdain for politics in general. If he goes on like this, in a few months he'll have turned into a systematic enemy of the left.

Friday 16
In class, they suggest that I should publish my lectures. Now isn't the right time, I tell them, I prefer to wait so that what I am attempting to do now, rather blindly, can be seen with more clarity in the future. I have an insight into how to participate and be heard in a situation as confusing as this one. That's what I would like to convey.

I should say: make recordings of the classes, slightly corrected, to be read as the starting point for a discussion.

I have many plans for short stories and essays; if I manage to write them, I'll then be able to dedicate myself to the book based on the diary. The short stories or nouvelles I have are fairly far along: a nonfiction novel based on real events but with a freely-constructed plot, which, in fact, is a concealed fiction. The story of Pavese, which develops in Italy during the days when the protagonist is living in Turin with the university fellowship, having left Buenos Aires in order to forget about a woman (but he finds her in Europe). The story of the suicide of a father as told by his son, traveling in the night after receiving the news.

Saturday 17
Series E. I return laboriously to the metaphysical reflections of my diaries from 1960 and 1961, an attempt to narrate my disturbed perception. A feeling that I lived through those months in a murky stupor, always with the sensation of being too slow and never reaching the speed necessary to live.

Tuesday 20
I am writing the essay on Borges. The notion of the fiction of origins is one I also used in my analysis of *Mad Toy* by Arlt, and I also have a very advanced hypothesis about the way in which Sarmiento turns into a writer (and how long that state lasts).

Connected to that, some "incidents": phone calls from Dipi Di Paola today, the telephone interview for *Panorama* magazine. My answers are too dry, and I imagine the effect they will produce in a piece that also includes interviews with Bioy Casares, Viñas, and Soriano, as though I were one of them, but I am not. I belong to another breed.

At *Los Libros*, I handle myself clumsily in the meeting with Beatriz and Carlos. I make jokes, tell stories about my nights in the casino, but I don't participate in the discussion of the magazine. Requests for lectures in Santa Fe, and also in Tucumán, which I turn down with unfounded pretexts.

Wednesday 21
I spend one hundred seventy-five thousand pesos per month, plus fifty thousand for rent and ten thousand for the woman who comes to clean. Anyway, as long as I continue with the course at CICSO (ten thousand per month), the work at the publishing house, and the notes for Luna, I can keep myself afloat.

I see Catalina, who comes from the remote past; she is a Spanish friend of Elena, the girl I went around with in high school in Adrogué. She stops by the bookshop to see me: she has aged (like me) and has a son. That was all.

Fiction. Writing a story, "Roberto Arlt's Murderer," another one called "Love Stolen" with the story of a lover who steals a set of silver utensils from his woman (she sees him and says nothing), "Suicide of a Father." Including them in a volume along with "Mousy Benítez."

Saturday 24

A beautiful day, warm and soft. I walk around the zoo, pausing a while at the lion cage. I go out and spend a couple hours in the Botanical Garden, not thinking about anything, trying to become a plant myself. I had ventured into the street after two days spent shut in. The metaphor of the outsider (the stranger), who does not belong to this place.

Sunday 25

Amanda comes, surely for the last time. She took her sketching board, and I accompanied her to the taxi. All with the greatest distance, neither of us inquiring into the other's current life. ("How are you?" "Fine," I said. "And you?" I asked. "Fine, more or less," she said.) The rest was an exchange of news. "I'm working on Borges," I told her, "because they're going to pay me a million pesos for the essay." She is making good money in an architecture studio, and she is successful in her theater class. Why do I record this? Because I want to retain the final image of her. Beautiful and, perhaps because of that, a bit out of focus. Cold; as always, she wants to show herself to be rational. A strange history coming to an end at the wrong time, leaving me with the anxiety of loss.

It isn't her, ultimately, who brings up this nostalgia, but it is her, yes, who opens my old wound from ten years ago, or rather, it's as though she embodies the other life I could have lived. A life, shall we say, simpler, without literature, working to build something (what?), a family, for example, or something of that kind. It is no accident that she came up from my past, from ten years ago when it was still possible for me to become someone else, and that now she is fading away because I have understood (or tried to understand) that not everything is possible for me. She is associated with a certain ease, and with everyday life. Someone else's life, it will belong to someone else, as it did before . . .

Monday 26

Unexpected happiness; or; rather, only the unexpected makes happiness possible for me, but yesterday and today were days with no order, with no routine, very improvised. I left Iris's house in the morning intending not to go to the publishing office, and I went walking down Callao without a fixed direction. Suddenly I was in Martín Fierro bookshop, restoring my friendship with Luis Gusmán after the disagreement with Osvaldo L. about my prologue to *El frasquito*; the megalomaniac idiot wanted me to quote him in the prologue and tried to engineer it with Germán and Luis. Everything worked out easily, I just told him: "I'll take the prologue and throw it in the trash. Tell Osvaldo that if he feels insecure, he can find someone else to quote him in whatever he writes." In the end I went to the publishing office and met with Néstor García Canclini who, according to him, put my name forward for a class at the University of La Pampa. Today I had lunch with Lafforgue in a bar, and he gave me the bibliography of Borges's work that he made for Beco and me. I finished preparing tonight's class on Wittgenstein and private language.

And so, he said, happiness appears and persists unexpectedly, the same as in childhood. Fulfillment depended on the feeling of discovering and becoming familiar with the new. There was a dangerous and off-limits street, my mother said, which led up the slope, and, as you climbed up, under the sun, you could see an unknown reality from afar. Now, instead, there is a freedom that comes like a breeze in the night.

Sunday, September 1

A peaceful day, it is raining outside, Iris and I went out last night and went around the clubs in Bajo until sunrise.

Plan. A book of short stories

1. Mousy Benítez.
2. This Business of Living (Pavese, set in Italy). The narrator carries a diary in which he writes down his impressions of Pavese's diary.
3. The Suicide. On the bus, returning home, after having stayed with his father who attempted suicide.
4. Roberto Arlt. A man who met Arlt is looking after some manuscripts. He knows a secret. Does he steal a text from him and publish it in his own name? In that case, I would write that story by Arlt and publish it as a conclusion to this story.
5. The Adolescent. The atmosphere of a student boarding house, a girl visits the house every two weeks and sleeps with all of the boarders, and rides around the city on a Vespa ("The Girl with the Vespa"), the country boy who falls in love with the prostitute. He steals in order to get the money to be with her (to make her undress).
6. Sentimental Education. The young man who steals a valuable object from his lover; she sees him and pretends that she didn't see him.
7. The Serene Man (a retiree). He is on vacation, then returns home and kills a neighbor for no reason (just to see if his revolver is working). He goes back to work as if nothing had happened.

Encounter with Arlt. An ex-journalist (or ex-wife) has a notebook with unpublished writings by Arlt. Has his letters. The narrator is preparing a "secret" biography of Arlt. Maybe has an unpublished and unfinished novel? Talks with Rinaldi. Everything is or is not apocryphal.

Sunday 8

China Ludmer comes over, then we go for a walk through the Botanical Garden and she tells me her theories about Onetti's *A Brief Life*, an extraordinary reading. She wonders, how should she write it? As always, the critic cannot take it for granted that the reader will be familiar with the book she is analyzing. So, should she explain it or summarize it? She seems to have chosen to employ a rather abstract "map" of the novel as a frame for the analysis. Better without that, I tell her; I prefer that it either be understood or not, but without a direct reference to the text being analyzed. A reading without reference, a way of bringing "the fantastical" into literary criticism. Instead of writing a critique of a book that doesn't exist, write an analysis of a book that does exist but is absent or unknown. She has already written a prominent work about *A Grave With No Name*, but she reduces the story to a matrix in it so that, more than summarizing the plot line, she rewrites it, or rather, conceptualizes it (all very brilliant and also very psychoanalytical, fashionable. A great deal of Lacan, in the style of *Literal* magazine).

A story. A woman, walking among the plants in the Botanical Garden, explains her reading of a book, and the narrator imagines what that book is like, a book he doesn't know, based on his friend's description and analysis.

Tuesday 10
Series E. I have less and less to say, and that is why I am now able to write. I also want to assume that everything is already known and write only what is left, the remains of common language, the references that I alone understand. That is the style I seek in these notebooks. The writer cannot tell himself what he already knows. If I am faithful to that motto, I will manage to produce some acceptable pages. Emptied of sentimentality and with no concrete information, only emotional information. The speaker seems to be in another world and, though he isn't talking to himself, he isn't talking to anyone else either. Journeys of perspective, displacements, conversations with strangers, showing the difference between the place I come from and the place I describe. Therein lies the tension and anger accumulated by the disparity (of the experience) in the city and the country, the metropolis and the province. And so I will travel to Tucumán, Córdoba, and Santa Fe in the next few days. I will arrive by plane or train or bus, at some hour of day or night, and I will be welcomed by an unknown man—or unknown woman—who will talk as though we were friends, greeting me at the terminal and driving me to the hotel, and the impossible conversation continues. He or she will

leave me there, in the place where I am to spend two nights. A hotel room with windows that overlook the park and a television facing the bed like a mirror for the sleeper to watch himself dream.

I wrote this down at some point, a few days ago, on a paper napkin from Los Galgos bar, but I can't understand my handwriting and can only decipher this phrase: "Happiness with Iris, every [*illegible*] closer to her."

What, in the end, does free association mean? I ask Doctor C., the man who listens to me talk in exchange for money. A great invention by Freud: the one who speaks has to pay. The solid core of life is that which cannot be associated (with anything). The rift, the schism—I have always lived in two places, ever since I was a boy—the wound. In my case it is (or they are) emptiness, distraction, fixed ideas.

Wednesday 18

It is clear that there is little to be said. I went to Mar del Plata and back, to my mother's house. I tried to keep myself busy and went up to the attic where my father kept his papers (and his father's), useless collections of newspapers that no one reads. For example: pieces of news that he underlined in red ink; he would look for information that confirmed his beliefs: he marked out some obituaries, weather reports, fluctuations in the Stock Market, some crimes (especially sexual ones), and also the results (the winning numbers) from the numbers game and the National Lottery. Numbers upon numbers in a mystical circle drawn by a red ballpoint pen, expecting some revelation encoded there (written in those figures). When he got out of jail, my father was no longer the same. He had stopped believing, and he continued to act but only in the theatrical sense of the word, like an actor playing a Peronist who in turn was playing a doctor who in turn was playing a man without hope.

I went to see Susana Campos under the delusion of sleeping with her, but she greeted me along with her boyfriend, both of them very intoxicated.

They were drinking from a bottle of cloudy liquid; in the water they had dissolved some amphetamines, an LSD tablet, and a few grams of cocaine, scattered like dust in the wind. They were tripping hard; the boyfriend had climbed into a tree and was speaking from above as though he were a preacher. They said they would smoke a joint to come down, and that would bring them back to reality. They spent almost two hours telling me about their incredible experience going to the movie theater on drugs. The film lasted for years, according to them, and was very intense. They kept having to interrupt it to go to the bathroom and sometimes didn't know how to get back to their seats.

Then I went to the casino, intending to get rich, and at the end of the night I left with "only" twenty thousand pesos in winnings. I walked along the boulevard, and, in the sea illuminated by the light of the sky, I saw a ray cutting through the water like an upturned crucifix, the fin of a shark gliding eagerly under the surface. Behind me, the illuminated windows of the casino made everything seem more surreal. A shark, I thought, swimming silently and seeking a victim while the stubborn and drunk gamblers comment on the bad luck they've had this time around. Maybe the shark is a man eater and always comes back to the beach in front of the Hotel Provincial, hoping to find another gambler—a systematic loser—who has decided to drown himself in the sea, another suicide victim for the great white fish to devour.

I returned to Buenos Aires on a night train, intending to relax and sleep for the whole journey, but it was impossible, and I spent the whole time restless, anxious, watching the darkness through the window of the train car.

When I arrived in the city I was immobilized: there was a transportation strike. So I went on foot from Constitución to Córdoba and Callao, along 9 de Julio, and spent the day with Iris, hoping to able to think "about something else" by being with her. For example, interference at the University, which is now controlled by the Peronist right. That has left her without a job. But, on top of that, a schizoid cousin who believed himself to be Jesus Christ committed suicide.

I left to take a walk down Corrientes, planning to spend some time (a lovely expression: "to spend time") in La Paz bar and look in the bookshops until the afternoon when the subway would start running again. Unexpectedly (as always), I found myself with Amanda; she was sad, desolate, crying, "because she decided to leave the theater." She sat down at the table with me, in the corner by the window, and I tried to calm her down while she started on "the end of her adolescent fantasies" (the same kind that I cultivate, although in another genre). "You'll never stop acting," I told her, "life is your stage." I didn't convince her; for her, the theater is a way to forget about her life and, above all, a way to feel—or imagine—applause, recognition. I picture her on a bus, carrying her straight to the asylum. But there is nothing I can do . . .

Now I am at home, alone. Secretly certain that I am in danger, threatened by demands from outside. Preparing a lecture on Sarmento to give in Tucumán and Santa Fe. Anxious because of reality and loss. I'm giving a talk about Wittgenstein's language games soon. There are also political demands. In October, I'm going to Córdoba for the meeting of cultural magazines.

Friday 20
I couldn't take a chance in the casino. I left when I won twenty thousand pesos instead of staying and risking everything to win two hundred thousand.

Saturday 21
Yesterday León R. comes over to combat his loneliness, crying in the dark. What can I do? I console him instead of crying along with him. A woman abandoned him. He can't think, can't understand anything about anything. (A novel could be written with the story of the great

philosopher who spends the night at a friend's house, crying over a woman.)

I look at the river through the window, it is five in the afternoon. If I'm unable to assimilate writing into my life, I will come to a bad end. I sustain myself with drugs and justify them with literature, but it isn't the truth; I use them for themselves, seeking extreme lucidity, and the literature is a pretense. I am a man alone in the city, watching the sunset, the river an ashen color, a pain in my left side. The disorganized writer, notes, photos, papers getting mixed together, a feeling of being smothered. On the table I see María Moliner's dictionary, Sartre's *Baudelaire*, Deleuze's *Proust*, Mannoni's *The Other Scene*, a Calvino novel, Martínez Estrada's short stories (a map of the confusion in my soul).

I reread my notebooks from ten years ago. Why don't I write a story about adolescence based on that material? Does it overlap with Pavese or complement him?

A short story. A woman masturbates on the balcony, alone in the city. The narrator spies on her with the binoculars that his grandfather brought back—as his only trophy—from the war.

How was it that in 1969, when I started editing the notebooks, I didn't see that the novel I wanted to write was right there? (And what am I missing now?)

I am going to go out and walk around the city trying to cut myself free from this disturbing vision and stop thinking. That is why one walks, so as not to see the lurking images, bloody and pale. Ambulatory obsession. I want, at least, to be able to read something.

I go to the magazine office to discuss the publication of the next issue. A girl started going after me, many games with her. What are you doing tonight? I don't know which of us asked that question. I invited her to go to the Tigre and see El Tropezón, the hotel where Lugones killed himself. Now they rent out rooms and, for the same price, offer you a guided tour of the room where the poet took his arsenic; they've left it just as it was, and it looks like a monk's cell. My attention was drawn to the blue bottle that they used for water at night, from what the lady told me. And she added: "He dissolved the poison in this glass." Finally, when I leave the magazine office, the girl comes out after me. "I'll take you?" she says, we go home in her car. I think: "I'll let her come up, sleep with her, and then I'll ask her to drive to the Tigre with me."

Sunday 22

I am on the Tigre with the girl, and the river calms me. I've spent the day going over old papers. I don't entirely recognize myself in the individual who has written certain events of my life there. That is the paradox: it is my life, we might say, but I'm not the one who writes it. The best part of my literature lies on that uncertain point. That being or not being is transferred to the content of the events, but the one who has written them stays in the margins, safe from uncertainty. That enunciation—so to speak—is what would justify publishing a selection of these writings. The material is true, it is real experience, but its writer—its speaker— does not exist. That is how I define fiction: everything is true or can be so, but the key to the method is that its narrator is an imaginary subject. The construction of this place, and the ability to make it convincing or credible, is the essence of what we call fiction.

I work on the transcription of the notebooks with the same spirit that earlier led me to make lists and lists of favorite or rejected objects, the finest movies, the finest women, the clothing I had to buy, the books I had read that month, the countries I thought of visiting, and the books I wanted to write. Truthful materials, delirious diction.

A curious situation, and once again the feeling of having gone down-hill. No interest in "my own" life. I prefer to live someone else's life or to tell my own life as though it belonged to someone else. Who is writing? That is the great question of autobiographies and diaries. It isn't true as Foucault says that Beckett says that "it doesn't matter who is speaking."

Monday 23
The drafts are now done, they "are up," they "erupt."

A certain dispersion, several simultaneous projects. I urgently need a working plan to sustain me and give me the drive to go onward. Otherwise, I worked on rewriting the editorial for the magazine. Political differences; Carlos and Beatriz support Isabelita with the formula of the Frente Único. But Peronism—most of all—will not resist the coup, and the right wing (López Rega and his minions) has already made agreements with the military and is acting covertly, determined to annihilate any last vestige of the politics of the left. Finally, at nine at night, we decide that the issue will go out with no editorial.

Tuesday 24
Pablo G., the owner of the apartment, comes over. He asks me to leave. To pay him a hundred thousand pesos. He's an economist and talks about nothing but money. Possibility: offer him seventy-five thousand per month. Save up, suppress superfluous spending, and live on two hundred fifty dollars per month; I would have savings for two years by doing that. An alternative is to take everything as it comes and live comfortably and easily until April. That is, spend the dollars and live with no savings. I could marry Iris—something I don't want to do—and shut myself in with her, at her place, living together to combine our expenses. I'm trying to see how I could make more money. In April I either leave the apartment or pay him the hundred thousand that he's asking for; the best thing would be to spend the money I have and then see.

Sunday 29
This morning I saw an excellent film by John Huston in the series at the Auditorio Kraft: *Fat City*, set in the world of wasted, poor boxers. I see

Máximo Soto, who lets me in and gives me *Filmar y Ver*. I stop by to see David; everyone is very worried about the assassination of Silvio Frondizi, the escape of Puiggrós, and the political situation. David feels threatened, and he has good reason. He is very exposed. He seems to have grown old and has no energy.

Wednesday, October 2
Today deserves to be recorded because it is like a snapshot of the current situation in the city. I spend all morning at Iris's house and write half a page about Brecht to introduce a short selection of his essays in *Crisis* magazine. León R. stops by to see me after calling on the phone. Fearful about the wave of attacks by the ultra-right and the Triple A, and about the repressive laws that the government is implementing in alliance with the military. He feels pursued, and he has good reason too. He has received threats and no longer lives in his house; he wants to leave for Mexico, for three months to begin with. He wants to stop writing. His state of mind is shared by the majority of the intellectuals, who are starting to flee en masse. And what do I intend to do? I'm not on the front lines, I'm not that well known and barely visible, though that doesn't guarantee anything. Danger can come from being listed in an address book that belonged to someone who was followed, imprisoned, or killed. After that at La Moncloa I meet Julia, beautiful and exceptional. She is going to Venezuela with Mario Szichman. She offers me her apartment on Cangallo and Rodríguez Peña (fifty thousand per month, with telephone); she will leave the furniture, and if they try to evict me, she says, I can tell them "we live together." Little games, as in the past; each of us, she says, was the love of the other's life. Before leaving, she tells me this anecdote: Amanda took Alberto Cedrón to my apartment in Canning while I was traveling in China. When he saw my photo there, he asked what was going on. "I'm a woman," she says, so then he puts on his pants (which he had taken off before he saw the photo) and leaves. After that I go to the publishing office, general panic. Alberto S. wants to sell everything and go to Mexico. I'm dealing with all that when Amanda calls. Just to find out how I'm doing, to tell me to please take care of myself. I finish

the day facing a group of six psychoanalysts who pay me one hundred twenty thousand pesos per month to speak to them about philosophy. One of them asks me: "Are you related to the older Renzi?" "I am," I tell him, startled by my fame coming from an older person. Finally, at *Panorama*, a series of photos and profiles of writers (myself among them) from Bioy to Viñas. I lie, as always. I have a book of short stories ready, and also a first version of *Artificial Respiration*.

Thursday 3

At seven in the morning, I take the train and go to Santa Fe. An introspective journey, I read Silvina Ocampo's—excellent—short stories. A cavalcade of activity when I arrive, reports in the papers and on the radio. I critique the right-wing offensive supported by the government. We're all in danger if the reactionary terrorists act with impunity. Finally, a short rest and then I give the lecture. Difficult beginning and solid ending. I travel back by night and change trains in Rosario. Traces of Saer everywhere: the bus terminal, the café on the balcony, the open-air grills along the river, the iced wine, the conversations that last all night long.

Saturday 5

Yesterday I got off the bus in the early morning, dying of exhaustion from two lost and sleepless nights on the journey. In front of the zoo, around Libertador in the pale morning, a surreal feeling, the atmosphere of a nightmare or a premonitory dream, because three cars with no license plates suddenly appear (green Ford Falcons), carrying plain-clothed men who show off machine guns and blast the sirens. In the stillness of the morning, covert repression and horror emerge like phantoms. The worst thing is the feeling of normalcy. No one seems to notice anything; the military cars, camouflaged, go around the city sowing terror and it seems like no one can see them.

Sunday 6

A beautiful day, an unexpected visit from Iris, always amusing and seductive. My intimacy with her is growing, I see some pages of my notebooks from 1960—they are lying open on the table, and she says that secrets are meant to be revealed and then laughs—and she amuses herself with the arrogant tone of the prose from those years, and finally we go to bed.

Monday 7
I am preparing a project for the course with the psychoanalysts. The notion of private language in W., the analytical situation in Freud, and the Socratic dialogues in Plato, a stage to make words possible (compare the three strategies). First issue: How does speech begin? How to get beyond the "inauthentic murmur?" None of the three seem to want to eliminate insubstantial speech, but rather start from it. One case has to do with questioning, the other has to do with establishing a "setting" (someone speaks to another person whom he can't see, and he has to pay the price in gold because of what he says and the ability to talk uncontrollably for fifty minutes: because someone is listening to him). Finally, the third form involves rules that determine ways of living, and what is said about life is a muddled record.

At the publishing house, I try to get the rights to the detective novel that Boris Vian wrote under an American pseudonym, that is, as though he were an American writer. It is called: *J'irai cracher sur vos tombes*. B. shows up and then Mario Szichman, who is trying to reestablish ties with me, in spite of (or thanks to) his relationship with Julia. My friends and I can only look at the women in our tribe and we circulate among them like cards in a rigged deck; no one can complain because we all do the same thing. For example, I am with Iris, who was with Osvaldo L. before me, who in turn used to be with . . . endogamy and cyclical passions. Sitting beside each other at La Moncloa, we make predictions about the political situation while our friends (David, León) plan to take flight abroad.

More and more interested in the project of writing a novel of (sentimental) education, based on the diary. "Without realizing it," I can see the narrator I have always sought appearing in these notebooks: furious, ironic, desperate, elliptical. Thus emerges the tone of a protagonist who is not me. There's nothing like autobiography to confirm that the writer is not who he is. (But who is he? A stupid question.) I think about that other writer along the lines of the imaginary writers I know well: Stephen Dedalus, Quentin Compson, Nick Adams, Jorge Malabia, Silvio Astier. The life of the hero before defeat.

Tuesday, October 8

I feel very well now, he said. A calm morning; I am writing notes for a possible future book (ultimately, they will be nothing more than the preliminary notes, the outlines). That's how the work would have to be, in progress, unfinished, fragile, its only subjects being the imminence of something that never comes and the joy of inspiration. The apartment is full of light. I got back at ten, after reading the paper and having breakfast with Iris. The process of creation matters more than the work itself.

After cooking roast beef for myself in the oven (with French fries), I went down for a walk around the Botanical Garden. Sitting on a bench under the trees, I finished putting together the reading report for the Centro Editor and brought it to the run-down main office of the publishing house (I earned twenty thousand pesos). I met Beatriz Sarlo and Carlos Altamirano: *Los Libros* received a letter—containing threats—from the Triple A. My friends go into exile for less than that, but we won't let ourselves be intimidated and will go onward (toward the abyss).

At night, class with the group of psychoanalysts. Language scenarios, the—non-verbal—conditions that make utterance possible. On my way out they pay me for the month: a hundred thousand pesos.

At the theater with Iris: *Morir en familia*, a detective story that makes you think of a clumsy reading of Faulkner. In the theater, you can clearly see when the methods of an author are stolen and adapted without citation. For example, *The Wrong Man* by Hitchcock, an illegal version of Kafka. *Taxi Driver* by Scorsese, based on—or rather, stolen from—*Notes from Underground* by Dostoevsky. Adaptation as plagiarism.

Wednesday 9
Memories of childhood. The plaza with aromo trees, the church under construction, my grandmother donating her copper pots (which she brought over from Italy) to forge the bell.

I stop by the editorial office of *Crisis* and drop off the piece about Brecht, earning seventy-five thousand pesos. (In fact, I have earned almost three hundred thousand pesos from extra work this month.) Several proposals from Galeano, for me to bring in a short story, for me to prepare something to be published in every issue. A freelancer can't reject any offer out of fear that the well will run dry, and so he loads himself down with work. How can I get the cash I need to clear away five or six months' worth of obligations and be able to write in peace?

Thursday 10
Reality insists. A professor comes from the University of La Pampa. A proposal for a course on Arlt and Borges in the first week of November. Three days in exchange for a hundred thousand pesos (which straight away doesn't seem like enough money to me). I (a desperate man) accept and start to prepare the course.

Saturday 12
I'm happy and free when I'm not writing, and if I write I can't be happy or free.

León came over, drowsy and melancholic. He has been left several times by the same woman, crying. A good discussion with him about Borges. His is the classic Sartrean reading, which does not read but applies existing molds.

Monday 14
Andrés comes over and I spend the morning with him. His son is dying, and it's as though he couldn't see him. Andrés goes back and forth about publishing a story in *Crisis* because he's afraid of drawing the attention

of the Triple A. He is a great detector of dangerous places and situations. He situates himself far from here, along with the right.

A dream. Borges dies drowning, I cry for him but then he appears alive, reborn with a clean appearance, white hair, round eyeglasses (I can't identify the hair).

Wednesday 16
On Monday night my father appears unexpectedly in a dream, almost like a hallucination, and when I see him I realize that it was his hair that I could not recognize in that dream. In fact, I have the feeling that I myself "hallucinated" my father in order to be able to understand the dream and so not have to go to the cemetery because of him.

Last night I dreamed that I had to pick up Dad's old Underwood typewriter (which had belonged to my grandfather Emilio) from someone whose name I don't remember. It was the machine I learned to write on, using two fingers. The chain of generations.

Friday 18
Another empty day, and now I want to go down to the bar on the corner and get drunk, erasing the pain in my chest (which will not let me be). Rapid images of a happiness I never had, but one I yearn for more with every passing day. To be with friends, to talk with them, in a house lit up by large windows with blue curtains. Amanda's face or some of her sayings as mementos of a passion. That room over the garden where I wrote the story about Urquiza. Getting on a train one sunny day with newly bought books and magazines and setting out on a long journey to the south, crossing the corridors of the sleeping car at night and going to the dining car to order French fries and a bottle of white wine, getting rid of the restlessness caused by the certainty that everything is lost and that the best times have already passed, the era of great projects, when hope was possible. Julia would be reading, lying on the large bed in a corner by the wall of the blue room in the boarding

house in Barracas, the sun coming in from the avenue through the wall of glass that stretched from the ceiling to the newly cleaned wooden floor. It has been five years since I began to capsize, and it is useless to try to save myself.

Saturday 19

I suddenly found the essence of the novel about the adolescent: his mother has a trunk with pornographic photos that her husband has taken of her over the years; in this trunk there is also a photo of the mother as the spring queen, the most beautiful woman, and also letters from an ex-lover. "Will I become my father's son?" he asks himself.

Thursday 24

This week, I have earned one hundred seventy-five thousand at Tiempo Contemporáneo, one hundred thousand from the course of the psychoanalysts, and seventy-five thousand at *Crisis*. Or rather, five hundred thousand pesos. Next month the same work will continue, plus one hundred thousand pesos for the course in La Pampa. That's how, by scattering himself, a writer—like me—makes a living in Argentina.

On Wednesday I see Roa Bastos, who has written an extraordinary novel (*I, the Supreme*) and asks me to write a review in *La Opinión*, but I decline and instead recommend China L., whom he praises: "No one writes better criticism than her." Then at Ramos I see Eduardo Galeano, who has written a bad novel. With both of them, I create the illusion that I have a finished novel and will give it to them to read.

Saturday 26

A beautiful day, Iris and I spend the afternoon in bed, adventures into fantasy.

A dark life. All the same, this month was one of the most peaceful since I began my descent (1971). All I want is to know more and write better.

Wednesday 30
I meet Norberto Soares, who calls me to ask for an interview about Borges. Then, hung up on my intention to improve the article and the reporting, I hate myself for accepting the proposal from the media. Now I'm waiting for Iris, and I'm going to take her to bed.

Thursday, November 7
Yesterday was the wake for Andrés's son. Vast silence. Roberto Cossa and Jorge Onetti were there with him. A feeling of helplessness in everyone who was there. The death of a young person is always impossible.

Friday, November 8
Sitting in the dining room of the hotel in Santa Rosa, La Pampa, killing time; in an hour I'll teach the second class in the series on Arlt and Borges. A curious feeling, time has been confusing for the last ten days. A provincial slowness here, along with the slightly earnest tone that everyone has when they speak.

I'm reading *A Journal of the Plague Year* by Daniel Defoe.

Saturday 16
How can I summarize these days? Back and forth from Norberto Soares's house, endless alcoholic discussions. On Thursday I went to Adrogué. A return to the past. The old houses, the streets of my childhood. Uncle Mario, accompanying me to the station and showing me the family's "historic" sites: the house where Mom was born, the McKenzies' cottage, Queen's College. Yesterday I bought clothes: shirts, pants, and shoes.

Sunday 17
A condensation of the story about Roberto Arlt. The writer is preparing an edition of unpublished works, he knows a man who has texts but shows no interest, yet after some prodding the man shows him a story by Arlt and the narrator pays him for it. Then, a short while later, the story appears,

published and signed (pseudonymously) by the man who sold it to him. The mystery is, why did he publish it?

Wednesday 20
If he had to define this era, he would say that everyone says he's doing fine, "much improved"; he thinks they say this knowing that he has lately started to die, and they want to cheer him up. Everything he has to do costs him an impossible effort. He passes his days trying to pass the days.

I meet Germán García and we talk about Borges, about his book on Macedonio, about Peronism. He is working on the relationship between rhetoric and psychoanalysis. He proposes that I teach a course at some Freudian school they're thinking about starting.

Friday
X Series. I spent the whole day shut up in a house on Avellaneda with four workers and Rubén K., a long discussion about Peronism and the current situation.

Sunday 24
I am working on the essay about Borges. I turn thirty-three years old today; my economic future is dark.

Monday
Uncomfortable reading the interview on Borges that Norberto Soares did with me for *El Cronista.*

Saturday 30
Passage: moving. Last night, Amanda, beautiful as always, calls me and we meet. She had decided to stop being the actress she never was. We end up in bed after having dinner at Hermann, enjoying that romantic atmosphere.

I am working on the article about Cortázar for *La Opinión*. The idea of exclusive consumption and the collector as a metaphor for the artist in Cortázar.

Thursday, December 5
It is not true that "everyone" wants to write, some imbalance is needed. It was no accident that I began to suffer from this mournful fever at age sixteen.

Friday, December 6
Beautiful women are tanning in the sun on the terraces: naked bodies, scattered among the geometric white spaces of the city. A surreal quality like that of a dream.

Amanda's gesture: after making love she holds out her hand and takes my wrist to look at the time. A beautiful, shameless gesture, it is a key, in the end, to the current state of our relationship, and one I have read—for a while—as though it were a caress. I embrace her then, and it takes me a second to realize my mistake.

I'm reading Freud's excellent work on Leonardo: the meticulous notation of the spending necessary for his mother's burial. A pathetic poem of the obsessive man's love.

"A man's position before the world must be as literary as possible. Any man of a less refined species would doubtless laugh about a race so corrupted that the literary is considered a vice of character. All great men have been literate," Bertolt Brecht.

The logic of contagion: media outlets copy one another, so that if a person shows up in one place, the others, who have only seen what is visible there, ask for more texts or put out articles. This deadly logic can bring fame to a writer who doesn't write, or rather, who only writes in the media. A fine way to glorious failure. This comes because I received a call from *Crisis* magazine (let's mention, for future readings, that this magazine is directed by Eduardo Galeano and is part of the establishment of the left): they need biographical information to write a profile in the section dedicated to writers. Of course, I did let them give me an interview in *El Cronista Comercial* and published an essay on Cortázar in *La Opinión* a few days later. Journalists only read newspapers and take everything they read to be real.

Saturday, December 28

I work for three hours and finish the first five pages of the story, intoxicated by tobacco and coffee. Last night, before going to sleep, I found a solution for how to narrate the father's suicide (after two years of not seeing the way). The whole story takes place on a bus ride to Mar del Plata. Narrating in third-person, he thinks about his father. At the first stop, he reads a letter and sees a woman who is traveling alone. At the second stop, he begins a relationship with the woman and says goodbye to her in the terminal. And then at the hospital where the father breathes, groaning. He can't bear it and goes down to buy cigarettes and sleeps with the woman. I worked on four possible endings and, in the end, chose the best one.

Monday, December 30

The best part of the year was the story "The End of the Ride," which I wrote in ten days at a rate of two pages per day.

8

Diary 1975

Thursday, January 2
A card came from Tristana. At night I go to the theater with Iris: *Chinatown* by Polanski. Really, the movie seems to be based on a novel that Chandler never wrote.

Friday
Maybe I could write a volume of short stories centered around a single protagonist ("En el Terraplén," "Tarde de amor," "En el calabozo," "Tierna es la noche," "The End of the Ride," "Pavese").

Tuesday 14
The newlywed who interrupts her honeymoon trip to carry meat, milk, and bread in a net bag to feed many people. I had breakfast in a café with a counter over the platform of Once station, and I saw her going by and heard the man next to me tell her story.

Tuesday
A meeting for *Los Libros* magazine at night in a café on Calle Corrientes. A violent argument with Carlos and Beatriz. I am against centering the next issue around a denouncement of the USSR. In the end they compromise, and I feel worse.

Thursday

I meet David, who left a message for me at the publishing office. Sitting at Ramos, I give him a summary of the general situation. He tells me about his escape from a hotel in Mexico, leaving without paying, and his visit to Trotsky's house. (According to him, in the end Trotsky raised rabbits, which reproduce quickly, to compensate for his political group's lack of growth.) Then he tells me about his secret work on the adaptation of Borges's story "The Dead Man" for the movies, which will be under Juan Carlos Onetti's name.

Tuesday 11

Carnival days. I think I have more or less resolved the structure of the *nouvelle* "Homage to Roberto Arlt."

1. The narrator speaks of the publication of an homage to Roberto Arlt. He puts an announcement in the newspapers. A notebook appears with notes and unpublished pieces, there are mentions of Kostia and a story Arlt is about to write.
2. He meets Kostia in the boarding house. They discuss Arlt.
3. A week later Kostia appears. He brings him the story. They talk on the phone.
4. Kostia comes to see him. He asks him for the story (as though it were a betrayal). He will not give it to him.
5. A few days later the story appears, published by Kostia in his name.

Alternatives:

a) Kostia publishes the story, gives the money back to him, and lets him know where the original is.
b) Kostia *does not* publish the story but sends him the original and the money.

Friday 14

The story about Arlt is coming along marvelously, the idea about the notebook makes everything work.

An unexpected appearance from Amanda, who as usual comes to see me when she feels lost. Nothing, except for some tension.

On Arlt. Careful, if the "novel" that appears in the notebook grows too much, the effect of the lost story will be lost.

Monday 17
Weekend on the Tigre, the river, my skin burning. Helios Prieto's short stories. The Dostoevskian scene of Indio Bonnet, who returns from Cuba with money for the ERP and stops over in Rome; he has the day free and leaves to walk around the city, letting himself be won by passion and daring. In a plaza he bets in the shell game, three cups hiding a little black marble. He loses two thousand dollars . . .

I reread my essay "Roberto Arlt and the Fiction of Money." Written in 1973, about to come out.
    "Borges: The Two Lineages," written in 1974, about to come out.

Wednesday, February 19
I finished a first draft of "Homage to Roberto Arlt." Kostia's mystery is that Arlt, short on money, has rewritten a story by Andreyev. But the narrator *does not* know it.

Friday 21
I finished the first revision of "Homage to Arlt": the footnotes and the other story still have to be done.

Last night an encounter with Amanda. We ate in the restaurant on Carlos Pellegrini and then went to La Paz. We went back to her place to listen to the Charlie Parker record that I gave her at the beginning of everything. No desire, nothing, except nostalgia for other days.

The book of short stories (I still don't have the title) is finished and is fairly good.

For the first time, I have confirmed that literature does not solve life's imperfections. Write a work. And what do you do with that? A curious confirmation at this age.

Thursday 27

I meet David at La Paz at noon; he brings me the Cuban edition of my first book of short stories and tells me his misfortunes working as a ghost writer on the script of *The Dead Man*.

Saturday, March 1

I go to Martín Fierro in the morning, and in the bookshop I run into Gusmán. (The caves or crevices where his family's "accomplices" shut themselves in.) Difficulties, on my part, in talking about the fiction I write.

Two titles for the book: *Partial Vision* or *Assumed Name*.

Monday 3

I'm buried in Stendhal, from whom I learned *all* of my creed in 1963: strategy, control, clear prose.

I spend the afternoon sorting through my library, throwing out papers, not getting around to going over the short stories I've written (I don't want to read them again).

Tuesday 4

I want to clarify that, in rereading, I like the stories less and less.

Wednesday 5

I go to *Crisis* magazine to drop off my story "The Price of Love." I meet with the successful "young" writers (Eduardo G., Jorge A.) who discuss their literature in the way it was discussed ten years ago. Presumptuous, self-satisfied. Eduardo G. talks about the letters that his readers send him and reads a letter from the woman who translates him into Czech. Jorge A. "quotes" his own novels. No future in that direction. Aníbal Ford seems more promising, he has written a good short story with an indirect tone and a "simple" character, a truck driver. Lastly Juan Gelman, asking them to write to Spain for his newly published book, etc.

Tuesday 11
Dream. The crime is in the handkerchief, someone says. A puzzle can be seen, and in the dream it remains unsolved. Suddenly we are in the theater: all improvised.

Thursday
Opposite, in the window, two young people eat lunch as though on stage in a theater. I have nothing to eat; I'll have to go out despite the rain and walk to the deli where they sell prepared food.

Friday 21
At Jacoby's invitation, I'm going to give a course at the CICSO on Arlt and Borges on Monday nights at nine thirty.

Wednesday 26
Yesterday José Sazbón spends the afternoon at my place. We talk about Borges, listen to songs by Brecht. He remains the same, very intelligent and very shy.

Rumors of a coup d'état are growing.

April
I have finished correcting *Assumed Name*. Except for some roughness in the style, this book is good enough to show how far I can go at this time. The prose could possibly be improved, but the book was written in a short time, in a sort of blind space where I had little choice.

In a sense, "The End of the Ride" brings the poetics that I began in 1961 with "La honda" to an end; it is impossible to go any further. It contains the Americans, Pavese, "narration." "Homage to Roberto Arlt," on the other hand, opens a certain path, the possibility to "think" in the middle of a story and break the structure. In any case, I can't comment on the value of these stories. I have few illusions, as though I have finally managed to write with no pretense other than following the rhythm of the prose. This explains the indifference, the strange lethargy that rereading it causes in me, as though someone other than me had written it.

Wednesday 2

I rediscover a certain lost emotion of the city, intermingled with the empty hours. The walk along Corrientes, the bar on Santa Fe and Pueyrredón with the veneered walls and the young girls who laugh and drink beer. I end up at the theater, watching a regular film (*Rosemary's Baby*) among the single men there to kill the tedium of the afternoon.

Earlier I saw Germán, Oscar Steimberg, Luis Gusmán; they have veered toward the baroque, studying rhetoric. Some emotional bond, anyway, especially with Luis (who has dedicated his novel to me).

I kill time in another bar, read a Borges story, an anachronistic utopia, men of the future complaining, gloomy.

Thursday 3

Norberto comes over, the critic acts stubborn toward everyone as a mask for all of the texts he announces and does not write. He will say the same things about me that he says to me about others.

I've decided to quit *Los Libros* magazine. My differences with Carlos and Beatriz are more and more definitive; it isn't about literary discrepancies, which have always been there, but rather political views, which so far have always determined the positions I've published (for example, renouncing *El Escarabajo de Oro* for jumping on the Communist Party bandwagon). I never publicly discuss literary matters or cultural positions that refer to me, I never respond to reviews and try to never get into useless "artistic" polemics, but I do have qualms with political labels. In this case, opportunism toward López Rega, ravings about a supposed Soviet strike . . . Anyway, I won't be able to leave until the next issue. I see Beatriz (having said nothing to her), and she talks about my article on Brecht, which is already written.

At Juárez's house with Julio G., who seems intimidated, undecided, outside of politics. I remember him years ago in the College as an optimistic militant of the CP; I had lost the election for president of the Students' Center by three votes, and Julio got up on a table and proclaimed that the defeat was a victory. It has always been hard for me to take in the idiotic optimism of progressivism.

Friday 4
Why was I astonished by Scott Fitzgerald, now so many years ago? (I read him for the first time in 1958 and have gone back to him several times since then.) Maybe it is his lyrical and nostalgic way of recounting failure, and at the same time a certain fragile arrogance; like him, I hoped "to be" better than any other writer in my generation.

Sometimes I would sit down to write only so that I could look at the river in the distance, among the buildings, especially at six in the afternoon when the sun was gone and the light was gray, the same color as the water.

Our enemy these days is one Luis G., stupid and pretentious; today in *La Opinión* he wrote a venomous critique of Ludmer's excellent work on *Toward a Nameless Grave* by Onetti. Before that, several references to me because of my prologue for Gusmán and my project on Borges, which he branded—like a good cultural policeman—"Maoist." He nicely expresses the dominant thought in the media and among people with little education; he demands simplicity, demands that writing be clear, that is, done in his heavy and mediocre manner.

At Corregidor publishing, Juan Carlos Martini offers to publish *Assumed Name* "without reading it." Schmucler is sick, so the Siglo XXI work is postponed.

I will let this month come to an end before I decide what writing to continue. Really, I should "have to" finish with Borges, but I don't have much desire to do it. I prefer to continue with the fiction, writing my bildungsroman (there are not many in this country: *Mad Toy* and *Betrayed by Rita Hayworth*). The only issue is that I detest autobiographies and so would have to write the novel in third person.

I am reading a biography of Scott Fitzgerald. Some scenes: Zelda ("crazy") who comes out of the house naked while Scott is playing tennis with a friend. Grand theme: success and collapse. (Fitzgerald and Pavese replace Byron and Rimbaud for us; they are our myths.)

As always, I try to read every novel by an author who interests me, in recent weeks it was Katherine Anne Porter, before her—long before—it was Stendhal, now it's Fitzgerald: his stories with ridiculous heroes, with inelegance as a mortal sin, are the signal (the oracle) announcing failure and death. To lose natural grace is to experience—ahead of time—collapse. His stories from the thirties—"Babylon Revisited" in particular—have a tragic strength and can only be written "with the authority of failure."

Saturday 5
It remains a joy, these days, to enter the study in the morning with the river in the background, where I sit down in the armchair and read the newspapers.

Over the last few months it is as if, for some reason I do not know, the writer I have been trying to construct for years has taken form. And so I feel myself detached and cold toward criticism (despite the fact that I will need it to earn my living in the coming years).

Fitzgerald's point of view, as in Conrad, can also be found in the work of Borges: the narrator is stunned, faced with a story he does not entirely understand. For me, on the other hand, the point is to maintain that uncertainty in order to think at that level. The witness avoids having to "heat up" the prose in relation to the storyline. I have to find something like that in the coming-of-age novel: maybe use him as a witness in La Plata and then turn him into a protagonist. For example, in *The Last Tycoon*, the point of view is shown in the middle of the story: "There was an eager to-do in the eastern sky, and Wylie could see me plain: thin with good features and lots of style, and the kicking fetus of a mind. I wonder what I looked like in that dawn, five years ago. A little rumpled and pale, I suppose." The witness describes himself in the way he imagines another sees, or has seen, him. That is also Chandler's method (that is why he calls his protagonist Marlowe, a narrative double of the Marlow in Conrad).

Today I saw a film by John Huston with Bette Davis, a cruel story with some memorable moments: Bette Davis steals her sister's husband. Bette goes to visit her, and the sister has the photo of the husband in her bed; she is lying there with the photograph. Bette takes the photo and stands there, staring at it.

Sunday 6
In the novel, I will try to narrate the way into that dangerous place where some lost desire is reactivated. That way in is motivated by the arrival of the student in La Plata. Remember what André Green pointed out: "The dominant feature is the distinction between the idea and the emotional state. Whereas the idea will be submitted to change, the emotional state will remain identical." This distinction is key for me and is tied to the relationship that the hero maintains with his own experience: when he narrates it, he is detached and looks with irony at his emotional state, which, nevertheless (and in spite of him), remains alive. Often, for example in Hemingway or in Conrad, narrators will tell the story from a time long after the events, and so they cannot transmit the emotional states they felt in the past but can contemplate them.

Green analyzes substance abuse, that is, addiction, as a shattering of the transactional ways of the ego: all mediations are lost. In my case, it has to do with the relationship between writing and the drugs.

Monday

I stop by *Crisis* magazine, where I receive eighty thousand pesos for the publication of my story "The Price of Love." Earlier, in the morning, I prepared the program on narrations of the ego for the course in Parera. They will pay me forty thousand per class (the dollar is at three thousand pesos).

Amid the rain I walk down Viamonte to *Los Libros*. I find Beatriz Sarlo in the office. We look at the proofs of my article on Brecht. Then I hand in my resignation. One phase comes to a close.

Tuesday 8

I spend the morning at a table in La Paz, overlooking the street corner, finishing my corrections on *Assumed Name*, and in the middle of my work Juan Carlos Martini appears and stays for an hour. I have lunch with Schmucler and leave the book with him, we'll see what happens. Then I go over the proofs for the essay on Brecht and don't end up writing a final version, as I had thought, so I'll turn it in as it is.

Wednesday

In therapy, C. says to him: "You give your father time, you hold back because of him, waiting for him." A strange history that he resists understanding.

A meeting with Beatriz Sarlo and Carlos Altamirano, rather gloomy. Carlos "politically" laments the end of our work together.

Friday 11

A melancholy and asseverative meeting with Andrés R., Norberto S., and Jorge F. Experience at *Los Libros*, critique of *Pasado y Presente*, the possibility of a new magazine, etc. Everything ends at three in the morning and I stay over at Norberto's house.

A meeting with Beatriz and Carlos at six in the afternoon where I submit my letter of resignation; little goodbyes and an end to my work at *Los Libros*.

I am reading *The Charterhouse of Parma*. The secret, the disguise, the conspiracy, the Bovarysme are built around Napoleon (Fabrizio in battle: he cannot understand what is happening and sees Bonaparte passing on horseback like a phantom).

Sunday 13
A peaceful day at Iris's house. We go to the movie theater and return in the rain.

Monday
A certain chain of memories that have remained fixed reappear, summoned by the present: that trip, sitting in the last seat of the bus from La Plata to Buenos Aires with Virginia, Manolo, and Pochi Francia. The discussion about the CP and Russian poets in Cuba. That morning at the end of 1967 when I peeked out the window of my room in the hotel on Rue Cujas and saw snow on the dark rooftops.

I see Gusmán, Altamirano, Steimberg, and Germán García in the bars near the Martín Fierro bookshop. A letter from Oscar Masotta in London, references to *Brillos* and to my prologue for *El frasquito* (Luis's first two books).

José Sazbón with his amusing son, who is growing up and worries him; he is always worried about money, always wise. With a smile he dismissed Emilio de Ípola and his thesis on Lévi-Strauss ("very superficial").

Tuesday 15
An invitation—via Germán García—to give a talk at the Escuela Freudiana de Buenos Aires (effect of Masotta's letter): I will talk about Borges, psychoanalysis of "Emma Zunz," equivalencies, substitutions, one name in place of another.

It would be interesting and enlightening to make an historical analysis of the successive speeches by the Commanders in Chief of the Army on

May 29 (Army Day). They have been delivering them since 1870: see whom they are directed to in each instance and who is the enemy.

A meeting at Siglo XXI to inaugurate a main office on Calle Perú. A dizzying succession of the faces of friends, acquaintances, and rivals. We took a photo in which China L., Luis, Pezzoni, Toto, and I are smiling. Schmucler (excessively) praises my "Homage to Roberto Arlt," but (I'm sure) they don't like the other stories. Luis G. detains me to talk despite the void that surrounds him. Tense because Lola Estrada is there, I take refuge with Iris in a corner, surrounded by Gusmán, Máximo Soto, and Urbanyi until Andrés R. and Norberto S. arrive. We end up in a restaurant in the area having dinner with lots of alcohol, and I decide out of nowhere to pay ten thousand pesos for a team flag of Peñarol de Montevideo.

Wednesday
Tired because of the two courses I teach every week, I take things calmly all the same. In the middle of the afternoon León R. comes over and then Tristana, who takes me for a car ride and gives me a memo book that someone left behind.

Thursday
Both courses are going well. I've made a hundred twenty thousand pesos from three classes with the psychoanalysts, and I'm at ease. I prepare for tonight's course on Borges; demands from outside erase the emptiness, and it seems that work (at least reading and preparing for the classes) may be something necessary, recalling the sailors' saying (sailing is necessary, living is not necessary).

Friday, April 18
I meet Schmucler at the Grill on Santa Fe and Salguero. We planned for one in the afternoon, and he's delayed. I order chicken and rice and convince myself that he isn't coming, that he has rejected the book. But instead he does arrive, excited about "Homage," and differing on the other stories in this decreasing order: "The End of the Ride," "Benítez,"

"The Price of Love." He suggests releasing the book before October and paying an advance of five hundred thousand pesos.

Yesterday was the first class in the course on Borges and Arlt at the CICSO. A full classroom, many enrolled, great interest. A divided audience: Iris, José Sazbón and a group of initiates, a group of literature students, some not paying attention (like the redhead who works for *Crisis*). Everything turns out well. I end the night with Iris, José, and other friends eating dinner at Hispano on Avenida de Mayo.

Saturday
Last night a barbecue at Vogelius's country house. An incredible place, a large library with an extraordinary periodicals collection, some very good paintings, a vast park, a Fitzgerald atmosphere (melancholy). Galeano, Conti, Asís, Pichon-Rivière, Perrone. I go there with Schmucler and dedicate myself to drinking and smiling in the face of the arrogant stupidity of the—young—Argentine writers. I drive back with Haroldo, who suddenly seems to have grown old, always with an expression like someone who just got out of jail.

> *Economy and literature*
> *Assumed Name*: five hundred thousand pesos (September).
> Arlt anthology: five hundred thousand pesos (June).
> USA short stories anthology: the same (April–June).
> Borges: one million pesos (November).

I spend the afternoon working on the course on nineteenth-century literature, we'll see if I can find a solid foundation: Mansilla and Hernández.

Sunday 20
A condemned man on a perpetual chain, locked up in a cell over the river, enjoying certain privileges (films, bars with friends, a woman). That is what I am. I can expect nothing but what comes from that very solitude.

"Things may, however, be condemned to be lost without their value having suffered any diminution—when, that is, there is an attempt to sacrifice something to fate in order to ward off some other dreaded loss," S. Freud, C. W., volume II, 2166.

"Once upon a time a valiant fellow had the idea that men were drowned in water only because they were possessed with the idea of gravity. If they were to knock this notion out of their heads, say by stating it to be a superstition, a religious concept, they would be sublimely proof against any danger from water. His whole life long [that man] fought against the illusion of gravity, of whose harmful results all statistics brought him new and manifold evidence," Karl Marx.

"A patient made a comparison that fits the case. He said it was as if he had fallen into the water with a towel in his hand, and someone were trying to dry him with the towel which had become wet along with his body," S. Freud.

Monday 21
I have to let everyone at the publishing house know that I arranged to publish my book at Siglo XXI.

Sazbón comes over, I have trouble paying attention to him because I'm half finished with the outline for today's class on death and religion in Freud. In that group, the psychoanalysts talk about painting while the youngest of the women, Estela, tries to seduce me.

Thursday
Under pressure from the courses, but happy because I have lots of free time. Every day, I arrive at nine and work until five in the afternoon; at noon today I made grilled beef with tomatoes and then gave in, waiting for the future.

Friday
Excellent "performance" in the courses this week. An experience more akin to theater than to writing; speaking in public fills me with uncertainty for

hours before I begin and gives me some nerves at the beginning of the talk. Then I forget who I am and let myself be carried off by the words. Now it is seven in the evening and I am drinking whiskey and reading Conrad, sitting in the leather armchair, killing time before I go back to see Iris. Amanda called me, we'll meet at her place tomorrow. Two years ago, she read my notebooks one day and everything ended. I am tempted to go; it isn't advisable, but I always find a way to get myself in trouble. I'm bringing *Assumed Name* to Siglo XXI on Tuesday, so I will try to correct it tomorrow. Today I saw Estela, who attacks psychoanalysis because she cannot find her place within it.

Monday, April 28
Tomorrow I will go to Siglo XXI to sign the contract. I have to correct the short stories ("Luba" especially) and decide whether to include "The Price of Love" or not. I hope they will pay me the five hundred thousand pesos.

An interview tomorrow with television producers who are offering me a spot on an afternoon program on Channel 13, five hundred thousand pesos per month. (I will say no.)

A competition for detective stories is announced in *Siete Días* magazine. Borges is one of the three judges. The prize is a week-long trip to Paris for two people. I would like to win it, but I don't know what to write.

May 1
An event in Plaza de Mayo in the light rain. Isabel Perón is inclined to affirm her personal leadership. I spend the morning reviewing my answers to the interview, Lafforgue is coming to get it in a while. At the Obelisco, young unionists start some trouble.

Sunday 4
Now I am alone in the evening, watching night come over the river. A long lunch with Julia and Mario Szichman (who has arrived from Venezuela),

with them is Pelín N., a Trotskyist student. It is impossible for me to feel comfortable in that company, as though I can only feel comfortable with my closest friends or when talking about literature, otherwise I'm inattentive and detached.

A strange era, leaving no mark. On Tuesday, getting off the bus that brought me back from Channel 13, where I had gone to turn down the job, I saw the issues of *Crisis* magazine with my short story being distributed on the corner of Callao and Córdoba. I sat down in the bar on Corrientes and Rodríguez Peña and flipped through the magazine. On Friday at Norberto Soares's house, Andrés Rivera calls on the phone, praising "Homage to Arlt," excessively, as always. Strangely, I am drifting farther and farther away from the book.

Tuesday 6
Subject: the Basques from Tandil. Siglo XXI. The "messiah," a witch doctor who mobilizes a street gang and cuts the throats of the Basque immigrants in the area. It coincides with *The Gaucho Martín Fierro*, 1872. A play could be written, along the lines of Brecht.

Wednesday 7
Last night I stopped to see Amanda at her house, melancholy and withdrawn. Bad and getting worse, espousing "seriousness," she has lost who she was, her seductive and charming ways. We had dinner at Arturito and she accompanied me to the subway, pulling her dog Bolero by the leash.

The issue of *Los Libros* comes out with my letter of resignation and the response from Carlos and Beatriz. Some sadness, but also the relief of breaking free.

Friday
A strange impression of finding, or rather, discovering the central axis of my work ten years after I started. Fiction tied to my passion for Argentine history.

There is a point at which a certain distraction is imposed as "legal currency," one acts in a strange way because it is better according to convention. For example, last night I met Alberto in the theater. I thought "he is here with another woman" and so I acted accordingly. I left the theater and it turned out he was with Clara, his wife; so I had been rude, evasive, etc.

Monday, May 12
On Saturday a party at Norberto Soares's house, I got mixed up in a disrespectful argument with Pancho Aricó that prompted the angry intervention of a beautiful and hysterical ballerina (we agreed that she only danced in order to be seen). Germán García, conspiring with me, got caught up in an easy speech to prove to the ballerina that she didn't understand. Aside from that, more praise for the story about Arlt. Aricó and María Teresa Gramuglio insist that I publish it on its own. Iris and I got back at four in the morning, walking along Callao, the street damp from the light rain.

Tuesday 13
It is raining, and I am working peacefully, not wanting to go out.

Yesterday a good class with the psychoanalysts about negation in Freud and negativity in Hegel. Before that I met Oscar Landi, who agreed with my resignation from *Los Libros*. We'll have to see how to put together a group of intellectuals (Landi himself, De Ípola, Menéndez, etc.) in the planning of "another" magazine.

Friday 16
After eating with Carlos Altamirano in the restaurant next door to the place where I lived for some happy years (on Calle Sarmiento, next to the entry door), I go to Siglo XXI to sign the contract for *Assumed Name*. Schmucler gives me a copy of a reading report with lots of praise, especially for the story about Arlt.

Saturday 17

I spend the afternoon reading Argentine literature. I discover Holmberg and the path of fantastical literature, which, through positivism, opens itself to the occult sciences and in a sense—via Lugones—will lead to Roberto Arlt. I read Eduardo Gutiérrez's melodramatic novels with great interest as well (*Moreira* and *Hormiga Negra*).

Saturday

At night I put some sugar in a yellow nylon bag and bring it to Iris because she can't get any. I wait for the subway, calm and exhausted, while a woman shows a man the tiles decorated with the picture of the Virgin of Luján. I play chess with Fernando on a wooden game board that scrapes when you move the pieces.

Sunday 18

It has been three months since I've written; all I do is read and prepare for classes. I have started having "bad dreams".

Tuesday 20

At noon José Sazbón comes over and we talk about my essay on Brecht; José is thinking of putting together a volume for Nueva Visión and including it there.

In the late afternoon I go to Martín Fierro and find Roa Bastos, who is signing books. Many people from Siglo XXI are with him; Marcelo Díaz, Tula, also Lafforgue all agree that I will win the *Siete Días* prize for detective stories if I enter. That certainty is enough to block me, and I can't think of writing for it.

Wednesday 21

Mario Szichman comes with a proposal for me to write two pieces per month for a Venezuelan newspaper for fifty dollars (which is almost two hundred thousand pesos). I tend toward dispersion and prefer not to make commitments.

Friday 23

I make progress on my theory about the relationship between the fantastical and the detective story at the end of the nineteenth century as two threads present in Roberto Arlt. Last night's class at CICSO was suspended because of the increase in repression following Numa Laplane's appointment as army chief and the strengthening of the most reactionary wing of the government (via López Rega).

Saturday

I am reading excellent political stories by Cabrera Infante, written in the style of Hemingway. I watch evening fall beautifully over the river.

I don't know how I can find a subject and write a detective story for the competition within a month. Plot: Almada takes photographs, Antúnez says goodbye to Larry. I have to construct a story in the midst of that, perhaps the two never meet.

Sunday 25

I dispassionately reread articles about the mass media for my class tomorrow. The uncertainty between truth and falsehood comes from the media (Enzensberger). Yesterday I went to the theater twice: alone, to free myself from the void, I saw *Los gauchos judíos* in the theater across the street from here and at night, with Iris, Losey's version of *A Doll's House*.

The detective story project has taken me over entirely, but, unable to write, I remain immobile, staring into the void.

Monday 26

I prepare for today's class with the psychoanalysts; it pains me to accept that I have to work to earn my living. I seek a "solution" to writing a ten-page detective story.

Saturday, May 31

Last night dinner at Carlos B.'s house, a plan to make a film of "Emma Zunz," Carlos holds himself up in a certain aristocracy of the artist. It is exactly what I try to avoid by "not doing" anything, only working; as for my fantasies, I have the courtesy not to communicate them to anyone.

Thursday, June 5

I meet Andrés and Norberto Soares in the café on Córdoba and Uruguay. Several different accounts of the political situation. Strikes in Córdoba, everything very unstable. A serious crisis following Rodrigo's economic plan.

Friday 6

I am working on the detective story but can't find the plot. Maybe I will focus myself on the death of the Chinese bartender. But I don't think I can write it until I have clarified the mystery. After almost six hours of working on the story, I am at the beginning. Almada is in love with Larry. In any case, I keep going without finding the mystery.

Friday 13

I discovered a new ending for the story. Maybe it is Almada who kills her.

Thursday

Today León R. showed up in the middle of the afternoon after months away; he continues with his ideas about Peronism for the book he wants to write. Very critical, he thinks the working classes support Perón because of immediate interests.

Friday

The political crisis erupts; the Minister of Economy refuses to accept the increases determined by the peer reviews (150 percent increase for the UOM), and the CGT decrees general shutdown. Aside from that it is raining, and so, between the political conflict and bad weather, I

476

shut myself in and after ten hours of work finally manage to write an acceptable story in the detective genre. It will have to be revised and cut down, but I think it can work. I will find a "linguistic" solution to the crime.

Saturday
I have written my thirtieth short story: "The Madwoman and the Story of the Crime." Apart from that are the *nouvelle* about R. Arlt and the failed novel about the criminals imprisoned in an apartment in Montevideo. Fifteen years of work, a sad assessment.

In the midst of my passion for writing, Tristana appeared with her tragedies: her husband has started sleeping with the maid again (like a Gombrowicz character), crisis, sleeping cure. She wanders around the city with no place to cling to, stretches herself out on the floor, her way of saying she wants to sleep with me. We spend the late afternoon in bed. Wicked and trivial thoughts at times: the work day cut short.

July
I finish a decent draft of the detective story. Hard work until I managed to establish a double story:
  I.   Almada-Antúnez (Larry).
  II. The madwoman who saw the crime.
  I still have to cut it down, bring it to eight pages, but maybe it will be enough to win the competition.

Tuesday 8
A little while ago I finished copying "The Madwoman and the Story of the Crime." Some stubborn confidence allowed me to write it.

In recent days the political crisis was unleashed, with worker mobilizations all around the country. The whole cabinet resigned, but Isabel supports López Rega.

Thursday 10

I occupy my morning with sending off the detective story for the competition; in the afternoon I go to Siglo XXI, and they confirm that *Assumed Name* will come out this year.

Friday, July 11

Perhaps studying the art of war is not a defense mechanism?

Couldn't the transcript of my diary from my trip to China be published as a book called *A Sentimental Journey*?

Saturday 12

Tristana arrives at midnight, a bit drunk just like every time she comes to see me. We stay together until this afternoon, not leaving bed until the end, before we say goodbye, when she sits in the tub under the shower. A final image I must not forget.

Monday 14

The same as with office workers, Mondays are the worst days for me (my course with the psychoanalysts). Also, I decided to let my beard grow out, but I think I may give that up. All the same, I'll make note of a superstitious procedure here: I won't shave my beard until I know the results of the detective stories competition. If I win (?), I will take photos of myself with the beard and then shave. If I lose, I will shave the day after I know the results.

Wednesday

Pay the rent, go to *Crisis* magazine, see Norberto Soares, write about Bellow, sort out the house.

At noon I go to Siglo XXI. Corrections for *Assumed Name* (which seems to me to be written worse and worse). It will go to the printing press soon. At Tiempo Contemporáneo, a call from David, who summons me to his house to argue about "literary criticism."

Thursday
Too much alcohol last night, I get up at noon, slightly dizzy. I read Laplanche's book on Hölderlin. Then Pablo G. appears, asking me for three hundred thousand pesos in rent for the apartment, so I offer him two hundred thousand. He refuses, threatening me with a lawsuit.

"The Foundling only perceived his parents in a general projection or identification which abolished their separateness; hence the ambiguity of his emotions and the incapacitating lack of conflict," Marthe Robert: *Origins of the Novel*. She works with Freud's model of the family novel.

Friday
I spend the whole day alone, shut in at my desk, without going out. Reading several books, warding off the cold and loneliness with a bottle of whiskey. I go in circles around the room, planning projects and searching for what can be "the most direct path" (to where?).

Tuesday 29
Entire days up in the branches; apart from that, vague anxiety and bad readings (S. Crane, V. Nabokov, W. Styron). Unexpected visits, Graciela came back looking for me for the third time.

In *An Expedition* . . . by Mansilla, the story of Corporal Gómez. The man stabs his wife because he dreams that she is sleeping with his enemy. He *believes* in the dream. A valiant man kills ("in his dreams") an officer who hit him in the middle of a battle. In reality he is drunk and kills another man, but he believes it was his "enemy." Mansilla tries to save him, but he is executed. His sister dreams he has died and comes from far away, certain ("I know") that her brother has died. A curious Shakespearean breath in this story.

The same thing in *Facundo*: the businessman enters a bar and does not recognize Facundo Quiroga (who is stretched out on the counter) and curses him because he owes him money. Someone talks to Facundo, says "my general." The man realizes who it is and gets on his knees and begs forgiveness. Quiroga laughs and lets him go with the money. Years later the businessman is a beggar, reminding him of the anecdote in the door of a church. Quiroga gives him a gold coin.

Another from *Facundo*: Quiroga is going to execute an officer with his own sword. The officer defends himself and takes the sword from him twice, giving it back to him with pride and honor. Facundo ties him up and then kills him.

On Saturday I assembled my work for the coming months, three courses, two of them on the same day. I will have more money and more work than ever before in my life. A man who earns his living by reading.

Wednesday 30
An excess of demand: in the newspaper *El Cronista* they ask me for a piece about Pavese and also a short story. In August, the lectures.

Yesterday seeing Pola, a long tiring conversation, dinner at the Agüero restaurant with memories of the past. In the end she doesn't want to go to bed and I return home alone in the early morning. At sunrise, not having slept, I think *Assumed Name* is bad and poorly written. I sit down on the bed and let myself go among those lost illusions.

Thursday 31
I have come back to Pavese, to the atmosphere of my beginnings. I remember that an article about him was the first thing ever I published, more than ten years ago.

Two days pass, and I don't make any progress. Captured here and there by some stray readings: Stephen Crane, William Styron.

Friday, August 1
The desire for an impossible desire? That is what his listener says. Veils: netted screens to cover nostalgia.

X Series. A long afternoon with Rubén K., sitting in a variety of bars. We know that, to me, he holds the prestige of revolutionary politics, a practice I have always thought of as done by others (Casco, Lucas), whom I have unhappily seen "selling out." Not Rubén, however, despite his constantly renewed optimism, his monotonous list of contacts (now via Cámpora). He does not seem to have a memory, and that must be a politician's "rationale": How long, for example, will he maintain the stupid pretense of expanding his group by capturing the pictures of other parties? In the end David, whom I had planned to meet, appeared, and then for the first time Rubén started to talk with a priestly tone with no content beyond a vague reformism: "allying" with Cámpora, Alende, etc. No political analysis at all; in short, the deficiencies that I endure personally.

A curious close to the night, I decide to go back along Corrientes and not by Callao to walk a bit further. Happy to go to sleep alone, aided by the wine. At La Paz, through the window, I see Tristana's face at a table with other women; Amanda is with a new companion, who starts talking about books as soon as he sees me come in. She seems more and more like a ghost, plays harmless games with Silvia P. and Tristana, and I pretend to be distracted while hearing the lines Amanda says, trying to let me know she's thinking about me. Why, in short, do I spend time on this nonsense?

Saturday
To Adrogué and back, to the neighborhoods of my childhood. I look at the old houses, saddened by the memories, the good times. At home I fill my time by organizing the boxes with Grandfather Emilio's archives. I spend the night reading letters, notes, and looking at photos. There are still tenants occupying the front part, kind and

generous people (he is a printer, fairly well known among my publishing friends.

Monday

I finish the night with Soares and Di Paola at La Paz, and Miguel Briante is there, as always. Long conversations and jokes. Miguel is charming, always telling his sumptuous anecdotes.

Tuesday 5

A beautiful morning, the city's fog against the river. Strange signs, destruction that retains its elegance.

Wednesday

I meet Tristana at the restaurant on Serrano and we spend the night together. She sits on the floor, her face to the picture window. She leaves me with the letters that she writes to me when she is alone.

Sunday 10

Yesterday a visit from Roa Bastos, he tells the beautiful story of the end of Solano López. He has written *I, the Supreme*, a masterwork, but that does not change anything. He is alone, sick, and penniless.

Monday 11

A meeting at the SADE, a list of writers for the elections. Castelnuovo, Kordon, Conti, Viñas, it reminded me of the meetings at the students' center. Then I have dinner with David and Conti. Political crisis, changes in the cabinet, rumors of a coup.

At noon Andrés R. visits me bringing a short story, *overwritten* and rhetorical ("La lectura de la historia").

Monday 18

The maté and the kettle on the desk, the clips that fasten the pages, the books, an open notebook, the lamp.

A possible version of Hamlet where he does not question the presence of his dead father and his ghost but only has doubts about his own reality. "Am I alive or dead?" the mourner wonders, sustaining himself on the repetition of the verb "to be."

Tuesday 19
Last night, after a melancholy meeting in the SADE with naïve young people and mature writers who delude themselves about winning the elections, I had dinner with David. As always, I let myself be pulled along by his enthusiasm and the amusing stories he tells me about his life. The trip to Bolivia in 1956 and his triumphs.

In a couple hours' work I make a clean draft of the article on Pavese. At three José Sazbón appears, fearful, very intelligent; he is preparing a course on history and literature. We discuss it. When he leaves, I work a little while longer and don't leave home until Hugo V. and his minions come over. A lackluster meeting, vague plans to produce a pamphlet about art and propaganda. At night I teach a fairly good class on negativity and evil to the psychoanalysts.

Thursday
Social life: Andrés R. at Norberto Soares's house. An article by Beatriz Guido on Conti, etc. News, jokes, rumors. In the Martín Fierro bookshop I see Pezzoni, who asks me to do a book on Borges for Sudamericana. But I have sworn never to write a book about Borges.

Friday 22
It is clear that my project has always been to become a well-known writer who makes a living from his books. An absurd and impossible project in this country. And so the need to find another path, but which? Not journalism; perhaps I will end up dedicating myself to teaching, but for now I live off my work as an *editor*. The risk is always that of being so present in the media as to turn into someone "well known," someone with a name but not a work.

I read fragments of Enrique Wernicke's diary in *Crisis*. Immediately I resolve to "improve" these notebooks, to *write them* and not reduce everything to these sporadic notes. This notebook, then, has lasted too long (five months). I've never known why I write them.

I'll spend the night alone, preparing tomorrow's class. Some peace in spite of the "night terrors." Who knows if I'll manage to free myself from the urgency that has separated me from everything for the last ten years, making me live behind a glass. I only know happiness retrospectively.

Saturday
A memory. The afternoon when I went out to walk around the city and saw a woman shouting back and forth with a man who was hanging from the roof.

The long passage of the courses, four hours of speaking to earn what I need.

Roa Bastos comes over, we have a faltering and erratic conversation about English books and Virginia Woolf. The best parts are the stories about his work; I listen to them as though they had been my own many years ago and I had forgotten them. He spends a year in a house in Mar del Plata, doing nothing other than writing, penniless and living on fish. For six months he got up at five in the morning and took amphetamines until he finished *I, the Supreme* (and had a stroke).

Sunday
I spend the afternoon reading *Cosmos* by Gombrowicz. Yesterday I received a letter notifying me of the eviction suit. I go to the theater with Iris in the rain to see an adaptation of *Daisy Miller*.

Monday
I'm going to go to the publishing house, I have to write a letter to one Zimmermann; David sent me his book on Goldman. And I have to go to the office of the attorneys who will defend me in the eviction suit.

Dinner with David and Norberto Soares. We talk about Armando Discépolo.

Wednesday 27
An empty day yesterday. I woke up feverish, with pain in my chest. I slept for twenty-four hours. Iris came and went, the room in shadow. A day erased. Today, in the newspapers, military propositions. Pressure against Numa Laplane from Videla. They are forcing him to retire, and Damasco as well (Minister of the Interior). Isabel Perón becoming more and more isolated.

I spent the day reading James Purdy.

Thursday
I'm still in bed, stretched out, setting deadlines for myself. I read, get bored, let go.

Saturday, August 30
At night, in Pichon-Rivière's house, a meeting of "young writers," Briante, Libertella, Soriano. The same nonsense as always, grand empty gestures. If these are my generational peers . . . Reuniting, especially with Miguel; I feel connected to him in a great mutual understanding. He too is growing old, like me.

Sunday 31
I hear the sound of military marches. I open the window, and it seems as though a circus is approaching.

Borges's "The Dead Man" in the theater, adapted—in secret—by David. Its merit is a certain quality in the details (searching for his bunk to sleep). Many errors, everything too explicit. Thus the possibility of a "tragic" western is lost.

Monday, September 1

I make a clean copy of my short story about the White Russians in Buenos Aires. A story that feels as if it were written by someone else, but I will earn fifty dollars for it.

In the Payró theater, many groups acting to finance the writers' campaign in the SADE. The "progressive" current, the same poems as always, the good intentions. I am there, anyway, and all of my efforts seem based in reversing and turning around everything they say. I make literature with "bad" sentiments, and I don't see that as progress.

Tuesday

A strange ritual. I sat down in a restaurant that specializes in meat and ordered a steak, as though I were a tourist wanting to try the specialties of the country.

Wednesday 3

Everything is possible. A certainty that has always accompanied me. Does that explain my disenchantment? I should make an inventory of my illusions. Disproportionate, no doubt.

Thursday

I begin a new course on Borges at the Institute on Calle Bartolomé Mitre. On the way out I have the thought that I was "too" brilliant . . . Am I going insane?

I have dinner with Julia. The same criticism as always. A dead man, someone who has no idea what to do. So it's impossible to think about crossing the city alone to return home. I sleep with her, rather, next to her, both of us dressed, not touching.

Saturday 6

I decide to call Iris on the phone in the the subway tunnel on Uruguay and Corrientes. "You won the competition," she tells me. Lafforgue called her to officially communicate that I am among the five winners of the detective competition. Some fantasies from age eighteen are achieved, a trip to Europe with her, sponsored by literature.

Sunday 7
Everything seems trivial; the story is nothing out of this world, and yet now it will be seen.

Monday 8
They announce that—along with Goligorsky and Antonio Di Benedetto—I have won the prize in the competition of detective stories with "The Madwoman and the Story of the Crime." The prize, a trip to Paris. Among the judges, Borges.

My friends call, congratulating me. I finish the night at dinner with Andrés Rivera and Norberto Soares.

Tuesday
I reread "The Glass Box," I could write a novel with the same method (a diary read in secret by someone else). Carlos stops by to see me. A strange emotion caused by Melina, the way she moves and talks about animals.

In spite of everything, this is a fortunate time, and with that sentence I conclude this notebook.

Wednesday
I meet Amanda at her place. She is waiting for me with champagne to celebrate the prize Fitzgerald-style, etc. Slightly tense but tender toward me. I spend the night with her because it is raining outside (she takes her dog out for a walk every afternoon; she wants a kid; she remembers her past with me nostalgically; she has many fears). She doesn't want me to go to sleep with my watch on.

Thursday 11
The political situation grows more and more sinister, the military officers taking center stage are reinforced. They plan to order the repression of the union movement. Isabel Perón, now along with Lúder, Lorenzo Miguel, and Calabró, seems weak and hesitant.

Series E. What can be done to improve the style of this diary? Maybe the time has come to type up the seventeen years' worth of notebooks in order to find the essence and the tone.

Friday
I can't bear to be alone at night; I want to look for a woman, get together with any one of them, the many who have accumulated from the past, and so I go out into the city. Dinner at Pippo, then the theater, a domestic film (*Una mujer* by Stagnaro) with unusual technical perfection, empty narration, a combination of commercial film and advertisement with an intellectual air, comparable to the young best sellers. I take a taxi back after having a couple of whiskeys at La Paz and inviting Dipi, Miguel and several strangers for a drink, as though I needed to burn through the money I don't have.

Saturday
I am reading Conrad, the coward as an epic and tragic subject—Lord Jim. *An Outpost of Progress* is a kind of *Bouvard et Pécuchet*.

Monday
I start to type up my first diary (1957–1962), but why? It's impossible that it could be published.

A meeting at the SADE: Costantini, Conti, Viñas, Iverna Codina, Santoro. We discuss the statements of Elías Castelnuovo (our presidential candidate) against González Tuñón. I go to dinner with David. Beba appears: strange games that I respond to with irony. I like her very much, but the same thing is happening with her as has happened with other women; I prefer to keep myself apart.

Tuesday

I receive an envelope with letters from Tristana, she has written down fragments of dialogues that seem to be said by someone else, but according to her they are my own words.

"I shouldn't ever sleep again. If only the day had thirty-five hours so I could read everything I want to read and write everything I want to write."

"You have to understand it, there's no other way I can explain it to you, but I'm empty (the description satisfied her, and I added), empty as an empty bottle."

Those are the things I apparently said to her.

One day I will write a story replicating the letters that a man might receive over the course of the years.

I meet Di Paola at the Ramos bar. He talks a lot, driven on by a strange mythology that dissolves his life and the lives of people around him. His father, who is burned-out and goes from one side of the city to the other, always on foot. Dipi fights with his wife: they hit each other like children, cry, and then embrace. Everything turns into a humorous tale. The best part was his recollection of an interview with Borges: he brought him an apocryphal prologue with which a Colombian poet had singled out his own poems. Borges never said the text was not his. Simply, while Dipi read it to him, he interrupted him with notes: "That line would sound better like this, no?" Or: "Don't you think it would have been more correct in this way?" In fact, by the end of the interview Borges had produced a text of his own: its subject, praise for a book of poems he had never read.

Thursday 18

Series E. In these notebooks I must respect one rule: never write extensive texts. Everything I may say must be less than three hundred words. Stories, memories, readings, reflections, meetings: I must discover a way to synthesize and concentrate; the diary is a fine-linked chain, like the chain my grandfather Emilio used to hold his pocket watch.

I will put a line from Borges at the beginning of my book *Assumed Name* but attribute it to Roberto Arlt: "One can only lose what one never had." The line does nothing more than synthesize what, for me, is the central "theme" of that book: loss.

According to Marx, Don Quixote's madness lies in that he "long ago paid the penalty for wrongly imagining that knight errantry was compatible with all economic forms of society."

Another from Marx: "In the twelfth century, so renowned for its piety, they included amongst commodities some very delicate things. Thus a French poet of the period enumerates amongst the goods to be found in the market of Landit, not only clothing, shoes, leather, agricultural implements, &c., but also *femmes folles de leur corps* (wanton women)."

Sunday
I force myself to rest from an overly agitated week. First I go to the theater to see Kurosawa's version of *Macbeth*, and then, once back, I sit in front of the TV to watch the 1950 Hollywood version of Fitzgerald's "Babylon Revisited," and when the program ends I go to my armchair, light the lamp and once again read Conrad's *Heart of Darkness* in one sitting. I consume foreign stories to erase my mild afflictions.

Series E. Two days for the transcription of the diary: (1) Call up all of the women who have the same names. (2) Include quotes from other authors without reference, as phrases that form part of the text. I'm going to write a story using the papers that appear in my notebooks: from what can be seen, I keep the same things there that I have in my desk, sentences, lists, schemes, plans, quotes, messages into the void.

Monday
(Notes from an old class with Nilda Guglielmi on medieval culture.)
    In the Middle Ages all readers were, at the same time, authors who copied interesting passages by the authors they read in their books. Then

they would add their own commentaries and the book would grow and take form in this way. The book is never "published," simply one day it would start to circulate from one person to another, while the author went on inserting new commentaries. The book never had a singular content—or theme or sphere of ideas—and would include all of the authors' centers of interest. Does a diary, ultimately, repeat this medieval technique? Dispersion, copy, a book to be read after death.

Wednesday
My notes on Pavese are published in the cultural supplement of *El Cronista Comercial*; a variety of offers come, trying to get me involved. Five hundred thousand pesos per month in exchange for two articles, selling the same pieces in Venezuela (via Mario Szichman) for one hundred dollars apiece. I can live off that easily; I could go from making a living on reading to making a living on writing, but I don't think so. As Pound said, speaking about Joyce: "He is also dead right in refusing to interrupt his stuff by writing stray articles for cash."

Friday
The double sustains the writing: it is the other who writes, and I attend to his work.

Lafforgue comes over. I correct the proofs of "The Madwoman and the Story of the Crime": I don't like the story very much, little space to develop the plot; still, the change in style is good, as is a certain density in the story that goes beyond the plotline.

Wednesday, October 1
Yesterday the prize was awarded. Borges appears, goes unsteadily down the stairs, as if in a dream. He sang old tangos in a proud voice; he likes prison lyrics, and his favorite is "Yvette." He made several political comments: we are worse now than in Rosas's era, it makes no sense to go into exile because when you return you always finds the government worse. He left on Donald Yates's arm.

I go to the Martín Fierro bookshop, then find Gusmán, Di Paola, Germán García, Pichon-Rivière, Norberto Soares at a table in Banchero: entertaining discussions about a variety of distinguished strangers.

Friday

A roundtable about Sartre last night at the Hebraica with Rozitchner, Matamoro, and another gentleman whose last name I forget. I say a few words about Sartre and literary criticism in Argentina. I argue with Matamoro about Masotta.

Sunday

Little by little, I regain my interest in my old work on Borges; I would like to write it in a fluid style, nothing technical. A thought that arose in bed as I was smoking the first cigarette of the morning after reading the papers and before starting work on tomorrow's class.

Today I'll stay in to watch the boxing match between Clay and Frazier that's coming on in a little while.

Thursday 9

The first galleys of *Assumed Name* are coming today, I'm going to get them and read the book once more in the dark bar on Diagonal, near Vivex. Some fear that I will find too many flaws that can no longer be fixed. Little by little, I am getting used to the idea that what I'm reading is my own book. I correct the proofs in Iris's house, improving the text as much as I can. Now we will see if it's possible to see the book in print before the end of the year.

Friday 10

It is beautiful to see the evening fall, the river is darkening, and the sun's last light reflected in the glass of a bank building looks as though it were catching fire. It is seven in the evening and I'm sitting in the leather armchair and writing this, drinking a whiskey, waiting for Lola, fantasizing. A strange mixture of desire and love.

Monday
A peaceful weekend, my mother was visiting, I took her to the theater. Then, last night, I stayed in to write the jacket copy for my own book, but it's impossible. What can I say about myself, someone I know less about than any other?

When I get home I see stains on the hallway floor. "They didn't clean," I think, but then I see that someone has scratched an insult into the door with a nail. The mark of evil. Who can it be? They don't write my name, only insult me. I remember writings on the wall of my childhood home, the same surprise in the face of anonymous hate.

It would be impossible for me to write a text about my own stories. All of the alternatives appear, alongside the faces of all of my friends. I could write many different texts, defending my writing with actions, between the stories and reality. Defending my experimentation in "Homage . . .".

Tuesday 14
The novel is coming together bit by bit in my head. I find the beginning: "I made the mistake of telling Maggi about the letters." Maggi is writing the biography of an unknown nineteenth-century hero.

On Friday I see Lola. We have dinner at Hansen and stay together all night. Today she comes back to end things. She managed to do what I wanted (to erase me from her life) and did it well. A very slight melancholy, and at the same time the certainty that it was the last thing (the only thing) I could do for her.

Tuesday 21
Circulations, digressions. The days are marked off by classes and meetings. Nothing worthy of being recorded. David, going to the United States; women, Julia, Tristana, Lola, entering and exiting my life.

Friday 24

At Siglo XXI today I saw the cover copy written by Schmucler, the usual annoyance at seeing something written about me, as though I were spying on a letter that was not addressed to me, in which I was being slandered or praised; what matters is the feeling that I am reading something that does not belong to me. Cuqui Carballo just showed me the proofs of photos for her cover design, images of the city. Slowly a fetish forms; once published, I no longer want to know anything about the books I have written, but they persist in me with the light of a dangerous and sacred object.

I should recognize the prosperity of this time, no economic distress, a book about to be released, and the trip to Europe with Iris in sight.

Monday

The final page proofs of *Assumed Name* at the publishing office. The days spent shut in, the empty years are all there. No illusion, rather the certainty of the rejection, or rather, indifference that will come from everyone. I will never produce a book that is at the level of my expectations.

Tuesday

I meet Mario Szichman at Ramos. He "buys" from me the notes on Brecht, the article on Arlt, the piece on Pavese (seventy-five dollars each). So my relationship with money is also improving these days. I would like to experience this era in the way I will remember it.

Obsessions, organizing the house, throwing out old papers, making another bookcase.

Monday 10

Circular digressions made even worse. A dark day on Friday, I meet Julia, who tells the truth about my life and destroys everything in order to let me know she has not forgotten me. Before and after that the course, classes, and discreet readings. Proposals for an article in *Crisis*, in *El Cronista*. A possible agreement with Fischerman to write a detective film. I live up in the air, I go to the movie theater every day in spite of everything and wait, not really knowing what I'm waiting for.

Complacency and acceptance, an inability to think intensely, except in limited circumstances, which I always know in advance (for example the classes, the interviews). I seek "harmony," nostalgia for a paradise lost, but discovering reality would make the world worse, would destroy the peace. Better that I connect myself with the ideas I don't want to think about. Am I a peaceful assassin?

Wednesday 12
Rage, the meaning of which I do not know. Is it from waiting for the book? I see women passing by, uncertain desires as I walk around the city.

Tuesday 18
I go in and out of darkness, a single essence that I don't want to see; I know what it is and lay it aside, as though someone were preventing me from seeing clearly.

At Siglo XXI today I see the book cover. No emotion. I came walking down Corrientes under the warm sun. Final proofs of the detective story.

Friday 21
Sitting in front of the typewriter, I rewrite old papers, the same ones I've looked at again and again for years. Many difficulties. I don't know how to talk about myself.

Exhausted from teaching courses, growing closer and closer to Iris, I only wait for a chance at relief. I will finally go to Europe in January, not too excited. Navigating.

Monday, December 1
Norberto Soares comes over, a confusing pretense that we should meet to do something I can't quite discern. Thus, my complicated relationships

with friends. Thus, the stifling drama from demands that others naturally lay upon me. I wander around the city, have to move and don't know which way to go.

Tuesday 2
I let myself go, read randomly. I also fill my time with Ludmer's book on Onetti, which I am reading with great interest. A good beginning, the first two chapters are excellent conclusions on the cutoff and beginning of the story, but at the same time there is something of an overinterpretation that makes you think about criticism going too far and adding its own meanings, so that it can be read as autobiography of critics themselves, unknowingly writing about themselves.

I enter and exit Argentine history. Now the origins of the theater.

I stop by Martín Fierro, Gusmán develops his theories with a certain brusqueness. He defends Medina and the best sellers. "We all benefit." There's always a realist thought underneath. It is clearly visible that the "avant-garde" subject thinks about the market as the future site of his texts.

Wednesday
According to the man who listens to him, his anxieties are no more than old beliefs that he will not relinquish. Anyway, a strong oppressive feeling since the beginning, a stone—one of those cement blocks used to build the jetties that hold off the sea in Mar del Plata—in his chest.

Slowly I get used to the idea of the trip to Paris. I meet Goligorsky, who has already returned. The hotel in Paris is splendid, and everything seems like a Fitzgerald story.

More and more, I think I must abandon politics before it abandons me. My relationships with Elías and Rubén fluctuate between boredom and distance. Maybe my qualms have to do with the rise of repression.

Thursday 4

Hours in the Civil Registry going through the process of changing my residence. The employee attending to me has a face like a bird, he talks forcefully and unexpectedly shows his knowledge of philosophy.

Friday 5

I return to the Police Department to renew my passport. The same as in '67 and '72, always in December. I sit down to wait in a bar on the corner and read the Quentin Compson chapter in Faulkner's novel.

Saturday

I see Norberto S., who tires me by always repeating the same thing about Armando Discépolo. We meet at his house to go over my interview, which he and the people from the newspaper think is "perfect, intelligent," etc., but I think it's terrible. I have to cut out one response and not refer to Marxism. I accept that without arguing because I don't want to make things difficult, and also because I think it's better not to classify one's thinking according to previous, recognized labels.

Tuesday, December 9

I talk as always from the public telephone in the dry goods store on Santa Fe and Canning. At Siglo XXI they confirm that the book came today. What do I think? Distant happiness, unreality. At the counter, one of the secretaries shows me the copy, a beautiful edition. I take twenty-nine and bring the book to Iris, then I meet Andrés at La Paz, he gets excited when I give him the book and rambles about the stories he is writing in his Faulknerian style, then I go to see Gusmán. I end up eating alone at Claudio, I reread "Homage . . . " which this time seems excellent to me.

Wednesday 10

At Air France, a final date for the trip: Monday, January 5 at 3:30 p.m. Everything is falling into place. In the afternoon, at Querandí, they take photos of me for the literary supplement of *El Cronista*. With Iris, before bed, I have a strange feeling when she critiques "The End of the Ride" (now that it can't be fixed). The worst part is that she's right, all stories can be improved. I support myself, nevertheless, on Saer's enthusiasm for the story, which he relayed in a very generous letter. I placed that story first in the book and am happy. Maybe because I couldn't have written it better.

Thursday, December 11
In the morning at the publishing office, the first copy of *Assumed Name*, the book is too expensive (twenty thousand pesos). Then I see Dipi, Soriano, Gusmán and ironically discuss the article by Enrique Pezzoni; in an evaluation of the year, he wrote that I am the best Argentine critic (because of my essays on Arlt).

Monday 15
I have lunch with Lafforgue, digressions and returns to the past. He gives me a copy of *Nuevas aguafuertes de Arlt*, and I give him my book.

An interview on Radio Rivadavia in the early morning, I improvise tired answers to add to the oppressive and melancholy atmosphere of the radio journalists. I return to the city that breaks apart at dawn.

Wednesday
First references to *Assumed Name*, someone saw someone reading it on the subway. My friends' tastes are divided between "The End of the Ride" and "The Price of Love."

Thursday 18
Series E. In the profile in *El Cronista*, I talked about this diary for the first time in public, shall we say. Now that I have made it known, it would be good if I finally started writing it well.

I go down to buy something to eat; in the shop, a climate of euphoria. The Aeronáutica rose up, the military coup is underway. A feeling of old catastrophes, my first thought: "I'll stay and live in Paris."

Friday 19
The crisis stabilizes. The aviators make their fascist programs known. Videla keeps the army as arbiter of the situation.

Sitting in the bar on Corrientes near Rodríguez Peña, I read my own words, my article on Brecht reprinted in Colombia. I kill time before returning home.

Saturday
A strange restlessness after seeing my photo taking up a whole page in the supplement of *El Cronista*. I can't read my statements, it's as though I were a stranger. News about the book, praise ignited by Pezzoni, Muraro, etc.

Last class with my group on Saturdays. We will resume next year.

Friday
A highly favorable review by Di Paola in *Confirmado*. A reading of the stories from my own point of view: the characters would perform social relationships. It seems unlikely that these opinions are the ones that will help me to believe in the literature I write. I'm looking for something, anyway, without quite knowing what it is.

I am in Mar del Plata surrounded by family, here to see my mother for the holidays the same as every year. All I do is go to the sea.

ABOUT THE AUTHOR

RICARDO PIGLIA (Buenos Aires, 1940–2017), professor emeritus of Princeton University, is unanimously considered a classic of contemporary Spanish-language literature. He published five novels, including *Artificial Respiration*, *The Absent City*, and *Target in the Night*, as well as collections of stories and criticism. Among the numerous prizes he received were the Premio de la Crítica, Premio Rómulo Gallegos, Premio Bartolomé March, Premio Casa de las Américas, Premio José Donoso, and Premio Formentor de las Letras.

ABOUT THE TRANSLATOR

ROBERT CROLL is a writer, translator, musician, and artist originally from Asheville, North Carolina. He first came to translation during his undergraduate studies at Amherst College, where he focused particularly on the short fiction of Julio Cortázar.

RESTLESS BOOKS is an independent, nonprofit publisher devoted to championing essential voices from around the world, whose stories speak to us across linguistic and cultural borders. We seek extraordinary international literature that feeds our restlessness: our hunger for new perspectives, passion for other cultures and languages, and eagerness to explore beyond the confines of the familiar. Our books— fiction, narrative nonfiction, journalism, memoirs, travel writing, and young people's literature—offer readers an expanded understanding of a changing world.